RIDE THE LIGHTNING

SINISTER IN SAVANNAH BOOK 1

AIMEE NICOLE WALKER

To the truth seekers, promise keepers, and the guarded hearts.
This one's for you.

RIDE THE LIGHTNING

SINISTER IN SAVANNAH BOOK 1

CHAPTER 1

"There's a vicious storm coming, love. I can feel it in my bones."

Jonah could hear his granny's voice as clearly as if she were standing right beside him. Maeve St. John, the daughter of a lifelong sailor, had predicted changes in weather better than any meteorologist on television. Some people had thought she was bat-shit crazy; Jonah had known she was pure magic. When others would seek shelter, Jonah and his granny had sat on the porch and reveled in the beauty of a thunderstorm.

"You're witnessing Mother Nature at her finest, Jonah. Life is like a thunderstorm—unpredictable, beautiful, and sometimes dangerous."

From Maeve, Jonah had inherited his black hair, olive-toned skin, and weird green eyes with a hue so dark they looked black in certain lights. She'd also taught him how to read the clouds and study the wind. A strong breeze blew across the parking lot, and the sense of trouble made the hair stand up on his neck.

He'd blamed his headache on stress after spending twelve hours in endless meetings where he'd had to defend his skillset to his immediate supervisor in front of everyone in their division, including the deputy director. Just another miserable Monday. As soon as he stepped outside to leave, Jonah discovered the shift in barometric pressure was the real culprit for the skull-splitting pain. Granny felt the weather in her bones, while Jonah felt it in his sinus cavities.

The temperature had dropped at least ten degrees and the wind had intensified since his lunch break. Jonah hoped he had enough time to run a quick errand on his way home before the storm hit. He wanted to watch the show from his front porch, just like he'd done at his granny and pop's house where he grew up. It wasn't a matter of *if* the severe weather arrived, but *when*.

Nighttime thunderstorms were the best. The lightning was brighter as it split the sky and arced toward earth, and the rumble of thunder sounded louder and more menacing. Could this be the weather front that matched or exceeded the intensity of the maelstrom raging inside him?

Jonah debated going straight home, but he needed his Caramel Bugles fix after a day like this, and he'd blown through last week's stash in two days. He loved his job as a criminal analyst for Georgia Bureau of Investigations, where he used technology to predict and prevent crimes and capture bad guys. He loathed his boss, Supervisory Agent Butch Trexler, just as ardently.

If brewing storms reminded Jonah of his granny, then Trexler reminded him of Pop. It wasn't a compliment either. Oscar St. John had been one mean son of a bitch who had bullied and brow-beaten everything and everyone into submission. Trexler seemed to live for the moments he could demean and humiliate Jonah and flex his power over him. If things didn't change at the bureau soon, he'd be forced to make a tough decision before the job took a hard toll on his health. Leaving was complicated. Someone dear to Jonah had stuck their neck out for him so he could get an interview for the position. He also didn't want to give Trexler the satisfaction of running him off.

Jonah mentally shoved the thoughts aside and concentrated on driving across town to his neighborhood. Part of Thomas Square Streetcar Historic District had undergone heavy revitalization. Investors bought the homes for a low price, renovated them, and flipped the houses for a profit, which brought an influx of hipsters to the area. The other half, where Jonah lived, was the exact opposite. Residents and businesses flooded out of the neighborhood, leaving abandoned homes and buildings that bordered on derelict. His destination, Ling's Corner Market, was the only surviving business in the strip mall on Bull Street near his house.

Several cars were in the parking lot, but only one caught his attention. The driver had backed into a spot instead of pulling in. When Jonah parked beside the car, he noticed the engine was still running. This wasn't the kind of neighborhood where you left your keys in the ignition unless you wanted someone to steal your car, or you planned to rob the corner market because you figured the elderly Asian-American owners made an easy target. He quickly exited the car and made his way toward the store. Jonah must've wrenched the door open with too much enthusiasm because all eyes turned to him. Mrs. Ling was behind the counter and smiled softly when their gazes collided. Maybe he'd overreacted to the car out front and someone was just passing through and didn't know better than to take their damn car keys with them.

No, his gut said he was right. Like the approaching storm, Jonah could smell trouble brewing. No one was acting suspicious as he scanned the customers. The patrons met Jonah's perusal with stares of their own, ranging from curiosity to fear and even disgust. He was used to it, even if the reasons had changed over the years.

He'd always stood out—pun intended—due to his height. He started kindergarten as the tallest kid in his class, a title he retained until he joined the military after graduation. The years in between garnered attention for his awkwardness, a nerdy brain, and his inability to use his size to achieve glory for the various sports teams, their coaches, or Oscar. He tried. God, had he tried.

These days, it wasn't his broad six-five frame that drew everyone's eye. It was the silver scar slashing diagonally across his face from above his right eyebrow to the left corner of his mouth. Some people seemed uncomfortable and broke eye contact. Others reacted to the scar with fascination and saw him as a challenge. He'd gotten laid many times by playing up the bad boy image.

Jonah caught sight of himself on the television screen showing the live security camera feed and nearly winced. *Jesus, St. John.* A lock of black hair had fallen across his forehead, nearly covering one of his oddly colored eyes. Obsidian, his granny had called them. The scowl on Jonah's face made him look much older than thirty-five. Forcing himself to un-clench his jaw and relax his shoulders, Jonah took his time perusing the aisles. One by one, the customers bought their items and exited the store, and yet, the car with the running motor remained parked out front.

"Hello, Jonah," Mrs. Ling called out as he approached the counter.

"Hello, Mrs. Ling," he replied, studying her for any signs of duress. "I'm here for my stash."

Every Monday, without fail, he picked up the ten bags of Caramel Bugles—never more, never less—the Lings set aside for him. It would be a perfect opportunity for Mrs. Ling to signal something was wrong by pretending not to know what he was talking about.

"Of course," she said.

After she ducked into the back room, Jonah walked through the market looking for spots where the asshole could be hiding. In the far corner, back by the beer coolers, he spotted a door with a sign marking it as employee use only. Jonah kept his tread light while approaching, not knowing what could be waiting for him on the other side. A knife? A gun?

Jonah yanked open the door. The young skinny white guy yelped loudly and tried to duck when Jonah reached inside to grasp his hoodie, but Jonah was faster. He dragged the guy out of the closet, then lifted him up until the tips of his toes were barely touching the ground.

"What the fuck are you doing hiding in the broom closet?" he asked angrily.

"I-I." Skinny White Guy emitted a high-pitched squeak, then his head fell forward, breaking eye contact. A strong ammonia smell made Jonah crinkle his nose. He looked down and saw the puddle of piss pool-ing at SWG's feet. The goddamned punk had pissed a river down his leg. Jonah took a quick step back to keep his shoes out of it but didn't let go of the weasel.

"Were you going to rob Mrs. Ling?" Jonah asked.

"No," SWG said quickly, shaking his head frantically. "I wasn't."

"Get your hands up and keep them there."

The kid immediately obeyed. Jonah reached inside the hoodie pocket and pulled out a small caliber handgun.

"What the fuck were you going to do with this?"

"It's not loaded," the guy said.

"And that makes it okay?" Jonah asked, giving the kid a good shake. "You were going to put that gun in Mrs. Ling's face and demand money?"

"I wasn't going to hurt her," he said, struggling in Jonah's embrace.

"Jonah, what's going on?" Mrs. Ling asked from the front of the store.

"Call nine-one-one. This little bastard was about to rob you."

"The gun isn't loaded," the guy repeated.

"People can't tell that when they stare down the barrel, you little fuck face."

The kid started to panic when he heard Mrs. Ling call 911, twisting and trying to break free. He stepped to the right and his foot landed in his puddle of piss. SWG's feet slid out from under him, wrenching Jonah off balance. He released the guy's hoodie to avoid slipping in the urine too. The prick went down hard, banging his head on the bottom of the shelf and knocking himself out.

"Huh," Jonah said, staring down at the prone man. He checked the gun, confirming it wasn't loaded, then tossed it onto the ground so the police would see it when they arrived. He didn't want them to shoot him first and ask questions later.

Two patrolmen Jonah didn't know responded to the call and quickly took over. Unfortunately for him, it meant he had to spend ninety minutes or longer answering questions. First with the patrol officers, and later, when the robbery detectives arrived on the scene. Some queries were legit, such as how he knew to look for trouble. Others were stupid, like when Officer Bauer asked why someone who worked for the GBI wasn't carrying a gun.

"I'm a criminal analyst, not a field agent," Jonah explained, hoping his annoyance wasn't showing.

"Huh," Bauer replied unenthusiastically.

Jonah could've taken the time to explain what he did for the bureau and the many ways he assisted SPD, but he wasn't in the mood. He only wanted to eat his Caramel Bugles on the front porch and watch a thunderstorm. Was it too much to ask?

Apparently so, since he forgot to buy his guilty pleasure during his haste to leave. Jonah swore a blue streak but kept driving toward his house. Tomorrow morning would be soon enough to pick up his Bugles and might even ensure that his stash lasted later in the week than Wednesday.

As soon as his house came into view, relief rushed in to ease the tension gripping his body. Jonah's shoulders slumped, and he breathed easily for the first time since leaving home this morning. He'd purchased his two-story Folk Victorian home three years ago and fixed it up as he found time and money. The house had been structurally sound with a solid metal roof, but the exterior and interior had needed a shit ton of TLC. He'd hired a contractor to deal with the biggest projects, such as replacing the windows and siding on the house. Jonah had tackled the smaller tasks himself. He liked expending the physical energy and seeing the results of his labor. His favorite endeavor was sanding and painting the wraparound porch and trim. He'd chosen a bright white hue which nicely contrasted against the dove gray siding and the black metal roof. Jonah needed new outdoor furniture for his porch to finalize the exterior makeover, but his granny's old rocking chairs would do for now. The interior, however, was another story. He'd upgraded the master suite and refinished the hardwood floors on both stories before he exhausted a good chunk of his savings. The kitchen was his next big project, but it would require a lot of capital, time, and sweat. He could make do with the raggedy cabinets and outdated tile a little longer. He'd at least updated the appliances, which was a huge expense out of the way.

When he turned into his driveway, Jonah's headlights illuminated the front porch like a spotlight, revealing Miss Marla, Savannah's legendary drag queen and his next-door neighbor, sitting in a rocking chair. She'd chosen a long, silver, satin nightgown with matching robe for her visit. The color looked amazing against her flawless dark skin. Beside her, a tall highball glass sat on the table, indicating she hadn't planned a short visit. Marla lifted her arm to shield her eyes, so Jonah cut his headlights.

"Well, this is a surprise," Jonah said when he got out of the car.

"People say the same thing about a herpes diagnosis," Marla quipped, her husky voice laced with her affection for him. Jonah liked it much better than the disdain she'd treated him to when he'd first moved in. Marla had pegged him as just another white guy who was hell-bent on gentrifying her neighborhood. He'd won her over after time, and she'd become a dear friend.

Jonah smiled as he recalled the first time he'd seen a crack in the veneer of Marla's contempt for him. He'd received mail addressed to Richard Bruce Barker once, and initially had thought it was a past owner until he'd noticed the address beneath the name. When Jonah took the envelope next door, Marla looked at the letter in her hands for several moments before meeting his gaze.

"These are my rules, and I expect you to obey them without question." She'd paused long enough to raise a perfectly arched brow. How could someone communicate so much with one little action? Marla had wanted to know if she should continue speaking or save her breath. Jonah had nodded for her to go on. "When you see me dressed like this," she'd said, gesturing to her red dress with white polka dots, "I expect you to call me Miss Marla or Marla. On the rare occasion you see me dressed as a man and not wearing a fabulous wig, you may address me as Ricky. Never Richard, Rick, and especially not Dick, unless you have plans to suck mine." Jonah had bit his bottom lip to keep from chuckling. Marla hadn't finished laying down the law though. "You will treat me with respect at all times. Am I clear?"

"Yes, ma'am," Jonah had said.

"And just because these are my rules does not mean they apply to all genderqueer people. Ask someone if you're unsure which pronouns to use. Don't be a jackass."

"Yes, ma'am."

Marla tilted her head and studied Jonah's face. She must've liked whatever she saw there because she stood aside, gestured for him to enter her home, and said, "Join me for coffee." She didn't ask or invite; she commanded, and he obeyed. Not much had changed since that fateful day.

In three years, Jonah had only seen Ricky twice. He was curious to know how old Marla was, but he'd never be stupid enough to ask. He figured a lady was entitled to her secrets.

Marla's visit made him curious. Not so much because of the time, but because she'd chosen his porch to wait for him rather than her own. Their homes were close enough that she would've heard Jonah pull in without having to watch out the window for him. There was something in her voice, a wisp of sadness that made him push aside his exhaustion and frustrations as he dropped into the rocking chair beside her.

"Late night, isn't it, darling?" Marla asked.

It was approaching ten, which wasn't late for most people's standards, but it was hours later than Jonah usually arrived home from work. "Meetings and more meetings."

Marla shivered. "Sounds dreadful."

Soul-crushing was a better adjective. "How was your day?"

"Very enlightening," she replied. "I listened to the new true-crime podcast you are making with your friends. I wasn't sure what to expect, but I enjoyed it. The three of you have vastly different personalities, but you complement one another very well." She sounded like an indulgent aunt or mother who acted as the sole audience member for a garage band's private concert.

Sinister in Savannah, a podcast he'd created with his friends Rocky and Felix, a private detective and an investigative reporter, was the subject of much scorn during his meetings. It had debuted the previous week to rave reviews and was already trending in the top ten of true-crime podcasts. He'd had the deputy director's blessing to participate, but Trexler thought it was a horrible idea. Jonah suspected Trexler's animosity stemmed from jealousy over the attention the show garnered, rather than genuine concern Jonah would leak GBI secrets during the segments. Trexler had doubled down on making Jonah look like a fool by trying to discredit the work he did with Stella, the supercomputer with artificial intelligence Jonah had built from scratch. Trexler belittled his efforts and dismissed every conclusion Stella came up with after analyzing files.

"How'd the three of you meet?" Marla asked, pulling Jonah's attention back to her.

"Through mutual friends with the Savannah Police Department." Jonah wasn't at liberty to discuss the investigation involving a serial rapist and killer that had brought them together since the case was still pending trial. "I don't suspect you've been waiting in the dark for me to come home just to discuss the podcast or my friends."

"No," Marla said softly.

"Then why don't you tell me what's troubling you."

"I'm dying, Jonah."

The tempest in his soul rumbled louder.

CHAPTER 2

Her words sucker-punched Jonah in the gut, and he was grateful he was already sitting down. He had to have misheard Marla. She was the kind of person who was larger than love and bolder than hate. A world without her was unfathomable. Jonah tried to speak but couldn't with his heart wedged in his throat.

The moonlight was strong enough for Marla to see Jonah's struggle. She reached over and gripped his hand. If he'd been more prepared, he would've tried to shield her from his devastation. What did it say about him that she was the one comforting him and not the other way around?

"I found out this morning that I have stage four liver cancer," Marla said calmly.

How could it be? He hadn't even known she was sick. He'd seen her several times over the past week, and she'd been her typical luminescent self—defying age, gravity, and gender norms. Jonah wanted to know why she hadn't told him sooner about her illness, but his tongue wouldn't obey his brain's command to speak.

"I've had all day to think about my situation, and I've decided not to seek treatment."

That detonation rattled him even harder, but it enabled him to speak again. "Bullshit," Jonah said fiercely. "The Marla I know doesn't give up without a fight."

"Baby, this isn't the same thing as teaching those snot-nosed punks down the street how to treat a lady. I am talking about the difference between the quality of life and quantity." She gestured to her ankle-length nightgown. "This queen won't settle for anything less than the best." Marla took a deep breath and released it slowly. "I promised the oncologist I would think about my options. He gave me an overwhelming number of pamphlets to take home, and I read every word, including the fine print and disclaimers. I've made my decision."

"But there are treatments—"

Marla lifted her free hand, signaling she hadn't finished speaking yet. "The cancer has metastasized, which means I'm not a candidate for a transplant. Those chemo and radiation treatments might extend my life, but they will not save it. I'd rather live my remaining days to the fullest, and for me, that doesn't include having poisons pumped into my body or getting nuked like a baked potato in the microwave."

Jonah was at a loss for words, so he went with the first thing that popped into his head. "You're such a damn diva."

Tilting her head back, Marla laughed hard and huskily. Normally, her bawdy sense of humor made Jonah smile, but tonight it just whipped his battered emotions into a frenzy. "Always and forever, baby, which is exactly how I want people to remember me. I'm so glad you get it," Marla said.

Jonah understood where she was coming from, but he didn't have to like it. He respected her right to choose her path, but he wasn't ready to say goodbye. How selfish was he? Jonah nodded because it was what Marla needed from him. The remaining tension in her lean frame eased, and she relaxed against the rocking chair.

"Do you want to go inside and talk? It will be more comfortable," Jonah said.

"If it's okay with you, I'd prefer to chat outside and enjoy these mild temperatures. May is my favorite month, and I want to soak up every second."

The heft of her unspoken words pressed heavily against Jonah's chest. It would be her last.

"There are two promises I need from you, Jonah St. John, and I will not leave your porch until I have them."

"You expect me to make promises without first learning what's involved?" Jonah quipped.

"Yes, because you love me," Marla said. And he did. "Tell you what, I'll explain what I need from you, so you can pretend to think it over. I'll still extract your promise, but in a way you can live with and not feel manipulated."

"Too late," Jonah said.

Marla's full-bodied laughter echoed off the house before the wind carried it away. They sat quietly, listening to the crickets for a few minutes before Jonah said what they both knew he would.

"I promise." He wouldn't deny her anything, so why waste precious time pretending otherwise?

"It's going to take Betty time to get used to you, so be patient with her," Marla said.

Jonah should've known Marla's top priority would be making arrangements for her French bulldog named after her favorite Golden Girl, Betty White. He'd always wanted a dog but never gave in to his desire because of his long work hours. He'd find a way to make sure Betty was happy, even if it meant using a doggy daycare.

"I will spoil her rotten," Jonah said. "What's the other thing I agreed to do?"

"This one is harder, but after listening to the kickass podcast, I think it's something you and your friends will love to tackle since none of you can stand an injustice," Marla said.

Intrigued, Jonah angled his body to face her. "An unsolved case? You have my attention."

"In 1982, a dear friend was brutally murdered. The cops didn't put much effort into solving Earl Ison's case because he was a gay man and a part-time drag queen known as Lola the Ice Queen. I, along with some of Earl's other friends, got tired of their bullshit and started harassing the police department, even though we knew we were putting our lives in danger. We staged protests and marches, knowing all along we were going to get arrested for stirring up shit, but it would've been a victory if one of those lawmen saw Earl as a human instead of a gay man who sometimes dressed in women's clothing." Marla grew quiet as she stared off into the night.

"Your plan didn't succeed?" Jonah asked.

"Yes, but not in a meaningful way or how we wanted." Marla pivoted in her rocking chair, angling her body toward Jonah and meeting his gaze. "In 1995, Bo Cahill, who was already on death row for another murder, confessed to killing Earl a week before his execution."

Jonah tipped his head to the side. "I thought you said it was an unsolved case."

"No, *you* said it was an unsolved case. I called it an injustice."

"How so, if the killer confessed?" Jonah asked.

Marla rolled her eyes. "Child, please. You can't believe every person who's confessed to a crime really committed the offense." Of course, he didn't.

"You're saying Bo Cahill gave a false confession," Jonah said. "Why would he lie? I understand when the reverse happens, but confessing to a murder you didn't commit doesn't make any sense."

"That's for you to find out, honey. I didn't believe his confession then, and I don't believe it now. The cops and DA were all too willing to accept the confession and close Earl's case, and my continuous harassment only spelled trouble I couldn't afford. I promised myself I'd find the truth someday, and I think I was waiting all this time for you to come along. Earl's killer is still out there, and I want to make this right for my friend before…"

She dies.

"This aging queen is asking a lot, but you promised me."

"Yeah, I did," Jonah said, nodding. "Tell me everything you know about Earl's death and what was going on in his life at the time. I know it's been almost forty years, but a minor detail could hold major significance."

"I can remember it like it was yesterday." Her dark eyes took on a faraway look. "Earl had started dating someone new and was really excited about it. The relationship wasn't without big issues though. His boyfriend wasn't out to his friends, family, or at work, and I don't think Earl had revealed Lola to him yet. I tell you, baby, I knew it was a recipe for disaster. Earl was so happy and in love, so I bit my tongue." Marla smiled wryly. "It was the last time I did so too."

"Had Earl's personality changed a lot after meeting this person? Were there any indications he was involved in an abusive relationship?" Jonah asked.

"He had changed a lot, but he hadn't acted jumpy or scared. Earl had just pulled away from his friends and spent all his free time with his boyfriend." Jonah heard a hint of bitterness in her voice which time, heartbreak, and loss hadn't erased. Resentment was a foe he knew all too well. "Earl never had bruises or scrapes he couldn't explain. He'd just turned dismissive as if he were too good for us once this guy noticed him. It also wasn't uncommon for some queens to tone it down for a man."

"Not you, I bet."

Marla laughed. "Never, sugar. There are certain things I am unwilling to compromise and staying true to myself tops the list. Love me as I am or get the fuck gone. My plan might've backfired a bit since I will die single."

Jonah hated how she could utter the hateful word with such ease. Marla was one of the most perceptive people he'd ever met, so it didn't surprise him when she squeezed the hand she still held.

"I've never been one to hide from the truth. I'm sorry if I've upset you."

Jonah's eyes watered, and his nose started to burn, but he blinked the tears away before they could fall. Him giving in to his grief was not what she needed right then. "Never apologize for being you, Marla. You might die single, but you will be loved, and you won't be alone. That's promise number three."

"I'd like to ask for a fourth, but I think I've already pushed my luck tonight." Or maybe she realized Jonah would agree to anything and didn't want to press her advantage. Jonah decided to push on with his questions so he could start looking into Earl's case.

"Confessions without corroborating evidence aren't admissible in court, so I'd like to think the cops working the case would go the distance to make sure Bo Cahill's confession was legitimate before they closed the case. Did the chief or the investigating officers discuss why they so readily accepted the confession?"

"The detectives working the case, Milton and Morrisey, told me Bo Cahill gave them details of the crime scene that only the police and the perpetrator would know," Marla replied. "I'd heard there was a GBI agent working the investigation, but I never met one."

"What reason do you have to believe they weren't telling the truth?" Jonah asked.

Marla tapped her temple, her heart, and then her stomach. "Instinct. I'm never wrong. I'm not saying Milton and Morrisey lied to me. Maybe they were nothing more than pawns, but something doesn't add up."

"You think someone fed information to Bo Cahill and walked him through a confession?"

"It's exactly what I think. I just don't know who."

"Why would he agree?" Jonah said.

"Maybe he was protecting someone he loved."

Jonah considered it. "The real person who killed Earl, maybe?"

"Could be, or maybe there's no connection at all. Bo just happened to be the first man up for execution after Earl's death. I think an ambitious person set the confession in motion. Maybe to shut me the fuck up so I'd stop coming into the police station and demanding to know the latest updates in Earl's investigation," Marla said.

Jonah wanted to say it was too big of a leap, but Bo Cahill confessing was a win-win for the DA and the police department. "I'll try to access the case file tomorrow. In the meantime, I need you to make a list of everyone you think I should interview—Earl's friends, cops, coworkers, and family members."

"I will start on that now," Marla said, untangling her fingers from his. She started to rise, but Jonah reached out and stopped her.

"Don't rush off," he said. "Tell me the tips and tricks I'll need to know about Betty."

Only when she talked about her beloved dog did Marla begin to cry. Jonah wrapped an arm around her slender shoulders.

"She's the best girl, Jonah. You're going to be damn lucky to have her in your life."

"I will show my gratitude for her every day," he promised. *And for you.*

"I'm glad you moved next door to me," Marla said tearfully.

"Me too, Marla. Me too."

CHAPTER 3

"**Y**o, Eagle," a voice called out from the back of the Humvee. "You sure got quiet last night after receiving letters from home. Is everything okay?"

Without missing a beat or taking his eyes off the convoy vehicle in front of theirs, Eagle replied, "I assigned you to look out for insurgents, not bust my balls about letters from my wife, Lion."

"Uh-oh," Cobra said in an ominous voice.

"Sounds like someone didn't live his time on leave to the fullest," Dragon added

"Fuck off. All of you," Eagle said, but there was no mistaking the humor in his voice. "Kirsten is pregnant. I'm going to be a dad."

Excited whooping erupted throughout the tightly packed armored vehicle.

"I take it back," Dragon said.

"Attaboy," Cobra cheered.

"I'm scared shitless, man. A baby," Eagle said, shaking his head. "I—"

A loud boom cut off his words as the Humvee in front of theirs exploded. Eagle cut hard to the right just as a secondary detonation went off, sending their vehicle into a sickening roll.

Rat-a-tat-tat-tat-tat.

Jonah jackknifed up in bed as another loud blast shook his house and the drumming sound intensified. Jonah's raspy breaths sounded loud in the silence as his brain registered he was in his bedroom and not back in Afghanistan. God, he'd never been so relieved in his life to hear thunder and rain splattering against the windows.

The respite was short lived. His friends were gone, and it was his fault.

Jonah flopped back onto his bed and willed his racing heart to slow down. That's when another thump sounded, but it had nothing to do with the storm raging outside his house. A loud moan and a giggle quickly followed the noise, which meant Kendall was home and he wasn't alone.

Like Marla, his friendship with Kendall had caught him off guard. He'd met the younger man at a club called The Cockpit where Kendall worked part-time, and they'd spent the entire weekend fucking like animals. When Kendall left his bed in the early Monday morning hours, Jonah hadn't expected to see him again unless he pursued Kendall at the club. In a weird twist of fate, Jonah received a call from his detective friend Royce Locke, asking him to verify Kendall's whereabouts over the weekend. Kendall had returned home to find his roommate dead, and the person who discovered the body is always at the top of the suspect list. Jonah's role in Kendall's life swerved from random weekend hookup to alibi.

Kendall's roommate wasn't just anyone either. Vivian Gross had been a prominent attorney for high-profile clients like Franco Humphries, the serial rapist and killer whose investigation brought Felix and Rocky into Jonah's life. Royce Locke, along with his boyfriend and partner, Sawyer Key, put a clandestine task force together to nail the man for the crimes he'd committed. They put the sick bastard behind bars and forged wonderful friendships.

Jonah hadn't known about the connection between his hot weekend hookup and the attorney representing one of the vilest men on earth, but then again, Jonah hadn't been interested in the other jobs Kendall worked or who he knew. They hadn't exchanged phone numbers because neither of them had wanted to pursue a relationship. Kendall worked two jobs and went to college, and Jonah wasn't in the right mental space to entertain a romantic relationship. He liked Kendall and had offered him the use of his guest room since the condo he'd shared with Vivian was a crime scene.

Seven months later, Kendall was still living in his house, but as a paying tenant. The two men shared an easy camaraderie that wasn't complicated by sexual tension since they'd worked it out of their systems.

Rapid thumping sounded from the room below his as Kendall's bed frame repeatedly banged against the wall.

"Yes! Fuck, yes!" Kendall said, urging his lover on. "Harder. Faster." Whomever he'd brought home complied. The headboard banging intensified in both frequency and speed.

Jonah's cock started to stir. Who could blame him? Hearing two men fucking always had that effect on him. Throw in his long-ass dry spell, and who wouldn't spring wood? Deciding to settle for a beer, Jonah threw back the covers and pulled on a pair of basketball shorts to cover his bare ass.

The sex sounds were even more intense on the first floor where Kendall's bedroom was located. His roommate moaned incoherently, and his guest grunted before they both fell silent. Jonah raised his bottle of beer to toast the pair and headed to the front porch, where he'd have a front-row seat for nature's performance.

The cool air felt wonderful against his heated flesh. Jonah breathed deeply, working to calm himself after his nightmare by cataloguing his favorite scents and remembering simpler times. The musky, pungent smell of freshly turned earth and the sweet, sharp scent of a newly cut lawn reminded him of the many hours working beside his granny in the yard. Oscar would get pissed about Granny making him a sissy boy and would drag him off to fish at the lake. Jonah had cried the first time Oscar put one of the worms on a fishhook. Oscar swore it didn't hurt the worm, but Jonah didn't believe him. From then on, Jonah had done his best to rescue every worm he'd encountered, especially after a hard rain flushed them from their hiding spots.

He reopened his eyes in time to witness a large bolt of lightning rip through the clouds, reminding Jonah of the restless energy surging inside him that had no way to escape. A loud clap of thunder boomed in the darkness, then rolled and rumbled for several seconds. Jonah recognized he was witnessing the tail end of the storm rather than the beginning. Too bad he couldn't say that about the maelstrom wreaking havoc on his psyche.

Marla was dying. It was beyond his comprehension, yet he'd seen the truth in her eyes. She had accepted her fate, even if Jonah was struggling to do so.

"I'm still here, baby," Marla had whispered when Jonah hugged her goodbye. "Please don't mourn me yet."

Jonah had nodded and forced a smile on his face. Sitting alone in the dark with his nightmares as company, Jonah didn't have to pretend. He allowed himself to grieve for baby Abigail who'd never met her daddy. He mourned the brothers he lost to Al-Qaeda forces in Afghanistan ten years ago. Mostly, he cried for the dear friend he hadn't lost yet.

Each remembrance of what he'd lost, or stood to lose, churned the emotional vortex stronger and faster until he thought his brain might explode. Another bolt of lightning rent the sky, reminding him of his granny's wise words.

"No matter the ferocity of the storm, it always passes."

Jonah saluted the sky with his bottle of beer. "Here's to you, Granny."

He sipped his beer and watched the resplendent display until he could no longer see the flashes of brilliant light or hear the rumble. Unfortunately for him, his private turmoil had only quieted instead of moving on.

Back in his bedroom, Jonah could hear Kendall and company starting up for round two. He buried his head beneath his pillow to drown out the sounds, but it didn't work. He tried thinking about complex coding techniques to distract his mind, but it didn't work either. The sounds of his roommate engaging in very enthusiastic sex steered his brain into a direction he seemed incapable of stopping. Behind Jonah's closed eyelids, visions of the unattainable man tormented him until he could no longer ignore his aching dick.

Jonesing after your intern. Could you be any more cliché?

Flopping onto his back, Jonah looked at his right hand and said, "I guess it's just you and me again, pal."

CHAPTER 4

The next morning, Jonah got the shock of his life when he returned to the corner market to pick up his Bugles and saw the skinny white guy standing behind the counter with Mr. Ling. The older man appeared to be teaching the leg pisser how to use the fucking thing.

"You've got to be kidding me?" he groused, startling a lady, who grabbed her kid's hand and bolted out the door.

Mr. Ling looked up and smiled happily. "Ah, it's Dirty Harry."

SWG snapped his head up. His eyes widened in alarm, and he began to tremble like a Chihuahua. *Good.* "C-c-c-can I h-help you?" he managed to stammer out when Jonah reached the counter. His name tag read Dakota, and the red polo uniform shirt made the acne on his face look more prominent. If the Lings hired him to work in the store, the guy was at least twenty-one. He sure didn't look it.

Jonah didn't bother hiding his contempt for the pissant. After a long staredown, he shifted his attention to Mr. Ling. "Are you sure this is a good idea?" Jonah asked, gesturing to SWG Dakota in case his question wasn't clear.

"Yes." Mr. Ling nodded. "We'll be just fine."

"I didn't rob the store," Dakota said softly. "I would still be in the broom closet if you hadn't yanked me out."

Jonah jerked his focus back to SWG. "So, this is my fault?"

"N-n-no," Dakota stuttered.

Jonah held out his hand, palm up. "Give me your ID."

"My ID?" Dakota asked.

"Dirty Harry is a cop. Good guy," Mr. Ling told Dakota. "Show him so he feels better about you working here."

Dakota quickly pulled his driver's license from his wallet and extended it to Jonah with a shaky hand. "Your name is Harry?" he asked.

Ignoring him, Jonah snapped a picture of the ID with his cell phone before returning it.

"His name is Jonah. I just call him Dirty Harry after my favorite character." Mr. Ling squinted up his face, formed a pistol with his right thumb and forefinger, and lifted his hand. Jonah knew what was coming, but Dakota moved out of the way like he was about to get caught up in the crossfire. Mr. Ling narrowed his eyes and began reciting the famous lines from Dirty Harry, where Clint Eastwood asks a perpetrator if they're feeling lucky. Dakota jumped when Mr. Ling put big emphasis on the word "punk" at the end.

Chuckling, Jonah said, "No, I'm not feeling lucky. I went home without my stash of Caramel Bugles."

"Oh, those were for you?" Dakota asked, then worried his bottom lip between his teeth.

"What do you mean *were*?"

Mr. Ling smiled apologetically. "I forgot to explain our arrangement to Dakota. He saw the delivery and assumed they were for sale and stocked them on the shelves this morning. I was arguing with distributors and hadn't realized what was happening until they were all gone."

"Sorry," SWG Dakota mumbled.

Jonah tamped down his disappointment. "It's fine."

"Mrs. Ling is gathering some from our other stores. You can pick them up on your way home."

"Thank you, Mr. Ling."

"So, Caramel Bugles, huh?" Dakota asked.

"You got something against caramel-covered corn snacks?" Jonah countered.

"Well, no, but you seemed so..." Dakota waved his hands around while presumably searching for the right words. Either no adjectives came quickly, or he wasn't willing to speak them out loud in front of his boss and ruin his second chance.

The phone rang, and Mr. Ling left him alone with Dakota to answer it.

"Who is Dirty Harry?" Dakota asked.

"It's a movie franchise starring Clint Eastwood. Mr. Ling just performed some of the iconic lines from it."

"Never heard of him," SWG said.

"Scott Eastwood's dad," Jonah explained.

Awareness sparked in Dakota's blue eyes. "Oh, I know him."

"He looks just like his dad," Jonah said.

"Where's your gun and badge?" Dakota questioned.

"He's not that kind of cop," Mr. Ling said as he rejoined them. He tapped his temples, and Dakota looked even more confused. "Uses brain to catch bad guys instead of a gun."

Jonah could happily go the rest of his life without holding a gun, let alone shooting one.

"I'm a criminal intelligence analyst," Jonah explained. "I have to take all the same training and certifications as the field agents, but my position doesn't require me to carry a gun."

"Brain is a weapon," Mr. Ling said emphatically.

"So, you're like a *cyber* cop?" Dakota asked.

Jonah wasn't in the mood to correct the kid's assumptions, so he said, "Something like that."

"How'd you get the scar?" Dakota asked. What the fuck was this? Twenty questions?

"Knife fight in a bar last year."

"Cool," the kid said nervously.

"Nonsense," Mr. Ling said. "Big joker, this one. He got the scar in war. He's a hero. Always be nice to him."

Hero.

Jonah mentally cringed but tried not to show his contempt in front of Mr. Ling, who thought he was bestowing an honor on Jonah. "I'm a survivor, but that doesn't make me a hero," Jonah said. When Mr. Ling went to answer the phone again, Jonah snagged Dakota by his polo and jerked him forward. "Don't you dare do anything to hurt the Lings. Don't steal from them. Don't show up for your shifts late or call in sick. Never make Mrs. Ling cry. If you do, I will come back here and show you how deadly a person can be without a gun. Am I clear?"

"Yes, sir," Dakota replied, nodding like one of those bobblehead dolls.

"I'll be watching," he said before releasing SWG's shirt and leaving the store.

The first thing Jonah did when he reached his office was run a background check on Dakota, who was surprisingly clean. He didn't like the Bugles blocker working for the Lings, but he had to trust their judgment.

Outside his office door, Jonah heard the familiar sounds of Avery's arrival. His accelerated pulse matched the resurging gusts inside him. This was the moment Jonah anticipated and dreaded the most each workday. Avery would open the door and enter, bringing the brightest ray of sunshine with him. It would pierce Jonah's gloomy universe, making it that much darker when Avery exited his office.

And, like last night's storm, it wasn't a matter of *if* he left. One of these days, Avery would leave for good, taking his warmth and brilliance with him.

Jonah hated clichés, but he was the moth to Avery Bradford's flame. Over the past eight months, he flew closer and closer, longing to feel Avery's heat against his skin just once.

Once was all it would take to reduce him to a pile of ash. Still, the lure became harder and harder to resist each day.

What have you done to me, Aunt Ellie?

A question he asked himself every day since his aunt, Ellen Rigby, the newly appointed police commissioner, had convinced him, and later the deputy director, that Jonah needed Avery's assistance. She said he was brilliant with computers and was eager to use his skills for the greater good, so they'd hired the guy sight unseen. No interview. No resumé. That was the kind of influence Aunt Ellie had over him, or maybe it was the caramel macarons her wife had baked for Jonah that had softened him toward her big idea.

Or was it a big mistake?

Jonah's door opened a few minutes later, and Avery breezed inside. He didn't have to glance at his intern to know he held two mugs. One would hold the nectar of the gods, coffee, and one would contain a liquid Avery called tea. Based on the stench, Jonah surmised the brewing method required leaves, dried flowers, and sweaty gym socks. "You won't believe the latest gossip," Avery said excitedly.

"I'm sure I won't care," Jonah replied drolly, not taking his eyes off his computer screen displaying Dakota's driver's license picture.

"Okay," Avery said coolly, placing Jonah's mug on his desk. "Please tell me you're not screening potential boyfriends."

Jonah jerked his head in Avery's direction. His intern's hazel eyes glittered with mischief, and Jonah flapped his wings closer to the flame. "Don't be ridiculous."

"That's right," Avery replied sagely, running his fingers over the row of buttons on his pale lavender dress shirt. Was it new or had he just never worn it to work before? The color made his hazel eyes look more green than brown and went well with his fair skin and golden hair. When Jonah had last seen Avery yesterday afternoon, his hairstyle had looked a bit shaggy with overlong bangs hanging in his face. This morning, Avery's fade looked tighter and his quiff smoother. A new shirt and a trip to the barber? Jonah resented noticing these things at the same time he cataloged them in his brain. "You don't do the boyfriend thing."

"I don't," Jonah agreed. He fucked. Just not lately. "This jackass tried to rob the corner market store in my neighborhood last night." Technically, SWG hid in the closet, then pissed himself, but it didn't sound nearly as interesting. "The owners showed the guy mercy and hired him instead of pursuing charges. I wanted to make sure he had a clean record."

"You don't think people deserve a second chance?" Avery asked.

"I do," Jonah said. "I also know that a high percentage of people don't appreciate them. I don't want to see Mr. and Mrs. Ling get hurt."

Avery smiled and his eyes sparkled with admiration. "You're a good man."

Jonah's skin heated, and his face felt like it was engulfed in flames. He usually recoiled when someone called him a hero or praised his character but not with Avery. He wanted to be the good man Avery saw, and on many days, Jonah could almost believe it was true.

Sensing Jonah's discomfort, Avery nudged his coffee mug closer to him and changed the subject. "Bill is back with Ashley again."

"Again? Does that make it the tenth time?"

"Aha! It's the eleventh. You do pay attention when I repeat the water-cooler gossip."

Jonah rolled his eyes. "I feign interest so you'll spit it out and get to work."

Avery studied him over the rim of his mug as he sipped his sweat-sock stew. He set his tea down and smiled devilishly. "You hang on to my every word. Admit it."

"Do not." He so fucking did. Sometimes Jonah watched those lips form each word, then replayed them later when he was alone. Especially in moments like these because Jonah could almost believe Avery was flirting with him.

"Is today the day you finally admit how much you like me?" Avery asked.

The corner of Jonah's mouth twitched. "Like is such a strong word." It wasn't strong enough.

Avery smirked but didn't press harder for an admission. "You look tired."

"I'm sure you heard how badly the meetings went yesterday," Jonah said. "I doubt anyone excludes me from the morning gossip."

"Definitely not," Avery admitted. "People go back and tell their assistants and interns how poorly Butch Trexler treats you, and they can't wait to fill me in. There's an office pool on how long you'll last at this job."

"How long I'll last?" He'd already worked for the bureau for three years. "Before I do what? Harm him or quit?"

Avery tipped his head to the side. "I'm not sure what 'Hulk out' entails."

"Did you bet against me?"

"What do you think?" Avery punctuated his question with an exaggerated eye roll.

Jonah wasn't sure he wanted to know. As his intern, Avery should be on his side. As Jonah goes, so does Avery, or something like that. He didn't like thinking Avery was rooting against him, or worse, plotting against him.

"I would never bet against you."

"Can we get to work now?"

"You're the boss," Avery said.

Jonah fumbled his coffee cup and nearly dropped it. He'd lain in bed the night before, fucking his fist while fantasizing about Avery saying that very same thing after Jonah ordered him to drop to his knees and suck his cock.

"What?" Avery asked. "You're not the boss?"

Jonah swallowed hard. "I am the boss."

Avery set his cup down on the desk and clapped. "That's good, Jonah. Now say it with more conviction."

Jonah traded the coffee cup for the legal notepad on his desk. He and Avery used it often to make notes for one another when they were working simultaneously on different aspects of their projects. Both men liked to listen to music while working, and constantly hitting pause to chat about different coding variables was just annoying. Most days, the notebook was filled with computer-geek jargon that most people wouldn't understand. In between those scribblings were messages they wrote to one another and sometimes a rousing game of tic-tac-toe. What Avery didn't know, and Jonah would never tell him, was that he'd kept every single page of gibberish in a drawer at home. So pathetic.

Jonah picked up a pen and wrote, *You're fired.*

Avery pulled another pen from the cup on Jonah's desk and wrote,

Ha! You're a funny guy. Then Avery returned the pen to the cup and smiled impishly.

Jonah had seen that same wicked grin behind his closed eyelids in the early morning hours. Recalling it in his office made him break out in a cold sweat.

"I don't know why you insist on goofing around when there's work to be done," Avery said in a mockingly severe tone. His lips quivered, ruining the effect, but he continued. "We're so close to completing your microchip design. It will change the way people view cybersecurity, so maybe you focus on that instead of Bill and Ashley."

Jonah grimaced. "Do I really come off sounding that douchey?"

Avery's eyes widened. "God, no. I was trying to imitate Trexler. Seems I need to work on my skills."

"Or, we could focus on the microchip," Jonah suggested.

"Fine. Be a thundercloud," Avery teased. "The storms woke me up this morning, and I started thinking about you."

Jonah quirked a brow, and Avery's eyes widened.

"I meant the chip. I have some ideas on how to improve it. To beat a hacker, you have to think like one. You"—Avery pointed at Jonah—"don't think like a hacker. Do you want to hear my suggestions?"

"Of course."

He'd be an idiot not to listen to Avery's suggestions because Ellen had been right about his intern's skillset. He was brilliant. Jonah just wished his admiration stopped there and didn't wander to Avery's lithe body, or his generous mouth, and pert ass. As fine as those attributes were, and he'd spent many hours thinking about them, Avery's feisty spirit was the irresistible flame Jonah couldn't ignore.

Too bad Avery's exuberance also meant he liked to gesture with his hands, sometimes wildly. It was how Jonah's coffee cup ended up knocked over a few hours later.

"Fuck!" Jonah said, shoving his chair back from his desk. He wasn't fast enough.

"Oh no." Avery's horror-stricken voice matched his expression. "Not again."

Jonah glared at his intern as he stood up. "Yes, again. I'm starting to think you're doing it on purpose," he said, striding toward the door.

"On purpose? For what reason?"

"To drive me crazy," he replied, picking up the pace.

"How's it working so far?"

Jonah yanked open the bathroom door down the hall and was relieved to see it was empty. "I found the perfect intern for you. You'll wonder how you ever survived without him," Jonah said, mimicking his aunt's voice.

"Oh, that's a great impersonation. Now, do me," Avery said.

Jonah jerked to a halt, pivoted, and strode toward Avery, who mistook the intensity on Jonah's face as anger. He backed up until his body pressed against the door, and there was nowhere for him to go. Avery notched his chin up higher, challenging Jonah.

"You want me to *do you*? Is that what you just said?" Jonah didn't press his body to Avery's, but he stood close enough to feel his intern's heat. Avery's soap or fabric softener smelled like rain.

Avery's pupils dilated, and he darted his tongue out to moisten his lips. Jonah couldn't tear his eyes away from the movement. What he wanted most in the world was within his reach. Avery emitted this little whimpering gasp that grabbed Jonah by the balls, and the moth glided closer. "It is what I said," Avery whispered. He started to lift his hand toward Jonah's face when a burst of laughter from the hallway startled him.

Jonah pushed off the door and walked over to the sink.

What have you done to me, Aunt Ellie?

Jonah rubbed a wet paper towel over the enormous coffee stain on the front of his dress shirt.

"You're not doing it right," Avery said as he approached.

Jonah jerked his head up and met Avery's gaze. "Absolutely no one has ever told me that before," he said huskily.

Avery swallowed hard as he took the wet paper towel from his hands. "You have to dab it," he said, demonstrating. "Otherwise you'll make it worse."

Jonah wrapped his hand around Avery's wrist, hating the fabric separating their skin. "I think I got it now."

"Are you sure? I don't mind showing you again."

"Yeah." He reluctantly released Avery's wrist one finger at a time. Reclaiming the paper towel, he added, "It's a good thing I started keeping extra clothes in my closet once you started working for me. At least you didn't scald my crotch again." Jonah ignored Avery's stifled giggle. "You seem extra animated today. What's up?"

"I have a blind date," Avery replied miserably.

That explained the shirt and haircut. "Tonight?" Jonah felt like someone had punched him in the gut, rendering him breathless.

"No," Avery replied. "At lunch."

"Who goes on a blind date during their lunch hour from work?"

"A person who knows nothing will come from it and wants a valid reason why he has to leave," Avery replied.

Jonah just blinked at him for a few seconds. "That's actually kind of genius."

"If it goes really, really bad, I can leave even earlier by using my asshole boss as an excuse?"

"Me?" Jonah asked. *Was he an asshole to Avery?*

"Yep. I can say you don't do anything for yourself, and I have to pick up your lunch, dry cleaning, or your boyfriend's birthday present."

"Boyfriend? Dry cleaning? How long have you been thinking up excuses to leave this date?"

"Since my best friend set it up," Avery replied. Jonah had heard Avery talk about Karlee enough to know she wouldn't fix him up with a loser. Avery stared him directly in the eyes and said, "He's not who I want."

The moth flew closer still. Jonah's body heated with the possibilities. *Who do you want?* They'd been dancing around each other for months. Four little words and he could learn the truth once and for all. That wasn't the question that came out when he opened his mouth. "How could you possibly know that when you haven't even met him yet?"

"I just do."

"Stop focusing on the negative things that could happen and trust your friend to have your best interests at heart. It's how I ended up with you as my intern. Maybe you'll have a great time."

Avery smiled. "An excellent point." He tipped his head to the side and scrutinized Jonah. "You seem extra broody. Is something wrong?"

The door swung open, and two agents entered the restroom, saving Jonah from having to answer. He wasn't ready to talk about Marla to anyone yet. He'd half-convinced himself he'd dreamed the entire conversation until Jonah saw her leaving in a cab at eight in the morning. Marla didn't like to be awake before noon or show her face to the world before two. Jonah regretted he hadn't insisted on driving her to her appointment with the oncologist.

"There will be times when I might need to take you up on your kindness, baby, but tomorrow isn't one of them," she'd said on his porch the previous night.

The two agents, Paxton and Meyers, looked between Jonah and Avery as if they'd interrupted something. Paxton wore a bemused expression while Meyers maintained his typical stony façade. The partners were as different as day and night—in looks as much as their temperaments. Paxton was tall and whipcord-lean while Meyers was short and built like a block of ice.

"Avery, Mary is looking for you," Paxton said after a few awkward seconds. "She said you have a visitor in reception."

Avery gasped. "He's here? I thought we were meeting at the restaurant."

"Hot date?" Meyers asked.

"Blind date," Avery said. He moved past the two agents to wash and dry his hands.

"During your lunch hour?" Paxton asked.

"You explain it to them," Avery said over his shoulder on his way to the door.

The two agents looked at Jonah expectantly, so he repeated what Avery had said.

"That's damn smart," Meyers said. Paxton nodded.

Standing around the men's room and chatting with these guys wasn't on his list of things he wanted to do. Jonah tossed his wet paper towel in the wastebasket and headed toward the door. "See you around."

"Hey, St. John," Paxton called out.

Jonah sent a silent plea for mercy as he slowly turned to face the men. "Yeah?"

"For what it's worth, I think you got a raw deal yesterday with Trexler," Paxton said.

Meyers nodded.

"The man has it out for you," Paxton said.

"Real bad," Meyers added.

"Thanks for the heads-up, guys," Jonah said, although they weren't telling him anything new. "See you later."

He retreated to his office and decided to work through his lunch hour since it might be the only free time he had to look into Earl Ison's murder.

Before Jonah had joined the Savannah branch of the GBI, the process would've required an agent to dig through moldy, dusty case files at a storage facility. Jonah had overseen digitalizing thousands of case files and uploading them into the system so Stella could access prior case history when looking for patterns in crimes. It was one of the things Butch Trexler bitched the most about because it had cost the agency a substantial chunk of money and time to make it all happen. It didn't matter what Trexler said, because Jonah and Stella had solved three cold cases and discovered patterns among unsolved investigations when no one else had. In each instance, it was the tiniest piece of evidence tying the crimes together. Jonah had also worked with Savannah PD on challenging cases to develop criminal profiles based on evidence they'd gathered. Trexler could bitch all he wanted about technology being unreliable, but Jonah's track record said otherwise.

Once back in his office, Jonah bypassed the GBI-issued computer on his desk and went straight to Stella, who occupied her own corner in his office. He typed Earl's name into the database, and within minutes, he had access to the entire case file, which was pitifully thin for a homicide investigation. There weren't pages upon pages of interview notes like he expected to find. The handwriting was barely legible on what was there, but Jonah managed to make out most of what the investigators wrote.

On June 12, 1982, a construction crew had found Earl Ison's body on a jobsite when they arrived for work. He'd been severely beaten, strangled with one of his stockings, and someone had shoved a pair of silk underwear in Earl's mouth. They were presumed to be his since his skirt was hiked up to his waist, exposing his bare genitals for everyone to see. The crime scene photos didn't show the staging, however, because the investigator documented that one of the workers on the crew lowered the skirt before the cops arrived. Jonah briefly wondered what pronouns he should use but decided to stick with Earl, he, and him because it was how Marla had referred to her friend, and she knew Earl best. Both of Earl's stilettos had come off during the struggle, and one heel had snapped off completely from the sole.

After studying the disturbing crime scene photos, Jonah continued looking through the rest of the file, noting a few meager interview notes with the construction workers but nothing else until October 1995 when Morrisey and Milton headed to Georgia State Prison in Reidsville to interview Bo Cahill after he confessed to killing Earl. The detectives hadn't documented any of the conversations they'd had with Earl's friends, family, or coworkers, and that was just sloppy policework. Marla claimed to have made a considerable nuisance of herself but none of that was noted in the file either. Cops often documented when someone was highly invested in a case because sometimes that person was the perpetrator making sure the police weren't getting too close to them.

According to the Cahill interview, Bo was in Savannah visiting friends when he met Lola at a bar. Bo didn't realize Lola was a man dressed in drag until they left together. He claimed to have gone into a rage when he found out. Cahill had punched Earl hard enough to knock him out with one blow, then drove him someplace isolated, which happened to be a new neighborhood under construction. Bo stated he dragged an unconscious Earl out of the car and into an empty house, then strangled the prone man to death with one of the stockings. Afterward,

Cahill reportedly masturbated with the silk panties and shoved them in Earl's mouth. He deliberately left the skirt up to shame him. Bo stated Earl had never regained consciousness and hadn't put up a struggle.

Morrissey or Milton had noted in the file that the underwear stuffed in Earl's mouth were not public knowledge, and the coroner had found trace evidence of semen on the purple fabric. Jonah rolled around what he knew about DNA testing. At the time of Earl's death, they weren't using the kind of sophisticated analysis they were today. Techniques would have been available when Bo confessed thirteen years later though. There was no record they tested the semen to tie it to Cahill. The confession matched what the physical evidence told them, and he stated details only the killer knew. Cahill was heading to the electric chair the following week, so why waste taxpayer money for tests that wouldn't be used to convict him? Was that the logic they used to justify policework that was negligent at best and criminal at worst?

There's no way in hell Jonah would've accepted that as the only bit of proof. They'd made no attempt to corroborate Cahill was even in the area when Earl died. Bo Cahill said, "I did it," and Morrisey and Milton said, "Okay." It was probably followed with, "Thank God. Now we can get that Marla bitch off our asses."

The chief of police at the time, Deacon Potter, signed off on closing the case, and that was it. Jonah shook his head, then began a new search. He typed in Bo Cahill's name and hit enter. His file wasn't one that had been digitized and uploaded, but Jonah could still see Bo's criminal record.

On June 10, 1982, Bo Cahill was arrested for the murder which had sent him to death row. According to the information, Cahill was denied bail and remained incarcerated before and during his trial. He would've been transferred to GSP upon his conviction.

June 10th?

Jonah returned to Ison's file again. He looked for any discrepancy in the dates, but Earl's death was consistently documented as June 12th.

If these dates were correct, Bo Cahill could not have killed Earl Ison.

Jonah looked for the name of the GBI agent who was involved in

Earl's investigation. Marla had thought one was assigned to the homicide, but Jonah couldn't find a record of that anywhere. If the file was in the database, it meant GBI had been given a copy at one time. Someone within the bureau had either requested it or SPD had sent them the file and requested their assistance. Had someone in the bureau been involved in the cover-up? Jonah wouldn't know unless he obtained approval to re-open Earl Ison's case.

CHAPTER 5

The proper protocol would've been for Jonah to take what he discovered about Earl Ison to his immediate supervisor, but since Trexler hated Jonah, it would've been a colossal waste of time. Trexler would've told him to send the information to him, and he'd look through it when he had time.

Time was something Marla might not have much of, so Jonah decided to go over Trexler's head and take the information to the deputy director, Charlie Malcolm. Jonah wasn't one to exploit Malcolm's friendship with his aunt, but this was for a worthy cause. Trexler would be furious when he found out, but Jonah felt his actions were justified.

He learned from Malcolm's personal assistant that the deputy director was out to lunch, but she said Malcolm had twenty minutes free immediately afterward.

"So, around one o'clock?" Jonah asked.

"Yes, unless he's running late," Desiree replied.

"I'll be there, Desiree. Thank you."

"No problem," she said. When she cleared her throat, Jonah realized she wanted to say more. "I heard what happened yesterday. Keep your chin up, Jonah."

Jonah winced. "Thanks," he said, knowing she meant well. God, he hated being the center of gossip. "I'll see you in a bit. I better head out and grab a bite to eat if I'm going to make it back in time."

"We wouldn't want you to get hangry," Desiree said.

"Get what?" Jonah asked.

"Hangry. It's when you get so hungry it makes you irritable and angry."

"Oh. Don't worry. I won't 'Hulk out' on anyone," Jonah said.

Desiree gasped. "You know about the office pool?" she asked. "Damn Avery and his big mouth."

"Sure do." Jonah's casual tone implied he'd known about the bet much longer than a few hours. "Did you bet for or against me, Desiree?" he teased, wanting to ease the awkwardness.

"I've sat in during some of those meetings, Jonah. You have the patience of a saint, so there's no way I'm betting against you. If you leave the bureau, it will be because you've set your sight on bigger goals."

Her kind words improved Jonah's mood, but not as much as a pastrami on rye with extra pickles and freshly made Saratoga chips would, so he politely ended the call and decided to bring her a few cookies from his favorite lunch spot, Bytes and Brew.

Luckily, the cybercafé was only a few blocks from his office, and the warm spring afternoon was perfect for walking. Jonah regretted his decision when he stepped inside the café and saw Avery sitting in a corner booth with his lunch date. Avery had his back to the door and didn't see him, but Jonah got to size up the competition. The guy looked almost as tall as Jonah, but that was where the similarities ended. Avery's date looked successful, handsome, and unscathed, where Jonah looked like he'd gone several rounds with the devil.

Avery's posture was relaxed, and he laughed at something the man said. *Guess he won't be needing an excuse to leave early.* He didn't want to think about why it bothered him so much.

Jonah carefully moved through the line, hoping not to do or say anything to catch Avery's attention. The last thing he needed was Avery flagging him over for an introduction.

Eating at the café was out of the question, so Jonah trekked back to the office and ate his sandwich and chips at his desk. He'd just cleaned up his mess when his phone alerted him to an incoming text from Kendall.

Sorry if things got too loud last night. A second message immediately followed. *And again this morning.*

Jonah sent him the middle finger emoji.

Kendall's response was swift and snarky. *Thanks, baby, but I'm worn out.*

Jonah snorted, then typed a reply. *You can make it up to me by bringing home Chinese and moving your headboard a few inches away from the wall.*

Deal. Smooches, Kendall replied.

Avery still wasn't back, and Jonah didn't want to think about why, so he forced his brain to think about Earl Ison's situation instead.

Why were Morrisey and Milton, along with the district attorney and police chief, so eager to close Earl's case and call it a day without taking any steps to corroborate Bo Cahill's story? Bigotry? Laziness? Or something more sinister?

He couldn't accuse them of neglecting the DNA evidence, because it wasn't a widespread practice back then like it was today. Even if they had sent Cahill's DNA off for comparisons, the results would've come back months, maybe years, after the correctional department electrocuted Bo Cahill. Maybe they could exonerate him for Earl's murder now. If the panties were stored correctly, the DNA analysis could tell them a lot. They'd need to obtain a sample from one of Cahill's living relatives for comparison if his DNA wasn't already on file.

Jonah opened a blank document on his computer and began typing what he knew so far, the reasons why they should reopen the case, and how he wanted to proceed. Sure, Malcolm might decide to kick the investigation to a different agent since Jonah didn't work in the field, but he sincerely hoped not. He couldn't risk someone tossing the file to the side and ignoring it since both men were already dead. Jonah would be the only one to investigate it with any vigor and urgency, so he had to convince Malcolm he was the right guy for the job.

A knock sounded on his door. Jonah jerked his head up and wished like hell he'd yelled "go away" when he saw Avery's gleaming eyes, flushed cheeks, and puffy lips. *Don't say anything. Don't say anything.* "Wow," Jonah said, ignoring his directive. "That must've been some lunch."

Avery's face turned pinker. Unfortunately, he stepped farther into the room instead of shutting the door and leaving Jonah alone. "Wow," Avery said, mimicking Jonah. "Your lunch must've been horrible because you're in a darker mood than you were before I left. You did eat, right?"

"Yes," Jonah said tersely. "I don't need you to mother me."

"Smother you?" Avery asked. "Did I hear you correctly? The thought has never crossed my mind. Not once since…an hour ago."

Ignoring him, Jonah returned his attention to the screen and resumed typing. He wasn't ready to put in writing his feelings about the shoddy investigation because law enforcement officers stuck together, even sometimes when they shouldn't. Malcolm might let him reopen the case, but he'd have to attack it from a different angle such as focusing on the differences between the DNA testing capabilities now compared to back then, or even the reporting systems and ease of use now.

"Um, hello," Avery said, not taking the hint. He shut the door, crossed the room, and dropped in the chair across from Jonah. His large desk might have separated them, but Avery still felt too close for Jonah's comfort.

"What?" Jonah asked, not bothering to hide his exasperation.

"You were going to tell me what's bothering you before Frick and Frack interrupted us in the men's room," Avery said.

Jonah snorted. Frick and Frack was perfect for Paxton and Meyers. "I was going to do no such thing." Jonah met Avery's gaze. "It would seem like you were worried about your blind date for nothing." He was Avery's supervisor, so he had to refrain from commenting on Avery's lunchtime activities.

"You're looking at me like you want to kill me?" Avery said softly. "What did I do wrong?"

"Nothing," Jonah said, shaking his head. "I'm just working on something I need to pitch to Deputy Director Malcolm."

"Is it something I'm familiar with?"

Jonah shook his head. "It was something a friend mentioned to me last night. I looked into it over lunch, and her hunch was right." He glanced at the clock and noticed he had five minutes to get to Malcolm's office, so he printed what he'd typed before crossing the room to pull it off the printer. "I need to meet with Malcolm, but it shouldn't take long. We can begin working on our next phase of cybercrime detection and prevention when I get back. Trexler really had a stick up his ass over it yesterday."

"You're going to meet the director wearing a coffee-stained shirt?" Avery asked.

Jonah had forgotten all about it and was glad Avery had said something. Rather than stare at the printer while it spat out his documents, he crossed to his closet. Jonah could feel Avery's eyes on him as he started unbuttoning his shirt, but it didn't stop him or even slow him down until he heard Avery suck in a sharp breath when he got an eyeful of the tattoo inked across his back. Jonah regretted his hasty action and quickly tossed the soiled shirt into the closet and pulled on a clean one. He'd nearly fitted all the buttons through the holes before Avery spoke again.

"Wow." Jonah imagined Avery's breath ghosting over his skin while he took a closer look, running a finger over the intricately inked design or traced the dark lines with his tongue. A shiver of arousal snaked through Jonah's body, which only made him angrier. "That is one magnificent beast," Avery continued, completely unaware of the storm gathering inside Jonah. "What is it? Something mythic?"

"No," Jonah said curtly. "It's deeply personal, and I don't wish to talk about it."

"Oh," Avery said sadly. "I'm sorry. I won't bring it up again."

He knew his intern would resemble a kicked puppy if he looked at him, so Jonah kept his back turned to Avery. He tucked in his shirt as best he could without unbuckling his belt and unzipping his pants. He wrenched open the door and left without another word. Jonah stopped short when he saw the vase of colorful flowers sitting on the corner of Avery's desk. He had the strongest urge to pick it up and launch it across the room. What the fuck? This wasn't the set of one of the reality house-wife shows Kendall loved so much. He didn't throw things in a fit of rage.

Jonah needed to get laid. His hand wasn't getting the *job* done, and it was making him jealous of anyone getting action. He felt downright mean, and it wasn't cool. Desiree's eyes widened when she saw him com-ing, so he got a grip on his emotions and forced a smile.

"Is he back?" Jonah asked, aiming for a friendly tone.

Desiree visibly relaxed. "Yes, and he's expecting you."

"Thanks, Desiree." Jonah handed her the cookies he bought from the café.

"You're so sweet. Can I get you some coffee or something?"

With his luck, Jonah would end up wearing another cup, and he was down to his last spare shirt at the office. "No, thanks." Then Jonah realized he'd left without grabbing the document from his printer. He briefly debated going back to get it but nixed the idea. He had the main details memorized, and he could always email additional information if Malcolm wanted more.

Jonah knocked on Malcolm's door.

"Come in," the deputy director said.

Jonah twisted the knob and opened the door. *Here goes nothing* was his first thought, but he recalled how much was truly at stake—jeopar-dizing his career by breaking protocol, rectifying injustice, and getting peace for a dear friend Jonah wasn't ready to say goodbye to yet.

Here goes everything.

CHAPTER 6

"Jonah, this is a pleasant surprise," the deputy director said jovially, greeting him more like a favorite uncle than a powerfully ranked member of the bureau. Smiling, he gestured for Jonah to take a seat in one of the chairs in front of his desk.

Charlie Malcolm was the kind of guy who maintained a youthful appearance well past the time most men started exhibiting crow's feet and laugh lines. He'd only recently started showing a bit of wear and tear, and his blond hair had begun to gray at the temples. If Jonah hadn't known better, he would've guessed the deputy director was forty years old instead of approaching sixty.

Jonah knew a brilliant mind lurked behind the sparkling blue eyes and brilliant smile though. The deputy director had worked in law enforcement for almost four decades, starting as a sheriff's deputy in Fulton County before moving back home and accepting a position with the Savannah Police Department. His first partner with SPD was a rookie cop named Ellen St. John. Everyone had expected Malcolm to climb the ladder at the police department, but he'd chosen to pursue a new path with the Georgia Bureau of Investigation instead, climbing to the second-highest rank in the department. His former partner, now Ellen Rigby, ascended to the highest rung at the SPD and wore her police commissioner title with much pride.

Malcolm had quipped more than once that his job was more on the political end of the spectrum instead of law and order these days. He performed the balance brilliantly, and it was only a matter of time before Malcolm became the director of the Georgia Bureau of Investigations. Jonah wished the office pool wagered on when the current director would retire instead of people guessing when he'd "Hulk out."

"Thanks for seeing me, sir," Jonah replied. "I won't take much of your time."

The deputy director shook his head and sighed. "How many times do I need to tell you to call me Malcolm when it's just the two of us?"

"At least once more, sir," Jonah joked.

"Fine. Have it your way," Malcolm said. "What can I do for you?"

Knowing the director was a busy man, Jonah got straight to the point. He filled Malcolm in on everything he knew so far, sticking to facts and leaving out Marla's hunches and his conjecture. Cops trust their own instincts but weren't as eager to rely on anyone else's. Jonah watched as the deputy director morphed from friendly uncle to intrigued lawman to shrewd politician in a matter of minutes. Jonah couldn't blame him. If he was correct, and he'd bet his next paycheck on it, reopening the case could have huge repercussions. Malcolm would need hard proof before he would be willing to take steps that could tarnish a lawman's reputation and bring unwanted attention on their agency or the police department.

"You have my attention," Malcolm said once Jonah finished.

"Sir, I can't see any other course of action except to reopen the Ison investigation."

Malcolm placed his elbows on the desk and steepled his fingers. "How certain are you of these facts, Jonah? What if Bo Cahill's arrest dates were entered into the computer incorrectly? Say the person transposed a number or used the wrong month. For the first ten years of marriage, I thought my wife's birthday was March fifteenth instead of May fifteenth. Danielle would smile and tell me it was better to receive a birthday gift two months early than two months late. Still, it's a miracle Danielle and I celebrated our thirty-fifth anniversary this past weekend."

"Congratulations, sir."

"Thank you, Jonah," Malcolm said, briefly slipping back into fond uncle mode before continuing. "What if he had been released on bail, but the details weren't properly documented."

Jonah wanted to dispute Malcolm's suggestion, but, how could he? Someone might have entered dates incorrectly or only included partial information. "Can I at least have your permission to request a copy of the file from DeKalb County?"

"Have you spoken to Trexler about this?" Malcolm asked, his right brow arching toward his hairline. "You know that is the proper chain of command."

Jonah barely bit back a frustrated groan. "I do know, sir, but you have to agree Supervisory Agent Trexler isn't very open to my suggestions." Trexler had a habit of dialing back his criticism of Jonah when Malcolm was present, but his contempt had been barely veiled the previous day.

"I know you think it's the case," Malcolm countered. Jonah wanted to ask the deputy director to name one idea of Jonah's that Trexler had liked, but the older man held up a hand before he could form the words. "Look, I know you have a strained relationship with Butch, but going behind his back will do nothing to repair the fractures. He will view our conversation as an act of insubordination and could write you up for breaching protocol, and he'd be well within his right."

Jonah recognized a losing battle when he saw one. He'd be wise to retreat to his office and come up with another battle plan to deal with Trexler instead of risking his good standing with the deputy director. "I understand, sir. I will take your advice. Thank you for your time."

"Hold up," Malcolm said when Jonah started to rise.

"Yes, sir?" he asked, sitting back down in the chair.

"I'm curious how you found out about this case? Was it something introduced through your podcast?" Malcolm asked.

"No," Jonah said, shaking his head. "Earl Ison and I have a mutual friend who was recently diagnosed with stage four liver cancer. She never believed that Bo Cahill killed Earl and would like to see the real killer brought to justice before she dies."

The deputy director's blue eyes softened, and he was back to Uncle

Charlie again. "It's a noble thing you're doing for your friend. Talk to Trexler, Jonah. I will back you up if he asks me for my opinion. He might surprise you."

I won't hold my breath. "Thank you, sir."

Desiree smiled at Jonah when he exited Malcolm's office. "Avery stopped by with this," she said, handing him an interoffice envelope. "He thought you might need it for your meeting."

Jonah wasn't surprised by Avery's thoughtful gesture even after his display of surliness and abrupt departure, nor was he a stranger to the guilt surging through his body.

"Avery looked like a kicked puppy," Desiree continued, jabbing a finger in his conscience. "Someone should do something nice to cheer him up." She batted her eyelashes innocently. Jonah didn't fall for her act. He met and held her shrewd gaze until the woman's cheeks turned pink, and she broke their staring match to roll her eyes. "Fine. I'll stay out of it." She wouldn't, but Jonah would take the reprieve for as long as it lasted.

Jonah's mood was darker than ever. Nothing about the past twenty-four hours had gone his way, and he was taking it out on the wrong people. He needed to get his shit together and put his energy where he needed it most, which was preparing—emotionally and physically—for a meeting with Trexler. He swung by the break room to get his caramel fix and was further irritated when he saw they were all out of Twix. He settled for a Milky Way and bought a package of Reese's Peanut Butter Cups for Avery since they were his favorite. It was lame as far as peace offerings went, but it was better than nothing.

Avery wasn't at his desk when Jonah got back, so he left the candy on Avery's desk and headed inside his office. The space often felt like the eye of a storm, peaceful and serene, allowing him to block out the chaos swirling like howling winds on the other side of the door. Sitting down at his computer, he pulled up their instant message system and requested a meeting with Trexler. Jonah expected his supervisor to ignore him, so he was surprised when a reply came through almost right away.

It will have to wait until the morning, Trexler replied. He imagined his boss's gruff voice when he read the words.

Jonah didn't want to delay the investigation another day, but his hands were tied. Plus, it gave him more time to come up with an argument even Trexler couldn't refute. His supervisor might insist someone with more field experience review the details. Trexler might even investigate the situation himself to earn extra brownie points with Malcolm. Jonah wouldn't like either of those outcomes, but he could live with it if someone pursued the case seriously.

Avery entered his office carrying Jonah's coffee mug and had Jonah's peace offering tucked inside his shirt pocket. "Permission to approach your desk?" Avery asked. Jonah was pleased to see the teasing light in his eyes.

"I don't know. How hot is the coffee?" Jonah asked, quirking a brow.

"Very. I just made it for you," Avery said.

Jonah scooted back from his desk, giving Avery a wide berth and nodded. "It smells delicious."

"I found these salted caramel coffee pods at the store last night, and they reminded me of you." Knowing Avery thought about him at random times did funny things to his stomach and delicious things even lower. "I hid them in my desk so no one else would drink them."

"That's very thoughtful. Thank you."

"I can be exceptionally nice sometimes." Avery set the mug on Jonah's desk.

The temperature rose inside the office, and the temporary peace Jonah had felt evaporated in Avery's warmth. The glint in his intern's eyes said *dance for me, moth.* Oh, how he danced.

"When you're not dousing me in hot coffee," Jonah quipped. "Speaking of, I know I've said this several times, but it bears repeating. I—"

Avery waved a hand and cut him off. "I know. I know. This isn't the fifties and making coffee or retrieving your lunch isn't part of my duties."

"Unless it's an excuse to get out of a lousy lunch date, then by all means." Jonah wanted Avery to tell him it had been a miserable experience and that he was never seeing the man again, but he didn't.

Avery laughed as he sat down across from Jonah. He tore open his candy bar and hummed happily as he chewed the first bite. "Thank you for the Reese's. I needed something sweet to counterbalance all the salty stuff I consumed at lunchtime."

Jonah nearly choked on his coffee. A dozen remarks came to mind, but he left them all unspoken because it would've been impossible to hide the innuendo or his jealousy. He didn't want to think about Avery's swollen lips, let alone talk about the activities leading up to the condition.

"Don't make a big deal out of it," Jonah groused. "Let's get to coding."

"I don't get you, Jonah St. John."

That makes two of us.

"I ordered enough food for ten people," Kendall said as he unpacked the delivery bags from their favorite Chinese restaurant a few hours later. "You could invite your podcast friends over. I can change and put on something nicer." Kendall gestured to the shortest pair of pale blue shorts Jonah had ever seen. They clung to his roommate's ass like a second skin.

"For future reference, neither Felix nor Rocky would be upset if you wore those shorty shorts around them. It might make it harder for the fellas to concentrate though."

"Good to know," Kendall said with a wink.

"If it's okay with you, I prefer a quiet night at home with just the two of us."

Kendall's head snapped up, and his perceptive gaze raked over Jonah's face. "What happened?"

Where did he start? His conversation with Marla the previous evening? Or the disastrous way his week had started with meetings from hell followed by the impending discussion with Trexler in the morning?

Jonah pulled a soda out of the refrigerator for himself and a bottle of strawberry-kiwi water for Kendall. He set them on the counter and met Kendall's curious gaze.

"Oh, honey. That bad?" he asked.

"I haven't said anything," Jonah replied.

"You didn't have to. I can see the storm brewing in your eyes and feel the tension rolling off you in waves. I know what you need," Kendall said. "I'll fix you right up."

Kendall put the beverages back in the refrigerator and removed the brand-new bottle of bourbon and two tumblers from the cabinet beside it. "On the rocks or straight up?" he asked, setting the booze and glasses on the counter.

Jonah smiled. "I'll take the first one straight up and add ice later to pace myself."

"Same," Kendall said, pouring a generous amount in both glasses. He picked up one drink and gave the other to Jonah. "I propose a toast."

Jonah didn't feel like he had a single thing to celebrate but kept his mouth shut as he held his glass in the air.

"To our fabulousness and the dumb fucks who don't deserve us," Kendall said. *Uh-oh.* Before he could ask questions, Kendall clicked his glass against Jonah's and said, "Cheers." Then he knocked back half the drink like a rum-guzzling pirate.

"Cheers," Jonah repeated, but unlike Kendall, he sipped the fine liquor. "God, that goes down so smoothly."

"That's what *he* said," Kendall teased, winking playfully at Jonah. When he followed it with a giggle-snort, Jonah knew Kendall was already feeling the alcohol. *Lightweight.* "I need ice."

"Yes, you do," Jonah said, taking the glass from Kendall and adding ice to his drink for him.

"Let's set up a buffet on the coffee table," Kendall suggested. "We can eat a little bit of everything."

"Sounds good to me."

Jonah retrieved plates from the cabinet, and Kendall pulled open a drawer and removed two forks. Then they each grabbed as many containers as they could carry before making a second trip.

"Looks like we're eating our emotions tonight," Jonah said, surveying the bounty.

Kendall hiccupped, then giggled. "And drinking."

"Cheers to that too," Jonah said, clinking his glass against Kendall's before taking a longer drink.

Their conversation stalled as they dished food onto plates and began eating. The lull in conversation allowed Jonah's mind to wander, and the path inevitably led him to his intern. He pictured Avery's enthralled expression while working out some of the kinks with Jonah's microchip design. He'd been so caught up in his work, Avery hadn't noticed Jonah watching him. Avery's tongue had darted out to lick his lower lip when he got close to figuring a problem out, or he'd chewed on his pencil when he felt frustrated. Jonah wanted Avery's tongue and teeth all over his body. He recalled the way Avery's long fingers danced over the keyboard and wanted to feel those nimble digits pushing all Jonah's buttons. And the gasp he'd made when he saw Jonah's tattoo? *Fuck me.* He would hear the sound during his fantasies for sure.

"What's troubling you?" Kendall asked, startling Jonah back to the present. "Is Trexler being a douche again?"

Jonah chuckled. "Still, not again. I'd say he's acting extra douchey." He poured them another drink and decided to skip the ice for the second round too.

He told Kendall everything, starting with the brutal meetings from the previous day and ending with Malcolm insisting Jonah discuss the Ison investigation with Trexler. He left out the parts about Avery spilling coffee on him or the moment they shared in the restroom afterward. Jonah would unpack that later when he was alone.

"You win the prize for the shittiest thirty-six hours," Kendall said softly. "I'm so sorry to hear about Marla, Jonah. It's a beautiful thing you're trying to do for her, and I know you'll get justice for Earl in the process."

"Thanks," he said awkwardly. It amazed Jonah how much easier it was for him to accept criticism over praise.

A full stomach and two potent drinks were making Jonah feel drowsy. Kendall poured a third drink for them both, and Jonah knew he wasn't the only one struggling with demons. "What's wrong? Whose ass do I need to kick for hurting you?"

Kendall snorted. "Mine. I should've ignored Travis's text messages. I knew he didn't want to meet for dinner to talk about old times, or at least it wasn't his only motivation."

"Is this the guy from last night?" Jonah asked.

"And this morning," Kendall said with a wry smile.

Jonah shot him the middle finger just like he had in his text. "Old times?" he asked. "How long have you known this Travis putz?"

"Oh, about sixteen years," Kendall replied casually.

Jonah turned his head too quickly and the room spun a little. He waited until he only saw one Kendall instead of two before he spoke. "Sixteen years?"

"Mmmhmm," Kendall said. "That's when his father married my mother. I was nine and Travis was eleven."

Jonah just stared at him for a few moments. "Travis is your stepbrother?"

Kendall grinned wickedly. "Uh-huh."

"So, how long have the two of you, um…"

"Been fucking?" Kendall asked nonchalantly.

"Yeah," Jonah replied.

"We fooled around when we were in high school, but it never went beyond mutual hand jobs until we were adults. I think Travis was a college sophomore by then, and I'd just graduated high school." Kendall looked at Jonah and smiled. "You should see the thunderous expression in your eyes. Travis didn't take advantage of me. Not then, and not now. I knew what I was getting into, and I was the one who invited him back here last night, all the while knowing he could never give me what I want."

"Which is?" Jonah asked.

"I don't want to sound like some stupid sap, but I want to be the most important person in his life." Kendall closed his eyes and took a deep breath. "He's so deep in the closet, J. I don't think he'll ever truly see the light of day. Even if he comes out to his family and coworkers, he will never pursue a relationship with me."

"Why not?" Jonah asked.

"For one thing," Kendall said, "he's the kind of guy with big career aspirations and banging his stepbrother would be frowned upon in any social circle." He smiled sadly at Jonah. "And even if that didn't bother him, my lack of education and my side hustle at The Cockpit embarrasses him."

"You're studying to become a paralegal," Jonah said. "How does he know what kind of establishment The Cockpit is if he hasn't seen the sexy aviator uniforms in person? He sounds like the typical self-hating, closeted gay."

"Uniform?" Kendall asked. "It's a pair of booty shorts, a mesh crop top, aviator glasses, and a pilot's hat."

"And you wear them so very well," Jonah said, smiling fondly at the memories of the night he met Kendall at the club. "Back to my point. How does he know about the uniforms?"

"You think you're the first guy I fucked in the back seat of a car during my dinner break, Jonah? That's the kind of guy I am, and it's not what Travis will be looking for *if* he ever comes out."

"You're worth so much more than you think. Someday, you'll find a guy who helps you realize it."

Kendall reached over and squeezed his hand. "You deserve the happiness you insist on denying yourself. Someday, the perky intern will help you realize it."

"You think so, huh?" Jonah asked drowsily.

"I know so."

Jonah sighed. "Won't be today."

Kendall pressed a cool hand to Jonah's cheek. "That's why we have tomorrows."

Jonah knew all too well they weren't guaranteed a tomorrow. "Maybe," he said, leaning his head back against the couch and closing his eyes.

The next thing he knew, his alarm clock was blaring. Jonah reached over and turned it off. The motion created a jolt of pain in his skull. What the fuck had happened to him? Was he involved in an accident? His mouth was dry and tasted horrible. What was that noise? Was someone singing?

He cracked one eye open and regretted it immediately. The room started to spin, making him nauseous as fuck. Jonah recognized the symptoms. He had a fucking hangover, a condition he hadn't experienced in a long time. He usually exercised more control and could handle liquor better than this. What the hell was that screechy racket? It *was* someone singing. Then Jonah heard the water running in his bathroom. Someone was singing in his shower. Who? It hurt to think, but he tried anyway. It had just been him and Kendall at home last night. They'd eaten Chinese food, drank excellent bourbon, and talked. Another recollection followed the first. And then another. Kendall helping him to the bathroom to throw up when he'd woken from his nap on the couch. Kendall pressing a cool rag to his forehead and cheeks. Kendall kissing his forehead. Kendall tucking him into bed, and Jonah reaching out to stop him before he could walk away.

"Stay," Jonah had begged.

"This isn't a good idea," Kendall countered as he pulled back the covers and slid between them.

Oh, God. What had he done?

The shower shut off and the singing got louder. After a few minutes, Kendall walked out of the bathroom, wearing nothing but a towel and a joyful smile on his face.

"Oh, God. What did we do?"

CHAPTER 7

"**Y**ou don't have to sound so goddamned stricken right now," Kendall said, placing his hands on his hips, nudging the towel a little lower. "You also don't have to imply I'm the kind of guy who sexually assaults another while he's too drunk to give consent. I might be easy, but I'm not sleazy."

Despite everything, Jonah's lips twitched into a semi-smile. Just that little motion reminded him of how miserable he felt.

"Furthermore, you couldn't have gotten it up last night even if Avery paraded around in front of you buck-ass naked."

"I wouldn't bet on it," Jonah said dryly.

"You know what today is?" Kendall asked cheerfully.

Jonah had to think, which was unbelievably painful. *How much bourbon did I drink?* "Um, Wednesday?"

"Yes, actually," Kendall said. "More importantly, it's the day you take the bull by the horns or the intern by the balls, and make shit happen. Plus, you're going to get justice for Earl and Marla."

Jonah groaned as the events from the past few days began to crystalize and take shape in his muddled brain. He couldn't afford to lie around and moan about his poor decisions when Marla needed him.

"I won't be taking Avery by the balls, K."

Kendall crossed his arms over his chest. "Why not?"

"He's seeing someone," Jonah replied.

"Since when?" Kendall scoffed.

"Yesterday."

"Ah, I see," Kendall said, fixing Jonah with a determined look. "One date or even night of sex isn't strong enough to extinguish the torch the sweet boy is carrying for you."

"Sweet boy?" Jonah asked. "He's twenty-five. Same as you."

"Maybe on paper, but I'm decades older in experience," Kendall countered.

Jonah's eyes snagged on the tiny scrap of blue fabric lying in the middle of his bedroom floor. It took him a moment to recognize them as Kendall's shorts. "Are you sure we didn't do *anything*?"

Kendall sighed. "I stripped out of the shorts on the way to the shower, not before I got in your bed. Pull back the blanket and look at yourself. Are you wearing underwear?" Jonah lifted the sheet and comforter and saw he was indeed wearing his boxer briefs. "There's your answer," Kendall said huffily. "I can't believe you question my character." He bent over to retrieve his shorty shorts with a dramatic flourish and ended up losing his towel in the process. "Oopsie," Kendall said, making no attempt to cover himself as he left Jonah's bedroom.

"I hope you saved some hot water for me," Jonah called out, wincing when the effort sent a stabbing pain through his brain. His water heater was starting to show its age, and he knew it wouldn't be long before he had to replace it.

Kendall's voice rang out from down the hall. "More than you deserve."

Jonah gingerly got out of bed and padded to his bathroom, where he took the hottest shower he could stand. After he finished and toweled off, Jonah saw Kendall had left a cup of hot coffee, a bottle of cold water, toast, and three Advil tablets on his nightstand.

He planned to thank Kendall for his kindness and apologize for jumping to conclusions when he got downstairs, but his roommate had already left. Jonah had to settle for sending a text instead. Even though Kendall didn't appear to be angry with him, Jonah had meant what he'd said at dinner. The guy deserved better treatment than he allowed. If Jonah wanted Kendall to believe it, then he needed to demonstrate his sincerity.

Kendall's reply was a simple xoxoxo.

He made a quick trip to Ling's to pick up his Caramel Bugles. "How's Dakota working out?" Jonah asked Mrs. Ling.

"He's a good boy. Just needs someone to care," she said with an easy smile. Mrs. Ling tried to give him the Bugles for free, but Jonah refused her kind offer.

Mrs. Ling wasn't one to take no for an answer and began negotiating a deal. Jonah ended up accepting a ten percent discount because he still felt like sunbaked roadkill, and he'd be sick if she called him a hero one more time.

Once at the bureau, Jonah kept his head down and didn't make eye contact with anyone as he navigated the labyrinth of hallways. He held up his hand in silent greeting to those who ignored his body language but didn't stop moving until he reached the blissful peace of his office. Let their tongues wag about his present mood.

"Whoa. You look rough as hell. Are you ill?" Avery asked softly as he entered the room with a steaming cup of coffee in his hand.

Jonah looked up and wished he hadn't. The expression in Avery's eyes was a mixture of concern, compassion, and something else Jonah was too afraid to acknowledge. If he did, there'd be no turning back.

"I might've had too much to drink last night. It wasn't my smartest move," Jonah said, his voice sounding as ravaged as he felt. He had to pull himself together before meeting with Trexler, so he reached for his vice. "Want some?" he asked, opening the bag and tipping it toward Avery.

His intern approached the desk cautiously. "In all these months, you've never once offered me one of your beloved Bugles. The end must be near."

In response, Jonah rolled his eyes and shook the bag to double down on his offer.

Avery slowly slid his hand inside the bag. It felt as intimate to

Jonah as if the younger man had ghosted his fingertips over his bare flesh. Avery snagged a few caramel-covered corn snacks before retreating. "Let's see what the fuss is all about," he teased, popping one into his mouth. "Mmmm."

"Now you get it," Jonah said before tossing back a handful of Bugles.

"What rattled you so hard that you went home and got drunk?" he asked. "Is it me? Have I finally driven you to drink?" Avery asked.

"Why? Is there an office bet on that too?"

"Jonah," Avery said somberly. "I'm serious."

"God, no," Jonah said. "I'm sorry the thought even crossed your mind." He gestured for Avery to sit down in the chair across from him, offering his bag of corn snacks again. Avery smiled but shook his head. "I received some terrible news about a friend on Monday night. She has terminal cancer."

"Oh, Jonah. I'm so sorry," Avery said, reaching across the desk and covering his hand. Jonah was momentarily stunned because it was the first time they'd had skin-on-skin contact. *Jesus.* How was it something so innocent made his pulse race and left him breathless? A buzz much stronger than awareness sparked along his spine, and he thought he saw the same reaction in the hazel-brown eyes staring back at him. Jonah had to battle the urge to rotate his wrist and lace his fingers with Avery's.

"Thank you. It really threw me for a loop. Marla seems so indestructible."

"Is there anything I can do for you?" Avery asked.

Let me count the ways. "There might be."

"Anything," Avery said breathlessly.

Pulling his hand back, Jonah made a fist beneath the desk. He wanted to hold on to the sensations Avery brought forth in him a little while longer. "It depends on how my meeting goes with Trexler this morning."

Avery blinked. "Meeting with Trexler?"

Tearing his eyes away from Avery's, Jonah checked the time and swore. "I'll have to explain later. Trexler's expecting me in five minutes."

He reached inside his middle desk drawer and pulled out the interoffice envelope containing his notes about the discrepancies in the Ison case. "Wish me luck," Jonah said, pushing back from his desk.

"Um, good luck."

"Don't eat all my Bugles, Avery," Jonah tossed over his shoulder on the way to the door.

"Yes, sir."

Jonah made the short walk to Trexler's office, arriving with a minute to spare. His assistant Tabitha looked up from her computer and smiled at him.

"He's just finishing up with a call, and he'll be right with you," Tabby said.

"Thanks," Jonah said, searching his brain for small talk to engage in while they waited. Weather was always a safe bet, so he went with it.

"Spring is my favorite time of year. I love seeing all the flowers in bloom."

A big smile spread across Tabby's face, and Jonah knew where the conversation was headed. "So, who sent Avery flowers?"

"I don't know," Jonah lied. "Avery didn't say, and I don't pry. They just appeared on his desk sometime after lunch yesterday." Then Jonah realized he hadn't seen the colorful bouquet on Avery's desk this morning, but it made sense that he would want to take them home.

The door behind Tabby opened suddenly, cutting off their conversation. "Sorry to keep you waiting, Agent St. John," Trexler said, offering an apologetic smile, which made Jonah uneasy. The man scowled, belittled, and frowned at him. He never smiled at Jonah, and he sure as hell didn't apologize.

"It's no problem, sir," Jonah said.

"Won't you come in? I'm sure you have better things to do than gossip with Tabby." His assistant stiffened and broke eye contact with Jonah. Trexler didn't wait for a response; he spun on his heels and headed back into his office, expecting Jonah to follow.

Jonah rapped his knuckles on Tabby's desk, pulling her gaze back up to meet his. He winked and smiled, hoping it would ease the sting she felt from her boss's crass treatment.

Closing the door behind him, Jonah entered Trexler's lair. His boss was already seated at his desk, waiting impatiently for Jonah to begin. Trexler looked as debonair as always in a black suit, light blue shirt, and a striped tie. Not a hair was out of place. Trexler had ten years on Jonah, and it had started to show.

"What did you wish to discuss with me?" Trexler asked, interrupting Jonah's thoughts. The man leaned back against his chair and studied him carefully. A half-smile tugged at the corner of Trexler's mouth, reminding him of a cat waiting to pounce. Worse, it was the same smug expression Oscar used to wear when he knew he had the upper hand. Jonah's unease quadrupled.

"I stumbled on to a closed case I feel was poorly investigated at best and criminal misconduct at the worst," Jonah said. He opened the inter-office envelope and pulled out the summary of facts he'd typed, then slid it across the desk to Trexler. "I'd like permission to request official files so we can determine if the investigation should be reopened."

His boss kept his eyes locked on Jonah's instead of looking at the document in front of him. "You're not a field agent," Trexler said. "How many times do I have to tell you that?"

Yep. Just like Oscar. Trexler unknowingly catapulted Jonah back to the summer he'd fallen from the treehouse and broke his arm.

"Boys don't cry, Jonah. How many times do I have to tell you that?"

He'd been seven. God, he fucking hated toxic masculinity.

"You're supposed to be using your supercomputer to solve crimes."

"I'm not experienced in the field, and I understand if you want to assign this investigation to another agent," Jonah said.

"How big of you, St. John," Trexler said snidely, shoving the document back across the desk to Jonah without looking at it. "You have two minutes to tell me why the case needs further scrutiny." Trexler looked at his watch. "Starting now."

Jonah quickly went through the facts he uncovered as succinctly as he could in the time allotted.

Trexler steepled his fingers at mid-chest. "I'm not willing to reopen a thirty-eight-year-old case on a whim."

"With all due respect, sir, it's not a whim. Bo Cahill couldn't have killed Earl Ison if he was incarcerated in DeKalb County. Can I at least have your permission to request their official file?"

"People could've entered the wrong dates, St. John."

"True," Jonah agreed, "and a quick look at the file will resolve the issue once and for all."

Trexler heaved a deep sigh. "You might be willing to stake your career on this, but I'm not willing to hinge the reputation of retired officers and prosecutors on your conjecture. I have faith in the system and trust that those involved practiced due diligence. As I see it, this is SPD's problem. If a mistake was made, it's their responsibility to investigate and correct their error. You may tell your aunt, the police commissioner, I said so. My answer is no, Agent St. John."

Jonah knew he should accept the verdict and leave, but he couldn't. He'd given Marla his word. "With all due respect, sir, the Ison file wouldn't be in our database if the GBI wasn't involved. We had either requested the information or SPD sent it to us when asking for our assistance." Jonah thought the latter was unlikely.

Trexler's nostrils flared as he jabbed the air with his finger. "All I'm hearing from you are assumptions, and I don't appreciate you wasting my time. Send this information to your aunt and let her sort it out and be ostracized by the public if what you discovered is true."

Trexler was on a roll and wasn't finished. "We went over your shortcomings in detail during Monday's meetings. Apparently, I need to reiterate a few key points."

Jonah sat ramrod straight, unmoving except for the ticking in his jaw.

"I know how highly you think of your criminal analysis and profiling skills, and you've even convinced Director Malcolm of your merit. The key fact remains that your primary task at this agency is to detect and prevent cybercrimes. You don't get to dust off your supercomputer and investigate crimes at whim, especially not cases that are already marked as solved. You are to wait until your assistance is requested and approved by me before you start feeding facts into Starla."

"Stella."

"Whatever," Trexler said dismissively. "What about this 'game-changing software' you're developing?" Jonah briefly fantasized about dislocating the fingers Trexler used to form his obnoxious air quotes. "Do we need to discuss how to best allocate your energy and focus? Again."

"It's a cybersecurity microchip, sir," Jonah said. He was impressed with how calm he sounded, especially since Trexler had been put in charge of a division he didn't even appreciate or understand. Whose dick had he sucked to get this promotion? Maybe someday Jonah would find the nerve to ask. "Software is too easy to hack and manipulate. I plan to finish the mockup today, which is a week ahead of schedule." He never missed a deadline and sure as fuck wouldn't start now.

"Then I expect to see the results of your trial runs by the end of this week instead of next. I can see that having too much time on your hands is detrimental."

"Yes, sir." Not that the idiot would understand the data.

"I knew allowing you to participate with the Sinister in Savannah podcast was a mistake, and I wish Director Malcolm would've listened to my opinion on the matter. It's obvious the success has gone to your head and made you think you're an amateur sleuth." Trexler took a deep breath. "It's also apparent you don't respect proper protocol since you went over my head and discussed reopening the case with Director Malcolm instead of coming to me first." Trexler opened a desk drawer, pulled out a piece of paper, and slid it across the desk to Jonah. "I think the director's friendship with your aunt has given you a false sense of security and importance around here. This," Trexler said, nodding to the paper, "should help you put things in proper focus."

Jonah glanced down at the document, and his gaze snagged on words like "insubordination" and "official warning." He glanced up and met Trexler's smug expression. No wonder the bastard had seemed happier this morning. Jonah had finally played into his hand and given Trexler a legitimate reason to write him up.

"I think you should be grateful it's only a warning this time. I could've suspended you without pay, but I chose not to."

Bullshit. Jonah's offense wasn't severe enough to warrant a suspension without prior written warnings. Was Trexler expecting Jonah to thank him? The supervisory agent's smug grin morphed into a joyous smile. Trexler knew Jonah was choking on bitterness and was daring him to pop off. Jonah would not let this asshole make him "Hulk out" at work, no matter what everyone thought.

Nope. Jonah needed to focus his energy on where it was needed most: making the person who betrayed him pay.

Trexler's phone rang, and he picked up. "Yes, Tabitha. Jonah was just leaving. Please send the call through once he steps out of my office. Thanks." He returned the phone to its cradle and looked expectantly at Jonah. "Did you have anything else you wanted to discuss with me?"

"No," Jonah said tersely.

"You can show yourself out so we can both get on with our workday," Trexler said.

Jonah snatched up his warning along with the summary he'd prepared, got up, and left the room. He passed Tabby's desk without saying goodbye because his brain was too busy trying to figure out who had betrayed him. Jonah knew damn well Malcolm hadn't ratted him out to Trexler, and he hadn't discussed the investigation with anyone else.

The truth hit Jonah with the force of a tornado, and he almost stumbled.

When he returned to his office, Avery was working on Stella. He was so engrossed in his project that he hadn't realized Jonah returned until he shut the door more forcefully than he'd intended.

Avery jumped, and the pencil he'd been gnawing on fell out of his mouth. "Jonah," he said, clutching his chest. "You scared the hell out of me."

CHAPTER 8

"**O**r are you just jumpy?" Jonah asked.

"I don't have a reason to be jumpy," Avery protested.

Jonah stalked across the room until he practically stood over him. "Is that so?"

Avery swallowed hard but didn't look away from him. "What's going on?"

"Did you read the document I prepared yesterday before you placed it in the interoffice envelope?" he asked.

"I glanced at it, yes," Avery admitted, raising his chin defiantly.

"Who'd you tell about it?" Jonah asked.

Avery's mouth dropped open in shock. "No one. I only delivered it to Desiree since I figured you would need it for the meeting. What's going on?"

Jonah shoved the insubordination warning at Avery, who looked at it, then gasped.

"Oh no." Avery pushed back his chair and rose to his feet, glaring at Jonah. "You think *I* told Trexler about your meeting with Malcolm? How could you think I'd betray you like that, Jonah? I know how much you can't stand the smug bastard."

Avery's anger took a little wind out of Jonah's sails, but he wasn't willing to dismiss his suspicions altogether. "Okay, maybe you didn't tell

Trexler directly, but you told someone during morning gossip, who told someone else, who—"

"Fuck you, Jonah," Avery snarled, stepping around him and walking quickly toward the door.

Jonah caught up to him in three strides, bracing his hand against the door to prevent Avery from opening it. "I'm not done talking to you." Jonah knew he was acting irrationally but couldn't seem to stop himself.

Avery's body vibrated. From anger? Or was it from lust pooling in his gut? Jesus. Heat rolled off Avery, making his rain-fresh scent stronger. Jonah had the insane urge to press his nose behind Avery's ear and inhale deeply.

"Take your hand off the door, Jonah. I don't want to be near you right now."

"Avery, I know how much you like to gossip with some of the ladies. Maybe you didn't mean for this to happen, but—"

Avery threw an elbow, driving it into Jonah's gut and temporarily cutting off his ability to speak. Avery followed it up by stomping on Jonah's instep.

"Fuck," Jonah groaned, limping backward.

Avery spun around and boldly strode toward Jonah, his nostrils flaring as he breathed heavily. "I told you to back off, and you didn't," Avery said, jabbing his finger in Jonah's chest. "Next time, I'll knee you in the balls."

For the first time since Jonah left Trexler's office, he started to second-guess himself. If Avery was lying to him, he was very persuasive. Jonah ran both hands through his hair.

"I told no one about what I read on the report. I didn't seal the interoffice envelope, so Desiree could've read it and told Tabby about it. They're cousins and probably wouldn't even view the exchange as gossip. Trexler is always on Tabby's ass, so she probably told him to score points. So, indirectly, I'm probably responsible, and I am sorry. I wouldn't intentionally betray your trust, and I'm hurt you think I would."

Jonah had the strongest urge to pull Avery into his arms, but he couldn't…wouldn't. "I'm sorry, Avery. I should've known better. I don't know what's come over me."

"You're not forgiven, Jonah. I need a few minutes to calm down before I can continue working," he said before spinning around and leaving Jonah's office.

Jonah walked over to his desk and flopped down in his chair. Snatching up the bag of Bugles, he devoured them in two minutes or less while white-hot rage burned through him. He couldn't believe Trexler refused to even consider requesting Bo Cahill's official case file from DeKalb County. Jonah wasn't buying his pomp and circumstance about protecting the law enforcement officers' reputation either. Trexler would throw his own mother under a bus if it meant advancing his career. Fuck. Had Jonah approached this the wrong way? He'd gone into the meeting armed with facts when he should've gone in there ready to stroke the man's ego. The thought left a bitter taste in Jonah's mouth, but his pride could've cost him the one chance to give Marla peace of mind.

"Idiot," Jonah mumbled under his breath.

"Well, I can see our little time-out wasn't long enough," Avery said from the open doorway. Jonah snapped his head up and found his intern scowling at him. God, he was so fucking cute when he was mad.

"I wasn't calling you an idiot, Avery. Get in here and shut the door so I can grovel in private."

"What if I want the entire office to witness you on your knees?"

Heat uncoiled low in his belly and spread upward as very tantalizing images flooded his brain. Jonah raised a brow.

Realizing what he said and how it could be interpreted, Avery started to sputter. "I…um didn't mean I wanted you on your knees for *that*. I meant begging for it." He gasped and choked. "No. Begging me." He shook his head. "I meant you should be on your knees, begging for my forgiveness. Christ. I *am* an idiot. You're right."

"You're adorable," is what Jonah wanted to say. Instead, he smiled and said, "Maybe we should start over."

"We can try, but it's not likely either of us will forget this disastrous morning," Avery quipped.

"Maybe it's for the best. Let's aim for learning from it instead."

"Deal," Avery said with a firm nod. "Let me grab my tea, and we'll start over."

Jonah scrunched up his face. "Gross."

"Don't you start with me," Avery tossed over his shoulder as he ducked out of Jonah's office. He returned with a cup of something that didn't resemble his usual sweat-sock stew. It smelled like cinnamon and cloves and other things he couldn't name. Black licorice? "Good morning, Jonah," Avery said, plastering a huge smile on his face. "Did you have a fun night?"

Jonah's expression must have given away his confusion.

"I said I wanted to start over, and you agreed," Avery said.

"I scoffed at your choice of beverage, and you consider it agreeing to your plan?" Jonah questioned.

"You didn't say no," Avery countered.

Jonah shook his head. "I didn't say yes, either."

"Quit splitting hairs and tell me about your night," Avery said.

"My roommate and I ate too much Chinese food and drank too much bourbon. What about you?"

"My night wasn't nearly as exciting," Avery said. "I ate a frozen dinner and drank pink lemonade."

"Those dinners taste better if you heat them up."

Avery gasped. "Why didn't I think of that?"

"What's in your tea?" Jonah asked.

Avery puckered his lips and blew his steaming brew before taking a sip. Jonah's tie started to feel like a noose. "It's called chai."

"Okay, what's in your chai tea?" Jonah tried again.

Avery laughed. "Chai means tea, so when people say chai tea, they're saying tea tea. This is a chai latte."

Jonah blew out a frustrated breath. "Avery, this redo isn't going much better than the first time around. What's in your *chai latte*?"

"Unlike English teas, it contains cardamom, cinnamon, black peppercorns, star of anise, cloves, and a few other spices. It's full of flavor and good for you. Would you like to try it?"

"Maybe later," Jonah said noncommittally, making Avery smile.

"So, you were telling me why you got hammered on a Tuesday night," Avery prodded, distracting Jonah by blowing on his steaming mug again.

"No, I wasn't," Jonah said.

"You were about to tell me," Avery amended.

"Was I?" Jonah asked. "Pretty sure I was going to tell you we need to buckle down and finish the final phase of our cybersecurity microchip. I kind of told Trexler we would finish it today, then he shortened our deadline for trial testing by a week."

"You kind of did what?" Avery asked. His mouth fell open, and his mug wobbled in his hand.

"Set your *chai* down before you spill it all over me," Jonah insisted.

Avery rolled his eyes but did it anyway. "A guy knocks over coffee one time..."

Jonah held up two fingers. "But who's counting?"

"You obviously are," Avery groused. "Why'd you guarantee we'll finish the final phase so quickly?"

Jonah sighed. "It wasn't my finest moment." He'd been reeling from Trexler's insults and dismissive attitude toward his abilities, but Jonah left his excuses unsaid. "Now, we need to find a way to finish the microchip and begin phases of testing."

"Sounds like we'll be ordering in lunch," Avery said.

"Maybe dinner too. Or do you have plans?" Jonah asked.

Avery broke eye contact by looking down at the cup in his hands. "No plans," he said softly.

What was the wistful tone all about? Was Avery pining for the new guy? Jonah wanted to ask more, but he needed to keep their focus on the task at hand and not open a can of worms. Instead, Jonah said, "Fine, but no eating or drinking around Stella."

Avery met his declaration with an eye roll, then finished his tea while they reviewed their plans for the final phase. Once they finished, Avery walked over to Stella, stroked her keyboard, and said, "Hello, beautiful."

Jonah felt the caress in his soul and barely suppressed a shiver. Damn, it was going to be a long fucking day.

Eleven hours, dozens of pages of scribbled notes, two rounds of take-out food, and three bags of Caramel Bugles later, they had reached the testing phase. Jonah intently watched his monitor as Avery attempted to hack through their new cyber-protection from his laptop. As the day wore on, Jonah's office seemed to shrink in size until it felt smaller than a coat closet. He'd lost his jacket and tie not long after they started their marathon of coding. At some point, he'd loosened three buttons on his shirt, and had caught Avery staring at the swath of tan skin exposed there every so often. Pointing it out would've embarrassed Avery, so Jonah silently basked in the attention and debated tempting the devil by undoing another button.

Jonah traced his bottom lip with his forefinger and watched with glee as their cybersecurity chip blocked Avery's attempts to breach the firewall. Each time he was thwarted, Avery made this adorable little grunt that had Jonah thinking dirty, dirty thoughts.

"I wish I'd thought to program sounds," Jonah teased.

"What kind of sounds?" Avery said without looking up from his laptop. His fingers flew over the keys as he continued trying to penetrate the fortress.

"Video arcade noises like when Pac-Man died. I could've rigged it to play every time you failed to breach the firewall."

Avery chuckled. "Explosions like Battleship?"

Jonah grimaced. "I'm not too keen on war games or explosions."

Avery's fingers stilled, and he looked up at Jonah with a horror-stricken expression on his face. "Oh, God. That was such an insensitive thing to say."

"Why?" Jonah teased.

Avery pinned him with an annoyed look. Apparently, he'd uncovered the truth about Jonah's injury. For eight months, Jonah had given a variety of reasons for his scar ranging from getting struck with debris while rescuing a kitten from a tree during a hurricane to battling a samurai.

"I won't get triggered and 'Hulk out' over loud noises and explosions," Jonah said.

Avery continued to glower, which Jonah much preferred over pity. "I never once implied such a thing."

"What happened to your flowers?" Jonah suddenly asked, opening the can of worms he'd vowed to leave alone.

Avery only gaped at him unblinkingly. Who could blame him? The question had come out of nowhere. "My flowers?"

"The ones Romeo brought you. I caught you making heart eyes at them every time I stepped out of my office yesterday."

"Don't be ridiculous," Avery scoffed. "I took them to my grandmother."

Of all the possible things Avery could've said, Jonah hadn't been expecting this one. "Why?"

Avery released a deep sigh. "I told you he wasn't the guy for me." It was Jonah's turn to just stare. "Here was this handsome, successful guy who seemed to be interested in me, but I felt…nothing. No spark."

Jonah snorted, and Avery scowled.

"What the hell is that supposed to mean?" Avery asked.

"No spark?" Jonah asked. "I'd hate to see how you return from a lunch date when you do feel chemistry with a man."

Avery stiffened in his chair. "What are you talking about?"

"Come on, Avery. Flushed cheeks and swollen lips. I recognize the signs of someone who has been thoroughly kissed…or more."

"You th-th-thought I… that we…" Avery stammered. He swallowed hard and briefly closed his eyes. "You're an idiot, Jonah. My pink cheeks and puffy lips were a result of a medical condition."

Jonah raised a brow. "Is that what they're calling it these days?"

"I had an allergic reaction to my lunch, asshole," Avery practically shouted. "I didn't see the little bites of heaven in my salad until it was too late."

"Little bites of heaven?"

"Avocado," Avery said. "I was stuffing my face while my date talked about his job. Suddenly, I noticed my face felt numb, and my lips were tingling. I shifted the lettuce around in my bowl and found the cause."

Jonah buried his face in his hands. "I'm the biggest dick on the planet."

"This isn't the time to brag about your dick size, Jonah," Avery chastised.

Jonah lifted his head and stared at him. "I said I *am* the biggest dick, not that I *have* the biggest dick. God, Avery, I'm—"

Avery held up a hand, cutting him off before he could apologize. "Stow it for another day when you make an even bigger ass of yourself than you have today." Jonah doubted it was possible, but he wasn't willing to wager on it. "Do you know what your problem is?"

"Is that a rhetorical question, or do you expect an answer?" Jonah asked.

Avery made a growly noise of frustration Jonah found sexy and sweet. "I could strangle you with my bare hands right now. You make me crazy with your hot-and-cold, push-and-pull personality. If you want something, then by God, go get it. Stop giving up at the first sign of a roadblock. Sometimes you go around the barriers and other times you run the fucking thing over."

Was Avery encouraging him to make a move? Jonah's pulse sped up.

"Take this Ison case, for example," Avery said, crushing Jonah's unbidden hope. "Trexler said no, so you're willing to let it go just like that. You have innumerable resources and contacts who could help you look into the case further if you're willing to set aside your wounded pride and ask for help."

Disappointment was Jonah's familiar foe. It was the uninvited dinner guest that popped by one night and never left. Avery was right. This wasn't about Trexler, his grandfather's ghost, his aunt's career, or even Jonah's pride. It was about Marla and Earl and Bo. He needed to find another way, even if it meant turning this over to Ellie. He trusted her beyond measure.

Jonah's computer chimed, interrupting his musings. He knew what it meant but couldn't look away from Avery's bright, passionate gaze. A wicked smile spread slowly across his intern's face, and he pointed at Jonah's computer screen. Jonah looked at his monitor and confirmed

Avery had broken through his firewall. He hadn't even realized Avery was still typing during his big speech.

A knight in armor marched across Jonah's computer screen, carrying a flag with a large letter A as trumpets blew victoriously.

"Checkmate, thundercloud," Avery said smugly. "Your move. The question is, are you going to give up or go through the roadblock?"

"I'm going to run the fucker over," Jonah replied.

The real question was, were they still talking about Trexler's objections or the barriers Jonah had erected to fight his attraction to Avery?

CHAPTER 9

"**E**arth to Jonah," Felix said, snapping his fingers a few inches from Jonah's face. "You've been staring off into space while swirling your French fry in ketchup for the last five minutes. Are you okay, man?"

Jonah blinked and refocused on his friend's worried face. Beside him, Rocky simply shook his head. The private eye was more stoic and less likely to show concern.

"You look like a zombie," Rocky said. "I've called you every filthy name I can think of, and you didn't react."

"I feel like a zombie," Jonah admitted, dropping his fry back into his take-out container. "It's been a rough week. Monday was the Monday-est Monday of all time with twelve hours of meetings where Trexler sharpened his teeth on my bones."

"I have a feeling the hits didn't stop there," Felix said.

Jonah shook his head. "Not even close. Thank God tomorrow is Friday, and we beat our deadline to submit test results to Dickface a day early. At least I should be ending the week on a bright spot," Jonah said.

"So, you spent a lot of time locked in your office with the adorable Avery this week?" Felix asked.

"How do you know he's adorable?" Jonah asked. "You haven't even met him."

Rocky snorted. "Dude, you talk about him all the time. The guy has you wrapped around his finger, so he must be irresistible."

Jonah could only stare at his friends for a few moments. "I wasn't aware I spoke about him so much."

Felix and Rocky just grinned.

"I sense there's something bigger going on that you haven't shared with us," Felix said.

"Marla was waiting on my front porch when I got home Monday night. She has terminal cancer and has decided not to get treatment," Jonah said.

"Oh, man. That's rough. I'm really sorry," Felix said.

"Me too," Rocky added.

"Thanks, guys. I'm having a hard time processing it all," Jonah admitted.

"We can skip the podcast production meeting if you want to go home and get some rest," Rocky suggested.

"I appreciate it," Jonah said, "but sleep has been elusive this week, and I don't expect tonight will be any different. I'd rather not sit home and stew over things I can't change."

"If you're sure," Felix said. Jonah nodded. "Then let's choose the subject of our next podcast episode."

"I think the Tess Hamilton case is interesting," Rocky said. "She's suspected of killing all three of her husbands for their insurance money. They could never prove it before she died last year."

"New evidence has come to light recently though," Felix added. "We can focus on how law enforcement officers were fooled by her June Cleaver looks."

"It would be easy to credit Tess's appearance for her success, but there had to be more to it. She was forty-two when her first husband died, so her demeanor and looks probably played a significant role," Jonah said. "What about later when she was sixty-five and eighty? She had to have made it nearly impossible for them to detect the poison in her husbands' systems."

"Or was some of her success due to luck?" Rocky asked. "All of the men had pre-existing health conditions, so the coroners weren't going to spend a lot of time looking for causes of death."

"None of them had the same health issue either," Jonah pointed out. "If all three men had heart issues, for example, it would make the pattern stand out more. Was that luck or part of her plan?"

"I don't think it was luck," Felix countered. "I think she was an evil genius. Hamilton moved around the state of Georgia so the deaths wouldn't be easily connected. She seemed to take her time remarrying and executing her plans. She poisoned them slowly, so their decline was gradual and not obvious."

"The only person who raised a red flag was the life insurance adjuster for her last husband," Jonah said. "If not for her, we wouldn't have known about Tess Hamilton's string of victims."

"True," Rocky said. "Maybe we could get the insurance adjuster to join the podcast for an interview."

"That's a good idea," Felix said, making a note. "I think this has excellent potential."

"What else do we want to consider?" Rocky asked.

They continued discussing some of Savannah's most sinister crimes for another hour. Being one of the oldest and most colorful cities in the United States, they wouldn't run out of unique stories to share on their podcast for years.

"I still think Tess is the most interesting," Felix said after they narrowed it down to their top five favorites. "What do you think?"

"Yeah, I agree," Rocky said. "Jonah?"

Both men looked at him. "Yes" was on the tip of his tongue, but he couldn't pull the trigger. As intriguing as this case was, he couldn't forget the pleading in Marla's voice. He couldn't ignore the tension in his gut when he'd discovered Bo Cahill was incarcerated the night someone killed Earl Ison.

"Lola the Ice Queen," Jonah finally said. Maybe he should've found another way to reopen the investigation that didn't involve his friends, but Jonah trusted them.

Rocky's brow furrowed. "That's what you want to name the episode featuring Tess Hamilton?"

"Lola the Ice Queen," Felix repeated, tipping his head to the side like Betty the French bulldog. "Where have I heard that name?" He straightened in his chair and snapped his fingers. "A drag queen who was murdered in the early eighties, right?"

"Yeah," Jonah agreed. "According to Marla, Lola was pretty new to the queen scene and hadn't fully conformed to her stage name. She refers to him as Earl."

"The case was solved, wasn't it?" Felix asked.

Jonah shook his head. "The case remained cold for thirteen years, and out of the blue, a man on death row for another crime confessed to killing Earl a week before his execution date."

"Do you think it's a false confession?" Rocky asked.

"I absolutely do," Jonah confirmed. "Days before Earl's death, DeKalb County Sheriff's deputies arrested Bo Cahill for the murder that sent him to death row. He was incarcerated and held without bail. Bo Cahill did not kill Earl Ison."

"Who were the investigators on Ison's case?" Felix asked.

"Milton and Morrissey with SPD," Jonah said.

"I've interviewed them before when writing articles on old cases," Felix said. "They were the typical cops of that generation. Milton and Morrissey didn't have much respect for the rainbow community, women, or people of color, but I never got the impression they were dirty. Lazy, maybe. Indifferent, perhaps."

"Marla isn't convinced they outright lied to her, and she's not sure they were responsible for coercing the confession. Maybe they were just patsies," Jonah said.

"If that was the case," Felix countered, "what did Bo Cahill say to sway them? There had to be more to it than him saying he did it."

"I was able to access Earl Ison's case file and read what the detectives recorded, which wasn't much. They either invested extraordinarily little energy in solving the crime or were too lazy to document the file properly. Cahill told them he'd masturbated with Earl's panties, then shoved them in his mouth. Since it was exactly what the killer did, they closed the case and called it a day."

"That is very specific information," Rocky said. "I assume it was a detail they hadn't shared with the press."

"It wasn't, but a construction crew found Earl. His killer had staged his body and hiked up his skirt to humiliate him. Any of the men working on the crew that day saw him and could've shared the details with friends and family," Jonah explained.

"Cops talk too," Felix added. "I have at least one reliable source in every county. Some talk because they like to feel important, and others are decent human beings that want to do the right thing."

"So, the information about the panties could've been fed to Bo Cahill, but why would a man confess to a crime he didn't commit?" Rocky asked.

"I've been asking myself the same question for days," Jonah said.

"What conclusion did you come up with?" Felix asked.

Jonah expelled a long breath. "Bo Cahill confessed to protect someone else. It's the only thing that makes sense."

"The person who really committed the crime?" Rocky asked.

"That's one possibility, but what if someone he cared about was in trouble with the law and he brokered a deal? His life for theirs? Cahill was already going to die, so what did he have to lose?"

Rocky and Felix contemplated his question for a few seconds before exchanging brief glances.

"I assume Marla brought this up recently," Felix said.

Jonah nodded, tried to speak, but couldn't get the words out past the lump in his throat. He took a drink of water and tried again. "She never bought the narrative. She wants justice for her friend before she…" *Goddamn it.* "Before she dies. I promised her I'd do everything in my power to make this right. I went to work the next day and accessed what I could, which wasn't much for Bo Cahill, beyond his arrest records and notes about him being held without bail. It took me two minutes or less to realize Marla's instinct was correct. I asked Malcolm for his permission to pursue it, but he reminded me of the proper chain of command and referred me to Trexler."

Rocky and Felix both groaned.

"Yeah," Jonah said. "The bastard wouldn't even entertain the idea. All I asked Trexler to do was request a copy of the file from DeKalb County. He shot me down and wrote me up for insubordination."

"Asshole," Rocky muttered.

Jonah nodded. "He gave me some song and dance about protecting the reputations of retired police officers and court officials, but he's not fooling me. He'd do anything to advance his career and playing the crusader wouldn't get him the kind of attention he needs to get promoted."

"Any devoted law enforcement officer should want real justice to prevail," Felix said passionately. He narrowed his eyes. "Do you think Trexler treats you horribly because you're gay?"

"It's possible, I guess," Jonah said. "I think his attitude is because he doesn't respect my skills, and he resents that Malcolm hired me because my aunt encouraged him to do so. I don't even know if Trexler is aware of my sexual orientation."

"Under the Georgia Open Record Act, I can request a copy of Bo Cahill's case file, and they have to provide it. I also have contacts at the DeKalb County Sheriff's Department who might be able to get me what I need quicker. I could run an exposé piece for my column, or we could do a podcast on it. Either way, the shit will hit the fan, and you won't avoid the splatter."

"Gross," Rocky grumbled.

Felix shrugged. "I'm a writer. I paint a vivid picture with my words."

Rocky shook his head, then said, "Your aunt Ellen will get caught up in the crossfire too."

"Yeah, I know. I'm not too worried about myself, but I don't want to drag anyone else down with me," Jonah said. "What if the dates were entered into the system incorrectly? What if Cahill had been granted bail and committed another murder while waiting to go to trial? I don't want to jeopardize your careers or my aunt's without more facts."

Rocky winked. "Trouble is my middle name. I can take care of myself."

"Minerva will have my back," Felix said, his fondness for his editor showing in his voice. "Let's get a copy of Cahill's file," Felix said. "Once we confirm dates, we'll talk about which route to take next. You could turn this over to Ellen, or we could pursue the investigation ourselves."

"Fair enough," Jonah said. "What do you think, Rocky?"

"I'm in. Trexler can come for me all he wants," Rocky said.

"I'll get on it first thing in the morning," Felix told them. "In the meantime, let's plan to produce our next podcast episode about Tess Hamilton. Maybe we end up bumping Tess for Earl, but let's be prepared either way."

"I agree," Jonah said.

Rocky nodded. "Sounds like a plan. Can we just make sure our podcast doesn't become the how-to guide for a new generation of spouse killers?"

Felix and Jonah laughed.

"Let's avoid lawsuits if at all possible," Felix said. "Rocky, you dig up everything you can about Tess Hamilton. Let's form a concise picture of Tess for our listeners. I want to know her education, her hobbies, and what her childhood was like. Let's assume her family are innocent victims in all this."

"Will do," Rocky said as he scribbled notes.

Felix looked at Jonah. "I want you to approach this as a profiler. Talk about the psychological aspects of how Tess was able to fool law enforcement."

Jonah nodded. "Sounds great."

Pointing his pen at his chest, Felix said, "I'll start requesting official documents like autopsy reports from medical examiners and death certificates. I'll also place a call to Jennifer Blossom, who was the insurance adjuster who connected all the dots."

Rocky rubbed his hands together. "I think this has the potential to be a fascinating episode."

"I agree," Jonah said. "We'll need to add a bunch of visuals to our official website so people can compare and contrast Tess's wholesomeness to her evil deeds."

"Excellent," Felix said, continuing to write in his notebook. "I think that's a wrap on this planning session." Felix dropped his pen, then glanced up at Jonah. "So, you were telling us about the hours and hours you spent locked in a room with Avery."

Jonah shook his head. "No, I wasn't."

Rocky waggled his brows playfully at Jonah. "Be honest. On a scale of one to ten, with one being only a little and ten being the guy has you by the balls, how fucked are you?"

Jonah heaved a deep sigh and said, "One hundred."

CHAPTER 10

On Friday, Jonah kept his head down at work to avoid attracting any unwanted attention. Trexler was moderately impressed with the program he and Avery designed, as well as the initial trial runs. The microchip would need to undergo strenuous testing before the agency would deploy it in real time, so that's where Jonah focused his energy.

Avery stood up and stretched his arms up over his head before bending his upper body to the left and right, stretching his back and abdomen. His untucked dress shirt had risen in the process, giving Jonah a peek at pale flesh that would contrast so nicely against his darker, olive-toned skin. Was that a cinnamon-colored freckle above the waistband of Avery's pants? Where else did he have freckles? Jonah wanted to lick a path between each one. A grown-up version of connect the dots.

"You need to get up and stretch to get the blood flowing."

Jonah's blood was pumping fine and heading straight to his dick. Standing up would not be in his best interest. "I'm good," he told Avery.

"We've been at this for hours, and your brain has been as busy as my fingers," Avery said, interrupting Jonah's thoughts before they could get too out of control.

"I don't know what you're talking about."

Avery smirked. "There's smoke coming out of your ears. Maybe you'll feel better if you get things off your chest. You've had a pretty shitty week. Let's get out of here and get some fresh air and a bite to eat."

Jonah's first instinct was to grab a snack and keep working, but he knew Avery was right. "Fine," he agreed after a few moments. "But no avocados."

"I have Benadryl in my desk," Avery grumbled.

"No avocados or no lunch date." *Oh, shit.* Why had he called it that? They'd had lunch together dozens of times since Avery started working for him.

Avery quirked a brow but didn't correct him. In fact, neither of them said anything until they exited the building.

"I took your advice and talked to Rocky and Felix last night about the situation with Earl Ison and Bo Cahill," Jonah said, breaking the silence.

Avery stopped suddenly and turned to look at Jonah, who was unprepared for the sudden move. He pulled up short, but Jonah's momentum carried him a few steps forward. He crashed into Avery hard enough to knock the much smaller man off balance. Jonah's hands snagged Avery's waist to steady him, and he didn't immediately let go.

"That was a close call," Avery said, placing his hand over Jonah's racing heart.

"Very close." Jonah knew he should drop his hands and step away, but he gripped Avery a little harder instead. He might not ever get another chance.

"What do they think?" Avery asked.

Jonah just blinked. What were they talking about again? "Who?"

"Rocky and Felix. What do they think about Earl Ison's case," Avery said, looking at Jonah like he'd lost his mind.

Avery had wanted to get Jonah's blood flowing, and by God, it was rushing south in a hurry. Jonah released Avery and stepped back before he made a bigger fool of himself.

"My partners agree that something isn't adding up, so Felix is going to request a copy of the case file under Georgia's Open Record Act," Jonah said, continuing toward Bytes and Brew. "He said he also has contacts in DeKalb County who will hopefully expedite his request."

Avery fell into step with him. "That's great, Jonah. What about Marla? How's she feeling?"

"She hasn't been home. I called her last night, and she said she and Betty were in Atlanta making peace with some family members. She sounded so tired. I just wanted to drive to Atlanta and bring her back home."

Jonah hadn't told Avery that Marla's illness was the reason he was pushing so hard to investigate Earl's case. He saw no reason to keep the information from him now. By the time they reached the café, Avery understood why Jonah just couldn't let things go.

"You're a great friend, Jonah."

"I learned the hard way to never take friendships for granted," he said solemnly. Jonah could tell by Avery's expression that he wanted to know more, but he didn't press him.

"Does she plan to return soon?"

"Monday," Jonah replied. "I hope to have some answers for her by then."

Until then, Jonah needed to keep busy to stay out of trouble.

Kendall didn't come home after his shift at The Cockpit on Friday night, so Jonah was stuck at home with no one to distract him from his thoughts. He'd never been good with idle time. On Saturday morning, Jonah went to the hardware store and purchased paint and a few home-remodeling magazines to get ideas for his kitchen. He spent the rest of the day painting his living room a bluish-gray color that reminded him of the sky just before it rained.

On Sunday morning, Jonah and the rest of *Savannah Morning News* subscribers got a shocking surprise. On the front page were side-by-side photos of Earl Ison and Lola the Ice Queen beneath a heading that read: *Who Really Killed the Queen?*

Jonah dialed Felix without reading the article.

"Hello," Felix said groggily into the phone.

"Thanks for the warning."

"What are you talking about?" Felix asked.

Jonah was too stunned to speak right away.

"Jonah? You still there?"

"I'm here. I'm referring to the exposé you published in the newspaper this morning."

"What exposé?" Felix asked, sounding almost shrill.

Jonah read the headline to him. "Front page and above the fold."

"Oh, fuck," Felix said, sounding truly horrified. "I got the file late last night from my contact in DeKalb. I spent a few hours going over every detail at least three times, then stayed up until after two o'clock this morning typing the article. I sent it to Minerva after the print deadline. Hell, she should've been sleeping. I had no idea she'd see it and possibly delay print production to include it. I never intended for it to get published before I had a chance to give you a heads-up. Your aunt is going to kill me."

Ellie was going to kill him when she learned about Jonah's involvement.

"I'm so sorry, J."

"I haven't read the article yet. Was the information I found about Cahill correct?" Jonah asked.

"Yeah, there's no way in hell Bo Cahill killed Earl Ison," Felix replied, then yawned.

"I'll let you get back to sleep. Call me later when you get up."

"Will do. Later, J," Felix said before hanging up.

Jonah read every word in the article twice, not because he learned anything new, but because Felix had irrefutably validated the information Jonah had found. Bo Cahill was arrested on June 10, 1982, for murdering Maurice Vanderwahl and held without bail until his trial. Upon conviction, he was transferred from the county jail to the state facility, where he remained incarcerated until his death thirteen years later. Who really killed Earl Ison on June 12, 1982? With or without GBI backing, Jonah was going to get to the truth.

His phone rang, and Jonah glanced down to see Rocky's name on the screen. "Hey, man. Did you see Felix's article?"

"I did. Why didn't anyone tell me Felix got his hands on the case files?" Rocky asked.

"He didn't tell me either. I found out by reading the paper just like you and everyone else," Jonah said, then shared the excuse Felix gave him for not calling them. Rocky didn't sound convinced. "Trexler is going to have a stroke, and I won't be there to witness it."

Rocky chuckled. "What do you think will happen when you arrive at work tomorrow?"

"Nothing fun. I should've at least given my aunt Ellen a warning."

"You would've warned her if Felix hadn't jumped the gun. I thought we were going to discuss our approach before moving forward," Rocky said.

"Me too," Jonah grumbled. "We'll be sure to bring it up when we talk to Felix. I have a feeling he's going to want to meet later. Will you be free?"

"I'll make time. Right now, I'm working on another cheating spouse case. The missus attends a high-dollar yoga class. The owner is this beefcake named Jacque. Dude is built like a bodybuilder. He looks familiar too, but I can't place where I recognize him from."

"I'm bored," Jonah said. "Send me a picture, and I'll run it through Stella 2.0 here at home. Her facial recognition software might give you the answers you need."

"Perfect," Rocky said. "I'll send them over soon. The missus is on the move again. I gotta go."

"Talk to you later."

Jonah puttered around his kitchen until he couldn't put off making the dreaded phone call another minute.

"Do you know anything about Felix's article?" Ellen asked, getting straight down to business.

Ellen was the younger sister to his mother, Jane Anne, or Janie to her friends and family. Janie had only been seventeen when Jonah was born, and she was ill-prepared for motherhood—then and now. Many people called her flighty and selfish, but Jonah learned she was just a free spirit, unwilling to be tied down to any one person, including her son. She refused to name his father, so Jonah had no paternal family to speak of. Oscar and Maeve became his guardians, and Jonah was grateful every day that Janie had left him behind when her wanderlust grew too strong for her to ignore.

Ellie was only fifteen years older than Jonah, so she was more like a big sister than an aunt. Ellie and Maeve's unconditional love more than made up for Oscar's belligerence and Janie's indifference. Ellie had always been fearless, placing herself between Oscar and Jonah when the old man was in his darkest moods. Oscar admired that about Ellie, even if he disapproved of everything else about his youngest daughter.

She'd stuck her neck out for him again to help him land an interview with the bureau. How had he repaid her kindness? By allowing her to get caught up in the kind of firestorm that ruins careers.

"Yeah," he admitted. "Felix hadn't expected the article to run today, which meant I should've had time to prepare you for the shit storm."

"I'm going to kick his ass the next time I see him," Ellen groused.

"He's prepared for it." Jonah took a deep breath. "As am I." Then filled her in on the rest.

"First, I am truly sorry to hear about Marla's cancer diagnosis. I know how much you adore her. There's nothing wrong with looking into an old case to ensure it was investigated properly either."

"Are you going to reopen Earl Ison's investigation?" Jonah asked.

"Of course," she said.

"Did you know Milton and Morrissey?"

"Yeah," Ellie replied. "They were getting close to retirement age when I joined the force. Both were absolute pieces of shit, so I'm not at all surprised by the lack of concern for a murdered drag queen. They didn't like anyone who wasn't white, straight, and male. I have no problem dragging their names through the mud if I find out they knew about the coercion." There was noise in the background, and he could hear his aunt's wife talking. "Sherry has lunch ready," Ellen said. "You want to come over and eat with us?"

He did, but Jonah knew he would make lousy company. "Nah, but thanks."

"Suit yourself. I'll save some gumbo in case you change your mind." Jonah whimpered and Ellie laughed wickedly. "I assume your podcast will continue investigating?"

"Yes, ma'am. I don't know how much time Marla has left."

"I understand and respect where you're coming from, but please don't do anything that will prevent us from getting a conviction. I want you to keep me in the loop. Pass along any important information you run across, and do not go public with anything else without my approval. Tell your asshole friend not to run any more articles, and I will guarantee he gets exclusive content once the case is solved. Fair enough?"

Fairer than he deserved. "Yes, ma'am."

"Love you, J. You know where to find us if you change your mind and want to eat gumbo."

"Love you too, Ellie."

He felt much better after talking to her, even though he still felt guilty for the firestorm she faced.

By early afternoon, Kendall returned home, looking so thoroughly fucked that the man barely had the strength to wave as he passed through the house. Jonah snorted and continued looking through the renovation magazines until Rocky's picture texts came through. Then he laughed until he cried. There was no need for Jonah to run the yoga instructor's photo through facial recognition software because he knew the man's identity. He quickly typed a message to Rocky. *The yoga instructor is named Randy Dagger. He's a gay porn star.*

Rocky immediately called him. "Ahhhh. That's where I recognize the stud from. The dude has a monster cock."

"Mmmhmmm," Jonah replied. "If your client's wife is cheating, it isn't with Jacque."

Rocky chuckled. "My motto is: if you must hire a PI to find out if your spouse is unfaithful, the answer is most likely yes. But this woman… She takes the kids to school, goes to church, yoga, and various committees for causes she supports. I rarely see her talking to a man. She has lunch with her lady friend and plays tennis at the club."

"Why are you assuming her affair is with a man?" Jonah asked out of curiosity.

"Oh, hell," Rocky said slowly. "Why the hell didn't I consider her lover could be a woman?"

"We're brainwashed with heteronormative bullshit from birth,"

Jonah replied. "Maybe the woman isn't cheating at all. Surely your clients' suspicions aren't always proven correct."

"They're right ninety-five percent of the time, which is the reason for my motto," Rocky teased.

"So, this woman is in the five percent, or she's having an affair with her lady friend," Jonah said. "What happens in the locker room at the tennis club, stays in the locker room at the tennis club."

"You're right, Jonah. I can feel it in my gut. I'll need to be creative to catch her in the act."

"Do you ever feel sleazy?" Jonah asked.

Rocky came back with a quick response. "All the time."

"It can't be fun exposing people's secrets. Maybe she's in the closet for a reason. What if her husband would sue for custody of the kids, or find ways to keep them away from her? Are you okay if that's the consequence of your investigation?"

"No," Rocky said after a long pause. "I'm also not comfortable lying to a client."

"How are you lying?" Jonah asked. "You've just told me you've seen no evidence this woman is cheating. How long have you been tailing her?"

Rocky heaved a sigh. "A week."

"How long does it usually take you to bust a cheater?" Jonah asked.

"A day, maybe two."

"I think you know what the right answer is, Rocky. You've tailed her for a week, and there is no evidence she's having an affair. Give him back some of his retainer if your conscience bothers you."

"Fucking Boy Scout," Rocky groused. "You're right. I'll just go home and watch my favorite Randy Dagger videos until Felix the Attention Whore gets his beauty sleep."

Jonah laughed. "Sounds like a plan. Talk to you later, Rocky."

"See you, J."

Jonah wouldn't call Felix an attention whore as Rocky had, but the reporter didn't shy away from the spotlight. He certainly had no qualms about going headlong into the fray, and it seemed like he'd done this without consideration to how it impacted Jonah. Rather than let his irritation fester and grow, Jonah decided to stay busy by doing things around the house. Unfortunately, his brain raced despite his best efforts. On the bright side, he had organized closets, clean bathrooms, freshly laundered and ironed clothes for work, and had a fully stocked pantry and refrigerator. He played music, audiobooks, and favorite podcasts, but nothing held his attention for long.

By the time Felix woke from his beauty sleep and called him, Jonah had worked himself into a tangled knot of frustration.

"What happened to us discussing the information in the file before deciding how to proceed?" Jonah asked.

"I know, Jonah. I'm used to working alone and got carried away. It's a piss-poor excuse, and I'm sorry," Felix said. Jonah heard the sincerity in his voice. "When I suggested the three of us work together on Sinister in Savannah, I truly meant the three of us had equal roles and stakes in the podcast. This isn't the Felix Franklin show."

"You've already been there and done that," Jonah quipped.

Felix laughed. "True, but I sincerely enjoy working with the two of you more than researching and recording podcasts by myself. I just need you guys to give me a bit of a learning curve. I'll do better. I promise."

"Fine. Why don't you guys come over for barbecue tonight, and we can discuss where we go from here."

"Sounds like an excellent plan. I'm starving," Felix said.

"Perfect. Now you get to call Rocky and eat crow while you invite him to dinner."

Felix moaned. "You want me to apologize more than once today?"

"If you truly meant what you said about us being a team, then yes."

"He'll take it better from you," Felix countered.

"Probably, but I'm not the one who owes him an apology."

"You're such a fucking Boy Scout, Jonah."

Jonah chuckled. "That's nicer than what Rocky called you."

"What did the sleazy bastard—"

Jonah hung up on Felix before he could finish asking his question. He felt much better after working things out with his friend and decided to give Felix the benefit of the doubt. A few hours later, Jonah could hear his two podcast partners squabbling on the porch before either of them knocked. In fact, they were so involved in calling each other names, they didn't hear him open the door.

"I meant what I said. You're an attention whore," Rocky told Felix.

Felix snorted. "Maybe I am, *Major*. Let's not pretend you've never gotten your hands dirty."

"Major?" Jonah asked, startling them both. "Is it short for Major Pain in the Ass, or are you terrible at insults, Felix?"

Felix rolled his eyes. "It's Rocky's first name."

Jonah looked at Rocky. "Really?"

The private investigator heaved a sigh. "Give me a beer, and I'll tell you the story."

"You've already told Felix?" Jonah asked. "And he's your nemesis."

Felix tilted his head back and laughed. "I didn't need him to tell me. Investigative reporter, remember?"

"Big fucking deal," Rocky scoffed. "So, you uncovered my full name."

"That's not all I know, stud," Felix said before sauntering into the house like he owned it.

Rocky met Jonah's curious gaze. "He's insufferable. Please tell me your sweet roommate is home. Seeing his pert ass would help offset your seriousness and Felix's dickishness."

Jonah laughed. "He's here but sleeping off his wild weekend."

"Damn," Rocky said, snapping his fingers.

"I'm making barbecue ribs, coleslaw, and collard greens for dinner if it makes you feel better."

"It's a good start," Rocky said before patting him on the shoulder and entering the house.

Never a dull moment.

"So, Major," Jonah said, following Rocky to the kitchen where Felix was twisting the caps off three bottles of beer. "What were your parents thinking?"

"My mom had a lot of complications during labor, and it was left to my dad to complete the paperwork. He told me he was an emotional disaster. He was excited to have a son but worried sick about my mom. A nurse took pity on him and helped him with the paperwork. She asked questions, he answered, and she would fill in the lines. When it came to my name, my dad told her they were naming me after a great-great-great-grandfather who was a Civil War hero named Major Rockford Michael Jacobs. My first name was supposed to be Rockford, but the nurse took him literally and entered my great-great-great grandpappy's title as my first name."

"Oh, man. Was your mom upset when she found out?" Jonah asked. Felix's eyes widened in alarm. Before Jonah could ask what his problem was, Rocky answered him.

"My mom died from her complications," he said softly.

Jonah felt like a complete ass. "I'm so sorry."

"It's okay," Rocky replied, patting him on the shoulder. "My dad remarried when I was five, and Michelle is the only mother I've ever known."

"I don't feel like such an asshole now," Felix said.

"Don't sound so smug. I still think you're an attention whore," Rocky told him.

The two of them verbally sparred for at least ten minutes before Jonah shoved them toward the backyard where he already had the ribs grilling.

"So, what did you find out about Bo Cahill?" Jonah asked Felix.

"He was a fifty-year-old black man who shot a twenty-six-year-old white man he caught raping his wife," Felix said. "This Vanderwahl guy also happened to be the sheriff's son. The prosecution claimed it was a consensual affair between Mrs. Cahill and Mr. Vanderwahl. They accused Bo Cahill of lying in wait to catch the two in the act."

"That's why they were able to convict him of murder in the first degree, which made him eligible for the death penalty," Jonah said.

"Yes," Felix said. "After reading the file, I believe Mr. Cahill was telling the truth. There's more than one travesty of justice here, fellas."

"Oh fuck," Rocky said. "And Cahill was the sheriff's guest until he was transferred to the state penitentiary after his conviction."

"What do you want to do next?" Felix asked them.

"We dig up every rock until we find the truth," Jonah said. "As expediently as we can because I don't know how long Marla has." He told them about Ellen's caveat, and they both agreed.

"It could unravel quickly once we start pulling strings," Rocky added.

Felix nodded. "The key is determining which are the right ones to tug."

They spent the next few hours eating and formulating a game plan on how to attack both investigations simultaneously. There was no tension or lingering bitterness between them. Still, Jonah couldn't shake the foreboding unease in the pit of his stomach. The repercussions of their investigations could be far-reaching, stirring up painful memories and trouble where they least expected it. He imagined the process was like poking a hornet's nest with a stick. Some people wouldn't want the truth to come out and would go to any lengths to keep it buried. Was Jonah prepared to feel the sting?

Hell yeah.

CHAPTER 11

On Monday morning, Jonah wasn't the least bit surprised when he swiped his badge and discovered his access to open the employee's door was denied. He walked around the building and entered the same door as their visitors would. The receptionist looked nervous as he approached.

"G-g-good morning, Jonah," she said, fidgeting in her seat and offering a nervous smile.

"Get him out here, Mary," Jonah replied in response.

Mary didn't ask which "him" he had referred to. She picked up her phone and dialed an extension while winding her pearl necklace around a finger. "Mr. Trexler, Agent St. John would like to speak—" Mary's gaze jerked up to Jonah's, and her pearl-winding halted. "Yes, sir. I'll tell him." She hung up the phone and grimaced. "He'll be here soon."

Trexler took his sweet time meeting Jonah in the lobby. "You had some nerve pulling a stunt like that, St. John," Trexler snarled, his complexion was ruddy with anger. "Did you think the deputy director and I would overlook such a gross display of insubordination?"

"I had nothing to do with the article, sir," Jonah said. It wasn't a lie. They had agreed to discuss their next move, but Felix made a preemptive strike on his own.

A bark of dry laughter burst from Trexler. "How stupid do you think

I am?" He held up his hand, showing his thumb and forefinger about an inch apart. "I'm this close to firing you outright, St. John. I would be well within my right."

"How so?" Jonah asked. "You can't prove I had anything to do with the article. I'm not named as a source, and I didn't write it."

"Your podcast butt-buddy did though."

"Butt-buddy?" Jonah asked. "Why, Supervisory Agent Trexler, surely you know that kind of language isn't acceptable in the workplace?"

Trexler's complexion went from red to a deep shade of purple, and his veins protruded from his forehead and neck, pulsing angrily. "Don't you turn this around on me, you arrogant prick. You're suspended without pay for a week. Surrender your badge peacefully, or I'll call security."

Jonah worked hard to keep his cool. He refused to "Hulk out" and give Trexler more ammunition against him, so he unclipped his badge from his belt and extended it to his boss. He tightened his grip on it when Trexler moved to take the badge from him. "Stella is my personal property. I built her before I began working for the GBI, and the agency has no claims on her. If any of you so much as touch her—"

"No one is going to fondle your girlfriend," Trexler said with condescension dripping from his tongue. Jonah could tell his boss wanted to say so much more. Maybe take another dig at his sexuality or call him a freak because he liked computers. It would be so easy to goad the man into telling Jonah what he really thought about him, which he could take to the deputy director. On the other hand, Mary raptly watched the exchange from her desk and could say Jonah had coerced or pushed Trexler.

With a week off work, he'd have plenty of time to dig deeper into Earl's murder and Bo's confession. So, he relinquished his grip on the badge, and said, "I'll be back in a week to collect that, so take good care of it." He smiled politely at the receptionist. "My apologies, Mary. I hope your day gets better."

She smiled timidly and nodded.

Jonah left the building without another word. Jonah texted Avery, who wasn't due in for another thirty minutes.

I was just given a week off without pay. I'll explain later. Watch your back.

Then he sent a group text to Rocky and Felix, who immediately responded with apologies.

Nah. More time to solve this case.

Rocky sent him a thumbs-up emoji and Felix blew him kisses.

Jonah chuckled and dropped his phone in his cupholder, then drove to the corner market to pick up his weekly stash of Caramel Bugles. Mr. Ling didn't question why Jonah was getting his weekly fix before nine in the morning instead of after six at night. He simply rang him up and handed over the goods, which was precisely what he needed.

A mid-eighties, red Cadillac convertible was parked in Marla's driveway when Jonah arrived home. It belonged to Amos Charles, Marla's on again-off again boyfriend. The top was up, the engine was still running, and he could see them inside talking. Anxious to see his friend, Jonah leaned casually against the side of his car and waited for them to wrap up their conversation instead of going directly inside.

Marla got out of the Cadillac a few minutes later. Her artfully applied cosmetics and big smile didn't conceal her exhaustion. She still looked beautiful in a pale pink summer dress and matching pumps. She waved at Amos, who glared at Jonah before he backed down the driveway and sped away.

"I knew you'd do it, baby. I just knew." She looked down at the white and black French bulldog sitting beside the suitcase at Marla's feet. "Didn't I tell you he would, Miss Betty?" The dog barked twice in reply. Marla looked at Jonah. "That means yes, darling. You better write it down and learn to speak Betty's language."

"Why don't you come over to my place so I can fill you in on the latest news. I need your help to really get this investigation going," Jonah said. He held up his canvas tote stuffed to the brim with Bugles. "I have sustenance."

Marla's eyes sparkled with mischief and purpose, eclipsing her fatigue. Feeling needed had a remarkable effect on the human spirit. "Do you also have bourbon?" she asked.

Jonah chuckled. "How about I make us some coffee, and we can pretend it's heavily laced with bourbon?"

"Deal, darling." Marla gestured to her luggage. "Be a dear and grab my valise, won't you? I will not have my best lace, prettiest dresses, and sexiest shoes stolen while crime solving."

"Sounds like you need a new costume for the caper."

"I have many superqueer-o costumes in my closet already, baby," she said, crossing the driveway with Betty close on her heels. "Do your business before we go inside the house, Miss Thing."

"Are you talking to Betty or me?" Jonah asked.

"You can piss in your own front yard if you want to. Who am I to tell you what to do?"

Jonah tilted his head back and laughed. God, how he loved her. Thirty minutes ago, Jonah would've thought himself incapable of joy. Two minutes with Marla and the world was a much better place. Then he remembered her diagnosis, and it felt like someone stabbed him in the heart.

Seeing his mood shift, she wagged her elegant forefinger from side to side. "None of that now," she said firmly. "I will not spend the rest of my time feeling sorry for myself, and I don't have the emotional energy to spend on making others feel better either."

"Yes, ma'am."

Marla gave a haughty nod. "All right, then. Let's get down to work."

Jonah retrieved her suitcase while Betty sniffed the grass until she found the perfect spot to pee. The three of them went inside. Jonah started a pot of coffee while Marla sat down at his ancient kitchen table, which was a representation of both the best and worst times in his childhood.

He'd dyed Easter eggs with his granny on the scarred surface and had completed his homework there after school every day while she prepared dinner. He could close his eyes and remember the smell of her freshly baked chocolate chip cookies. The kitchen table was also the scene of many standoffs between Jonah and Oscar when he hadn't wanted to eat something on his plate like liver or lima beans. It was during one of those battles of will that Oscar had called him Joanie for the first time.

"A sissy name for a sissy boy."

Oscar was smart enough to never say those things in front of Granny or Ellie, but he wore a hateful sneer on his face that let Jonah know when he was thinking them. The old bastard's tactics won every time, and Jonah had bent to his will.

He'd fallen into the same toxic paradigm with Trexler. Jonah needed to break the pattern before it broke him.

"I love the new wall color in the living room," Marla said when he carried two steaming cups over to the table. "It's very serene and peaceful."

"Thank you," Jonah said, taking a seat across from her. He reached beneath the table and rubbed a hand over Betty's smooth fur. She must've liked it because she stood on her hind legs and placed her front paws on his thighs. Scooting his chair back, he scooped the dog up and set her on his lap.

"Miss Thing, you know damn well you're not allowed to sit at the table," Marla said, but she couldn't keep the grin off her face. "Lord, she's going to have you wrapped around her paw in no time."

"She will," he replied, not bothering to deny it. Wasn't it better to let Marla see how much he would spoil her beloved companion?

Betty barked, and Marla laughed.

"You're not all that," Marla told her dog. "You snore, and you fart worse than any human."

Jonah laughed. "And here I thought you were bestowing a great honor on me."

Marla smiled. "I am, doll. I truly am." She reached inside her large pink tote and pulled out a notebook. Marla ripped out a sheet of paper and slid it across to Jonah. "These are all the things you need to know about Betty."

Jonah read the brand of dog food and snacks, as well as the dates for Betty's next annual checkup and the name of her veterinarian. Marla had included the brand of flea medicine and heartworm preventative Betty used and her schedule for taking them. He was not at all surprised by the care she put into the details.

"Thank you," Jonah said, winking at her. "So, how'd you find out about Felix's article? Did the Associated Press pick it up?"

"They might have, but one of my friends back here sent a link to Felix's article in the *Savannah Morning News*. I can't believe *you* didn't call me," she said accusingly.

"Well, Felix kind of jumped the gun a little bit and caught me off guard too."

Marla raised a perfectly arched brow. "Trouble in paradise already?"

Jonah smiled. "Let's just say we're still working out the kinks. It's more like growing pains instead of real trouble. The three of us have very different personalities, and we're used to working solo on projects for the most part. There is a definite learning curve in the process."

Marla cupped her mug with both hands and lifted it to her mouth for a sip. "Tell me everything that happened." So, Jonah did.

"Do you think the GBI is just being stubborn, or is there something more sinister at play?" Marla asked.

"I honestly don't know the answer to your question," Jonah admitted. "Trexler isn't old enough to have worked either case. Director Malcolm hadn't worked for either department at the time."

"Maybe neither of them is directly involved in Earl's or Bo's investigations, but it doesn't mean bias isn't at the root of their refusal to get involved now," Marla countered.

"I think Trexler may be a homophobe, but Charlie Malcolm has been one of my aunt's friends for decades. Ellie is a very out-and-proud lesbian."

Marla reached across the table and covered Jonah's hand. "Honey, it's easier for people to understand homosexual and bisexual people. Getting them to wrap their minds around transgender, nonbinary, or gender-queer people is a totally different ballgame. People fear what they don't understand and often hate what they fear. It makes them feel less power-less. Maybe Malcolm and Trexler aren't even aware their bias exists."

She made valid points they couldn't afford to ignore if they wanted to conduct an honest and thorough investigation. "You're right."

"I normally am, baby," Marla teased, patting his hand before retracting hers to take another sip of coffee. She set her cup back on the table and flipped her notebook to another page. "I made a list of Earl's friends for you to interview. I don't know if they'll remember anything more than I've already told you, but it's worth a shot." She ripped the page out and handed it to him.

There were only five names on the list. Jonah glanced up at Marla, and his surprise must've registered on his face.

She heaved a long sigh. "The eighties and nineties were brutal on our LGBTQ community, stealing our friends from us left and right. I feel lucky to have lived as long as I have," Marla said. She shook her head. "Nope. We're not going there right now. Not after the healing weekend I had with my family." Marla's bottom lip quivered for a few seconds, which she covered by taking another sip of coffee. "Doll, are you sure I can't have real bourbon in this coffee?"

Jonah felt the grip on his emotions slip and gave himself a mental shake and firm lecture. *Don't lose your shit and cry. If you could choke down liver and lima beans, you can choke back the tears until after she leaves.*

"Of course." Rather than set Betty down, he carried her into the kitchen. Jonah retrieved the liquor from the cabinet and set it down on the table in front of Marla, who giggled as she added a generous amount in her coffee cup.

She took a drink and said, "I should've asked you to pour out the remaining coffee to make room for the booze."

Jonah laughed despite his heavy heart and reclaimed his seat across from her once more. "I'll start talking to Earl's friends tomorrow. I want to track down the guards who worked at the county jail and prison when Bo was there. See what they're willing to tell me."

"They keep the death-row inmates isolated, but it wouldn't have been the case when he was in the county lockup," Marla pointed out. "I bet he talked to other inmates."

Jonah nodded. "That's on my list too. Talking to Bo's family is un-avoidable, but I want to postpone it for as long as possible. Scraping off the scabs on these old wounds will be painful for them, especially if my questions don't lead me anywhere."

Marla nodded. "I agree."

"So, what about Earl's family?" Jonah asked. "You said the names on the list are his friends."

"Like so many others, his family disowned him once he came out as gay. For all I know, one of them killed him after learning he'd started dressing in drag." Marla tipped her head and narrowed her eyes. "Why the hell didn't I think of that sooner?" she asked.

"When a person is suddenly and violently killed, it's common to focus on new people who'd entered their lives," Jonah said. "Subconsciously, it's scarier and harder to believe the killer is someone you know well."

"Well, damn," Marla said. "Maybe I've barked up the wrong tree all these years. Maybe it wasn't the new boyfriend but his brother, his father, or a cousin instead."

Jonah acknowledged the possibility with a nod. Maybe he didn't have much field experience, but he knew statistics, and Jonah knew human behavior. Those two things should never be discounted during an investigation. "Do you know much about his family?" he asked.

Marla pulled out a pen from her tote and began writing notes on a new sheet of notebook paper. "Not a lot," she said, "but I'll tell you everything I remember. Sandy Jasper knew Earl the longest. I'd start with him. They were childhood friends, and I didn't meet Earl until we were in our late teens. He's the one who sent me the article link."

Jonah glanced down at the notes Marla had made. She'd included addresses, phone numbers, and places of employment. It listed Sandy as owner of The Cockpit. Jonah's brow rose. Kendall might be able to offer some insight into the club owner since he worked weekends there. Marla's throaty laughter caused him to jerk his gaze up. She was grinning from ear to ear.

"Bet I know where your mind went just now," she teased. "Be careful you don't drag home another roommate if you visit Sandy at the club. This place will become Jonah's Home for Lost Boys."

Jonah narrowed his eyes. "How'd you know what I was thinking?"

"Your face got pink, and your eyes glazed over just like most men's do when they see those little aviator uniforms for the first time."

Jonah chuckled because it was true.

Marla took another sip of coffee, then yawned. "I should really get home and catch a nap. I spent most of my time talking to my parents, aunts, and cousins, making up for lost time." Her voice cracked on the last part. Marla heaved a sigh. "You ready to go home, Miss Thing?"

"Stay a little longer," Jonah suggested. "We can watch episodes of *The Golden Girls*. Betty can help me do some research in my office while you rest. I can fix us some lunch when you wake up."

"That sounds lovely," Marla said, rising from her chair slowly. Jonah wanted to offer his hand, but he recognized the proud look in her eyes. He had to trust Marla would ask for help when she needed it. "You know what sounds lovelier?"

"A soft blanket and a pillow?" Jonah asked.

"The recliner will do," Marla said. "I think I'd like you to design a brilliant new computer and name her Marla. She needs to be as smart as Stella but look snazzy while working her magic."

"So, like a glittery exterior?"

"Glitter," Marla scoffed. "I said snazzy, not tacky. This blush pink is my signature color in case you haven't noticed."

"I have," Jonah replied.

"Instead of boring-ass black plastic, why not make a blush pink computer with silver or gold accents?" Marla said as she walked to the living room.

Jonah and Betty followed her. "That's not a bad idea." He draped a soft blanket over Marla, then gently settled Betty on her lap.

"It's a brilliant idea, which is why you should name a supercomputer after me."

Now that Marla had planted the seed, ideas began to take root. Jonah was suspended from work and needed to stay busy, after all.

Marla and Betty were fast asleep before Rose shot Blanche's vase in Jonah's favorite episode. He took the lists Marla made him and tiptoed down the hall to his home office, where he made measurements and looked for blush pink computer components. Then Jonah buckled down and searched for information on the list of people Marla made for him. She might've known where they lived and worked, but he wanted to know things they might've kept secret from her, such as their criminal history. Since his GBI access was locked down, Jonah used the same kind of service PI's used to search public records. He found a few misdemeanors for some of Earl's friends, but nothing that concerned him.

A few hours later, he checked on Marla and saw she was still sleeping. Betty stood up and looked at Jonah with expressive eyes.

"Do you need to potty?" he whispered. Betty's entire body vibrated as she wiggled her ass end. "I'll take that as a yes," Jonah said, getting her down so she could follow him out the front door.

He sat on the porch steps while Betty sniffed every other blade of grass until she found the perfect spot to take a shit. She kicked up her legs afterward and trotted back to Jonah with a hopeful look in her eye.

"I don't have any of those Beggin Strips you like, but I'll stockpile them soon." Jonah heard a car slowing down in front of his house and got the surprise of his life when he glanced up and saw Avery pull into the driveway. Jonah stood up and crossed the yard with Betty right on his feet, barking as viciously as she could. "Exit the car at your own risk," Jonah said when Avery pushed his door open.

Laughing, Avery got out of his car and squatted down to greet Betty, who'd charged fearlessly toward him. "I didn't know you have a dog. I would've pictured you with something bigger and meaner to help push the badass image you try to project."

"I don't have a dog...yet," Jonah said, ignoring Avery's other remark. "This is Marla's dog. Her name is Betty."

Awareness washed over Avery's face, softening his beautiful eyes. "Hello, Betty," he said, extending a hand for her to sniff. Betty must've liked what she smelled because she stood on her hind legs and placed her paws on his dress pants. "I'm glad you'll have each other," Avery said, looking into Jonah's eyes.

"So am I," he admitted.

Avery scratched behind Betty's ears and under her chin before running a hand down her sleek back. Jonah had never been jealous of a dog before now. "You're the best girl, aren't you, Betty?" The dog barked twice and collapsed onto her back. Avery laughed at her antics and rubbed her tummy.

"That means yes," Jonah said, wondering what Avery would do if Jonah threw himself down and presented his belly and other things for rubbing. "I think she's enjoying the belly rub a lot."

Avery must've heard something wistful in his voice because his head snapped up, and their gazes collided and held. Avery rose to his feet and smiled nervously. "I bet you're wondering what I'm doing here."

"I am," Jonah said, closing the distance until there was only a foot separating them. Avery hadn't even acknowledged the text he sent earlier.

Avery swallowed hard, then reached into his pocket and withdrew a flash drive. "I copied everything I could find about Earl Ison and Bo Cahill."

Jonah accepted the flash drive from Avery without tearing his gaze away and slid it inside his front pocket. His fingertips tingled after brushing against Avery's palm. "I hope you were careful. I'd hate for you to get in trouble because of me. Besides, Felix already has a copy of Bo's case file from DeKalb County. That's why he was comfortable going public."

"Trexler requested the case file last week, even after he told you no."

Jonah's mouth fell open. "Where'd you hear that?"

"From Desiree who'd heard it from Tabitha. I told you the cousins liked to talk," Avery replied. "Anyway, I hacked into Trexler's computer and copied the files for you."

"Avery," Jonah sighed. "You shouldn't have done that. What if—"

Avery's scoff interrupted the flow of words. "I was cautious, and there's no way Trexler will know I was in there poking around. I wanted you to have the information in case DeKalb County deliberately withheld information from Felix."

"What makes you think they wouldn't withhold the same information from the GBI?" Jonah asked.

"They may have, but someone else in law enforcement is more likely to help cover up a botched investigation than an uncompromising reporter like Felix," Avery said.

Jonah nodded. "Good point."

"I'm very astute, Jonah," Avery said. He'd struck a playful, teasing tone, but the devilish look in his eyes was pure mischief. "You know what else I *observed* last week?"

"What?"

Avery closed the small distance between them until there were only a few inches of air between their bodies. His nostrils flared as he took a deep breath. "You didn't like it when I went on a date."

Deny. Deny. Deny. Jonah opened his mouth to dispute Avery's accusation, but the truth spilled out instead. "No, I didn't."

"Why?" Avery asked.

Jonah didn't trust himself to speak, so he shrugged.

"You were furious when you mistook my allergic reaction for the aftermath of a serious make-out session. Why?"

Jonah's mouth was suddenly too dry to speak, so he shrugged again.

"Bullshit," Avery growled. He rose on his tiptoes, gripped the back of Jonah's neck, and pulled him down into a kiss.

Jonah stiffened at the first tender press of lips against his because he'd fantasized about kissing Avery for so long. His hesitation made Avery second-guess himself, and he started to step back.

"I don't fucking think so," Jonah roughly growled, pulling Avery into his arms and slanting his mouth over the younger man's.

Avery gasped either in surprise or pleasure, and Jonah took advantage, slipping his tongue inside Avery's mouth to tease and explore. Avery moaned, fisted his hands in Jonah's hair, and melted against him.

Jonah backed Avery up against his car and ravaged his mouth. Every fantasy he'd had over the past eight months paled in comparison to the real thing. Heat, longing, and lust slammed together, twisting and swirling through Jonah's body like a cyclone, threatening to wreak havoc on him and everyone who stood in the way. Still, Jonah couldn't get enough. He slid his hands down to cup Avery's firm ass, loving the way the smaller man canted his hips toward Jonah, seeking friction and heat.

Avery sucked his tongue, and it took everything Jonah had not to throw him over his shoulder and carry Avery off to his bedroom.

Honk. Honk.

The blaring car horn startled Jonah and Avery apart.

CHAPTER 12

"**D**o that shit inside your house," a snarling punk yelled out the window of a passing car.

"This has been one of the strangest days in my life," Jonah muttered as they watched the bright yellow Honda Accord disappear around the corner. "I wouldn't be screaming at people from a vehicle that recognizable."

Avery mumbled something indecipherable. Jonah hooked his forefinger beneath his chin, lifting his head until Avery met his gaze.

"What was that?" Jonah asked.

"It's not all bad, right?" Avery asked.

Jonah traced his thumb over Avery's thoroughly kissed lips. He liked being the reason for Avery's flushed cheeks and plump mouth instead of an avocado. "I said strange, not bad, and some of it's been pretty fucking amazing."

Avery nipped Jonah's thumb. "You're not freaking out?"

"Oh, I am," Jonah countered. "But I don't regret it."

Avery heaved a relieved sigh. "I should probably head back to work."

"Is Trexler treating you okay?" Jonah asked, brushing his knuckles along Avery's cheekbone.

Avery leaned into his touch. "You're making it hard to be good."

"Sorry," Jonah said. He started to lower his hand, but Avery made an adorable growling noise, so Jonah continued touching him. He would've encouraged Avery to do the same, but it could result in them getting arrested for indecent exposure. He settled for tracing Avery's jawbone before resting his palm against his neck, smiling when he felt the erratic pulse throbbing beneath Avery's skin.

"Um, I forgot what I was going to say," Avery whispered.

"I asked if Trexler was treating you okay."

"Oh, him. Yeah," Avery said, nodding. "Too nice. I think Trexler's going out of his way to prove he's not the problem in your dynamic. Everyone knows better."

Jonah hated knowing everyone talked about him. Pitied him. Placed bets on him. He needed to reevaluate how badly he wanted to continue working in a hostile environment. Was it worth the stress? He shoved the thoughts aside to focus on the man in his arms. Jonah lowered his head and kissed Avery long and slow, loving the way Avery clung to his biceps.

Avery broke the kiss suddenly and panted for air. "Jonah, if we don't stop now, I will drag you into the house and do wicked things to your body."

"Get it, honey," Marla said from a rocking chair on the porch. Betty barked twice from her perch on Marla's lap. "Miss Thing agrees."

They'd been so wrapped up in one another that neither had heard Marla come out of the house.

"You must be Avery," Marla said.

"Yes, ma'am," he replied, sounding pleased that she'd heard of him.

"You're as cute as a button. No wonder you have the big guy tied up in knots."

"Okay," Jonah said, cutting her off before she could say more. He looked back at Avery. "Can I call you later?"

"I'll be pissed if you don't."

Jonah reluctantly released Avery and took a few steps back.

"It was nice meeting you, Marla," Avery said. The French bulldog barked sharply. "And you too, beautiful Betty." He raked his eyes over Jonah one last time before getting in his car.

Jonah waited until Avery drove away before returning to the porch. He flopped down in the chair beside Marla and began rocking.

"Attaboy," Marla said proudly.

Jonah laughed. "Ready for lunch? I have plenty of leftover barbecue from last night."

"No, thank you," Marla said. "I think I'll just head home. I think I'll make some soup before conquering my mighty to-do list."

"Is there anything I can do to help you? I'm pretty handy."

Marla patted his knees. "I know it, baby, but it's not *that* kind of list. And besides, you're already tackling my number one priority. Knowing you're doing all you can for Earl has helped me far more than the medicines my doctor has prescribed to keep me comfortable. The little nap in your recliner was the best I've slept in weeks. I will never be able to thank you enough." She stroked Betty as she spoke. "Well, I'm giving you this incredible dog to look after you when I'm gone, so maybe we are even."

"Your friendship is the only thanks I need," Jonah told her.

"Boy, don't you get all maudlin on me. There's no time for that," Marla said, rising to her feet. "I have one more favor to ask."

"Name it."

"Drag my heavy-ass valise over to my house. Lord, why I packed so much for a weekend in Atlanta is beyond me." Marla smiled wistfully. "It was worth it."

Jonah wanted to ask about the visit with her family, but he didn't want to pry. Instead, he stood up and said, "I'm surprised Amos's old car made it to Atlanta."

"Her paint might be fading, but her engine purrs strong under the hood. Kind of like Amos." Marla cackled and slapped Jonah's arm as she passed by him. "Come along now. You have work to do and supercomputers named Marla to build."

"Yes, ma'am."

Once Jonah got Marla settled, he returned home and got busy ordering the parts he needed to transform Stella 2.0 into a Marla the Magnificent instead. Afterward, Jonah planned out his interview strategy for the next day. There were only five people on the list, so he should easily knock out those interviews in one day and hopefully find out more about Earl's family.

He had time to kill and decided to visit to the Carnegie Library on Henry Street. Jonah headed to their genealogy and history section to look through their *Savannah Morning News* Obituaries Index, which dated back to 1913. As he suspected, the newspaper didn't publish an obituary for Earl Ison. His family had rejected him, so they wouldn't have gone through the effort and expense to place an obituary notice in the paper. They would've quietly buried their shame along with Earl. He switched to the digital copies of news publications.

The library had millions of statewide newspaper publications for their patrons to view, spanning from 1786 to 1986. They proved to be an excellent source of information about Bo Cahill's alleged crimes. Jonah noted the names of Bo's family members in his phone, then went back to looking for any information about Earl. He only came across one small article in a Fulton County press that was published the day after the construction crew discovered Earl's body. The heading read: *Local Man Found Dead by Construction Crew*. It listed Earl's name and age but didn't provide the name of the men who'd found him. That information was also omitted from the official SPD case file.

It made sense that the police didn't release the men's names to the media, but to not even document the file? Why?

It was presumed the perpetrator chose the kill site because it was relatively secluded since all the homes in the subdivision were still under construction. What if there was something more significant about the site? Did the cops look for a connection between Earl and the men who found his body? What about the men who owned the construction companies working in the subdivision? There would've been several subcontractors involved. If Milton and Morrissey spoke to them, they didn't note it in Earl's file.

Again, Jonah wondered if the detectives were lazy, incompetent, or corrupt.

When his stomach started rumbling to protest his lack of attention, Jonah glanced at his watch and was shocked to see it was almost six. He'd skipped lunch, thinking he wouldn't be at the library long, but he should've known better. He had a lifelong habit of skipping food in favor of exploring.

"A boy can't chase his dreams on an empty stomach," Granny had said nearly every day before school. Jonah had never cared for anything heavy on his stomach first thing in the morning.

"A boy won't grow to be a man if he skips meals," Oscar had countered. "Eat your oatmeal, boy."

Granny made it more palatable by sprinkling brown sugar and adding fresh fruit to his bowl. Just thinking about fresh peaches and brown sugar made his mouth water, and he knew it was time to call it a day.

Even though he had plenty of food at home, he still swung through Arby's drive-thru for a beef and cheddar sandwich, curly fries, and a milkshake. He could worry about calories, carbohydrates, and cholesterol another day.

Jonah started on the fries and shake right away but saved the messy sandwich for when he got home. He practically devoured the entire thing in four bites and immediately regretted his life choices. The only thing making Jonah feel queasier than consuming fast food was the idea of calling Avery. What would they talk about? Would it be awkward after everything that happened? Would sexual tension render him stupid? Probably.

After ten minutes of freaking out, he picked up his phone to call Avery, but his tormentor beat him to the punch.

Jonah's heartbeat accelerated as he accepted the call. "Hello."

"I could hear you freaking out clear on the other side of town," Avery told him. "I thought I'd put you out of your misery and call you instead."

"I wasn't freaking out. I had just picked up my phone to call you." Avery snorted. "Uh-huh."

"Fine. Don't believe me," Jonah said casually. "How was your day?"

"Oh, the usual. Copied some files, met a cute pup, and kissed a guy."

Jonah's laughter rumbled deep and low. "All in a day's work, huh?"

"Something like that, although, I think my afternoon would've turned out better if I'd listened to my gut."

Alarm rippled through Jonah. "Why? Did Trexler do something to you when you returned after lunch?"

"Oh, I wasn't referring to the job," Avery said. "I meant the instincts that urged me to drag you into your house so I could live out every dirty thought I've had about you over the past eight months. No one would've noticed I was missing."

Jonah's breath snagged in his throat. "Avery," he whispered, sounding both turned on and shocked.

"Don't bother clutching your pearls, Jonah. I felt how your body reacted to our kiss. So, how about a nooner tomorrow?"

"Avery," Jonah repeated, but this time his voice was raspier and full of need.

"This better not be the part where you start expressing regrets," Avery said.

Jonah chuckled. "Regret is the last thing on my mind right now."

"Were you going to lecture me about how it's inappropriate for you to get involved with your intern?" Avery asked, pushing on. "I'll quit tomorrow if that's what it takes."

"No," Jonah said firmly. One day Avery would leave. It was inevitable. When he did, Avery would cast Jonah back into the depths of gloom where sunlight and heat couldn't reach him. *Not yet. Please, not yet.* "It is inappropriate, but I don't care."

"Senators, judges, and presidents do it all the time," Avery argued. Like that was a ringing endorsement. Then he quieted when Jonah's words finally sank in. "Oh."

"Avery, will you go out on a date with me?"

Crickets. Jonah pulled his phone away from his ear and looked to make sure he hadn't accidentally disconnected the call. He hadn't, so Jonah pressed the phone to his ear again. "Um, hello?"

"I'm here," Avery said breathlessly. "Did you just ask me to go out on a date?"

"I did," Jonah confirmed. As exciting as a nooner sounded, hookups and meaningless sex were all Jonah had known for years. Avery made him want things he'd stopped believing in.

Maybe love wasn't just for other people.

"I thought I was going to have to battle much harder," Avery replied. "I was prepared to fight dirty too."

Jonah chuckled. "I have no doubt. What do you say?"

"Hell, yes. When?"

The case would monopolize most of his time over the next few days. He wanted to spend time with Avery outside the office and to share more kisses, but he had to put Marla's needs first. "Friday night. You can pick where we eat and the movie we see."

"So, you want me to put in all the effort," Avery said. "Just like I carry your ass at work."

Jonah snorted. "Dream on."

"Friday feels like a million miles away."

"Will it help if we have nightly chats like this one?" Jonah asked.

Avery hummed. "Will they involve dirty talk and heavy breathing?"

"Maybe," Jonah teased.

They talked for a few hours, discussing anything and everything. He learned Avery passionately hated olives and pickles but willingly devoured avocados, even though he was allergic to them. Jonah confessed how much he hated avocados, and Avery promised not to hold it against him. He told Avery his secret obsession with manga and anime, and Avery got Jonah to admit how much he loved *Yuri On Ice*.

"Your secret is safe with me," Avery said around a yawn.

Jonah chuckled. "We should probably hang up so you can get some sleep."

"You have a big day tomorrow too," Avery countered. "I'm jealous you get to investigate a crime while I dodge Trexler."

"Just keep running those trial tests. Be good to Stella for me."

"Stella is sad without you," Avery said. "She misses you thundering around."

"Stella misses me, huh?"

"Stop fishing for compliments, Jonah. It's not attractive."

Jonah chuckled. "Goodnight, Avery."

"Sweet dreams, thundercloud."

Jonah's dreams that night were a little bit sweet and a whole lot naughty.

CHAPTER 13

Even though Jonah didn't have to adhere to a strict schedule, he wanted to catch Kendall before he left the next morning.

"Why aren't you dressed for work?" Kendall asked when Jonah came downstairs wearing sleep pants and a T-shirt.

"I got suspended without pay for the article Felix published in Sunday's paper."

Kendall screwed the lid on his travel mug and looked up at Jonah. "What article?"

He quickly brought him up to speed.

"You'll want to head to the club this morning if you want to talk to Sandy there," Kendall said. "He comes in early and gets his work done before lunchtime. His nephew carries the brunt of the workload on his broad, sexy shoulders."

"What's the nephew's name?"

"Drew Callahan," Kendall said dreamily. "He isn't old enough to know who Earl Ison is, but he sure is pretty to look at."

"I'll keep it in mind," Jonah said dryly. "What's Sandy Jasper like?"

"Intelligent, kind, and very creative. Sandy just doesn't have the greatest head for business, which is why he's relied so heavily on business partners and his managers over the years. Many have taken advantage of Sandy's kindness and lack of business savvy. Drew's first act when he joined the crew was to fire a douchebag manager who used his position to gain sexual favors. The staff enjoys working for Drew."

"Thanks, K," Jonah said. "I hope you have a good day today."

Kendall heaved a sigh. "It's going to be a long one. I'm working extra hours this week to assist with a big case. I still haven't adapted to some of the other attorneys' personalities. I miss Vivian every day, but I've really struggled at work lately. She worked hard but never took the staff for granted. She'd treat us to lunch on grueling days. These other guys just keep expecting more and more."

"Have you considered looking for another job?" Jonah asked.

"Absolutely," Kendall said emphatically. "I need to finish getting my degree first. My final exams are next week, which is why I'm going to a study group after work tonight. The finish line is so close, and I cannot afford to fuck it up right now."

"You're going to do great," Jonah assured him.

Kendall crossed his fingers, blew Jonah an air kiss, and headed out the front door. Before he could shut it behind him, Jonah heard Kendall say, "Well, hello there, sexy. This is a pleasant surprise."

Who the hell was on his porch so early?

"Let's go back inside, and I can turn a pleasant surprise into a stupendous one," said a familiar voice.

Rocky Fucking Jacobs.

Jonah rolled his eyes and crossed to the front door. "Rocky, can you even spell stupendous?" he asked. "Leave Kendall alone. He needs to get to work."

"You just want to keep the prettiest boys to yourself," Rocky said. "Have a great day, darlin'."

"You too, handsome," Kendall said, blowing Rocky a kiss.

"I will punch you in the balls if you pretend to catch the air kiss," Jonah groused.

Rocky turned to face him. "What the hell is your problem this morning?"

"What are you doing here at eight thirty?" Jonah asked instead of answering his friend.

"I cleared my schedule so we can conduct interviews." Rocky raked his eyes over Jonah's T-shirt and sleep pants. "Is that what you plan to wear?"

"I just got out of bed, fuck face."

"Wow. Someone needs caffeine. Why don't you go upstairs and get ready while I make some coffee? I could use another cup too."

Jonah crossed his arms over his chest. "Why are you coming with me to interview Earl's friends?"

"Because you don't have a badge right now," Rocky said.

"Marla has probably told them to expect me, and none of them will be hostile."

Rocky nodded. "That's true, but what if they give you new leads? Those people might be hostile or refuse to talk because they don't trust you."

"And they'll trust a private investigator?" Jonah asked.

"They're more likely to trust a PI or a reporter over a cop. Felix is tied up today, so you're stuck with me. If a situation warrants it, I'll introduce myself as a PI and you as my associate. It's not likely they'll want to see your license once I show them mine."

It made sense, and Jonah was relieved Rocky wasn't tagging along because he didn't trust Jonah to get the job done right. "Exhibitionist," Jonah teased before heading upstairs to get ready.

Jonah returned downstairs showered, dressed, and raring to go twenty minutes later.

Rocky glanced up from his phone when he heard Jonah's approach. "I wasn't sure how you take your coffee, so I didn't doctor a cup for you."

"No problem."

"I'll drive while you navigate," Rocky said when they stepped onto the porch a few minutes later.

"The Cockpit is our first stop," Jonah informed him.

Rocky set his travel mug in the holder and rubbed his hands together gleefully. "This is going to be a great day."

The club wasn't open to the public until lunchtime, so Rocky and Jonah parked in the employee lot at the rear of the building. There was an intercom with a call button by the back door for delivery drivers to announce their arrival. Jonah pushed it twice before someone answered it.

"Yeah?" a gruff voice asked through the speaker.

"My name is Jonah St. John. I'm a friend of Marla's and—" A loud buzzer cut Jonah off before he could finish. He smiled in triumph and opened the door, gesturing for Rocky to go first.

A man built like a rottweiler waited for them at the end of the hall. He ran a hand over his silver crew cut. Was he impatient or nervous?

"Jonah St. John," he said, extending his hand to the man. "Are you Sandy Jasper?"

He shook Jonah's hand and jovially said, "I am. It's good to meet you."

"Likewise," Jonah returned. "This is my friend and fellow investigator, Rocky Jacobs."

The two men exchanged pleasantries before Sandy showed them to his office. The space was ample and comfortably furnished. Large pictures hung on the wall showing the various aviation themes the club had featured over the years.

"Would either of you like a cup of coffee?" Sandy offered.

The two men both declined. Jonah had debated his approach during the drive over. Rather than dive straight into the interview, he wanted to gauge the mood and let Earl's friend set the pace. The technique wouldn't work with everyone, but there was no need for him to crash into their lives like a bull in a china shop.

"I wanted to believe Bo Cahill killed Earl because it was so much easier than accepting Earl's killer was someone he trusted. It caused a lot of friction between our surviving friends over the years." The older man briefly closed his eyes and sighed deeply. "There aren't many of us left. God, it's a miracle any of us survived the eighties. If HIV or AIDS didn't get us, the bashers did. There was so much hostility and hatred directed toward us."

"I can't imagine," Rocky said sympathetically, surprising Jonah. The PI was always so bold and brash, but it made sense he could stow it away when necessary. "We're sorry for the hurt we're causing by reopening the case."

"Don't apologize," Sandy said. "Earl deserves to have justice, and Mr. Cahill ought to have his record cleared of the confession. It won't bring the man back, but maybe it will bring peace to his family."

"Did you know Mr. Cahill?" Rocky asked.

"No. The police said Mr. Cahill was visiting friends in Savannah when he ran into Earl, but I couldn't tell you who those friends were," Sandy replied. "No one in our circle recognized his name or picture."

"Marla told me Earl had started dating a new guy before his death. She also said he'd started distancing himself from the group. What can you tell me about that?" Jonah asked.

Sandy leaned back in his chair. "The only thing I knew for certain about Earl's boyfriend was that he was in the closet."

"How are you certain?" Rocky asked. "Did Earl specifically tell you he was?"

Sandy nodded. "I think Earl got a thrill out of the clandestine meetings at first. Everything was so shiny and new, but it didn't take long for the tarnish to appear."

"Did Earl ever use a nickname when talking about his boyfriend or give you any hints on his occupation or stature in the community?" Jonah asked.

Sandy thought about the question for a few moments before answering. "Earl only referred to the guy as his beau in my presence. Based on the conversations we had, Earl was the guy's first male lover. He never said anything about his beau's occupation, but he once remarked how much he loved the man's callused hands. I assumed he was a laborer of some sort, so most likely not a wealthy man or local politician who was dabbling on the wild side."

Laborer. As in a construction worker?

"Do you think Earl's boyfriend was married?" Rocky asked.

Sandy shook his head. "Earl never said or implied his beau had a wife. The presents he gave Earl weren't overly expensive, so I don't think he came from a prominent family. Earl treated his gifts as reverently as crown jewels. His favorite was a silver necklace with a heart-shaped pendant. He never took it off."

Earl hadn't been wearing the necklace in the crime scene photos Jonah accessed. Had it fallen off during the struggle, or had Earl's killer removed it? Taken it for a souvenir?

They shifted their questions to the last weeks of Earl's life, focusing on any known altercations. Sandy reiterated what Marla had told Jonah. Earl had started to pull away from them more and more, so he couldn't be sure about quarrels with anyone.

"What can you tell me about Earl's family?" Jonah asked.

"Nothing nice," Sandy countered. "Not that my family was much better back then." The older man's eyes took on a faraway look as he recounted what it was like for him and his friends back in the eighties. "Perverts and pedophiles, they called us. When the AIDS crisis hit, Earl's father, Thomas, looked him right in the eyes and told him he hoped he caught the disease. It's a horrible thing for a parent to say to their child."

"It's unfathomable," Jonah agreed. Had Earl's father hated him enough to kill him?

"What about his mother? Did he have any siblings?" Rocky asked.

The question snapped Sandy back to the present. "I grew up next to the Isons, and they were always so warm and friendly, until Earl came out. The sudden shift was a staggering blow for Earl. Mona Ison, his mother, wasn't as cruel as Thomas, but she didn't stick up for Earl, nor did she reach out to him privately. She only said she'd pray for his soul. Mona is living at Twilight Years Estates but is still sharp as a tack from what I've heard. Earl has a sister and a brother, Ava Dixon and Dennis Ison. As far as I know, both still live in the area." Tears filled Sandy's eyes, and he swiped a hand over his face to wipe away the ones that escaped. "They didn't even attend his funeral service." Sandy's lips trembled, and his voice broke when he said, "Earl's family refused to even claim his body. They would've allowed him to be buried in a potter's field. Earl's friends pooled their money together to pay for cremation and a burial plot."

"Do you think any of them could've been responsible for Earl's death?" Jonah asked.

Sandy sighed. "I can't point to a single incident that would make me think any of them were capable of killing Earl, but I wouldn't have predicted the cruel way they treated him either. You think you know someone until circumstances reveal their true colors."

Jonah and Rocky spent the next few minutes getting as much information about the Ison family as Sandy knew. "Ava was away at college when Earl died. Dennis Ison was around though. He and Thomas both worked for the area's biggest concrete contractor."

Jonah was immediately intrigued to find another possible connection to the kill site. "Do you remember the name of the company?"

"Locke-Tight," Sandy replied.

Locke? Was the owner related to Royce? Jonah and Rocky exchanged a quick glance, and he could tell the PI was wondering the same thing.

"Would Locke-Tight have poured the foundations and driveways in the subdivision where Earl's body was discovered?" Jonah asked.

Sandy straightened in his chair. "I never thought about the connection, but yeah. The owner was a young guy who'd inherited the company from his father. There were two sons, Jerry and Eddie. Jerry was younger than Eddie by a few years, but lightyears ahead of his older brother in brains and maturity. Eddie was the kind of guy who pissed away every good opportunity and never lived up to his potential while blaming everyone else for his failures. Jerry, on the other hand, took to the business like he was born for it." Sandy shook his head. "I can't believe I forgot this, but Earl worked for Jerry for a short time also. It didn't work out and was a big source of contention between Earl, Thomas, and Dennis. Then he came out, and they had bigger reasons to hate him."

Bingo.

"I've never heard of the company," Rocky said. "Are they still in business?"

"Nah," Sandy said. "The construction industry took a big hit during the recession in the early eighties. The subdivision developer filed bankruptcy, and most of the contractors lost everything, including Jerry. He moved to Florida in 1983 or 1984, I think."

They chatted a little while longer but didn't learn anything that tripped additional red flags. Sandy thanked them for looking into his friend's death as he walked them out. Rocky opened the door to leave and jerked to a stop. A sexy guy with broad shoulders stood on the other side. Based on Kendall's description, Jonah figured they were gawking at none other than Drew Callahan.

"Drew," Sandy said, confirming Jonah's suspicions. "You're earlier than usual."

The dark-haired behemoth with pale eyes and an engaging smile looked from Jonah to Rocky before focusing on his uncle. "I wanted to chat with you before you left."

"Okay," Sandy said. "I was just seeing my friends out, so I'm all yours now."

"Why don't you introduce me to your handsome friends?" Drew asked, studying them carefully.

"Rocky Jacobs," the PI said, extending his hand. "We just met your uncle today."

"They're responsible for the police reopening my friend's murder investigation," Sandy said proudly. "Rocky is a private investigator, and Jonah is with the GBI. He also is good friends with Marla."

Drew smiled when he heard Marla's name. "She's such a firecracker."

"That she is," Jonah agreed, shaking the hand Drew offered him. "It's good to meet you."

"Same," Drew said, returning his attention to his uncle. "I can come back later if this isn't a good time, Uncle Sandy."

"Nonsense," Sandy said, then faced Jonah and Rocky. "I want you fellas to join me for lunch soon. We have the best chicken wings in town."

"I'd love to," Rocky said, not tearing his eyes away from Drew. "I'm embarrassed to admit this is my first visit."

"Do you have a business card?" Drew asked. "I'd love to call you and set up a private tour."

"Oh, um," the usually unflappable man stammered. "I do somewhere." He patted his pockets, smiling like he'd struck gold when he discovered one. "It has my office and cell phone number on it."

"Great," Drew said. "Expect to hear from me soon."

Rocky and Jonah exchanged farewells with Sandy and Drew, then retraced their steps to the back door.

"Oh. My. God." Rocky sounded as winded as if he'd just finished a 5k race.

"Going to be okay to drive?" Jonah teased.

"Why aren't you flustered?"

"He's a good-looking guy, but he doesn't crank my gears like he does yours," Jonah said. "Seriously, do you want me to drive us to the next interview?"

"Fuck you, St. John," Rocky snarled as he increased his stride. "Just try and keep up."

Their next stop was Daisy's Place, where they hoped to find the owner, Daisy Gallagher. Marla said Daisy was another queen from back in the day who'd turned her love of cooking into a successful business. She'd noted that Daisy made the best pies on the planet. Seeing the dessert display made Jonah's mouth water.

"Do you mind if we get a bite to eat while we're here?" Jonah asked Rocky. "I'm starved."

"I could eat," Rocky said.

"Yo, Dais," yelled a burly man wearing head-to-toe leather. "I found one of your fake fingernails in my scrambled eggs."

"The fuck you did, Edgar," a deep voice said from the kitchen. "Keep it up, and you'll be digging them out of your ass."

Edgar's laughter rumbled and crackled like a Harley Davidson motorcycle. "Oh, baby," the man yelled back.

A few seconds later, a six-foot drag queen stepped out of the kitchen wearing a cotton candy-colored wig the same hue as her waitress dress. She carried a heavy tray laden with plates and cups, but it didn't prevent her from stopping at several tables to dish up sass. As she neared them, Jonah saw the name Daisy stitched across one chest pocket.

"You boys sit wherever you like, and I'll be right with you," Daisy said, smiling at them. "Don't pay any attention to my Edgar and me. We've been yelling at each other for twenty-five years. Keeps the fire burning, if you know what I mean. I promise you nothing weird is in the food, and I never threaten to shove my fingers up anyone else's ass."

Nonplussed, Rocky said, "Good to know."

Jonah followed Rocky to a booth in the middle of the room. He was aware of curious eyes on them and figured Daisy's was the kind of place that drew a steady crowd of regular patrons. If Rocky noticed the attention, it didn't seem to bother him. He flopped down on the bench seat. The menus were tucked behind the condiment holder. Jonah grabbed two, handing one to Rocky before opening his own.

"I want one of everything," Jonah said to Rocky.

"Just the breakfast menu, or lunch and dinner too?" Daisy asked when she arrived at their table with a pot of coffee in her hand.

Jonah laughed, "I meant breakfast, but now I'm not so sure."

"Everything is made from scratch, so you can't go wrong with anything you choose," Daisy said. "Are you gentlemen drinking coffee, or can I get you something else?"

"Coffee for me," Rocky said, flipping the mug right side up so she could fill it.

Jonah did the same thing. "Can I also have a glass of orange juice?" he asked.

"Sure thing, love," Daisy said. "Are you boys new to my diner? I don't remember seeing you here before, and I never forget a handsome face."

"Quit flirting and get back to work," Edgar shouted from the opposite side of the diner.

Daisy ignored him except for extending her middle finger in Edgar's direction.

"This is our first time eating here, but if the food is half as good as your sass, I see many returns in my future," Rocky said.

"Aren't you scrumptious?" Daisy cooed. "Listen, I'll let you fellas look at the menu for a few minutes while I go squeeze your orange juice for you." She used her arms to push her breasts together and did a little shimmy.

Jonah laughed at her antics. He could see how she and Marla had been friends for so long. "Stay," he said, stopping her before she could leave. "I'm Jonah. Marla might have—"

"Oh my!" she exclaimed, covering her heart with her hands. She sat down in the booth beside Jonah. "I'm so happy to meet you. Marla said you'd be stopping by soon. Thank you, thank you. From the bottom of my heart."

"Cold black heart," Edgar said as he approached the table. He extended his hand to Jonah first, then Rocky.

"Want to join us?" Rocky asked, scooting over.

Edgar dropped a kiss on Daisy's forehead, then sat beside Rocky.

The interview didn't last as long as Sandy's because Daisy hadn't known Earl as long, but she seemed to love him as much as Marla and Sandy had. Daisy refused to let them pay for breakfast and hugged them fiercely before they left the diner.

"I'm so stuffed," Rocky said on the way to the car.

"That's what you'll be saying after Drew Callahan gets ahold of you," Jonah teased.

Rocky laughed, looked skyward, and steepled his hands in prayer. "Please. I don't ask you for much." Once inside the car, Rocky turned to Jonah and asked, "Where to next?"

He gave Rocky the address for Monique Drake's house. When they arrived, an elderly woman greeted them and said Monique was doing story time at the Carnegie Library at the top of the hour, so they headed in that direction.

Jonah and Rocky stood in the back of the room and observed Monique reading a children's book to about two dozen five-year-olds and their guardians. Monique changed up her voice for various parts, engaging the children and making them laugh. They all clapped when she finished. Monique stood up and curtsied.

"Thank you, thank you, my little loves," she said. "You know the routine by now. It's time for cookies and punch."

Some of the kids rushed for the cookies and punch while others ran to Monique to hug her. Jonah could tell by the smile on her face she genuinely enjoyed interacting with them.

They waited until the last kid scrambled off before they approached her.

"Monique Drake?" Jonah asked.

She rolled her big green eyes. "What did some religious zealot accuse me of doing now, officers?" she asked. "Lord, I pray for patience every day, but it gets harder and harder to find."

"We're not here because of a complaint," Rocky said.

"I'm Marla's friend, Jonah."

"Oh, honey," Monique said, throwing her arms around his neck before hugging Rocky too. "Who are you, lamb chop?"

"Rocky Jacobs," he replied.

"The private investigator. I've heard about you."

"Do you have a few minutes to talk to us about Earl?" Rocky asked her.

"Absolutely. My next gig doesn't start for another hour. Do you mind if we walk down the street to the coffee shop? I need more caffeine."

Over coffee, they talked about Earl. Monique mostly spoke about her friend and how he made everyone around him feel good. She didn't offer additional insight into his family or contribute names to their suspect pool. It was still beautiful to hear her thoughts on the man.

Rocky got a phone call on their way to The Dive Bar, where Marla said they'd find Brandy Wyne and the bar's owner, Willie Monahan. The conversation was terse and brief, and Rocky looked irritated when he disconnected the call.

"Something tells me that wasn't Drew calling you to arrange your private *tour*," Jonah said.

Rocky sighed deeply. "God, how I wish. It was my business partner, Pete. Remember the client I discussed with you the other day?"

"The one who suspects his wife is having an affair?"

"Yeah," Rocky said. "The asshole isn't taking my word for it. He's accused me of being lazy or lying to him."

"Even after you offered to return part of his retainer?" Jonah asked. "He must be extremely paranoid."

"His gut says she's cheating, and he wants the physical proof to back it up. I told Pete the same story I told my client, so he wouldn't be forced to lie. Pete accepted my word, but the client is adamant that I finish the job. He's threatening to trash our reputation if we don't."

"Isn't that an odd reaction?"

"Very," Rocky replied. "Pete insists I meet him now, so we can decide how to proceed. I'll probably end up tailing her again tonight, looking for the money shot. I don't want to ruin this woman's life." Rocky slammed his palm against the steering wheel and growled. "Hanging around you has made me soft, Boy Scout."

Jonah snorted and rolled his eyes. "Drop me off at my place, and I'll do the last interview on my own."

"Call me later and let me know if you learn anything. We need to interview the construction crew and Earl's family. You have to wonder if he was dating one of the guys he met on the job."

"I agree," Jonah said.

The drive to Jonah's didn't take long. He got out and ducked down to look at Rocky. "I hope Drew calls soon."

Rocky waggled his brows. "Me too."

Jonah shut the door, and Rocky drove off. Instead of going into his house, Jonah got straight in his car and drove to The Dive Bar. He was expecting a run-down structure with a seedy interior, but the bar was quaint and had a fun vibe in the air. Even though it was early afternoon, there were several patrons inside eating and enjoying the live entertainment.

The bartender looked to be the right age for Willie Monahan, so Jonah strode over and sat in a seat. The bald man with bulging biceps ambled over. "What can I get you?"

"Are you Willie?"

"Depends on who's asking. Are you the IRS?"

"Not even on my worst day," Jonah quipped.

The grisly bartender laughed. "How'd you get the scar?"

"Snagged my face on barbwire when I was fleeing vicious dogs."

The bartender chuckled. "Did the husband come home too soon?"

"Nah."

"Wife?" he asked Jonah.

Chuckling, Jonah replied, "Burglary gone wrong."

"Uh-huh. What do you really want?" Willie asked.

"Marla sent me."

"Well, hell. Why didn't you say so in the first place?" He reached across the bar and shook Jonah's hand. They talked for a long time, and when the performer finished singing on stage, Willie waved her over to join them. The singer turned out to be Brandy, the final person on his interview list.

The pair turned out to be great company but didn't offer any new information. Jonah stayed much later than he'd anticipated but switched to soft drinks after one glass of bourbon. The sky was starting to turn dark with the promise of a rainstorm by the time he said his goodbyes and headed out to his car.

Jonah jerked to a stop when he saw someone had slashed all four of his tires.

CHAPTER 14

"**S**on of a bitch," he said, running his hands through his hair as thunder rumbled in the distance.

Jonah had a Triple-A membership, so this was more of a nuisance than anything. They'd send a tow truck out to haul his car to a body shop of his choice, and Jonah knew there was a Tire Discounters nearby. He just needed someone to drive him home. Rocky and Kendall were out. Marla didn't own a vehicle. He could try Felix or order a ride on his Lyft app.

Or...

Jonah grinned as he dialed.

Avery answered on the second ring. "Hello, Jonah. How was your day?"

"Well, it was going great until I came out of my last interview and discovered some prick had slashed my tires."

"Oh, no."

"I need a ride home. Think you can come and get me?" Jonah asked.

"It depends," Avery said.

"On?"

"You are aware that I'm not just going to drop you off at your house and leave, right?"

"I fucking hope not," Jonah said.

"Text me the address," Avery said, then hung up.

The evening had certainly taken an unexpected twist, but Jonah wasn't mad about it.

A fat raindrop smacked him in the forehead as he finished texting his location to Avery, so Jonah ducked back inside The Dive Bar to call Triple-A. They said it would be forty minutes before a tow truck arrived, but he didn't need to wait around for them. Jonah confirmed which Tire Discounters location he wanted to use, then headed back to the bar to chat with Willie while he waited.

Willie glanced up from drying a glass with a white towel. "Back so soon?"

"Waiting on a ride," he said. "Some asshole slashed my tires."

Willie set the towel and glass down. "Oh, man, I'm sorry to hear that."

"Don't suppose you have security cameras set up?" Jonah asked.

Willie shook his head. "I know the neighborhood is a little rough, but I've never had trouble here besides the occasional fight."

Jonah stroked his chin. "No vandalism to parked cars besides mine, huh?"

"Not that I'm aware of, and I'm sure someone would've filed a police report or at least mentioned it to me." Willie furrowed his brow. "What are the odds you would be the first victim?"

"And on the same day I started asking questions about Earl Ison," Jonah added. It wasn't a coincidence. Someone was either pissed about him poking the hornet's nest or they were trying to scare him off. They'd have to work much harder.

"Since you won't be driving," Willie said, "let me pour you another drink."

"Deal," Jonah said.

He sipped his bourbon and enjoyed a few of Brandy's songs in her next set while he waited. Jonah knew the moment Avery stepped inside the bar because the storm inside him surged. For eight months, Jonah had clamped down every urge to touch Avery. Not today.

Once Avery reached his side, Jonah cupped his nape and pulled him into a kiss.

"Mmmmm," Avery said when they pulled apart. He looked pointedly at the almost empty tumbler on the bar before meeting Jonah's gaze. "How many of those have you had?"

"Just two."

"Separated by two liters of diet soda," Willie teased, extending his hand to Avery and introducing himself.

"Good to meet you, Willie," Avery said before turning to Jonah. "Ready?" They both knew he was talking about more than leaving the bar.

Jonah knocked back the last swallow and stood up from the stool. "So ready." To Willie, he said, "I'll be in touch."

"Have a good night," Willie said.

The rain was coming down hard when they stepped outside, so they got drenched during the mad dash to Avery's car.

"I think I'm too big for this tight space," Jonah said, pushing the seat back as far as it would go.

Avery snorted. "Where there's a will, there's a way."

The tension was thick inside the car, and like Jonah's dick, getting thicker as Avery drove toward Jonah's house. Rain pelted them and lightning streaked across the sky. The only thing louder than Jonah's pounding heart was the rolling thunder, and the only thing spinning faster than his brain was Avery's tires.

What were they doing? There'd be no going back once they crossed the line. As much as he wanted Avery in his bed, he didn't want to risk—

Jonah nearly jumped out of his skin when Avery squeezed his thigh. He'd been so lost in thought he hadn't seen Avery reach for him.

"I won't bite...too hard," Avery said. He stroked his finger over the inseam of Jonah's jeans, stopping just shy of his crotch. "Stop thinking so much."

Jonah ached to feel Avery's hand on his cock, but his brain hadn't relinquished full control to his libido yet. "Avery," he said, his voice sounding jagged and raspy, "I want to take you out on a date."

"We're going on a date on Friday. Remember?" Avery asked, sliding his finger farther away from where Jonah wanted it instead of closer.

"Mmmhmmm," Jonah managed as he squirmed in his seat. "I meant before we, um…"

"Fuck?" Avery asked, stroking back toward Jonah's crotch. This time, the edge of Avery's pinky finger brushed against Jonah's erection. Avery sucked in a sharp breath, while all the air hissed out of Jonah's lungs.

"Uh, yeah," Jonah wheezed. "Get to know each other and stuff."

"Oh, I'm planning on getting to know you very well tonight." Avery squeezed his cock, and Jonah canted his hips, pushing harder against the contact. "I need to know what drives you wild."

"It's you," Jonah admitted. "You're my undoing."

Avery sighed as a shiver rolled through him. "This weather is the perfect soundtrack for us. The sexual tension has been building like a storm for so long. You've blustered and huffed and puffed, and now I'm going to blow…you." Avery stroked Jonah's rigid length through his jeans, squeezing with the perfect amount of pressure and making Jonah's eyes roll back in his head. "Dinner and a movie sound like a lot of fun, and I'm looking forward to it, but I've had enough foreplay the past eight months." Avery released Jonah's cock and placed his hand back on the steering wheel. Damn tease. He wanted to snatch that hand back and grind against it.

"I think our idea of foreplay is very different," Jonah said.

Avery shook his head. "The spilled coffees, the petty arguments, and the way you thundered around the office all led us to this point."

Avery's boldness and sass appealed to Jonah as much as the man's lean body, kind heart, and brilliant mind. Jonah had spent so much of his life hiding and pretending. He had hidden his sexuality from his family, friends, and the army. He'd pretended to be a soldier at war, but his hesitation to pull the trigger at a critical moment resulted in immeasurable loss. Some people saw Jonah as a scarred freak, some viewed him as a computer geek, and others mislabeled him a hero. Not Avery. He just saw a man.

Jonah felt like he was on the cusp of something truly special. He just had to be brave enough to reach for it. Was he?

"Do you trust my judgment?" Avery asked as he pulled into Jonah's driveway and parked. After turning off the car, Avery removed his seat belt and turned his body toward Jonah.

Jonah swallowed hard. "Yes."

"Then stop trying to talk yourself out of us," Avery said fiercely as he crawled across the console and straddled Jonah's lap. Avery removed Jonah's seat belt and attacked his mouth with hungry kisses.

Jonah gripped Avery's ass and held him tightly, deepening the kiss until they were both panting and breathless. Avery started rocking his hips, grinding their groins together. "I don't want to come in my pants."

Avery grinned wickedly. "One of these days, I do want to drive you that crazy, but not our first time together."

"First time, huh?"

Avery pressed his lips against Jonah's for a quick kiss. "Don't think for two seconds that we're going back to way things were. You're going to admit how much you like me, and I'm going to make you realize just how badly you want to do the boyfriend thing with me."

Jonah smiled at the audacious man on his lap. "Is that so?"

"Yes." He moved to get off Jonah, but the big man just tightened his grip on Avery's ass and pushed open the car door. "Wrap your legs around me," Jonah said as he stood up with Avery in his arms.

"Mmmmm. I've been waiting to hear you say those words to me," Avery purred as he complied.

Having Avery's arms and legs entwined around him felt so right that Jonah nearly stumbled.

"Whoa there, big fella," Avery said, shamelessly grinding himself against Jonah's straining erection.

Jonah stopped when he reached the front porch, setting Avery on the railing and ravishing his mouth. The rain continued to pelt them, but it felt good against Jonah's overheated skin. Lightning continued to streak across the sky, flashing against Avery's fair flesh like a strobe light.

"The front door is just a few feet behind you," Avery said, panting against Jonah's lips. "Unless you plan to fuck me out here on the porch." He reached down and gripped the railing, giving it a good shake. "Seems steady enough."

"I initially only planned to set you down long enough to remove my house keys from my pocket."

"Oh," Avery said excitedly. "Let me help you." He shoved his hand in the left pocket, which was the direction Jonah's erection leaned. Jonah's keys weren't in there, but Avery already knew it and continued to tease his cock through the thin fabric. His tormentor's mouth fell open, allowing a soft gasp to escape. The noise was precisely what Jonah imagined Avery would make when he slid his dick inside him. "You're not wearing any underwear."

"Quit teasing me and retrieve my keys from the other pocket so you can find out."

Avery ignored him and squeezed along the length of his dick. "I know full well you don't free-ball it when you wear dress pants to work. I've stared at your ass enough to see the outline of your briefs. Do you only go commando when you wear jeans?"

Jonah retrieved his keys before hoisting Avery in his arms once more. The lithe body felt so fucking right against his, even better than he'd imagined in his horniest fantasies. Avery sucked and nibbled on his neck while Jonah unlocked the deadbolt and stepped inside his home. He fumbled his keys and dropped them on the floor when Avery bit down on his earlobe. Jonah growled as his dick throbbed even harder.

"Oh, I'm sorry," Avery said. "Too hard?"

"No," Jonah said. When he moved to kiss Avery, the man squirmed out of his arms. Jonah was momentarily confused until Avery dropped to his knees.

Glancing up the length of Jonah's body, Avery said, "The least I could do is pick them up for you since I made you drop them." Avery made no move to pick up the forgotten keys; he reached for Jonah's belt instead.

Jonah ran his thumb over the plush lips that would soon be wrapped around his cock. Avery bit down on his thumb, then licked it. The sight of Avery's pink tongue swirling around the tip of his digit threatened to make Jonah's knees buckle. "We should take this to my room."

Avery shook his head as he unbuckled Jonah's belt. "Too far away."

Cupping Avery's face, Jonah said. "You don't even know where my room is."

Avery popped open the first button. "Doesn't matter." Then the second button. "Anything beyond this spot is too far." He leaned forward and kissed the bare flesh he exposed as a third button came loose. "I want you right here." Jonah's cock sprang forward once the fourth button was freed. "Right now." Avery's hot breath ghosted over Jonah's cock as he released the final button. Then he yanked the denim to mid-thigh.

"Kendall could come home and—" The last word died in his throat when Avery extended his tongue to trace the flushed head. Wrapping his lips around the crown, Avery swirled his tongue beneath the sensitive underside. "Right here is good," Jonah whimpered, staring into the hazel-brown eyes which had always seen right through him. He traced Avery's stretched lips while praying he didn't make a fool of himself by coming in thirty seconds.

Avery gripped the base of Jonah's cock and eased his mouth further down his shaft until the broad head nudged against the back of Avery's throat, making him gag a little. Avery's eyes widened and began to water. Jonah started to pull out of his mouth until Avery lightly grazed his bottom teeth along the underside of Jonah's erection. Then Avery swallowed more of his cock.

"Fuck. Oh fuck," Jonah said, slipping his fingers into Avery's silky hair. "Feels so good, but be careful." It took all his control not to fist the strands and fuck Avery's face.

Avery maintained eye contact with Jonah as he hummed happily, sending tiny vibrations along his shaft like electrical currents to zap his nuts. Yeah, he wasn't going to last long if he didn't put a stop to this.

Jonah wasn't the kind of guy who lauded his strength over other people, but he made exceptions when it was essential. Hauling the little minx to his bed seemed very necessary, so he hooked his arms under Avery's armpits and pulled him to his feet. Avery was so stunned, Jonah had him hoisted over his shoulder by the time he realized what was happening.

"Stay still," Jonah said, slapping Avery's ass when he started to squirm. Avery grunted but immediately settled down. Jonah yanked up his pants so he wouldn't trip going up the stairs to his bedroom. "Hold on."

Jonah made the trip to his room in record time. His long legs gave him a considerable advantage, allowing him to take the steps two at a time. He didn't set Avery down until he shut his door and locked it.

Jonah crossed the room to dump Avery on his bed. He wasn't gentle, but the gleam in Avery's eyes said he liked it a lot.

"Do you want this?" Jonah asked, fisting his erection, jutting from the gap in his jeans.

Avery groaned and licked his bottom lip. "You know I do."

Jonah toed out of his shoes and shucked his jeans down his legs, removing them along with his socks. Then he lifted his shirt over his head and tossed it onto the pile of clothes on the floor. "Behave and let me take my time."

Avery sat up and reached for his shirt, but Jonah stepped to the bed and wrapped his hand around Avery's wrist.

"Let me." Jonah bit back a chuckle when Avery flopped back with an adorable pout on his lips. Jonah removed Avery's shoes and socks, rubbing his thumbs along the arches of his feet. "I like you Avery. A lot," Jonah said hoarsely.

Avery sucked in a sharp breath. "Jonah."

"Mmmmmm. There's that sound again," Jonah said, massaging Avery's calves, the back of his knees, and his thighs through his jeans as he inched closer to his waistband. "Are you going to gasp so prettily when I slide my dick inside you?"

"I'll probably embarrass myself and cry because I've wanted you for so long."

"That makes two of us."

Jonah veered to the center and squeezed Avery's erection through his clothes, making the man squirm and moan. He unbuttoned his jeans and tugged the zipper down, exposing light blue underwear. Noticing the damp circle from precum, Jonah leaned forward, pressing his nose against the spot and breathing him in deep. *Heaven.*

Avery bucked beneath him and cried out his name desperately. Jonah raised up and locked gazes with Avery, who lifted his hips to make it easier for Jonah to remove his jeans and underwear. Avery slid his hands in Jonah's hair when he hovered over Avery's bare cock for too long. Jonah knew what Avery craved. He wanted it also.

Jonah fisted the base of Avery's cock and took him to the back of his throat.

"Oh, fuck!" Avery cried out, snapping his hips up and driving his dick deeper into Jonah's mouth. Reaching between Avery's spread legs, Jonah cupped and massaged his smooth balls while working his mouth up and down Avery's cock. "You better stop," Avery said, his voice trembling. "I really want to shoot down your throat, but not yet."

Jonah chuckled and released Avery's cock. Pushing Avery's shirt upward, Jonah kissed each inch of smooth, pale skin Jonah exposed, lingering on that cinnamon-colored freckle near Avery's belly button. Jonah lavished a lot of attention on Avery's hard nipples, licking, sucking, and tugging them with his teeth.

"Pin me to the bed. I want your weight on me," Avery moaned.

Jonah lifted his head and stared into Avery's eyes. He'd be lying if he wasn't worried about the differences in their sizes. Not just Jonah's weight either. As if Avery read his mind, a sly grin slowly spread across his face. *Uh-oh.*

"I've been practicing," Avery whispered.

Practicing? What the hell did that entail? He scowled at the idea of Avery fucking other men, which was ludicrous since he wasn't the Boy Scout everyone claimed he was.

Avery slapped his bicep. "Not that kind of practice, idiot. More like training."

"Not sure I like that verb any better," Jonah admitted.

Avery snorted and lifted his legs toward his chest. Jonah smiled when he understood what Avery had meant. He grabbed Avery's firm ass cheeks and spread them further apart before gripping the base of the butt plug and twisting.

Avery's eyes widened, and his mouth fell open. *Like that, did he?*

Jonah pushed the toy again, knowing it pegged Avery's gland. Avery whimpered and clung to Jonah's biceps. "Need you. Now."

Avery sounded like he was seconds away from spurting all over himself, and Jonah liked it…a lot. With his shirt rucked up and forgotten, his mussed hair, swollen lips, and blown pupils, Avery looked the part of a shameless imp. Fuck if it didn't push all Jonah's buttons.

"You were awfully sure of yourself," Jonah said, running his finger along the puckered flesh stretching to accommodate the intrusion.

Avery's body tensed, and his back bowed off the bed. "Not really," he panted. "I mean, I figured this weekend was a sure bet, so I started my training tonight when I got home from work."

Jonah closed his eyes, moaning as he imagined how sexy Avery had looked while lubing and inserting the plug inside his ass. Did he make the sexy little gasp? Did Avery think about Jonah and get turned on? He nudged the base again, and Avery's breath hissed between his lips.

"I was going to graduate to a larger one tomorrow, an even larger one the next day, and so on to get prepared for Friday. I'm not a virgin, but I was pretty certain you have a horse dick, so…"

Jonah lowered his head and licked the precum dripping onto Avery's abdomen at the same time he twisted the butt plug again.

Avery fisted both hands in Jonah's hair. "Fuck me, damn it."

"I don't know," Jonah teased. "If you just started stretching—"

"I put the biggest one in after you called me. I. Am. Ready. Get the lube, get the condoms, and—"

Jonah cut off his bossy tirade when he sucked Avery's dick into his mouth, swallowing him down to the root. Avery squeezed his thighs against Jonah's head, lifting his hips and fucking Jonah's face. He placed his hand on Avery's abdomen to hold him still, then bobbed his head up and down on his cock. Avery's head thrashed from side to side, and his fingers tightened in Jonah's hair.

Jonah used his distraction to remove the plug from Avery's pucker before letting his cock slide free from his mouth. "Would you look at that?" Jonah said, watching Avery's entrance flex. "It's begging for me to fill it."

"Told you so."

Instead of retrieving the lube and a condom, Jonah lifted Avery's ass higher in the air, shoved his face between his ass cheeks, and made a feast of it. Avery cried out the second Jonah's tongue traced the rim of his pucker and continued to get louder and bossier as Jonah worked him closer and closer to the precipice. He knew when Avery had reached his limits because his words were incoherent.

Jonah released Avery's legs and retrieved protection and lube from the nightstand. "Are you sure? We can't undo this, and it might make things difficult for us at work."

"You're asking me that *after* you tongue-fucked me?" Avery asked, recovering his ability to speak.

"I'm serious."

Avery snorted. "Fine. I quit. Now fuck me."

Jonah tore the condom wrapper open and rolled it on before smearing lube down his length. Turning his attention to Avery's hole, Jonah stretched and prepared him further. Once he was satisfied Avery was ready, Jonah got onto the bed and lay down on his back instead of positioning himself between Avery's parted thighs.

Rolling to his side, Avery glared at him.

"You want me to pin you to the bed and fuck you?" Jonah asked, tucking his hands beneath his head.

"I was pretty clear about it."

Jonah smiled at him. "Prove you can take me."

The twinkle of mischief grew brighter as Avery crawled toward him. "You're going to regret putting me in charge."

"I've said the same thing at least once a week since you became my intern," Jonah quipped.

Avery raked his eyes over Jonah's stretched-out body. "So, what? You're just going to lie there and make me do all the work?"

Jonah ached to kiss his smart mouth. "Just this once."

"More like every day at work," Avery fired back, heaving a sigh like he was really put out. "If I must." Avery straddled Jonah's thighs and reached between his legs. "I love your hairy balls," he said, massaging Jonah's nuts with one hand. "And this too," he added, tugging Jonah's trimmed pubic hair with his other.

"Goes with my hairy ass," Jonah said, cupping Avery's face. "I love all the ways you're different from me. Soft where I'm rough and smooth where I'm hairy. Ride me."

Avery positioned himself and aligned Jonah's cock to his pucker.

"Nice and slow," Jonah cautioned.

Avery lowered himself onto the first few inches, releasing a whimpering gasp that clawed at Jonah's control. Bracing his hands on Jonah's pecs, Avery rocked his hips until he'd buried Jonah's cock to the hilt inside him. "I feel so full."

Jonah kept his hands tucked beneath his head, but he really wanted to hold on to Avery's hips while he fucked himself on Jonah's erection. Avery smiled wickedly, sensing Jonah's struggle and reveling in it.

"Look at those straining biceps," Avery murmured. "You want to touch me so badly."

"I am touching you," Jonah countered. "In the most intimate way possible."

"Mmmhmm," Avery said, slowly grinding his hips. "I like the hair on your chest too. Not too thick but the perfect amount to run my fingers through or hold on to when I'm fucking you." Avery demonstrated by fisting one hand in Jonah's chest hair and tugging it while rocking his hips faster. "Makes me want to pet you."

"Pet me," Jonah said.

He'd never given his chest hair much thought. He knew a lot of guys shaved theirs off, and maybe he would too if he'd sported fur like an animal pelt. Jonah was so damn grateful he'd left his alone when Avery started purring in the back of his throat while smoothing a hand over Jonah's chest.

Jonah stifled the urge to roll Avery to his back and pound his sweet ass. "I'm at your mercy," he reminded Avery.

Avery chuckled, and his fluid hips momentarily faltered from their hypnotic rhythm. "We both know you're much stronger and could do whatever you wish to me."

"I am bigger and stronger, and I could hurt you, but I won't. Not ever. When you believe me, I'll pin you to the bed beneath my weight and fuck you."

Avery moaned, rocking his hips faster. "So, this is a trust-building exercise."

Jonah grinned. "I take my role as a mentor *very* seriously."

"Mmmm," Avery agreed, releasing his grip on Jonah to run his hands over his own smooth chest while riding every inch of Jonah's throbbing cock. "And here I thought it was a test of wills." Avery's breath hitched every time Jonah's dick nudged his gland. "You don't want to lose control, but I want you to so very badly."

It was almost Jonah's undoing, but he just fisted his hands tighter.

Avery licked his swollen lips. "So close."

"Are you talking about my control snapping or your orgasm?" Jonah asked, his voice sounding hoarse and raw.

"Both," Avery said, his voice a higher octave as he inched closer to climax. Jonah expected Avery to reach for his dick and start jerking himself off, but he grabbed onto Jonah's pecs again. Avery rode Jonah faster and harder, his tight ass bouncing against Jonah's strained thighs until he cried out and splattered Jonah's abdomen and chest with cum.

"I win," Avery said, smiling triumphantly down at Jonah as sweat trickled down his body. He swirled a finger through the mess he made.

Jonah's tenuous grip on his control snapped. He snaked a hand forward and grabbed Avery's wrist, lifting the dripping finger to his lips. He sucked the digit into his mouth, tasting Avery's salty essence. After he finished, Jonah released Avery. "You finished first, but you didn't win," Jonah said.

In the next heartbeat, he'd grabbed Avery's hips and rolled him to his back, pinning the smaller man beneath him. Jonah gave them both what they wanted, snapping his hips forward hard enough to make Avery's eyes roll back in his head. "We're both winners."

"Yes!" Avery cried out.

He fucked Avery relentlessly, reducing his lover to a quivering, moaning, and groaning mess. Jonah shouted victoriously as he came, pumping the condom full. When he finished, he moved to roll off Avery, but he tightened his arms and legs around Jonah, keeping him in place. They both knew Jonah could break the hold just as they knew he wouldn't.

Avery slid his hands into Jonah's sweaty hair and pulled him down for a long kiss. When they broke apart several minutes later, Jonah eased out of Avery, then lay down beside him.

"Now comes the favorite part of my fantasy," Avery said. Jonah's brain was too fuck-blissed to even guess, but luckily, Avery took pity on him. "After-sex cuddling." Jonah lifted his arm and Avery tucked himself up against his side, resting his head on Jonah's chest. He made these little contented purring noises that made Jonah smile. "God, cuddling with you is even better than I imagined. If this is a dream, I don't want anyone to wake me up."

"Does this mean you like me too?" Jonah asked.

Avery raised his head and looked into Jonah's eyes. He expected a sassy or snarky response, but the tenderness in Avery's gaze stole his breath. "More than you're ready to hear."

Jonah opened his mouth to say something, anything, but no words tumbled from his lips. So he kissed Avery again, hoping he could feel how much his confession pleased Jonah.

Once they parted to catch their breath, Avery smiled impishly, then said, "Now I want to live out my second favorite part of my fantasy." Jonah quirked a brow. "Showering together. I want to run soapy hands all over your body. I hope you have a good hot water heater."

Jonah mentally crossed his fingers that the appliance had one last ride.

"I guess we'll find out."

CHAPTER 15

The next morning, his ringing cell phone woke Jonah from the deepest sleep he'd had in years. He glanced at the time and noticed it was only seven in the morning. Why the hell was Felix calling him so early?

"Hello?" he said gruffly.

"Be ready at eight."

The ensuing groan disturbed Avery, who Jonah discovered slept like the dead. The phone hadn't woken him, but the sound of Jonah's distress stirred him. Jonah ran a hand along Avery's spine to soothe him back to sleep, but his touch had the opposite effect. One moment, Avery was sound asleep, and the next, he was scooting beneath the sheets. Jonah's eyes rolled back in his head when he felt the first press of Avery's tongue at the base of his semi-erect penis.

"What was that noise?" Felix asked.

"Noise?" Jonah asked breathlessly. "I didn't hear anything." Avery giggled beneath the sheets. "Where are we going?"

"Jesus Christ," Felix groused. "Don't you know better than to answer your phone during sex? I'll be there at eight thirty. Be ready." Felix hung up before Jonah could respond. Avery sucked one of Jonah's balls in his mouth, and he lost the ability to do anything but cry out Avery's name.

Unfortunately, it happened at the same time Kendall burst through his bedroom door, shouting Jonah's name. He was soaking wet with a towel haphazardly wrapped around his waist and soapy hair sticking up in all directions. Beneath the sheet, Avery stilled for a second before tickling Jonah's taint with the tip of his tongue.

"Shut the door and go away," Jonah growled at Kendall. He grabbed the pillow Avery had slept on and hurled it at his friend.

Kendall ducked to avoid it but didn't step farther in the room. "Oh, wow. You have company."

"You don't have to sound so shocked," Jonah groused.

"Forgive me," Kendall said. "You've just lived like a monk for so long."

"I'm not into voyeurism, K. Get out," Jonah repeated.

"Oh, for fuck's sakes," Kendall said, rolling his eyes. "I didn't come here to watch or join in."

"Then leave," Jonah said, his voice straining as Avery sucked on his taint.

"The hot water heater crapped out in the middle of my shower. I must insist you fix it right away."

"Sure thing. Now get the fuck out of here," Jonah said tersely.

Kendall waggled his brows, then shut the door loud enough to make Avery giggle. Jonah reached beneath the sheets and tugged Avery up until he sprawled across Jonah's chest.

Jonah nuzzled his nose against the sensitive spot beneath Avery's ear. "Good morning."

"Not yet, it isn't," Avery said. "I was trying to make it one."

Jonah brushed a lock of hair off Avery's forehead and took in his disheveled appearance and soft eyes. "It's perfect."

"I had big plans to make you messy," Avery countered. "Maybe we need to alter them a little bit since you won't be able to take a shower, and it sounds like there's someplace you need to be soon."

"I have ninety minutes before Felix picks me up to drive me God knows where. I'm willing to get creative if you are," Jonah said, lifting his head and kissing the softest lips he'd ever known.

"What did you have in mind?" Avery asked in between kisses.

He rolled Avery onto his side with a playful growl. Jonah repositioned himself so his head was facing the opposite end of the bed. He would much rather have Avery straddling his face in a sixty-nine position, but this allowed Avery to have more control.

Jonah would've loved to drag out their pleasure and include more teasing foreplay, but things were still so damn new and thrilling. They spilled down each other's throats without much effort or fanfare, but neither of them complained as they lay panting in the bed.

"I wish I could stay longer," Avery said, pressing a kiss against Jonah's chest. "There's so much of you I haven't explored yet, but I need to get home and get ready for work."

Jonah held him tighter. "Don't wash my scent off you yet." He liked knowing Avery would go to work smelling like his soap and shampoo.

"I didn't plan on it," Avery said, smiling at him.

Jonah patted his ass, then eased out of bed. "I'll go get your stuff from downstairs." They'd washed their wet clothes after their shower and tossed them in the dryer before going to bed.

"Like that?" Avery asked, gesturing to Jonah's nude body.

Jonah smiled sheepishly as he pulled a pair of basketball shorts from a drawer and put them on. "Better?" he asked.

Eyes locked on Jonah's crotch, Avery said, "Barely, but I'll take it."

Jonah wished he could make Avery a cup of tea before he left, but he didn't keep any on hand. He made a mental note to pick some up along with Betty's preferred dog treats from the store. Avery hated coffee with a passion, so Jonah didn't bother offering him a mug or make any for himself. He could wait until he gave Avery a proper send-off which included a lot of tongue and touching.

Avery sighed happily and leaned against the driver's side door of his car. "I thought you'd be freaking out this morning."

"Me too," Jonah admitted. "It might come later."

Avery laughed. "I'll be ready. Have fun with Felix. Call me later."

"I will," Jonah said softly, kissing him once more before releasing him. "You were right, by the way."

"I so often am," Avery replied cheekily. "Care to elaborate?"

"You make me believe the boyfriend thing is a good idea."

"With me," Avery amended. "Don't leave out that part."

"With you."

"It's a fucking great idea," Avery said. "You'll see."

Felix arrived at eight twenty, and he didn't show up empty-handed either. He'd procured donuts and two tall coffees from Hermes, a Savannah landmark built in the late eighteen hundreds. The bakery was on the first floor of the massive Queen Anne corner store, and the Hermes family lived in the residential area above it. Sometime in the 1920s, the Gottlieb Bakery moved into the building. The bakery became Hermes-Gottlieb, but most locals still just called it Hermes. The stately building had recently undergone renovations to preserve history while bringing the beautiful structure up to current code. The current owners upgraded their menu to appeal to a broader customer base, but they never fucked with the original recipes that had made the pastries a household name.

"I hope they put enough syrupy bullshit in there to please you," Felix said when Jonah got in his car. "This is some sea salt caramel concoction."

Jonah took a sip and hummed appreciatively. "It's perfection."

"Glad you like it," Felix said while reversing out of Jonah's driveway. "I grabbed a variety of pastries since I didn't know what kind you like." He wouldn't know Jonah's coffee preferences either if Jonah didn't have a terrible habit of drinking coffee in the evening.

"Did you see iced coffee on their menu?" Jonah asked.

Felix had just taken a bite of a glazed donut covered in cinnamon sugar, so Jonah had to rely on his partner's scowl as an answer until he finished chewing.

"Coffee is supposed to be hot," Felix said after taking a sip of his brew.

Jonah chuckled. "Does that mean iced coffee is on the menu, and you don't approve?"

"It means I didn't notice if iced coffee was on their menu because I wasn't looking for it," Felix countered.

"And here I thought reporters were observant and noticed everything around them."

"I observe you're filled with piss and vinegar this morning. You remind me of Pul after he's taken a shit."

"Uh, thanks, I guess."

Felix chuckled and shook his head. "It wasn't a compliment, jackass."

Jonah laughed. "Who's Paul? Your latest plaything?"

"Plaything?" Felix asked, disdain dripping off his tongue.

"You're the slut puppy in this trio," Jonah replied.

"Oh, man. I don't think I'll ever recover from such a harsh insult."

Jonah laughed. "Who's Paul?"

"I said Pul not Paul. It's short for the Pulitzer Prize I'm going to win someday. He's a fucking cat, dick breath."

Jonah did indeed have dick breath, but he didn't say as much. "You own a cat?"

Felix laughed. "No one owns a cat. The cat owns you."

"Ah," Jonah said. He'd witnessed the way Locke and Key pampered their ginormous Maine Coon cat named Bones. "I'm having a tough time picturing you spoiling a pet."

"I'm not capable of affection? What do you call the donut you stuffed into your mouth in two bites?"

"I didn't say you're incapable of affection," Jonah rebutted. "I just have a hard time picturing you using a baby voice when talking to a cat."

"Pul would slit my throat in my sleep if I ever pulled a bullshit stunt like that. He has too much dignity." Felix took another sip of coffee. "Don't think all this talk about my cat is going to distract me from asking about your overnight guest. I'm assuming it wasn't Kendall I heard in your bed."

"Kendall and I are just friends," Jonah replied. "Avery and I have…" How did he put it? Were they officially dating? How could they be when they hadn't gone on a date?

"Avery yanked your head out of your ass," Felix supplied for him.

"With both hands," Jonah said, grinning from ear to ear.

"Good for you," Felix said. "You look like a different man."

Jonah felt different too. He hadn't just touched the sun and survived; Jonah carried Avery's warmth inside him, and it quieted the howling winds of discontent. "Thanks," Jonah said simply. "So, where are we going?"

"Roswell," Felix replied.

"Are we investigating aliens?" Jonah teased.

"Roswell, Georgia, not Roswell, New Mexico. It's a suburb of Atlanta." So at least a four-hour drive on I-16.

"Who lives there?"

"Agnes Cahill, the widow of Bo Cahill, her son, Darnell, and her daughter, Amelia, who goes by Millie. They saw my article and reached out to me late yesterday afternoon before I had the chance to track them down. I didn't tell you last night because I was waiting for them to confirm the interview time via email, which didn't come until this morning."

Jonah bumped the fist Felix held up. "That's awesome news. How'd they seem?"

"Eager to clear Bo's name of this crime, at least," Felix said. "How'd it go with you and Rocky yesterday?"

Jonah filled him in. Felix shared his enthusiasm for the new leads to investigate. "Earl's father and brother both worked for the concrete company responsible for pouring the foundations, driveways, porches, and patios in the subdivision. Earl briefly worked for Locke-Tight also. We can't chalk it up to coincidence."

"Locke-Tight, huh? Any relation to Royce?" Felix asked.

"I'm going to call him today and ask. I think we have to look at the subcontractors involved in the subdivision project. We can't afford to assume the location didn't hold more importance to our killer than convenience and privacy in the early morning hours."

Felix nodded. "I agree. Did you learn anything else interesting?"

"Earl's boyfriend had given him a silver necklace with a heart-shaped pendant. His friend said Earl never removed it, but he wasn't wearing the necklace in the crime scene photos, and it wasn't collected for evidence either."

"You think the killer took it?" Felix asked.

"I think it's possible. Or maybe Earl and his boyfriend had a big fight, and Earl returned it. The necklace feels significant to me."

"Every new clue we uncover is important. We're going to solve this case," Felix said excitedly.

Jonah hoped liked hell his friend was right.

Agnes Cahill sat regally, if not a little stiffly, in her son and daughter-in-law's dining room. Jonah understood the wariness in her eyes when they introduced themselves. He was asking Agnes to turn her life inside out all over again and expose her wounds and heartache to complete strangers. It wasn't easy for him, so it sure as hell wasn't a walk in the park for her. She'd survived a brutal assault only to have her husband taken away from her. Thirteen years later, their name would make the papers again when her husband confessed to a crime he couldn't have committed. Jonah had lost people he'd loved dearly, so he understood exactly what he was asking her to do. He didn't take it lightly.

Darnell had come home for lunch, and Millie took the day off, knowing how hard the interview would be for her mother. Darnell's wife, Trista, a thoracic surgeon, wasn't home, and his children were at school, so the five of them sat in the dining room. They made small talk at first, learning Millie was an elementary school teacher and Darnell was an architect. When Darnell and Trista decided to start a family, Agnes moved in with them to help look after the kids.

"What about James?" Felix asked. He'd obviously done some homework before the interview.

"Jamie," Agnes corrected with a smile. "He's the baby and has a touch of wanderlust. He's a jazz musician and travels around the world. He makes a home in New Orleans when he sets his trumpet down for more than five minutes."

"We'd like to speak to Jamie also, if he's willing," Jonah said.

"He's currently on a European tour," Agnes said. "I will ask if he's inclined to talk to you over the phone or on one of those video calls."

"Thank you. We greatly appreciate it," Felix said. "You already have my contact information, but Jonah will leave a business card for you also." Jonah removed one from his wallet so he wouldn't forget later.

Agnes accepted it with a gentle smile. "Jamie knows we're speaking with you today, and I won't say he disapproves, but he's hesitant to dig up the past again."

"I completely understand," Jonah said. "Before we begin, I do want to apologize. This can't be pleasant for you, and we wouldn't be here if we could clear Bo's name without talking to his family. We want to aggressively investigate Earl's death, but in a way that causes the least amount of trauma for your family."

"Furthermore, I think your husband is a hero," Felix said.

Agnes searched Felix's face before making eye contact with Jonah, who nodded. His ties to guns and violence were too complicated to express in a few words. He'd pulled the trigger more times than he wanted to remember, but he'd faltered the one time it mattered most.

Bo Cahill had not failed; the system had failed him.

"Thank you," she said softly.

"Jonah and I are just trying to figure out why Bo would've falsely confessed to killing a man," Felix said.

Agnes shifted in her chair. It was subtle but still there. "We, unfortunately, don't have those answers for you. You can rest assured I demanded to know why Bo would confess to killing a man he'd probably never even met. He just told me he knew what he was doing, and I had to trust him. We didn't have much time left, and I wasn't going to spend it arguing with him."

"You might have the answers we need and just aren't aware," Felix corrected. "It's our job to parse the truth from perception."

"Fair enough," Darnell said, joining hands with his mother and sister. Tragedy either destroyed a family or bound them closer. The Cahill family seemed to fall into the latter category.

"To the best of your knowledge, did Bo even know Earl Ison?" Jonah asked.

"I don't think so," Agnes said, shaking her head. "Bo had never mentioned the man's name to me."

"Did Bo have friends in Savannah?" Felix asked.

"No," Agnes said emphatically.

"He sure as hell wasn't a homophobic asshole either," Millie said. "Our uncle Mickey, his brother, was gay. Daddy loved him."

"I cannot even believe my father's mouth formed those hateful words," Darnell said.

Jonah stroked a finger over his chin while he thought through the possibilities. "Could your uncle have been friends with Earl?"

"Mickey did have friends in Savannah, but he had already died in a car accident before someone murdered Earl Ison," Agnes said. "Bo was devastated when Mickey died."

"Have you ever met any of Mickey's friends from Savannah? Did he talk about them? Was he into the drag scene?" Felix asked.

Agnes tipped her head to the side for a few moments. "I don't think Mickey dressed in drag, but I wouldn't be surprised if he enjoyed watching their performances. I'm sure he talked about his friends, but I can't remember any names after all these years. Like I said, Mickey had passed away before all this happened."

It sounded like a dead end to Jonah, but he'd ask Marla about Mickey next time they spoke. "Was Mickey's last name Cahill also?"

"No," Darnell said. "His last name was Reeder."

"Bo's daddy passed away when he was a little boy. His mama remarried and later gave birth to Mickey," Agnes explained, playing with the gold cross hanging from a chain around her neck. "I was heartbroken when my mother-in-law died early in my marriage, but I'm so grateful she didn't live to see what happened to her boys."

They chatted for another thirty or so minutes, hoping to find new leads from the family. Agnes did recall the name of one of the prison guards working at the county jail, Opie, and one who worked at the state facility, Bird.

Felix looked up from his notes. "Do you think Opie is a nickname?"

Agnes smiled. "He had red hair and many freckles, so probably. Pretty sure Bird is a nickname too because he looked a lot like the basketball player for the Celtics."

"It's still beneficial," Felix assured Agnes. "If they're still living, we'll find them."

After concluding the interview, Bo's family walked Jonah and Felix to the door.

Darnell shook their hands and said, "Even though clearing his name won't bring Daddy back, this means a lot to us."

"We'll do everything we can," Jonah assured them. "If Jamie decides to speak to us, please let him know the time of day doesn't matter. I'll rearrange my schedule however he needs it."

"I will pass your message along," Agnes said.

Neither man said anything until they were driving away from Darnell's house.

"Do you think Agnes knows why Bo confessed to killing Earl?" Felix asked. "She could be protecting someone just like Bo had."

"Possibly," Jonah said. "Who? Jamie?"

"He was awfully young at the time his dad confessed to killing Earl, but maybe he had a juvenile record. I will see what I can turn up."

They stopped at a steakhouse outside of Macon. They'd seen the billboard along the highway and decided it sounded good. As much as Jonah wanted to eat a thick, juicy steak, he settled for a massive grilled chicken salad. Felix wasn't worried about his waistline or cholesterol. He ordered a steak that was bigger than his head and onions rings that were the size of Jonah's fist.

"You can have one," Felix said when he caught Jonah staring at them and salivating. Jonah took two. "What's next?"

"I need you to drop me off at Tire Discounters when we get back to town," he said.

"I wondered where your car was," Felix said, spearing a bite of steak.

"Some asshole slashed my tires when I was at The Dive Bar interviewing two of Earl's friends."

"What? Why are you just now telling me?" Felix asked.

Jonah shrugged. "I can't prove it had anything to do with our investigation."

"Come on, computer geek. You're probably pretty familiar with probability and statistics."

"Very," Jonah said, nodding. "I agree it's improbable the two things aren't connected, but I'm not ready to start pointing my finger yet."

"We'll be extra cautious going forward."

"Agreed," Jonah said. "After I pick up my car, I need to purchase a water heater to replace mine. It died this morning." He told Felix about Kendall bursting into his bedroom, and Felix laughed until tears streamed down his face.

"If you didn't have bad luck, you wouldn't have any."

Jonah nodded. "True."

They left the restaurant a short time later. When they neared Savannah, a promo came on for the nightly news. "Who killed Earl Ison?" a familiar voice asked. "That's what I'm going to find out. Tune in at eleven and—"

Felix growled and stabbed a button on the radio to change the station. "Fucking Jude Arrow."

"Not a fan of The Straight Shooter?" Jonah asked, straightening in his seat. He'd started to get drowsy with a full belly, but Felix's irritation perked him up.

"He's a sanctimonious prick," Felix snarled. "I'd like to give the arrow shoved up his ass a good twist."

"Whoa," Jonah said. "Such hostility. How do you know him? He hasn't been with the local news for long."

"Journalism school," Felix spat out like the words tasted terrible. "He went to Atlanta afterward and became a big deal. If I cared about him even slightly, I'd find out why he left Hotlanta for a much smaller market."

Jonah looked at his friend and noted Felix's rigid posture, firm jaw, and white-knuckle grip on the steering wheel. Yeah, he didn't care even the tiniest bit. Jonah let it go because he wasn't an annoying shithead like Felix and Rocky.

Oh, fuck that. Being a shithead was much more fun. "Or you could use your investigative reporter skills to ferret out the information. If you cared, that is."

Felix released the steering wheel with one hand so he could flip Jonah off. "Kiss my ass."

Felix's ass was definitely not the one Jonah longed to kiss.

CHAPTER 16

By the time Jonah collected his car and drove home, it was already after six. He'd spent the last leg of their journey back to Savannah on the phone looking for a plumber who could replace his water heater. Everyone he called was booked solid for weeks, and none of them offered emergency services, which was odd since they could charge double for their labor.

Defeated, dingy, and wishing he could shower, Jonah changed into a pair of clean sweats and a T-shirt before calling Royce.

"Hey, big guy," Royce said when he answered the phone. "Why do you sound like Eeyore?"

Jonah chuckled, then explained his predicament.

"This is your lucky day," Royce said enthusiastically.

"It is?"

Royce laughed. "I just happen to know a guy who has amazing plumbing skills." Jonah heard a loud snort coming from the other end and suspected it came from Sawyer. "What?" Royce asked.

"Do you remember the last time you tried to help a friend with a plumbing issue?" Sawyer asked, his voice heavy with sarcasm.

"It was a freak thing," Royce said defensively.

"You nearly flooded Candi's upstairs bathroom," Sawyer said. "You can't be trusted."

"Oh, yeah?" Royce asked. "I haven't begun to show you my prowess around the house yet."

"I've got your prowess right here," Sawyer quipped.

"I've changed water heaters plenty of times," Royce argued.

"How many is plenty?" Jonah asked, reminding them he was still on the phone.

"At least twice," Royce replied. "It's easy. Have you already purchased a replacement water heater?"

"No. I've been out of town interviewing people for our current podcast investigation," Jonah replied. "I can get one pretty fast though, except I don't have a vehicle large enough to haul it."

"I got you covered there too. I have this new badass SUV, and the only thing I've hauled so far is groceries," Royce grumbled. "Call Sal at Sal's Hardware. He'll know everything we need to replace the water heater. You can pay for the order over the phone, and I'll swing by and pick it up in about an hour, then head over to your place."

"This *is* my lucky day," Jonah said.

"Famous last words," Sawyer warned, raising his voice to be sure Jonah could hear him.

"Why are you yelling in his ear?" Royce asked. "I have you on speakerphone, asshole."

"Shut up and drive, dickhead," Sawyer returned.

Jonah laughed at their antics. "Strangers observing you two would think I'm deranged for envying your relationship." But only because they'd be focusing on the wrong things. Yeah, Royce and Sawyer called each other names, but if you paid attention to the tone of voice and sappy look in their eyes, you'd see how much they loved each other. Asshole and dickhead were their pet names for each other.

"Do you hear that?" Royce asked. "He admires us."

Sawyer laughed. "Jonah, you need new friends."

He thought about the new people who'd entered his life over the past year, Royce and Sawyer were among them. Jonah's mind snagged on the image of Avery sleeping in his arms that morning. "I think I'm doing pretty good."

Since Royce was coming over, Jonah didn't bring up the real reason he called. They said their goodbyes and Jonah called Sal's. Just as Royce said, the owner helped him place the order after telling Jonah how to find the size of the tank he currently had. Jonah paid for the purchase and told Sal that Royce would be by to pick it up in about an hour.

"That one is pure trouble," Sal warned.

"Yes, sir," Jonah agreed. "Thank you for your help tonight."

Feeling relieved, Jonah called Avery. His call went straight to voicemail, so Jonah left a message.

Avery immediately sent back a text. *Can't talk right now. Sorry. I'll call you later.*

Jonah stared at the cryptic message. Should he respond to let Avery know he'd read it? Or would it be another interruption? Not replying felt rude but interrupting something important was too. This was Jonah's first attempt at a relationship in years, and he was already fumbling. He sent a quick thumbs-up and set his phone down.

Luckily, Royce arrived and saved Jonah from himself.

"This is a nice big utility room," Royce remarked once they carried the new water heater inside. The room was shaped like a large L and housed his washer, dryer, water heater, furnace, and a chest freezer. "The last time I changed a water heater, the tank was tucked into a closet, which made it difficult to work around."

"Is the homeowner still talking to you?" Jonah teased.

"I'm the homeowner, although I signed the house over to Jace and Holly when I officially moved in with Sawyer." Jonah had met the oldest Locke brother and his girlfriend, who happened to be Royce's childhood friend and a fellow detective on the force. "They haven't said anything about a busted water heater, and as you know, neither of them is shy."

"True," Jonah said.

"We need to drain the old water tank, but we want to shut off the water and electricity first. No one wants to get electrocuted." Royce surveyed the room. He crossed to the electrical panel, opened it, and read the labels above each breaker. "Aha," he said, flipping one of them to off. "There should be a drain built into the floor somewhere to catch runoff from your furnace."

"It's around the corner," Jonah said, showing Royce where it was located.

"Do you have a garden hose you can spare?" Royce asked.

"Yeah," Jonah said, heading out to the shed where he'd stored it for the winter.

When he returned, Royce connected one end to the water heater tank and unfurled the hose until it reached the drain. Then he reached into his back pocket and removed a utility knife and sawed through it, cutting off the excess length. "Now, we need to shut off the water and drain this bad boy." Jonah watched Royce move deftly around the room. "Let's hope your drain isn't clogged," he said, turning a valve.

Jonah held up crossed fingers as the water gurgled through the hose and down the drain. "So far, so good," he said.

"We'll hang out and keep an eye on it just in case," Royce said, leaning his hip against the chest freezer. "I bet you're glad you called me."

"I am, even though the water heater wasn't the reason I called you," Jonah quipped. "I wanted to know if you're related to Jerry Locke?"

Royce's right eyebrow curved upward. "Yeah, he's my uncle. Seems like a good enough guy."

"Seems like?" Jonah asked. Wouldn't he know?

"He's my dad's younger brother. My dad resented the hell out of the fact Jerry took over the business when their father retired. So, I only heard hateful things about the man while growing up. The first time I met him was at my mother's funeral when I was ten. Jerry was really nice to us kids."

"I'd heard he moved out of state," Jonah said.

"Yeah. My dad said the economy went to shit in the early eighties, and the housing market went to hell in a handbasket. My dad said Jerry lost his ass, got out of the business, and moved to Florida. Good ole Eddie took great pleasure in Jerry's failures. Why are you asking about my uncle?"

Jonah told him about the investigation and the connections to Locke-Tight. "What do you know about him?"

Royce blew out a whistle. "I can't really tell you much, and what I know is tainted by Eddie. He used to make a lot of scathing remarks about Jerry's Christianity. Looking back now, my old man just seemed jealous of Jerry's life. My aunt Tipsy had always said nice things about Jerry. Namely, she'd say my mom married the wrong Locke brother. I trusted my aunt's instincts more than anyone's. I should get to know Jerry better now that he's back."

Jonah perked up. "He's moved back to Savannah?"

"Yeah. Jace ran into him recently. Jerry and his wife are both retired now. One of their kids moved to Savannah for work, and they moved too because they wanted to stay close to the grandkids. You should definitely talk to Jerry about his employees at the time. Maybe he can tell you more information about Earl's brother and father."

"Or anyone else on the crew Earl might've gotten close to while working for him," Jonah said.

"He gave Jace his phone number, so I'll get it for you." Royce checked the flow of water into the drain. "I think we're good to go now, big guy."

They worked together to remove the old tank and set the new one in place. Royce pumped his fist in the air when everything lined up correctly, and he didn't need to cut or solder anything.

"Maybe your luck really is changing," Royce said.

"I deserve a break after the crazy week I've had."

"It's only Wednesday," Royce pointed out. "Plenty more time for fuckery to ensue."

"God, I hope not," Jonah said. "What do I owe you for your time?"

"I don't accept money for helping my friends," Royce said, patting him on the back. "I will accept food or booze, however."

"Sounds like a backyard barbecue to me," Jonah said. "Do you prefer ribs, steaks, or chicken?"

"Yes," Royce replied.

Jonah laughed. "How does Saturday sound?"

"I'm not aware of any plans, but I'll check with Sawyer and let you know when I get Jerry's number for you."

"Perfect. Thanks, Ro."

"Anytime, big guy."

It felt like the most protracted few hours of his life while waiting for the tank to fill and the water to heat up so he could take a long shower. He vowed to never take hot water for granted ever again.

When he stepped out of the shower, he found Avery sprawled on his bed. "Kendall said I could come up. I hope you don't mind."

Kendall hadn't been home yet when Jonah got in the shower, so he must've arrived minutes before Avery showed up.

"Mind?" he asked, loosening the towel around his waist and dropping it to the floor. He strolled to the bed, loving the way Avery's gaze raked over his body.

"It was a bit presumptuous of me," Avery said breathlessly.

Jonah stopped at the side of the bed and ghosted his fingers over Avery's heated cheeks. He took Avery's right hand and placed it against his hardening erection.

Jonah slid his hands in Avery's hair and placed a kiss on his neck. "How was your day?"

Avery's breath hitched. "It sucked because you weren't there." Jonah's heart tripped over itself. "Do you really want to talk shop tonight? I can think of better ways we can spend our time together."

Jonah popped open the button on Avery's jeans. "Such as?"

Avery released Jonah's balls to pull his shirt off over his head before reaching for his zipper. "You wrecked my ass good. I felt you all day, and I want you to make sure I feel you again tomorrow."

Jonah stilled Avery's hand so he could be the one to strip him bare. "You wrecked my world, so we're even." Jonah placed Avery's hand on his chest. "Just don't wreck my heart."

Avery's eyes widened as if it never occurred to him that Jonah would give him that kind of power. "Never," he whispered.

Could it be that easy?

Did he dare believe?

Avery licked his plump bottom lip invitingly.

Yes, goddamn it. He fucking dared.

CHAPTER 17

Jonah walked Avery to his car the following morning, intending to give him a brief kiss before he left, but Avery melted against him. Short and sweet turned into long and lazy. Avery made a happy little humming sound when Jonah broke their kiss.

"Keep making those noises, and you'll be really late for work."

Avery's eyelashes fluttered before opening to reveal a lust-drunk gaze. "You can't possibly be ready to go again." Oh, the funny things that came out of those sexy lips.

"You're pressed against my body, so you tell me."

Avery closed his eyes again as a full-body shiver rolled through him.

"Aren't you the one who said you wanted to feel me all day?" Jonah whispered in his ear before biting down on the lobe.

Avery's sexy gasp drove Jonah crazy. He slid his hands beneath the hem of Avery's T-shirt. He wanted to kiss that cinnamon-colored freckle once more and was just about to drop to his knees when a sharp whistle split the air, snatching Jonah out of his fantasies.

"Lord, child," Marla said from her front porch, "take the boy back inside and do it right." Betty, who'd been squatting to pee, straightened her hind legs and gave two short barks. She agreed with her human, who was dressed like she was going to church.

Jonah narrowed his eyes as he cataloged everything about Marla and this moment, unwilling to forget even a second. The ivory dress with yellow and pink flowers looked terrific against her dark skin. She'd matched it with a yellow cardigan, a straw hat with a pink ribbon and yellow flowers, and high-heel sandals. He thought they were called wedges. "It's Thursday," Jonah called out across their yards."

Marla lifted her white-gloved hands and slowly clapped them. "That's good, honey. Now tell me what year it is."

Avery, who'd rested his forehead against Jonah's chest, laughed hard.

"Don't encourage her," Jonah admonished playfully.

"Oh, please, do encourage me, baby," Marla quipped.

Jonah looked down into Avery's smiling eyes, and even though he hated to let him go, Avery needed to head across town to get ready for work. He couldn't afford to be late and give Trexler a reason to make his life hell. "I better see what she's up to today," Jonah said, then kissed Avery's lips once more. "She rarely gets up before noon, and she's dressed like she has an appointment with the queen."

"I do have an appointment with my drag mother, but she's always a queen to me," Marla said, laughing when Jonah looked at her. "Ain't nothing wrong with my hearing."

Avery laughed again. "Good luck today. I hope you blow the case wide open."

Royce had texted Jerry Locke's number to him that morning. He'd also said he and Sawyer had plans for Saturday night if the criminals of Savannah behaved long enough for the busy homicide detectives to have the night off. He asked if they could get together the following weekend instead, and Jonah agreed.

He'd shared his enthusiasm over both bits of news with Avery, who seemed more excited about the potential interview than attending the barbecue. Not for the first time, Jonah wondered about Avery's past with the Savannah Police Department. How had he come to know his aunt and the two detectives who made him as nervous as a whore in church when they visited the GBI offices. He'd seen Royce and Sawyer speaking to Avery in hushed tones more than once. Their body language was always engaging and noncombative. Avery never looked scared, but dark shadows appeared in his eyes for a little bit after each encounter.

He could've asked Avery how he came to know his aunt and detective buddies, but Jonah had a good idea. Right before he'd met Avery, a vigilante group called The Purists had pervaded the city of Savannah with chaos. They used arson and various intimidation tactics to terrorize people they felt betrayed those who believed in them. Ellen had sent Royce and Sawyer to meet with Jonah to develop a criminal profile on the mastermind behind the group. The Purists had started off by sending threatening letters to their victims but quickly moved on to the internet when their need for attention grew. Jonah had promptly recognized the person cutting out individual letters from magazines and newspapers wasn't the same individual who had created an untraceable website. The skillsets and mindsets for the two approaches were vastly different. Jonah quickly realized The Purists had found themselves a very gifted hacker.

Ellie had decided Jonah needed an intern soon after Royce and Sawyer solved the case. Avery was the most skilled hacker Jonah had ever met. The timing could be a coincidence, but Jonah didn't believe in them. He'd been hesitant to take Avery on as his intern, but then he met Avery and understood why Ellie wanted to help him. Recognizing Avery's potential, Ellie would've wanted to give him a second chance. Jonah was certain that *if* Avery had done The Purists' hacking, he hadn't done so willingly.

"I better go. Call me later," Avery said, stepping out of Jonah's arms to open his car door.

"I will." Jonah watched Avery back out of the driveway and waved as he drove off. Turning his attention to Marla, Jonah asked, "Why are you dressed up for Sunday church on Thursday morning?"

Marla snorted. "As if. The building would catch on fire if I crossed the threshold."

"Bullshit," Jonah countered. "Why are you dressed for the Kentucky Derby, then?"

Marla laughed hard at his remark. "Stop acting like a fool," she said, stepping off her porch and walking toward him with Betty right on her heels. The French bulldog ran to Jonah, who scooped her up and kissed the top of her head. "You two are going to be just fine," Marla said. Jonah didn't hear sadness in her voice; he heard relief.

"Amos will be here in a while to pick me up. We have some business to take care of—things I should've done before now."

"Do you have time for a cup of coffee on the porch?" Jonah asked.

"I'll make time."

Time. There was that fucking word again.

"Oh, good. I can bring you up to speed on the investigation," Jonah said.

As if someone lit a fire beneath her, Marla increased her stride, and the familiar spark returned to her eyes. "Tell me all about it, baby."

"Do you want your coffee with or without booze?" Jonah asked.

"Without. I can't have alcohol on my breath when Amos gets here, or it will give him the wrong impression."

Jonah went inside and fixed two cups of coffee and joined her in the rocking chairs while Betty gnawed on a stick in the yard.

"Do you know a good place to get tea?" Jonah asked her.

Marla looked at him curiously before rattling off the name of a specialty store.

"Do you think they sell chai?" he asked.

"Are you converting?" Marla asked, sounding genuinely appalled by the idea.

"No, but Avery refuses to change his wicked ways. He loves chai, but I don't have any here."

"You are the sweetest thing," Marla said. "You look so big and mean, but you have a marshmallow center."

"I assure you that I don't."

Marla snickered. "Chai is very popular, so I'm sure she sells it. One of my friends is a tea connoisseur, and he said they have hundreds of options from around the world." She reached over and patted his leg. "Tell me about Earl's investigation."

Jonah told her every detail as he remembered, including his observations to make the retelling entertaining.

"I'd forgotten Earl briefly worked for the same concrete company as his father and brother," Marla said. "I think it was only for a few weeks." She started giggling. "I loved Earl Ison with every fiber of my being, but I'd never met a clumsier man than him. He lacked any sort of grace *until* he put on a pair of high heels. Then he became as captivating as Tina Turner." She smiled at Jonah. "For a scrawny white dude, he did a fabulous job at impersonating her." Marla giggled harder, making him laugh too.

Once they quieted again, Jonah asked, "Did Earl ever mention someone giving him a hard time at work? Coworkers, other subcontractors, or maybe a boss?"

Marla shook her head. "Never. It's probably why I forgot he even worked there. You're really convinced there's a connection between Earl's death and the subdivision, aren't you?"

"Convinced? No. I just think it's as likely as an angry lover. Yes, Earl pulling away from friends could mean the new guy in his life was possessive, but these past few nights with Avery reminded me what it's like when a relationship is new and hormones are running rampant."

"This is why I needed your help," Marla said. "I was too close to the situation, and I let my emotions cloud my objectivity."

"Does the name Mickey Reeder sound familiar to you?" Jonah asked.

Marla tilted her head to the side. "No, but so many of us went by our drag names back then. Who is Mickey?"

"He was Bo Cahill's brother. According to Bo's widow, Mickey was openly gay, and Bo loved him dearly. They were adamant he wouldn't have killed Earl even if he hadn't been incarcerated at the time."

"That's interesting."

Jonah spotted a red Cadillac coming down the road. "Why does Amos dislike me so much?" It had always bothered Jonah, although he couldn't say why. He wasn't the kind of person who needed to make everyone his friend.

Marla cackled as she rose to her feet. "The old fool was jealous of you. Amos was convinced there was something more between us than friendship. He thought you were my boy toy."

Jonah reached out and snagged her gloved hand. "I do love you."

Marla beamed at him as tears filled her eyes. She patted his hand. "I know, baby. I love you too. Amos just didn't understand the kind of love friends have for one another. I think that's sad, don't you?"

Jonah practically choked on the lump in his throat. "I do," he agreed.

"Well, he understands things better now," Marla said, pulling her hand free and patting her leg for Betty to follow her. "Come now, Betty. Mama needs a witness."

Amos, who'd gotten out of the car and walked around to the passenger side, nodded at Jonah. It was a considerable improvement over the silent scowl Jonah typically received. He noticed Amos was dressed up in a pale gray suit, which accentuated the silver hair threading through the cobalt black strands. He'd paired the outfit with a yellow shirt and a floral tie similar to Marla's dress, and Jonah knew it wasn't a coincidence. Just what were they up to?

"Woman, a dog won't count as a legal witness," Amos said as Marla sashayed near.

"She will if I say so," she countered sassily.

Jonah had a sneaky feeling he knew what was going on. "Give me five minutes to get dressed, and I'll be your witness."

Amos smiled at Jonah for the first time since they'd met, and Marla rocked on her high heels a bit. "Much obliged," Amos told Jonah.

"Honey, you have a murder to solve," Marla protested weakly.

"It can wait until after I give you away," Jonah said. "Give me five minutes."

"Take ten," Amos said generously. "Our appointment isn't for another half hour."

Jonah darted inside the house and up the stairs. Before going to his closet to pick out an appropriate suit, he sent a group text to Marla's wonderful friends he'd met on Tuesday. He didn't expect them all to drop everything and rush to the courthouse, which was the only place they'd be getting married on a Thursday morning. Her friends could at least throw her a party to help her celebrate life and love. Wouldn't it be better to do that with Marla while she was still alive rather than after she passed?

He didn't wait to see what kind of replies they sent. Jonah had accomplished his goal and shifted his focus to getting ready. He chose a gray suit that was slightly darker than Amos's and a yellow dress shirt he'd forgotten he owned. He completed his outfit with a simple gray tie and black dress shoes. He wished he had a hat to wear, but he wasn't cool enough to pull it off.

Marla was sitting primly in the front seat of the Cadillac with Betty on her lap. Amos had lowered the ragtop down, so Jonah placed his hand on the side of the car and vaulted himself into the back seat.

"I've always wanted to do that," Jonah said, smiling at Marla's reflection in the side mirror.

Marla and Amos were shocked when every one of the people Jonah texted showed up to witness their wedding.

"What are y'all doing here?" Marla asked, turning a suspicious gaze on Jonah. "How'd you have enough time to make this happen?"

"Group text," Jonah said. "I usually hate them, but you can't deny how convenient they are sometimes."

"I cannot believe you dropped everything to share this day with Amos and me," Marla said, placing a hand over her heart. "I love y'all so very much."

There was a group hug, and then it was Amos and Marla's turn to get married. Jonah and Betty walked her down the aisle to stand before the judge with Amos and exchange their wedding vows. There wasn't a dry eye in the courtroom, including Judge Jackson, who turned out to be Marla's drag mother.

Afterward, the friends decided to do brunch at Daisy's Place, but Jonah begged off so he could work the investigation. Amos and Marla dropped him off at his house before heading to the diner. He debated on calling Jerry Locke first or just showing up at his front door. One option was more polite, but it also gave Jerry the chance to dodge Jonah. That wouldn't do because Jonah didn't have time for games.

Jerry Locke lived in Southbridge, a prestigious golf club community with immaculate lawns and stunning homes. It seemed like the man had bounced back pretty nicely if he could afford to retire in this neighborhood.

His house was a massive replica of Tara from *Gone with the Wind*. Pretty, but not Jonah's style. He parked behind a newer Mercedes Benz before walking up to the home and ringing the doorbell.

When the door opened, Jonah didn't need to confirm the identity of the man who greeted him. It was uncanny how much this man looked like Royce Locke. If Sawyer wanted to know how well Royce was going to age, all he had to do was meet Uncle Jerry. The answer was really fucking well. The man's blond hair was still thick and shot through with only a hint of gray. The laugh lines next to his eyes and mouth added character instead of detracting from his appeal. It was apparent he worked out and maintained his body well. Most noticeable was the appreciative once-over Uncle Jerry gave Jonah.

Jerry met Jonah's gaze and smiled. "Can I help you?"

"Are you Jerry Locke?" he asked.

"Yes," Jerry said, his smile never faltering.

"I'm a friend of your nephew's," Jonah replied.

There went the smile, and Jonah wondered if maybe he shouldn't have led with that. "Which one?" Jerry asked warily.

"Royce," Jonah replied, hoping it was the right answer. He knew there was a younger brother he hadn't met yet.

The smile returned, and Jonah breathed a sigh of relief. "Would you like to come in?"

"Don't you want to know why I'm here first?" Jonah asked. It never ceased to amaze him how trusting some people still were.

"I mean, if it makes you feel better to tell me, then sure," Jerry quipped.

"My name is Jonah St. John, and I'm with the Georgia Bureau of

Investigation," Jonah said, hoping Jerry didn't ask to see his badge. "I'm investigating the 1982 murder of Earl Ison. I'm interviewing anyone who might've worked with him before his death."

"Oh," Jerry said softly. "I'd read about the new information in the paper. It wasn't that I've never thought of Earl, but I at least felt some sense of closure when I thought his killer had confessed and was dead."

Jonah recognized the emotion washing over the man's handsome features. It was the same expression he saw when he interviewed Earl's friends and in Agnes Cahill's eyes when she spoke about her late husband.

Grief.

Jerry Locke wasn't just Earl's former boss. Their bond was much tighter, possibly intimate.

"Can I still come in?"

CHAPTER 18

"Oh, yes. Sure," Jerry said, gathering himself. "Forgive my rudeness." He stepped aside and gestured for Jonah to enter the house. "Would you like to sit out back on the patio and talk? It's my favorite spot."

"Sounds great."

The glimpses of the interior Jonah saw were as expensive and impressive as the exterior. When they reached the back patio, Jonah understood why it was Jerry's favorite part. He'd only met the man two minutes ago, but the comfortable seating area, built-in barbecue, and pool felt more like his style than the fussy furniture he saw during his quick pass through the house.

"Is that one of those brick pizza ovens?" Jonah asked.

"It is," Jerry said, nodding. "We only moved into this house last month and haven't tried it out yet."

"You have a beautiful home."

"And you're wondering why a concrete guy like me lives here, right?" Jerry asked.

"Not really."

"You want to know about Earl," Jerry said, breaking eye contact and looking out over his back yard. Jonah followed his gaze. Beyond the ornamental fence marking the property perimeter, a golf cart drove along the lushly green course. "It feels like an eternity since I've even spoken his name."

"Did Earl work for you long?" Jonah asked. He wanted to start out with questions he already knew the answers to so he could gauge Jerry's honesty and willingness to speak openly to him.

Jerry met his gaze once more, and a wry smile spread across his face. He shook his head and said, "Earl was all thumbs and two left feet. He might've lasted two weeks."

Jonah laughed. "That's what Marla said."

"I recognize the name. She was Earl's best friend—the one who encouraged him to start performing."

"Marla is my neighbor and a dear friend. She's the reason why we've reopened the case," Jonah explained. "She never believed Bo Cahill killed Earl."

Jerry ran a hand through his hair. "How could she know that?" he asked.

"Marla has amazing instincts, and she's better at listening to hers than most people. She was right. There was no possible way Bo Cahill could've killed Earl," Jonah said.

"Did I read that the man was already in jail for killing someone else?" Jerry asked.

"Yes. Bo Cahill was in a county jail awaiting a bail hearing when Earl died." Jonah explained what had happened to Agnes and the circumstances surrounding Bo's arrest.

Jerry scrunched up his face. "How was that possible?"

"Which part?" Jonah asked.

Jerry huffed a sigh of frustration. "All of it. The system is broken, and I've been too ignorant my whole life to realize it."

"No one wants to think that innocent people land in prison, especially not on death row. History has taught us otherwise, and I'm afraid some people weren't paying attention to the lessons."

"My wife would love that saying. Sheila is a history teacher and retired after forty years with teenagers. Do you mind if I borrow it?" Jerry asked.

Jonah smiled. "Sure."

"What can I tell you about Earl?" Jerry asked, getting them back on track.

"I really wanted to ask you about Earl's father and brother."

"Thomas and Dennis?" Jerry asked. "You can't seriously think Thomas would've killed his own boy."

Jonah tipped his head to the side. "How supportive was he when Earl came out as gay?" he asked instead of answering Jerry.

Jerry puffed out his cheeks as he released a big breath. "Thomas was furious. He kicked Earl out and told him to never come around. Later, Thomas told Earl that he hoped he died of AIDS." Jerry shook his head sadly. "I cannot fathom a single circumstance which would make me turn my kids away." He swallowed hard. "From an investigator's standpoint, I know it makes Thomas a top suspect, but I just can't see it."

"Why? Because he was a Christian?" Jonah asked.

Jerry scoffed. "No. I'm saying Thomas would've had to care about Earl to kill him, but Earl was already dead to his family. Earl was also much taller and stronger than his father and could've fought him off."

"Logic and reason go out the window when someone you love turns their rage on you. Someone knocked Earl unconscious before strangling him. It doesn't take brute strength to catch someone by surprise," Jonah said. "What about his brother, Dennis?"

"I don't think Dennis felt the same way as his parents but was too cowardly to speak up. Earl told me Dennis frequently checked up on him to make sure he was doing okay. He'd given him money for food and even helped Earl cover his rent for a few months. I cannot see Dennis turning on Earl in such a brutal way."

"You seem to know Earl's personal business pretty well for someone who only worked for you for a few weeks," Jonah remarked.

Jerry looked out over the golf course for a few moments before locking gazes with Jonah again. "We both know there was more to my relationship with Earl, or you wouldn't be here."

He was wrong. Jonah wanted to know about the people who had worked with Earl, either directly or indirectly. Finding out Jerry was the secret boyfriend was just a bonus. "I suspected." *Not until I saw your reaction, but why split hairs?* "Did you ever come forward and speak to the police?"

He shook his head. "To the best of my recollection, they only interviewed the guys who'd discovered Earl's body. My crew had already moved on to another project by then."

"Did Earl work at the location he was killed?" Jonah asked.

Jerry furrowed his brow. "I honestly can't say off the top of my head. We were so busy that summer. Believe it or not, I've kept all my records. I could dig through them and find out which projects Earl worked on and the other people on his crew."

"Oh, wow," Jonah said. "That would be very helpful."

"My wife thinks I'm nuts for holding on to all that old stuff, but I loved running my own company. I was proud to take the business over from my father. But between Earl dying and my business going bankrupt..." Jerry sighed.

"I needed a brand-new start somewhere else. I moved to Florida and attended community college for a few years before transferring to a university, where I earned a bachelor's in business and met my wife. Later, I got my master's degree and worked my way up to a CEO position for a telecommunications company, which paid well and kept my brain engaged."

"Did Earl ever tell you about having issues with anyone on the crew?"

"Not that I recall, but he probably wouldn't have told me anyway. Earl wouldn't have wanted to get someone fired or draw attention to our relationship for my sake."

"You weren't out as gay?" Jonah asked.

"Bisexual," Jerry corrected. "No. I didn't come out until much later. I told Sheila when we started dating, but no one else until my children were old enough to date. I wanted them to know I'd love whoever they did."

"Did your closeted status cause a lot of problems between you and Earl?"

Jerry narrowed his eyes. "Should I have an attorney present?"

Jonah chuckled. "You can call a lawyer if you wish, but I'm not trying to trip you up and get you to confess to killing Earl."

"I probably shouldn't take your word for it, but I will," Jerry said. "Earl and I had broken up before he died, but it wasn't because I was in the closet."

"Did it have to do with his performances?" Jonah inquired.

"No," Jerry said, shaking his head. "I was surprised to find out Earl had decided to develop and nurture a drag persona, but I wasn't mad or turned off by it." Jerry shifted his attention to the golf course again, and Jonah waited patiently for him to speak. When their gazes met again, Jerry's eyes shimmered with tears, but he wore a beautiful smile. "I was his first audience. I couldn't believe how graceful Earl was in those high heels. I teased him and asked why he couldn't have been that dexterous while working on my crew. He laughed and told me it was because I wouldn't let him wear heels." Jerry chuckled. "I loved Earl. All I ever wanted was for him to be happy. I even bought him a necklace as a good-luck charm to wear for his first performance."

The same missing necklace Earl wore every day? "A silver heart-shaped pendant?" Jonah asked.

Nodding, Jerry said, "He loved the inexpensive piece of jewelry as much as I loved him. I never would've ended our relationship. I would've eventually found the courage to come out to be with him."

"Why did Earl end it?"

"He'd met someone else during one of his performances. Earl had said he cared a great deal for me, but he'd felt a connection with the new guy like nothing he'd ever experienced. I was crushed. Earl died maybe a month or so later." Jerry shook his head. "Damn, such a waste. Earl was a beautiful person."

"Did Earl tell you he met this new guy at a club during a performance or did you assume it?" Jonah asked.

"He told me so," Jerry replied. "I'd asked Earl why he was breaking up with me, and he'd originally said things just weren't working out for him. I knew something else was wrong because he'd been just fine the previous week. I'd asked Earl to be honest, and that's when he told me he'd met a guy at a club. As painful as it was to hear, I needed to know, so I didn't make a fool of myself trying to get him back."

This was new information. None of Marla's friends could tell Jonah how Earl had met his new beau. If Earl had told Jerry the truth and had met this guy at a club, then chances were, they'd met him too. Jonah clamped down his excitement to focus on what he should ask next, but he shouldn't have worried. Once Jerry started talking about Earl, he didn't seem to want to stop. Rather than discourage him, he let Jerry get the things off his chest he'd carried around for thirty-eight years.

"I knew I liked both boys and girls at an early age." Jerry took a deep breath and continued. "Anyway, I'd never given in to my attraction to men until I met Earl. I'd never encountered anyone with as much joy and zest for life as him. I was a goner after one kiss." Jerry's cheeks turned pink, and his bottom lip trembled. "He was my first boyfriend and my first sexual experience. I'm sure I was clumsy and not too good in bed, but Earl was patient and loving. I only have one regret, Jonah. I wish I'd been brave enough to love him openly. Earl had deserved it, and it took me a very long time to realize I did too. I don't want you to think my sadness is because I'm unhappy or don't love Sheila. You just never forget your first love, and I refuse to deny Earl that title."

"I'm not judging you, Jerry," Jonah said softly. He steered the conversation to a less personal topic by asking for the names of the other subcontractors who worked in the subdivision. He'd hoped Jerry would remember some of the other companies, but Jerry knew them all. There were surprisingly few subs working to develop the subdivision.

"You had to know somebody who knew somebody to land contracts like government jobs and big projects like residential subdivisions. Back then, a new kid on the block didn't have much of a chance."

"And you knew somebody?" Jonah asked.

"My father did," Jerry replied. "As much as I resented him at times, he could network like no one's business. I had a tough first year trying to convince everyone I was as good as he was, but my hard work paid off. I took an already solid business and made it even bigger until the economy took a nosedive in the early eighties and killed the industry."

Jonah asked a few more questions and made more notes before he thanked Jerry for talking so candidly with him.

"It's a great thing you're doing," Jerry said after walking Jonah to the front door. "Good luck."

"Thanks, Jerry," Jonah replied, knowing it would take more than luck to get justice for Earl.

On the way home, Jonah stopped at the specialty store to get tea for Avery. Marla's friend hadn't been exaggerating about the selection. He stood in the center of the room feeling foolish for thinking he could just walk in and snag some chai for Avery.

"Can I help you, dear?" a kindly woman asked. "You look overwhelmed."

"I never knew there were so many different types of tea. Growing up, my choices were sweet and unsweet iced tea," Jonah teased. "I want to buy a gift for a friend."

"You've come to the right place. My name is Janice. I'm the owner of The Tea-Totaler. I offer selections from all around the world. Do you have something specific in mind?"

"My friend loves chai, and I'm just grateful it doesn't smell like sweaty gym socks," Jonah replied.

Janice laughed. "Not a fan of tea?"

"I prefer coffee," Jonah admitted.

"I won't hold that against you," she said cheekily. "I offer many varieties of chai." Janice gestured to a section along the back wall and began talking about the different nuances each chai offered. "And this one," she said, picking up another pouch, "has hints of chocolate and chili. It reminds me of Mexican hot chocolate. It's very popular." Janice glanced up at Jonah, who'd fallen quiet as he tried to guess which one Avery might like best. She chuckled and patted his bicep. "I've overwhelmed you, haven't I? Why don't you give me an idea of how much you would like to spend, and I'll put together a gift basket for you."

"I didn't have a limit in mind," Jonah said. "I just want to buy something thoughtful."

"Must be a very special friend," Janice said as she started choosing a variety of pouches.

"He is."

Janice chose five of her top-selling chai blends, then talked Jonah into buying an electric tea kettle and a little ceramic pot with a removable steeping basket. She even demonstrated how to use everything to make a perfect cup of chai.

Once Jonah arrived home, he changed out of his suit and started looking up information on the subcontractors Jerry gave him until someone rang his doorbell.

Jonah smiled when he saw who stood on his porch. "This is a nice surprise," he said.

Avery held up a bag of food in one hand and a drink carrier in the other. "I wanted to make sure you're not working through mealtimes."

Guilty. Jonah took the food and drinks from Avery and set them on the table. Then he pulled Avery into his arms and kissed him. "I have something for you too," Jonah said once they broke apart for air.

"I just bet."

Jonah gave him a quick kiss, then left him at the dining room table to retrieve the gifts he'd purchased for him. "I wasn't sure what all you'd need to make tea for when you stayed over. Marla told me about this specialty store that sells teas. I never knew there were so many different types of chai."

Avery oohed and aahed over each one and ran his finger over the curve of the teapot. Jonah had to admit it was cute as hell. "This is seriously the nicest thing anyone has ever given me." He rose on his tiptoes to kiss Jonah's cheek.

"You need nicer friends," Jonah said, feeling his cheeks heat.

"Stop it," Avery said, slapping his bicep. "I love it so much. Thank you."

Several moments and a long, breathless kiss later, Jonah looked into Avery's twinkling eyes. "Be honest," he said. "Is lunch the real reason why you came over?"

"It's only part of my motive," Avery admitted. "Fancy a nooner?"

Jonah feasted on Avery before the food and didn't feel an iota of guilt when his intern returned to work late and rumpled.

Jonah spent the remainder of his suspension running down leads and interviewing as many subcontractors as he could with either Felix or Rocky acting as his sidekicks. Even though their names weren't included in the official police report, the guys managed to uncover the names of the three construction workers who'd discovered Earl's body.

John Chambers, an electrician, Doug Haverty, a plumber, and Rex Miller, an HVAC contractor, were hesitant to answer questions until Felix assured them that he'd keep their names out of the press or their podcast.

"Why aren't the cops the ones knocking on my door?" Chambers asked. "I saw the police commissioner's interview about reopening the case, and I've expected a visit from SPD every day since then."

"I can't answer that," Felix said.

Jonah could, but he didn't. Milton and Morrissey had omitted their names from the file.

The three men all worked for different subcontractors but knew each other well. They admitted to seeing Earl around the jobsites while he worked for Jerry, who had contacted Jonah and confirmed that Earl had worked at the site where his body was discovered. Chambers, Haverty, and Miller all said Earl seemed like a nice guy. He was clumsy and awkward on the sites, but he tried really hard. They couldn't remember seeing Earl argue with anyone.

The interviews didn't garner new leads, but Jonah gave their names to Ellie when they met for lunch on Friday.

"Nice work," she said. "I asked Milton and Morrissey why they excluded the names of the construction workers who'd found Earl in their official reports."

"And?"

"They told me to go fuck myself," she said with a grin.

Jonah and Felix didn't even get that much during their attempt to interview the crotchety bastards later that same day. Milton and Morrissey both slammed their doors shut in their faces before Jonah or Felix could identify themselves.

Frustration mounted when it seemed like they'd hit a wall, but Jonah pushed on. Giving up wasn't an option.

The investigation claimed his days, but Jonah reserved his evenings and weekend for Avery. They cooked together, attended a drag cabaret at The Dive Bar, watched thunderstorms on the front porch, and played a rowdy game of poker with Marla and Amos. Jonah enjoyed watching Avery brew his chai and claiming each new flavor was his favorite. Every moment Jonah spent basking in Avery's sunny warmth only made him crave it more. He kept going back to touch the sun again and again and again. When Jonah returned from his journeys unscathed, the light inside him expanded, chasing away the shadows. Something new stirred inside him. No, not new. Reawakened. Restored.

Hope.

Maybe, just maybe, love didn't have to burn.

CHAPTER 19

Jonah could easily list a dozen ways he preferred to start out his first day back to work after his suspension. Walking through the visitor's front door at the bureau and waiting once again for Trexler to meet him was not one of them.

Mary, the receptionist, was a quivering mess once again when she paged Trexler. Jonah's temperament was much improved over the last time he stormed through the door like the thundercloud Avery accused him of being. That didn't seem to ease her nerves.

Trexler took his sweet time meeting him. Jonah forced a natural smile on his face, ignoring the smug expression his supervisor wore. "Good morning, sir. My badge, please."

"Not so fast," Trexler said. "Follow me."

"Of course," Jonah said, then smiled at Mary. Just like the previous time, she'd raptly watched their interaction. "Have a good day, Mary."

"You too," she said after a brief hesitation.

Trexler didn't say a word as they traversed the halls, saving his tirade for the privacy of his office. Jonah listened to a twenty-minute lecture that Trexler wrapped up with, "I hope you've learned a lesson."

"Absolutely, sir," Jonah said stoically. Their conversation ebbed into an awkward silence when neither of them had anything left to say. Trexler wanted Jonah to ask for his badge back again; Jonah would prefer someone douse him with honey and cover him with fire ants. He'd out-wait the fucker all damn day if he needed to.

"Well, then," Trexler said after the uncomfortable stillness stretched unbearably long. Reaching inside his desk drawer, he pulled out Jonah's ID badge and extended it to him. "Guess you'll want this now."

"Thank you, sir," Jonah said, accepting the thing that had defined his existence for the last few years. The badge had once represented a fresh start and a new journey. Lately, it had felt more like an albatross.

With a jerky nod, Jonah exited Trexler's office. Avery had stayed over-night and showered with him before work, but Jonah's heart still raced at the prospect of seeing him again.

Keep it together, St. John.

In his absence, Avery had neatly sorted and stacked his mail, casefiles, and project updates on his desk. A bag of Caramel Bugles sat in the center of the piles. He'd been too preoccupied with making Avery climax to save time for eating breakfast, so he tore into the bag and started in on his favorite treat while reading over the project report update Avery had left for him.

Jonah heard a noise outside his closed door a few minutes later. His heart thudded heavily as he waited for Avery to open the door and poke his head in. A minute ticked by, then two, and before Jonah knew it, ten minutes had passed without Avery approaching him. He began drumming his fingers against his desk.

Where is he? Was Avery avoiding—

The door burst inward before Jonah could finish his thoughts. He held two mugs like usual and wore a devilish smile on his lips. That wasn't what caught his attention, though.

"Have you been eating avocados?" Jonah asked.

"Who, me?" Avery asked, setting Jonah's coffee down on his desk. "What makes you say that?"

"Flushed cheeks and swollen lips. For Christ's sake, Avery. I saw you not more than thirty minutes ago."

Instead of dropping in his usual chair across from him, Avery skirted around the desk and planted his sweet ass on Jonah's blotter. "Avocado toast is my weakness."

"What am I going to do with you?" Jonah asked.

Avery waggled his brows. "Do you really want me to answer that, or would you prefer to hear about Bill and Ashley's breakup?"

"Again? What happened this time?"

"Ashley slept with his cousin."

"Again?" Jonah repeated.

"Aha! You do pay attention," Avery said. "Different cousin."

Jonah choked on his sip of coffee. "Are you fucking with me right now?"

Avery shook his head and his eyes glittered with mirth. Jonah barely resisted the urge to pull Avery onto his lap and kiss his lips. "It gets better."

"How?"

Leaning forward until their foreheads nearly touched, Avery said, "Bill got revenge by sleeping with Ashley's sister."

Jonah crooked his finger and Avery moved even closer. "I'm putting twenty bucks on them getting back together by the weekend."

"No way," Avery said, shaking his head. "Banging someone's sister is a deal breaker."

Jonah looked up at Avery with as much seriousness as he could muster. "I promise to never sleep with your sister."

Avery laughed hard. "I don't have a sister."

"Watch the swamp water," Jonah said, pointing at the cup teetering in Avery's hand. "I keep forgetting to replenish my spare clothing in the closet."

"Knock it—"

Jonah's door opened suddenly, and Avery stood up so fast his stinky brew sloshed over the side and landed on Jonah's pant leg. *Great.*

"Is this a bad time?" Deputy Director Malcolm asked.

"No," Jonah and Avery said at once.

"I'll just get started on the assignment you gave me," Avery said before hurrying from the room.

Malcolm chuckled when Avery closed the door.

"Sir, I can explain."

Malcolm held up his hand as he dropped into the chair across from Jonah. "No need. I just stopped by to see if you were doing okay, but I can see you're just fine."

"I'm a little embarrassed," Jonah admitted.

"Don't be. I won't be able to attend your cybersecurity microchip presentation this afternoon. I was hoping you could give me an advance peek at the data."

"Absolutely," Jonah said, pulling out the report Avery had prepared in his absence.

Malcolm took his time poring over the extrapolated information. "This is very impressive, Jonah. Your microchip will greatly reduce the risk of hacking, spamming, and data mining."

"I had a lot of help, sir. Avery assisted with development and continued to run the trial testing while I was out last week."

"He's clearly an asset to you and the bureau. I'm glad I listened to Ellen's recommendation, although I doubt she saw the full potential there," he said with a wry smile.

Jonah's face heated.

"You do great work here, Jonah. Your skillset is valued and needed. Guys like you and Avery play a critical role in crime solving as the world becomes more digitized. Keep your head in the game and your priorities straight, okay?"

"Yes, sir."

Malcolm gave him one of his Uncle Charlie smiles. "It is my hope that you and Butch can find some common ground to stand on. It's in the best interest for you personally and the bureau as a whole. I've told Butch the same thing."

"I will do my best, sir."

Malcolm nodded and rose to his feet. "I won't keep you any longer. Good luck at the meeting."

"Thank you, sir."

Malcolm left and Jonah started counting the seconds until Avery popped in. He made it to ten.

"Jonah, I'm so sorry," he said in an agonized voice. "I shouldn't have sat on your desk."

"You should've sat on my lap."

Avery's mouth fell open on a soft gasp.

"Have a seat."

"On your lap?" Avery asked hopefully.

"I wish," he replied. Heeding Malcolm's advice, Jonah gestured for the chair the deputy director had just vacated. "We have some work to do before we make our presentation this afternoon."

"We?"

Jonah nodded. "You've worked your ass off on this project and have earned a spot at the table," Jonah said.

"Oh, I'm not prepared."

"You will be," Jonah assured him.

They went over the presentation slides and devised a plan of how to divide and conquer. Jonah had hoped to take Avery to lunch, but he'd already made plans with his friend Karlee.

"Would you mind bringing me back something? I want to do some digging around on Earl's case."

Avery slid the notepad to him. "Write down what you want."

Jonah drew him a picture.

Avery looked down at Jonah's stick figure with the raging boner and smiled. "I can cancel with Karlee. Tell her something's come up."

"It will still be up when you get back from lunch. Have fun."

"Fine. I'll grab your usual from Bytes and Brew."

"Thank you."

Jonah's gaze lingered on Avery's ass as he left, then he gave himself a mental shake. *Big head in the game, St. John.*

Curious to see if there was any internal movement while he was gone, Jonah typed Earl's name and hit enter.

Access denied.

What the fuck? He thought maybe he'd typed the name in wrong, so he tried it again.

Access denied.

Jonah tried the case file number since he'd memorized it.

Access denied.

Jonah sat staring at the computer for a long time, trying to assess all the possibilities. Then he typed in Bo Cahill's name and received the same message. He typed in the names of cases Trexler had assigned him, and those he could view.

Fuck me.

Someone had restricted his access to only the cases he'd been assigned. It didn't take a fucking genius to figure it out. Why hadn't Trexler rubbed it in Jonah's face during their meeting? He figured Trexler would relish having a conversation like that.

He could poke around in the system and find who restricted his access, but he wasn't as skillful at hacking as Avery. He risked a chance at getting caught.

Jonah sure as hell couldn't make the request through the bureau's IM system or ask over the phone. He had been suspended to discourage him from pursuing the investigation further. Someone had slashed his tires. Maybe it was coincidence or perhaps it was because he hadn't heeded the warning. Now his access to case files was restricted. Jonah was getting close to answers, and someone didn't like it.

But who? Trexler?

Jonah's adrenaline spiked, making him fidgety and edgy. Was it excitement or paranoia setting in? Jonah was aware of how similar the emotions affected the body.

When Avery returned with his lunch, Jonah crooked his finger for Avery to lean over his desk so he could show him that his clearance was restricted. Avery's brows dipped into a deep V. Jonah flipped over the top sheet with Boner Man, then wrote a message for Avery.

Will you see who restricted my access? I think it's important. Suspension. Slashed tires. Now this...

Avery gestured for Jonah to give the notepad to him. He picked out a pen from the cup on Jonah's desk and wrote a response. *Leave it to me.* Then he pivoted and left Jonah alone in his office.

Forcing his frustrations aside, Jonah dug into his lunch so his blood sugar wouldn't tank and impede his presentation. He would not give Trexler a reason to humiliate him again. Unfortunately, a stress headache had already started to form, which only intensified as the meeting time neared.

His phone vibrated with an incoming text from Avery. *It was Trexler. 2:36 pm. Yesterday. Remote laptop.*

Thanks. See you in the conference room, Jonah replied.

Son of a bitch. Why? Trexler wasn't old enough to be involved with Earl's death unless he'd been killing drag queens at the age of ten. But he could be protecting someone now just like Bo Cahill had back then.

Jonah sent a quick text to Rocky, asking him to dig up as much as he could find on Butch Trexler and his family. The man was going too far out of his way to protect retired officers that weren't connected to him.

Rocky quickly responded. He would start as soon as possible but warned there could be a slight delay since the cheating wife case was taking up so much of his time.

Jonah rose from his chair, grabbed the presentation materials, and exited his office. Avery wasn't at his desk, so he continued to the conference room.

"St. John," said the devil as he approached from behind, "I hope you're prepared for the meeting."

Jonah halted and turned to face his boss. Avery was a few paces behind Trexler, watching their interaction.

"I'm more than prepared," Jonah said. "Avery and I are looking forward to sharing our exciting news."

"We are," Avery confirmed, handing Jonah a steaming mug of coffee.

Trexler scowled at Avery and Jonah in turns. "He's joining us?"

"He is," Jonah said without quantifying his reason.

Trexler stormed off without another word.

I'm onto you, you sanctimonious prick.

CHAPTER 20

The presentation went amazingly well. Trexler tried his best to trip him up but failed miserably. Jonah knew the chip inside and out because he and Avery had built it from scratch. He focused on what the latest cybersecurity would mean to the bureau, then asked Avery to present the data from the trial run.

"I can't believe you're developing it for us when you could sell it for a huge profit," Agent Paxton said. "You could probably get millions and spend your days on a boat or a beach instead of chained to a desk in here."

The thought had crossed Jonah's mind once he realized how unhappy he'd been at work lately.

Trexler quickly moved the meeting along once the attendees started heaping praise upon Jonah and Avery. No way the traitorous fucker would stand for that. Jonah only gave half his attention to the meeting and let his mind wander.

Why had Trexler restricted his access? So the bureau could avoid sharing the blame for the botched investigation? Or, was there a clue to the killer's identity Jonah had overlooked? Thankfully, he had a copy of the file on the flash drive Avery made for him. Jonah would prefer to examine the actual evidence collected at the crime scene, but he'd have to get someone at SPD to—

Wait a minute. He recalled seeing the storage location noted in the records, and it wasn't an SPD site. That was the proof he needed to show GBI had taken over the investigation at one point? When? And who? Since he'd memorized the case file number, he didn't need to swing by his house first to get it.

The meeting ran much later than it should have, since Trexler was in love with his own voice. Several agents had follow-up questions for Jonah about the microchip, and he stayed to answer them. Avery took off because he had dinner plans with his family.

By the time Jonah logged off and secured his computers, Avery was already gone. He'd left a note on his desk.

You'll be my dessert. I'll call you when I'm done.

Jonah swung through Arby's again on the way across town and ordered his favorite combo meal, but his stomach was too upset to eat it. He decided to leave the food in the car and reheat it later at home.

The sky had started to darken with impending storms by the time he reached the storage facility, a windowless warehouse. It housed rows upon rows of dusty metal shelves jam-packed with decades' worth of evidence from solved and prosecuted cases. Because the risk of theft and tampering was low, they didn't keep a clerk on site. This was also where all the old files had been stored before he'd digitized them, so Jonah knew the access code unless someone had changed it. He tapped it in and held his breath while waiting for the system to respond. The red light turned green, and the lock disengaged.

The setup reminded Jonah of a library, but instead of using alphabetical letters, they sorted and stored the boxes numerically by case number. Jonah went to the section where Earl's evidence should've been and found an empty spot on the shelf. There was a disturbance in the dust which signaled recent activity.

Son of a bitch. Of course, it wouldn't be as easy as he'd hoped. Jonah was disappointed but not surprised. No wonder Trexler didn't change the access code. Why go to all that hassle when you could just make the evidence disappear?

The headache he hadn't been able to shake had intensified from stirring up dust and other allergens. When he stepped outside, Jonah noticed the sky had darkened further. The wind had kicked up considerably too. It whistled and howled between the warehouse buildings the city used for various things, swirling dust and debris in miniature dirt devils. It wasn't loud enough to drown out noises coming from around the side of the building.

"Dammit," a gruff voice muttered.

Instead of heading for his car, Jonah poked his head around the alley between two buildings. An older man wearing filthy, frayed clothing stood looking angrily at the dumpster. He pushed an old grocery cart with one hand and held a dingy teddy bear in the other.

As wretched as his grandfather could be, Oscar St. John had a soft spot for homeless people. Jonah remembered the surprise trip to Atlanta when he was ten years old to see his very first Braves game. Jonah had never seen a homeless person before and was shocked to see how mean people were to them.

"Get a job, you bum," one lady had said to an elderly man who'd stretched out a paper cup to her as she walked by.

Not Oscar. He slipped some folded bills in the cup. "No one would choose to live on the streets," he'd said. "That man is probably a veteran who lost his mind after seeing horrible things in a war."

"Do you know him?" young Jonah had asked.

"No, but I can see it in his eyes."

There was so much admiration in Oscar's voice when he spoke of someone who'd served in the armed forces. He had been declared medically unfit to serve, but his brother had died in Vietnam.

That moment between Oscar and the homeless man outside the ballpark was one of the few times Jonah ever got a glimpse of the humanity his grandfather hid beneath the gruff exterior, and it stayed with him all these years. It was also the reason Jonah joined the army when he graduated high school. He wanted Oscar to speak so reverently about him... just once. He'd let Oscar down so many times over the years, but being a soldier was something he could do. Jonah had looked forward to graduating from basic training and having his picture taken with Oscar and Granny after the ceremony, but it wasn't meant to be. Oscar had died while he was in boot camp.

He'd been a colossal fuckup as a soldier too. He now understood the look Oscar had spoken about because he'd seen it in his own reflection. In this moment, he could honor the good part of Oscar who showed kindness to those less fortunate than him.

"Hey, buddy," Jonah said softly. He was careful not to advance toward the man and startle him. "Can I help you with something?"

"I'm Hank," the man said. Then he held up the bear. "This is Buddy."

"It's nice to meet you both. I'm Jonah. Do you need my help?"

"I'm okay, but Buddy isn't."

"What can I do for Buddy?"

"He's hungry. The dumpsters are empty."

Jonah remembered the uneaten food in the car. It would still be warm. "I have extra food I can share with Buddy. If that's okay with you, Hank."

Hank narrowed his eyes and assessed Jonah, nodding after a few moments. "Yeah, I guess that's okay."

Jonah hurried to the car to get the food. He slowed down when he approached the alley because he didn't want to frighten the man. Hank still stood by the dumpster, but he'd place the stuffed bear in the front of the cart so it sat up like a toddler.

"Is it okay to approach?" Jonah asked.

"I don't bite," Hank said.

Jonah smiled as he approached the man and extended his offering. "Beef and cheddar, curly fries, and a Coke. How does that sound to Buddy?"

"Sounds delicious. Do you think Buddy will share?"

"I bet he will if you ask nicely," Jonah replied.

"Thank you, mister."

"Is there anything else I can do for you? Anyone I can call? Can I give you a ride someplace? A nasty storm is brewing."

"Nah. This is enough. Bless you."

Jonah swallowed hard and nodded. "Take care. It was nice meeting you, Hank. And you too, Buddy."

Jonah exited the alley and headed back to his car. The wind picked up, and the increased cloud cover made the shadows shift all around him, making the hair stand up on the back of his neck. He heard the scuffle of shoes behind him while he was midstride. Had Hank followed him? He attempted to stop and pivot, but it was too little too late.

Someone delivered a blow to the back of his head. The pain was immediate and blinding. Jonah staggered forward, trying to get away, but he only managed one step before the world spun around him. He was unconscious before his body crumpled to the ground.

CHAPTER 21

Rat-a-tat-tat-tat.

Jonah's face felt like it was on fire when he regained consciousness. He tried to open his eyes but couldn't see for the blood in them. The metallic, coppery liquid filled his mouth, threatening to choke him. He was going to drown if he didn't move. It took all his strength, but he managed to turn onto his side.

His ears rang with a high-pitched noise that made him recoil. Acrid smoke mixed and diesel fumes filled the air, burning his throat and nose.

Eagle? Cobra? Dragon? Lion? He tried to speak but couldn't move his lips. God, he hurt so bad. Was his face on fire? Was he in hell?

Rat-a-tat-tat-tat.

He recognized the rapid fire of the Al-Qaeda's AK-47. Fuck. They were sitting ducks. Jonah couldn't see a fucking thing, so he strained to listen for signs that his brothers were alive. He heard nothing but rat-a-tat-tat-tat and the high-pitched ringing.

Peaceful darkness pulled at him, but Jonah fought to stay awake. He had to get his guys to safety.

The gunfire stopped, and the silence was far scarier.

They were coming.

Drip. Drip. Drip.

Water splatted against Jonah's face, a few droplets at first followed by a deluge. Where was he? Had enemy fighters captured him? Would they torture him?

When Jonah opened his eyes, clarity didn't come to him right away. It came to him in stages—excruciating ones because his head felt like someone had sawed through his skull and removed half of his brain. First, Jonah realized he wasn't in Afghanistan. He was lying facedown in a dark parking lot with his cheek pressed to the hard pavement. A flash of lightning streaked across the sky, and he comprehended the water was rain and not a form of torture. Thunder rumbled loudly, matching the thudding of his heart.

Where was he? What happened to his head? He needed to get to his feet and find shelter from the storm. Knowing what he needed to do and accomplishing it weren't the same thing.

Even in the rain, Jonah could smell the metallic tang of blood. Whose blood? He opened his mouth to call out for his brothers until he remembered they were already dead. Jonah's eyes fell shut, and darkness beckoned. It was peaceful there. All he had to do was stop fighting its pull.

Another flash of lightning rent the sky, and it was so brilliant Jonah could see it behind closed eyelids. The violent clap that followed shook the ground. *There are worse ways I could die.*

A phone started ringing. Whose was it? "Help me," Jonah whispered gruffly. No one rushed to aid him as Mother Nature's temper tantrum intensified. The phone quieted, then immediately started back up again. The cool rain helped clear his brain enough to realize it was his phone ringing. Jonah supported his weight on one arm and reached into his pocket with the other.

The caller ID looked blurry, but he could still read the name. *Avery.*

Jonah stabbed his finger at the phone to accept the call, as the gulf between consciousness and oblivion grew wider.

"Help me," Jonah said into the phone as he tumbled over the edge.

Jonah's next lucid moment came when he was getting wheeled into the hospital on a gurney. The EMTs were giving a full report to a blonde-haired ER doctor, who kept glancing down at him as she ran alongside him.

The overhead lights were too bright, and they took on a strobe-like effect as Jonah moved beneath them. Jonah squeezed his lids shut, but it was too little too late. The lights and movement made his stomach revolt, and he made a gagging noise.

"Stop," the doctor demanded. "Roll him to his side."

They raised the head of the gurney up. Jonah turned his head and leaned as far as he could to empty his stomach on the tile floor. The smell and splattering sound made Jonah retch even more. His entire body tensed and seized up until fingers slid into his hair once more to soothe him.

"You're going to be okay."

Avery. But how?

Jonah's teeth began to chatter, and his body shook, making him realize how cold and wet he was. The jarring motions exacerbated the pain in his skull to the point where he thought he might be sick again.

"We need to get him into a room and get those wet clothes off him," the doctor said. "Let's go."

They started started moving, and the world started spinning again. Jonah closed his eyes, hoping to ward off another round of violent puking. He was so relieved once the gurney stopped inside an exam room. Everyone around him burst into a flurry of motion with the doctor calling out orders. They removed his clothes, cutting through anything that gave them fits before covering Jonah with heated blankets. The weight and warmth made him relax into the bed. Darkness was calling for him again, and he had no reason to resist.

"Stay with me," the doctor said sharply.

Jonah snapped open his eyes and stared in the green assessing gaze of the blonde doctor.

"I'm Dr. Sheridan. Can you tell me your name?" she asked him when she noticed his eyes had opened.

"Jonah St. John," he replied. It felt like he was shouting, but she bent closer to him as if she couldn't hear him.

Dr. Sheridan shone a penlight in his eyes, then continued asking him more questions. She wanted to know things like what year it was, who the president was, where Jonah lived, and his date of birth. "What's my name again?" she asked.

"Um, Dr. Sheridan," he whispered. Just answering those few questions had exhausted him.

"You've got one hell of a concussion," Dr. Sheridan said. "Let's run some tests to see the extent of his brain trauma." Brain trauma? That sounded bad. Really bad. She rattled off the tests to the team, using acronyms. He recognized one or two from his previous injuries ten years ago. "We need to get his head wound to stop bleeding so we can assess the damage there. Any idea what his attacker struck him with?" Dr. Sheridan asked.

"No idea," Avery said.

"The weapon wasn't on the scene when I arrived," said another voice he didn't recognize. A cop? A paramedic?

"Can you get Detectives Locke and Key here?" Avery asked.

"Sure thing," the man said. Footsteps echoed and Jonah caught a glimpse of him as he passed Jonah's bed. It was a patrolman.

The machines in the room beeped and whirred to life as the nurses moved around Dr. Sheridan hooking him up to things. A new sound joined the medical equipment. Ringing. A phone?

"Hi, Commissioner Rigby. It's Avery. Jonah's been injured," he urgently said, then rattled off the hospital. "Someone hit him on the head. The doctor said something about a concussion, but they're running more tests." How had Avery found him? Jonah vaguely remembered Avery calling him when he woke up.

"Doc, radiology is ready for him now," someone said.

"Let's move him," Dr. Sheridan said.

Wait. He needed to tell Avery to get far, far away from him. It wasn't safe. Jonah opened his eyes and realized the hospital bed was moving again. Big mistake. He began dry heaving, sending jolts of pain to his brain every time his body tensed in preparation.

"Poor guy," someone on the team said. "Let's get moving again. The sooner they assess the head injury, the faster they can pump medications into him."

The bed started rolling once more, and Jonah tried his best to relax into the thin mattress. He prayed for the blissful darkness to swallow him up again and got his wish.

The atmosphere was drastically less chaotic when Jonah resurfaced the next time. He was also in far less pain, and his stomach wasn't in turmoil. Jonah remained still, assessing his surroundings. He could tell by the antiseptic smell, uncomfortable mattress, and beeping machines that he was still in the hospital. God, he fucking hated hospitals. Jonah mentally slammed on the brakes before his brain could take him down memory lane. He didn't want to think about the field hospital where they'd stabilized him for the long flight to Ramstein Air Force Base in Germany, then on to Landstuhl Regional Medical Center. Jonah had stayed there for a while to heal and recover before heading home to the States, where they began reconstructive surgery on his face. Jonah would give almost everything he possessed if someone could erase the memories of the emotional trauma and physical pain he'd endured during those long months of recuperation.

Hushed whispers snagged his attention. Jonah cracked open his eyes. Avery, Royce, Sawyer, Ellen, Rocky, Felix, and Marla stood in a small huddle, talking quietly. Jonah only had eyes for one of them. He raked his gaze over Avery's face, noting his puffy, red eyes and pale face. Regret and guilt squeezed Jonah's heart like a vise grip. He must've made a sound of distress because all eyes turned on him.

Even though his arm felt like it weighed two hundred pounds, he raised it enough to crook his finger.

"Which one of us is he beckoning to?" Royce asked.

"Doubtful it's you," Sawyer said. "It was probably your big mouth that woke him."

"You love my big mouth, asshole," Royce said softly.

Sawyer glared daggers at Royce, but Jonah saw his mouth twitch.

Avery shushed them and hurried to Jonah's side. "Hey," he said softly. "How are you feeling?"

"Like roadkill," Jonah replied. His mouth felt like sandpaper, and his throat was as dry as a desert. "How'd you find me?"

Avery removed a reusable plastic water bottle and straw from the cellophane, then filled it with ice water from a pitcher. "Here, drink this." Avery placed the straw against Jonah's lips, and he complied. "Some guy named Hank picked up your phone after you passed out. He gave me a general location, and I got in the car and drove around until I found you." Avery's eyes watered. "Hank stayed on the phone with me until I got there. He told me what you did for him and Buddy."

Jonah let the straw slide from his lips when he was done. Avery pressed the back of his hand against Jonah's cheek. He couldn't resist leaning into his touch, soaking in his warmth. After a few moments, Jonah wrapped his hand around Avery's wrist and pulled his hand away. "Avery, I think you should leave. Get as far away from me as you can."

Avery sucked in a sharp breath and recoiled, almost dropping the water bottle. He set it down and fell into the seat beside Jonah's bed. He looked dazed for all of three seconds before he straightened his shoulders and crossed his arms over his chest. "The hell I will," he said.

"It's time for us to step out and give these gentlemen some privacy," Marla whispered.

"But, *Mom*," Royce whined, "we're just getting to the good part of the show."

"Out now, before I drag you out by your ear," Marla said forcefully.

"Will there be spankings if we're really naughty?" Royce asked.

Marla giggled. "You're too eager. Come on, now," she said, herding them all out the door.

Once alone, Jonah reached out and caressed Avery's face. The firm press of lips and determined expression let Jonah know he was facing a losing battle. To be honest, his attempt was feeble at best. "You know that tattoo on my back?"

Avery nodded.

"It's to honor my four friends who died in combat because of a horrible mistake I made. I can't let this go until I solve what really happened to Earl Ison. I couldn't live with myself if something happened to you because of me."

Avery leaned into his touch. "Nothing will happen to me. You and your friends will see to it. I'm more worried about you. You could've died tonight."

"If he wanted me dead, I'd be dead. It was a warning. One I will not heed."

A promise made was a promise kept.

CHAPTER 22

Jonah woke a few hours later and found Marla sleeping in the chair beside his bed. As if she sensed him stirring, Marla sat up straighter and reached for his hand.

"Where's Avery?" he whispered hoarsely.

"I sent the little lamb home to get some rest."

Figures Avery would listen to Marla. Everyone did. Jonah snorted, then winced when just that motion sent pain reverberating through his skull.

"How you feeling, baby?" she asked.

"Bad," Jonah admitted. "Really fucking bad."

Marla caressed his face with cool hands. "I'll get a nurse for you."

Jonah gently wrapped his hands around her wrist to stop her. "Go home to Amos. You can't rest comfortably in these chairs. It's not safe to be around me right now," Jonah replied.

Marla gave him one of her patented, long-suffering sighs. "What is some big baddie going to do to me that cancer isn't already doing?" Her response caught Jonah off guard, allowing her to continue arguing unopposed. "I'll spend the rest of my fucking days doing what I damn well please, and it pleases me to look after my dear friend, especially since he's in this mess because of me."

"None of this is your fault."

"Let's make a deal," Marla said. "I will stop believing your injury is my fault as soon as you stop blaming yourself for every terrible thing that happens to the people you love."

Jonah wished he could just flippantly agree to her bargain, but he couldn't. Or maybe he just wouldn't. It was easier to keep people at a distance than to lose them after they got too close.

"I see," Marla said after a long pause. She pulled her hand free of Jonah's loose grip, pressed the call button for a nurse, then settled back in her chair. And that was the end of the argument with Marla.

Against Dr. Sheridan's medical advice, Jonah signed himself out of the hospital the following morning. "I suffered a much worse concussion the time I bounced face-first down the side of Kilimanjaro." Jonah pointed to the scar on his face. "It's how I got this."

Dr. Sheridan snorted while Marla just shook her head.

"I'll pull the car around front," Marla told Jonah.

"I thought you couldn't drive."

Marla rolled her eyes. "Just because I choose not to drive doesn't mean I don't know how."

"I beg to differ," Jonah groused during the short drive home. Marla had taken corners too short and waited too long to apply the brakes as she approached stop signs and red lights.

"You're not supposed to stop *in* the crosswalk," Jonah teased.

"Keep it up, wise guy."

Over the next few days, Marla oversaw Jonah's care, playing both nurse and psychologist to him. She also made his meals and herded cats, which is what she called policing his many visitors. Avery came over every evening after work and stayed until the sun went down, but Jonah talked him into going home to sleep in his own bed since he was still getting up several times a night.

His dreams were as turbulent as his sleep, replaying that fateful day of the IED explosion over and over again. To add insult to injury, his brain placed Avery in the Humvee with them, reminding Jonah what—or who—was at risk if he fucked up again.

"What the hell are you doing?" Marla asked when she entered his room one day toward the end of the week. "You're not supposed to be on your phone."

Jonah glanced up from his phone, then grinned from ear to ear. "Am I convalescing or attending a Reba McEntire concert?" He lived for her multiple wardrobe changes each day. The red satin, floor-length gown worthy of an Oscar appearance didn't disappoint.

"Reba?" she scoffed. "You mean Celine Dion, right?" Marla crossed the room and snatched his phone away.

Jonah would've shaken his head, but he still had a headache. "This is Georgia, so Reba reigns supreme here."

Marla tsked. "We'll just have to agree to disagree. And for your information, I've amassed these amazing outfits over the years and want to wear them all again before I die." Then she started a Reba-versus-Celine debate, which lasted at least thirty minutes. Typically, Jonah would've surrendered much quicker, but seeing her riled up was the best entertainment he'd had since leaving the hospital.

"Marla, I'm bored," Jonah whined.

"Fine. I'll talk about my recent weekend in Atlanta."

"Okay."

"I needed to atone for my stupidity and arrogance," Marla said. "That's what wise people do. You see, my family reacted badly to finding out I'm genderqueer, although we didn't call it that back then. They eventually wanted to understand and even made attempts to set things right, but I rebuffed their efforts. It was too little, too late. I felt like they had rejected me, so I gave them a taste of their own medicine. For more than three decades, I deprived myself of spending precious time with my family because of my foolish pride. I should've given them time to come to terms with things and allowed them the opportunity to get to know who I am. Instead, I ran off and didn't look back. It took a death sentence for me to acknowledge I'd made mistakes too."

Marla smiled wistfully. "I got to meet my nieces and nephews and hug my mama and daddy. I tell you," she said, covering her heart. "No one gives better hugs than my daddy." Marla nudged Jonah's shoulder.

"You come really damn close though. You've been my family for the past three years, and I love you more than I can ever express."

Jonah closed his eyes, but the tears still spilled down his cheeks. If he thought that would stop her, he didn't know Marla very well.

"And my Amos…." Her voice wobbled, so she cleared her throat and continued. "The man has the patience of a dozen saints. For decades, I've felt unworthy of love and pushed that man away. He kept coming back time and time again. Amos's love is unrelenting." Marla patted his chest. "Your feelings for Avery are strong, and I know they scare you. Resolve whatever demons are haunting you, cut those fucking chains, and allow yourself to love and be loved in return. You deserve it, baby."

Did he? God, he wanted to believe it was true.

Rocky and Felix showed up later that afternoon, saving Jonah from drowning in his misery. Felix was doing his best to run down leads because he wasn't about to let Jude Arrow gain the upper hand on the investigation. Jonah liked to listen to The Straight Shooter's segments on the evening news so he could rile Felix up with what he heard. Rocky was still caught up in the cheating spouse case but intensified his efforts to get dirt on Trexler after Jonah got injured. Both of them were keeping an eye on Avery for Jonah. The three of them agreed it wasn't safe to investigate the case alone because someone wanted to keep the truth buried at all costs.

Later that night, Jonah was awoken by a solid thud. He just figured Kendall brought someone home again. He rolled over and buried his head under his pillow, hoping they'd finish soon so he could go back to sleep.

Someone suddenly opened his door and flipped on the light. "Jonah," Kendall yelled out. "Are you okay?" Then he burst into laughter. "Oh, it's you. I heard someone climbing on the roof outside Jonah's window and figured they were coming to finish him off."

"What the fuck?" Jonah groused, tossing the pillow aside and gingerly sitting up. Avery was sprawled on the floor beneath his open window. Jonah turned to Kendall. "Finish me off?"

Kendall shrugged. "I can see you don't need my help. Goodnight."

He was dreaming, right? Jonah rubbed his knuckles over his eyes. He looked down, and Avery was still there.

"I can explain," Avery said as he sat up.

Jonah lifted a brow. "I can't wait to hear it."

Avery heaved a sigh. "I just needed to see for myself that you're okay. You were sleeping when I stopped by earlier, and I didn't want to wake you. Then you didn't respond to any of the texts I sent."

"Marla took my phone away. This was the most I slept at once. I must be healing."

"Oh, good. I, um, will just head back home and let you get back to sleep."

"Avery."

"Yes?"

"Come here," Jonah said, patting the pillow beside him.

Avery looked hopeful but also afraid to move. "Um, is that you talking or your medication?"

"I'm only taking ibuprofen," Jonah replied, patting the pillow again. "I want you in my bed."

The tension faded from Avery's lithe body. He stood up and stripped down to his underwear before crossing the room to flip the light switch off.

Jonah sighed in relief when the bed dipped beneath his weight. "You're a stealthy hacker, but you'd make a horrible cat burglar."

Avery giggled. "Don't quit my day job, huh?"

"Yeah," Jonah whispered. "Avery?"

"Hmmm?"

"Scoot closer," Jonah whispered.

"I don't want to jostle you," Avery said, sliding into Jonah's open arms.

Jonah melted into Avery's warmth and kissed the top of his head. All was right in his world again.

Avery didn't respond, only cuddled closer.

In the morning, Jonah woke up with a hard-on, a sense of purpose, and an empty bed. He started to believe he'd dreamed Avery's late-night visit until Jonah saw the impression in the middle of the pillow he'd used.

Jonah ran his fingers over it, then brought the pillow to his head to breathe in Avery's shampoo. Jonah's sense of purpose grew stronger as did his determination to make peace with his past.

He'd need some allies since he wasn't allowed to drive.

CHAPTER 23

"**G**ood morning, baby. You're looking much better this morning," Marla said when Jonah came downstairs fully dressed for the first time in days. She raked her eyes over him from head to toe. "Might it have something to do with your late-night visitor?"

"Did Kendall tell you?"

Marla snorted. "Honey, you know I'm a night owl. I watched the entire thing. I sent Amos out there to spot the silly fool and to catch him if he lost his footing." She shook her head in disbelief.

"Amos is a good man," Jonah said. He'd enjoyed getting to know Marla's husband better over the past week.

Marla nodded. "He's the best." She scrutinized Jonah's face some more. "You look determined. You weren't thinking about driving off someplace, were you?"

"Ellie is on her way to pick me up. I'm taking your advice and resolving my demons." *Trying to anyway.* Jonah gestured to Marla's plum purple ballgown with a plunging neckline and strappy silver heels, which made her nearly as tall as him. "What exactly is the *vibe* you're trying to establish this morning? Are you entering a beauty pageant?"

Placing her slender hand on her throat, Marla tilted her head back and laughed. "Oh, honey," she said, daintily rubbing a knuckle beneath her artfully painted eyes to brush away mirthful tears. "It wouldn't be fair to the others if I did."

"Too true."

"Where are you and Miss Ellie heading off to so early?"

"Bonaventure Cemetery," Jonah said. "We want to get there before the guided tour groups start."

Marla arched an elegant brow. "Please tell me your activities won't involve voodoo or resurrecting actual demons."

"Not today," Jonah quipped.

Bonaventure Cemetery was the burial place of several famous and infamous people from military generals to the award-winning lyricist Johnny Mercer. The book *Midnight in the Garden of Good and Evil* made the serene resting place a hot spot for tourists when the cemetery's famed Bird Girl statue appeared on the cover.

Jonah was only interested in visiting two of the cemetery's residents—his grandparents. Their grave markers weren't as macabre as the grim reaper statue that drew so much attention, nor were they thought provoking like the angels tucked in among the Spanish moss-draped live oaks, or as austere as some of the crypts belonging to some of Savannah's wealthiest families.

He shared a cup of coffee with Marla on the porch while waiting for Ellie to arrive. Jonah stood and kissed Marla's cheek when his aunt pulled into his driveway.

"Watch out for ghosts," Marla called out as he walked away.

Jonah waved to acknowledge her advice, although he was more concerned with the specters haunting his soul than some ethereal beings traipsing through the cemetery.

"You look so much better today," Ellie remarked when he got in the car.

"I feel better," Jonah admitted.

"Good," Ellie said. "Now that you do, we need to discuss the Earl Ison investigation."

"I'm not backing down."

His aunt scoffed. "You think I don't already know that? Quitting isn't in your DNA."

Jonah carefully turned and looked at her since sharp movement still triggered debilitating headaches. Ellie kept her eyes on the road, but Jonah could tell by her stiff posture that she was worried about him.

"I just need to know what you've discovered to trigger such a violent reaction. Do you have a lead?"

"Didn't I promise to share vital information with you?" Jonah asked.

"Yes," Ellie acknowledged, "but surely you can understand my concern."

"Am I talking to the police commissioner or my aunt right now?" Jonah asked.

Ellie stopped at a red light and glanced over at him. "They're one and the same. I am concerned about your safety and making sure I find out who really killed Earl Ison."

"Honest, Aunt Ellie. The only trouble I've stirred up is at work."

"Explain."

Jonah told her the sequence of events that culminated in his suspension and the restricted access. "After Trexler suspended me, someone slashed my tires. Trexler restricted my access, so I went to the storage facility to look through the evidence, which is now missing, by the way."

"Son of a bitch," Ellie growled.

"Then I got bashed over the head when leaving the facility."

"What about the homeless guy? Could he have hit you?"

"He could have, I guess, but to what purpose?" Jonah asked. "Hank didn't steal my wallet or my phone. In fact, he helped Avery find me. It wasn't him."

"Who knew you were going to the warehouse?" Ellie asked.

"No one."

"Someone must be following you," Ellie said, then instinctively checked her rearview mirror. "But who? Trexler?"

"Who else? He's the common denominator in all of this."

"Butch Trexler can be an absolute asshole sometimes, but I find it hard to believe he's trying to kill you." Ellie took a deep breath. "We can't afford to rule anyone out at this point."

"Rocky is digging into his background to see if Trexler has ties to anyone connected to either investigation."

"Tell me everything you've uncovered so far in your investigation."

Jonah started at the beginning and recanted each of the interviews, starting with Sandy Jasper at The Cockpit and ending with Milton and Morrissey slamming the door in their faces.

"The only one left to interview is the guy Earl dated after he broke up with Jerry," Ellie said. "Any idea who it might be?"

"None," Jonah admitted. "Nothing I uncovered would want to make someone kill me. I'm not any closer to solving this case than when I started."

"They might not know it."

"How'd they get inside a GBI facility to steal the evidence?" Jonah asked.

"We can't say for certain someone recently took the evidence, Jonah. There's a vacant spot on the shelf where Ison's evidence box *could've* been. Maybe it was a different investigation from the same year, which would have a similar case file number. We can't possibly store the evidence from every investigation."

"Maybe," Jonah admitted. "Any luck on finding my attacker?"

"Nope," Ellie said. "Locke and Key have talked to the owners of the surrounding warehouses and none of them have exterior security cameras. They haven't been able to locate your friend Hank either."

Jonah hoped to run into the homeless man again someday so he could thank him. He also wanted to find a way to get Hank off the street, if possible.

"My vice cops are asking around too," Ellen continued. "So far, we've got zilch." Jonah wasn't surprised. "The official police report for your *mugging* is temporarily stuck in our internal reporting system. Modern technology is great when it functions properly."

Jonah chuckled. "Is that the official excuse you're going to give if anyone requests the incident report?"

"Yep," Ellie replied. "I can't tie it up forever. How do you want me to proceed?"

"What do you mean?"

"Well, if someone at GBI requests a copy of the incident report, they'll see you were attacked at one of their storage facilities," she said. "I'm sure many questions will follow."

Jonah thought about it for a second. "I emailed the doctor's orders to HR. It detailed the injuries I received from the mugging, the number of days I'd need to miss, and the limited activity I'd need to adhere to upon returning. That should be enough, and I can't see why anyone would go beyond that to request the official police report. If they do, so be it. I'll let the chips fall where they may. I won't ask you or anyone else to lie and fudge a police report to protect my job."

Ellen reached across the console and covered his hand. "Just be careful. You're my favorite nephew, and I love you so much."

"I'm your only nephew," Jonah quipped.

She giggled. "And I love you so much."

"I love you too, Aunt Ellie."

By the time they reached Bonaventure Cemetery in Thunderbolt, Jonah's head was starting to hurt from thinking too hard.

Ellie looped her arm around his as they strolled through the serene grounds. "We'll make this right, Jonah. I promise."

That was all he needed to hear at the moment. Ellen Rigby was a woman of her word. That too was built into their DNA.

Jonah was momentarily struck speechless when they arrived at the black marble gravestone marking the burial spots for Oscar and Maeve St. John. These two people had molded and shaped him, but with such different methods.

"How'd you forgive Oscar?" Jonah asked, breaking the silence after a long pause.

"I just did," Ellie said. "I got tired of feeling like I'd never live up to his expectations no matter what I accomplished. I grew weary of never feeling like I was enough. No matter how many times Sherry or the kids expressed their love, I never felt worthy. How could I be if my own father didn't love me?"

Jonah put his arm around Ellie's shoulders and pulled her close.

"I woke up one day and said enough is enough. By that time, Daddy was already gone, so I started writing in a journal about all the complexities of my relationship with him. I expected to just write about all the things I resented about Daddy, and I admit it started out that way. Then, I noticed a shift in tone. I started including all the little things Daddy did for Mama to make her happy, and the way he smiled when you graduated high school as the valedictorian." She took a deep breath. "I realized he was imperfect and flawed, but I still loved him. Daddy did the best he could, considering he grew up in a generation where men weren't allowed to be sensitive and considerate. I ultimately made the decision to forgive Daddy for my own good." Ellie turned in Jonah's embrace and looked up at him. "I just showed up here one day and said, 'Daddy, I forgive you.' My spirit felt so much lighter afterward, and I'm a better person for it."

Jonah stared at the tombstone until his eyes watered, allowing himself to remember the good parts of Oscar St. John. He remembered Granny giggling girlishly when Oscar snagged a bundle of wildflowers from the lake when he went fishing. Jonah recalled the compassion he'd shown to the homeless man. Then there was the time Oscar went with him to the recruitment office to enlist in the army. Flawed. Imperfect. Human.

Jonah placed his hand on top of the cool marble. "I forgive you, Pop."

"Feel better?" Ellie asked.

Jonah nodded. He couldn't deny his soul felt lighter, but the thunder inside him still rumbled softly.

"Good," Ellie said. "Now you need to forgive yourself, Jonah."

Felix's old Woody Wagon was parked in his driveway when they returned. Ellie had a meeting with the mayor, so she didn't stay to say hello or bust Felix's chops.

From the porch, he heard Felix's and Rocky's voices followed by Marla's throaty laughter. Jonah entered his house and found Marla sitting in Rocky's lap, running her fingers through his blond hair.

"You sure are a pretty one," Marla told him. "Ruggedly handsome looks and a devil-may-care gleam in your light blue eyes." She ran a fingertip over the PI's scruffy jawline. "Tell Mama, has someone already claimed your heart?"

"Someone has already claimed *yours*, Mama," Jonah said, snagging their attention.

Rocky and Felix looked over at him, but Marla dismissed Jonah with a graceful wave. "Ignore him, Blue Eyes."

Rocky smiled up at her. "I think maybe I've been waiting for you."

Marla kissed his cheek, then stood up so she could kiss Felix's cheek too. "You boys behave today and don't let Jonah do too much. He's only allowed to look at computers, phones, or other electronic devices for thirty minutes at a time."

"Yes, *Mama*," Jonah said.

Marla presented her cheek for Jonah to kiss before exiting the house in a swish of plum fabric and leaving behind a cloud of Chanel.

The room was duller without her in it. Jonah absently rubbed a hand over his chest as if it could somehow make the pang in his heart go away.

"Wow," Felix said, grabbing his attention. "Jonah looks so much better today, doesn't he, Major?"

Rocky glared at Felix. "Don't start with me, or I'll eat your favorite donut and spit in your coffee when you're not looking."

"Don't the two of you have something better to do on a Friday morning than babysit me?" Jonah asked as he looked inside the bakery bag of donuts. "Do I spy caramel icing and bacon crumbles?"

"Nothing but the best for you, big guy," Felix said, pushing a drink carrier toward him. "Here's your caramel syrup, milk, and sugar with a splash of coffee. It should still be warm."

"You guys are the best," Jonah said before taking a massive bite of his donut. God, he loved the combination of sweet and salty things.

"You feel up to working a little?" Felix asked.

"God, yes," Jonah replied.

"Are you answering Felix's question, or are you having a foodgasm over the donut?" Rocky asked.

"Both," Jonah said, sitting in the chair across from them. "What's on your mind?"

Rocky and Felix exchanged a quick glance, and it made him nervous. He knew he wouldn't like what they were about to tell him.

"I figured out how your attacker knew to find you at the bar and storage facility even though you didn't tell anyone where you were going," Rocky said, glaring to show his displeasure about the last part.

"The goon didn't follow me on both occasions?"

"How would he have known when and where to start?" Felix asked. "You didn't broadcast your intention to go to The Dive Bar to anyone outside our inner circle."

"And besides, I drove for most of the day. We only split up after I got the call from Pete. So, it's possible someone staked out your house on the off chance you might investigate the case on your own while under suspension. They could've followed us around all day long and continued to tail you after we split up, or—"

"They put a tracking device on my car," Jonah said.

Rocky and Felix nodded.

"Your office is also bugged," Felix said.

"But your house is clean and so is Avery's car," Rocky added.

"Fuck." Jonah set the rest of his uneaten donut on the table. "How do you know about my office and Avery's car?"

Rocky's grimace was all the answer Jonah needed. He stood up fast, and his chair scraped against the floor before tipping over. The pain shooting through his brain reminded Jonah he hadn't fully recovered yet. He placed both palms on the table to steady himself.

"Careful, big guy," Felix said gently.

"How could you involve Avery?" Jonah asked.

Rocky kept his eyes locked on Jonah's. "He wanted to know how he could help you. I knew there was no way in hell he'd be able to get me inside the space so I could sweep it."

Jonah swallowed hard. "I asked you guys to keep him safe, not put him at greater risk."

"Jonah, Avery was going to insert himself into the situation regardless of what you or anyone else said," Felix pointed out. "He cares about you a lot. It's safer for him to work with us than go off half-cocked by himself and stumble into trouble."

"I let him borrow a sweeping device and showed him how to use it," Rocky said. "I'm not sorry. You could've died, Jonah."

Felix nodded. "The bullshit ends now."

"We know who's behind this," Jonah groused.

"Proving it might be harder than we thought," Rocky said. "I've been unable to find any dirt on Trexler. The man doesn't have so much as a ticket for jaywalking, and I cannot connect him to Ison or Cahill."

"What about the prison guards?" Jonah asked Felix. "Have you had any luck there?"

Felix shook his head. "Opie was Joshua Matheson, who passed away in 1997. I haven't been able to track down Bird yet. I figure he's the one we really need to speak to because he worked at Georgia State Prison when the coercion would've happened."

"I have connections at GSP," Jonah said. "Let me take a swing at it."

"Thanks," Felix told him. "I also reached out to the Ison family this week. Dennis was friendly and eager to talk about his brother. The sister, Ava, slammed the door in my face. I decided to take a chance and interview Earl's mother at the nursing home. Dennis gave me permission and said his mother was still sharp and alert to what's going on around her. When I showed up, she was in the community room watching *Drag Race* of all things. The other residents were loving it, but Mona Ison looked sad. I introduced myself and told her why I was there. She was polite, but her gaze kept shifting to the television. She pointed at it and said, 'I bet my Earl was magnificent.' I've never heard so much regret in anyone's voice. She remembered Earl's death like it was yesterday. She and Thomas were out of town at the time. Police notified Dennis, who tracked them down in Sarasota. Thomas definitely has a solid alibi, and I think we can safely eliminate Dennis. Maybe it's someone from the construction crew, but it wasn't them."

"More dead ends," Jonah said.

"Maybe we can trace the listening and tracking devices back to someone," Rocky suggested.

"How?" Jonah asked.

"Avery sent me pictures of the bug he found planted in the receiver of your phone. I took pictures of the tracking device on your car. Both are the kind law enforcement agencies use in their investigations," Rocky said. "Someone had to put in a request for them. We just need to find out who."

Felix tipped his head to the side and tapped his index finger against his chin. "If only we knew someone who could sneak in like a ninja hacker and find proof that Trexler is the one who requested those devices."

Avery.

"It's too risky. No matter how talented he is, Avery could get caught. Then he'd go to prison."

"Avery said he has a contingency plan for that too," Felix replied. "First, he laughed at us and explained he wasn't using an ordinary laptop that you can get at Best Buy. Then, he used a bunch of cyber-geek speak but it was something about the dark web and how anyone looking too close will blame the Russians."

Jonah narrowed his eyes. "If he gets hurt because of me…"

"We're keeping him safe and will continue to do so until you get back on your feet," Rocky assured Jonah.

"What will we do once we can verify Trexler is the one who planted the devices?" Jonah asked.

"Use them to our advantage and set a trap, of course," Felix replied, smiling like a Cheshire cat.

CHAPTER 24

After Rocky and Felix left, Jonah took some Advil and kicked back in his recliner, intending to take a brief nap. Sunlight bathed his chair, and the gentle breeze coming through the open window ruffled his hair. Jonah closed his eyes and imagined he was lying on a blanket with Avery on the beach. Nope. He'd had enough sand to last him a lifetime. A picnic? Yeah, that's better. Blanket, sunshine, and Avery. It was a good start.

They'd just finished eating and decided to stretch out on the blanket in the sun like lazy dogs. Jonah imagined reaching for Avery's hand and lifting it to his mouth so he could kiss Avery's palm. Then maybe he would press a kiss to Avery's pulse point on his wrist before working his mouth higher along Avery's arm, stopping when he reached the junction of his shoulder and neck. The curve was the perfect place to lick, kiss, nibble, and mark. Jonah's body started to come alive as his brain relaxed further into the fantasy.

Avery would make those whimpering gasps that drove him crazy. Jonah wouldn't be able to resist licking upward to Avery's earlobe and biting the tender flesh once there.

The next logical step would be to cover Avery's body with his own, to give him the weight and heft Avery craved. Avery would look up at him with trust and want. Capturing Avery's mouth in a long, lazy kiss had to be the next objective. Jonah would slide his hand inside Avery's hair, anchoring his head in place. He imagined Avery parting his lips to grant him entrance. That's where things could get dicey. One taste of Avery and Jonah wouldn't want to stop. But they were on a picnic blanket in a park. A public indecency charge wasn't something either of them would want.

This is a fantasy, dumbass. Strip him naked. You know you want to.

Jonah tasted the sunshine on Avery's skin as he removed each piece of clothing. *Oh, yeah. Now, we're talking. Picnic porn.*

The breeze kicked up again, and Jonah was confused if it was happening in real life or his imaginary picnic. Who cared? All he needed was to keep kissing Avery, to keep soaking up the sunshine. Jonah's breathing deepened and his body felt heavier.

Beep. Beep.

A car horn jolted him awake. Glancing at his watch, Jonah was shocked to see he'd slept for two hours. He hoped to catch Avery at lunch and sent him a quick text.

I'm thinking about having a pizza picnic in my living room and watching a movie. What do you say?

Sounds fun. Who's your lucky date? Avery asked.

Avery's sass did more to ease Jonah's dull headache than the ibuprofen or nap. *He's an irresistible guy with a quick wit and a smart mouth.*

Irresistible, huh? I'll be there by six if you can agree to a few terms.

Jonah chewed his bottom lip while he tapped out a reply. *Such as?* He couldn't wait to see Avery's list of demands.

No mushrooms on the pizza. Everything else is fair game, Avery wrote.

Jonah grinned. He hated mushrooms with a passion, so it wouldn't be a problem. He'd missed bantering with Avery something fierce, so he didn't submit easily. *Deal breaker?*

Yes. Avery didn't beat around the bush.

What if we do half with mushrooms and half without? Jonah questioned.

Avery sent a thumbs-down emoji before explaining, *I won't be able to relax and enjoy my pizza if I know there's a possibility a mushroom might be hidden beneath the cheese.*

Jonah laughed. *Are you allergic? Wait. That's never stopped you.*

I hate mushrooms. I. Hate. Them. I will puke if I feel one squish between my teeth. Consider yourself warned.

No mushrooms on the pizza, Jonah conceded. *What are your other terms?*

No horror films. I hate feeling scared, Avery wrote.

Define horror.

Jonah!

Avery's annoyance came through loud and clear. *Seriously! Sappy rom-com is scary to me. What's scary to you?*

Slashers. Monsters. Blood. Gore. Gratuitous violence.

Jonah wasn't a big fan of those things either. *Even if I'm here to save you?* He'd also add war movies to his do-not-watch list. He'd seen enough of the real thing to last five lifetimes.

Not even then, Avery replied.

Do you like action films?

I love action and adventure and psychological thrillers. I just can't handle horror.

Not a problem. What else?

Avery took a long time to respond again. *We'll play the rest by ear.*

The rest? Like having sex or Avery staying overnight?

I've missed you, Avery.

I've missed you too, thundercloud. Gotta run. Can't wait to see you.

He had to wait another six hours to see Avery. How the hell was he going to stay out of trouble for that long? The parts to turn Stella 2.0 into Marla the Magnificent had arrived earlier in the week. That would keep his mind occupied while on leave from GBI. Again.

Jonah lectured himself all afternoon about keeping his hands and lips to himself. He wanted Avery to know he meant more to Jonah than just a good fuck. Avery's sweet smile tested his mettle right off the bat, and he wanted to taste it. Instead, Jonah tucked his hands in his back pockets.

Avery raked his gaze over Jonah's white tank top, faded blue jeans, and bare feet. Then he looked at the living room, smiling when he noticed Jonah had moved the furniture around in the small space to spread out his comforter. He'd placed pillows at the end opposite the television so they could lie down and watch the movie after they ate. A wicker basket sat in the center of the blanket. Jonah worried it would come across as cheesy, but Avery's expression transformed from happy to wolfish in an instant.

Jonah cleared his throat and rocked back on his heels. Why was he so damn nervous? Because Avery mattered to him. So damn much. "The pizza should be here any minute."

Avery closed the distance between them, crashing into him. Jonah staggered back a few steps, banging into the kitchen table before finding his balance. The jarring motion rattled his brain, but he sure as hell wasn't going to complain. Jonah must've winced though because Avery made a horrified gasp and started to pull back.

"Huh-uh," Jonah said, snagging him at the waist and hauling him back against his chest. "I like you here, and I much prefer it when you whimper from pleasure instead of distress."

"I am just so happy to see you looking better," Avery said, nuzzling his nose against Jonah's neck.

Jonah cupped the back of his head, and Avery looked into his eyes. "I want to kiss you."

Avery hummed happily. "Yes, please. Nice and gentle."

Jonah laughed. "Are you instructing me or warning yourself?"

"Both?"

Jonah slowly lowered his head and kissed Avery the way he'd fantasized about earlier. Avery blessed him with one of his little whimpers, and Jonah nearly lost his mind. He'd just slipped his tongue inside Avery's mouth when someone knocked loudly on the screen door. Jonah begrudgingly pulled away from Avery, hopefully only long enough to retrieve the pizza and tip the driver.

Avery placed a hand over his pounding heart, halting him. "Do you know what my favorite part of picnics was when I was a kid?"

"Baked beans?" Jonah guessed.

Avery snorted. "Huh-uh. Climbing trees. I'm looking for more adult activities involving *wood* these days."

Jonah could feel his grip on his good intentions slipping. "Ouch," he said, sucking air between his teeth and cringing. "Think of the splinters."

Avery trailed his hand lower, stopping just above the waistband of his jeans. "You're the tree, Jonah."

"Pizza delivery," the driver said through the screen. "I have several others to make."

"I'm coming," Jonah said.

The teenager snorted. "Yeah, I can see that."

Jonah pressed a quick kiss against Avery's lips before walking to the door to pay the kid and get his pizza.

"Where were we?" Avery asked once they were alone.

"We were about to sit down and enjoy a pizza picnic and watch a movie," Jonah said, tipping his head toward the blanket.

"The basket is a nice touch," Avery said. "I can't believe you had one sitting around here."

"I didn't," Jonah admitted. "I still can't drive, so I enlisted Marla's help setting this up. She happened to have a picnic basket from a drag performance of *Wizard of Oz*."

Avery laughed. "I'm starving."

"It's from all your sleuthing, Velma."

"Velma?" Avery asked.

"You are familiar with Mystery, Inc., right? I mean, I know we have a ten-year age gap, but I thought everyone knew *Scooby-Doo* and the gang."

Avery glared at him. "Of course I know who they are. I was just surprised you called me Velma."

"Why? She's the smartest one."

"True," Avery said, preening a little before grinning at Jonah. "And who exactly would that make you? Fred?"

Jonah snorted. "God, no. Felix is Fred. The man is all about setting traps. He even owns a van he sometimes uses for investigations.

It's white and blends in everywhere, but maybe we could talk him into painting it psychedelic colors instead."

Avery laughed so hard he nearly fell over onto the pillow. If that happened, Jonah's control would snap, and he'd forget all about the pizza and his attempt at chivalry. "Who's Daphne?"

"Rocky," Jonah said without missing a beat. "He uses his good looks like a distraction device. Someone so pretty can't be smart too, right?"

"So, are you Shaggy or Scooby?"

"Shaggy, of course. I'm a bottomless pit," Jonah said, patting his stomach, "and a loyal friend." Then he aimed what he hoped was a seductive look at Avery. "Plus, Shaggy has a thing for Velma."

"I love your *thing*," Avery said without missing a beat. "Since when does Shaggy have a thing for Velma?"

"In the updated reboot."

"Have you been watching a lot of *Scooby Doo* this week?" Avery teased.

"Listening to episodes with my eyes closed," Jonah said. Anything to distract himself from boredom and pining for Avery. It obviously hadn't worked worth a damn. His favorite thing to pass the time was harassing Felix after listening to The Straight Shooter's investigative reports. Man, he'd missed the opportunity this morning, but who could blame him for being distracted? Bugs, tracking devices, and Avery thrusting himself in the middle of the investigation. "Rocky told me about the bugs."

"The pizza is getting cold," Avery said.

"Fuck the pizza," Jonah growled. "I don't want you to get caught up in the middle of this, and it makes me sick to think of you injured because of me."

"Arrogant ass," Avery muttered.

"What?"

"How do you think I felt when I called your cell phone and discovered you were injured?" All traces of happiness on Avery's face vanished. Misery marred his adorable features and pretty eyes. "Of course, I'm going to do everything I can to help you."

He reached for Avery's hand, brought it to his mouth, and kissed his palm.

Such a simple gesture, but his lips against Avery's flesh sent sparks throughout Jonah's body. Mirroring his fantasy, Jonah pressed a kiss against the inside of Avery's wrist, licking his tongue over his racing pulse. Avery rewarded Jonah with one of his whimpers, so he gave Avery's arm a gentle tug, urging him to cross the space separating them. Avery came willingly, crawling the few feet and settling in Jonah's lap. He slid his hands into Jonah's hair and massaged his scalp.

Jonah nuzzled the sensitive skin beneath Avery's ear. "I'm so glad you climbed through my window last night."

"Skills I learned from family picnics." Avery rocked his hips forward, grinding his groin against Jonah's. "Maybe the landing wasn't the best. I can work on it."

Gripping Avery's hips, Jonah stilled him. "I'd prefer you didn't."

"Too soon for your head?" Avery asked.

"I meant that I'd prefer for you to come through the front door," Jonah replied. He snagged a pizza slice and held it to Avery's lips. "No mushrooms."

Avery took a bite and chewed thoroughly. "This is much better than a restaurant. They wouldn't like me sitting on your lap while you fed me."

Jonah took a bite before offering the slice to Avery once more. "Probably not," he agreed.

Jonah moved the pizza box so he could remove two bottles of Avery's favorite cream soda. It looked enough like beer that Jonah had teased him about drinking on the job.

Avery smiled at Jonah as if he'd presented him a chest of jewels. "You remembered."

"I remember the look on your face after you took the first sip. Later at home, I thought of all the ways I could put that blissful expression on your face."

"Oh," Avery said breathlessly. "Were you naked?"

Jonah winked. "And I was touching myself."

Avery swallowed hard, setting his and Jonah's drinks down before scooting off Jonah's lap.

"Where are you going?" Jonah asked.

"*We're* going upstairs. Right now," Avery said, rising to his feet. "I want a demonstration."

"Why, Avery," Jonah said with a mock gasp. "I'm stunned by your audacity."

Avery slipped his T-shirt off over his head and tossed it to the ground, then pivoted and headed up to Jonah's room without waiting to see if Jonah followed. Of course, he fucking followed. "You better not be wearing underwear," Avery called from the stairs. "You're not the only one who has fantasies."

"I guess you'll find out."

Avery was sitting on the edge of the bed when Jonah entered his bedroom. He hadn't removed his shoes or jeans yet, which was fine because Jonah loved stripping him bare. Jonah kept walking forward until he reached the bed. Placing his palm in the center of Avery's chest, Jonah gently pushed the star of his fantasies on to his back. He removed Avery's shoes, dropping them with a loud *thunk* against the floor, before divesting him of his jeans and underwear.

Avery gripped his dripping cock and started stroking it, then reached down to fondle his balls with the other. "Tell me about your favorite fantasy."

"I'm fucking living it right now," Jonah replied huskily, removing his shirt before reaching for the buttons on his jeans.

"Go slow," Avery demanded, making Jonah smile.

"I can't dance without a brain injury, so don't expect me to now."

"Got it. Unbutton your jeans and start telling me how you've imagined me naked and wanting in your bed."

"Bed, in the car, on top of the car, in the shower, stretched out on a picnic blanket—"

"Picnic blanket, huh? I didn't know I'd stepped right into one of your fantasies. Do tell."

Jonah slowly opened the buttons on his jeans, loving the hunger in Avery's eyes as he talked about trailing kisses up Avery's arm and neck. Avery moaned and released his balls to circle his puckered rim.

Jonah shucked his jeans and stepped fully naked between Avery's parted thighs. "I fell asleep before I got to the sexiest parts. Why don't I start here?" Jonah asked, capturing the hand Avery used to stroke his cock. He lifted Avery's wrist to his mouth and demonstrated the kisses until he reached Avery's mouth. "And see how it plays out."

Avery scooted back on the bed to make room for Jonah, who joined him. They lay on their sides, touching and kissing as desire built inside them. Jonah resented his limitations, but they were only temporary. Fisting both their cocks in his hand, Jonah stroked them off together.

"What about your fantasies?" Jonah asked.

Avery blushed, and Jonah found it utterly endearing. "How can you expect me to think right now?"

"Tell me. I want to know."

"Bent over your desk," Avery blurted out. "Hard and f-f-fast." His eyes rolled back in his head as Jonah increased the tempo. "S-sometimes I straddle your lap or blow you under the desk while you're on a conference call."

Jonah's balls drew up as he shuttled his fist up and down. He wasn't going to last much longer and wanted to make sure Avery was right there with him. "Good thing I have a home office downstairs. I will put your legs over my shoulders and hammer that sweet spot until—"

"Oh! Oh, God!" Avery called out. Hot cum covered Jonah's hand and dribbled down his shaft.

Rolling Avery to his back, Jonah straddled his hips and began jacking himself off as if his life depended on it. Jonah braced one hand on the bed next to Avery's head to steady himself. "Look what you do to me," Jonah growled. "Only you." He painted Avery's chest and abdomen, and it felt more significant than just a sexual release. He was marking his territory. "Mine," Jonah said, smearing his cum with his dick.

Jonah lay beside Avery and pulled him into his arms. They kissed lazily for a long time. Neither seemed to be in a hurry to clean up the sticky mess that would soon act as a binding agent if they weren't careful.

Jonah finally released Avery's lips and eased apart from him. "If you want me to keep the chest hair you seem to love so much, then I better get cleaned up."

They kept the mood playful and fun when they got in the shower. Avery wanted the honors of washing him, and Jonah couldn't find a legitimate reason to tell him no. Avery's deft fingers moved boldly and confidently until Jonah presented his back to him.

He could feel Avery's fingers trembling as he traced sections of the beast tattooed on his back. "This is stunning artwork, Jonah. The artist has wicked talent."

Jonah took a steadying breath. "His name was Danny Valdez, but we called him Dragon. He was the first friend I made at boot camp. The man was never in a bad mood, but he was fiercely loyal and protective like a dragon. There was no one else you wanted by your side in a firefight." Avery's fingers continued to move, finding the parts of the tattoo that represented the dragon. "Then came Evan Deluca, but we called him Eagle because he had the sharpest vision. He never missed anything. Eagle was Italian through and through. He held nothing back." Jonah waited while Avery located the inked feathers representing Evan.

"Who's the cobra for?" Avery asked softly, tracing over the snake fangs coming from the lion's mouth as well as the eyes above the jaguar nose.

"Cody Walker," Jonah said. "Texan. Everything is bigger in Texas, you know. In Cody's case, it was his ego, but he set it aside for the good of the team. Lyle Leonetti is the lion. Lyle came from Boston and had a thick accent. God, we ribbed him endlessly for dropping the R in words. Cah? What's a cah? No, man. We want to go to a bar, not a bah." Jonah chuckled at the memory even as pain welled in his chest.

Avery slid his arms around Jonah's waist and pressed his lips to his back. "You're the jaguar, right?"

"I am," he said. Jonah felt so far removed from the powerful predator they'd dubbed him. He turned around and faced Avery. "The four of them died when the Humvee in front of ours ran over an IED. Our Humvee avoided most of the blast, but it rolled, and we came under fire." He pointed to the scar on his face. "That's how I really got this scar."

Avery bit his lip and nodded as tears filled his eyes. He reached up and traced his finger over the silver diagonal slash marring Jonah's face.

"Danny drew this design on our final leave, and I asked his mother if I could borrow it after I woke up from my coma. She'd already removed his belongings from our place. She mailed it to me and told me to keep it. Once I recovered enough, I sat through several sessions until it was complete."

"Did it hurt?" Avery asked.

"Yeah, but that was the point. I was looking for physical pain to relieve the emotional trauma. It only worked for a little while, and I kept adding tattoos."

"They're beautiful," Avery whispered, running his finger along the intricate designs of his sleeve tat. Then he rose on his tiptoes and kissed Jonah. "I've always known you and tragedy were familiar friends."

"That's just the tip of the tragic iceberg," Jonah said, holding Avery tighter.

"We don't need to talk about it," Avery said. "Let's get dried off so we can eat pizza, drink cream soda, and watch our movie."

"Can we finish the picnic in my bed? It would be more comfortable."

"Absolutely."

He'd chosen the movie *Blackhat* because it was about a convicted hacker who had to work with authorities to save the day. Jonah's favorite part was listening to Avery pick the technical stuff apart.

"I thought you'd just enjoy watching Chris Hemsworth," Jonah said playfully.

"He's okay," Avery said with a shrug.

Jonah fell asleep before Chris could save the day. When he awoke hours later, Avery was sitting up beside him in bed, typing away on a laptop Jonah had never seen at the office before.

"What are you doing?" Jonah asked groggily.

Avery smiled sheepishly. "Online banking."

"Uh-huh. Are you having any luck?"

Avery grimaced, and Jonah knew he wasn't going to like what he had to say. "Initially, I thought I hit the jackpot. I'm surprised I didn't wake you up when I fist-pumped the air in victory. Once I started digging deeper, a troubling pattern emerged."

Jonah sat up and looked at him. "What is it?"

"I traced the listening and tracking devices to Trexler," Avery said somberly.

"Okay. What's the bad news?"

"They were signed out at times he wasn't in the office. I think someone is framing Trexler to be the fall guy for whatever they're planning for you."

Avery's ominous words made Jonah shiver. "Are you sure?"

"I'm positive," Avery replied. "Things were slow and dull when you were gone, which gave me plenty of time for office gossip. When I see his assistant cubicle hopping for the latest scoops, I know Trexler is out of the office. Trexler ducked out early, and he wasn't the only one who got a head start on their weekend."

"Who?" Jonah asked.

"Trexler left at twelve, and Desiree followed at twelve thirty, so there were tons of nooner jokes." But Avery wasn't laughing, and neither was Jonah. "Anyway, look at the time Trexler supposedly signed for the listening and tracking devices." Avery turned the laptop for him to see it.

"Fourteen thirty," Jonah said. Trexler couldn't have signed for them at two thirty if he left at noon. "Are you sure he didn't come back?"

"Positive," Avery said. "And it gets worse."

How could it get worse? "Go on," Jonah said.

Avery turned the laptop around and started typing. "Do you remember me telling you Trexler used his remote laptop to change your clearance access?"

"Yes."

"Except Trexler reported his laptop stolen the prior week," Avery said.

Jonah's heart sunk. "I was certain Trexler was the one behind it all." This was why investigators couldn't afford to put all their eggs in one suspect's basket. He'd been blinded by his dislike of his supervisor and allowed it to poison his investigation. Jonah had made it personal.

Avery turned the laptop toward him again. "I found the incident report in Trexler's outgoing email. He claimed he left it in his car overnight and must've forgotten to lock the doors. With enough time, I could probably track its location if it hasn't been destroyed."

"You can try. If we find the laptop, we'll find who's behind it all," Jonah absently said as he stared off into space.

Avery slipped his fingers between Jonah's. "What are you thinking?"

"I'm trying to figure out which guy at the bureau hates me more than Trexler."

"Did you ever consider it could be a woman?" Avery asked. "Slashing your tires and clubbing you upside the head doesn't require a lot of strength. So far, your nemesis is cunning and has stayed one step ahead of you. There's no physical evidence pointing to a man as the perpetrator."

"You're right," Jonah said. "I've been making too many assumptions. Maybe I should stick with analyzing data and writing code instead of investigating crimes."

"Stop being so hard on yourself. You've obviously touched a nerve with your work so far."

Jonah chuckled. "And got my brains scrambled as a result."

Avery winced. "So, what do we do next?"

Jonah looked at the time and grimaced. "I need to call Rocky and Felix and bring them up to speed."

"At midnight?" Avery asked.

Jonah didn't really want to call them so late, but he knew they'd be upset if he didn't apprise them of the latest information. The person was stepping up their attacks to avoid getting caught, and Marla... He couldn't finish the thought. Jonah's phone rang on his nightstand, and he nearly jumped out of his skin.

"Fuck," Avery said, covering his heart. "That scared me to death."

Jonah squeezed his hand to reassure him, then picked up his phone. "It's Rocky and Felix on FaceTime," he told Avery, who tugged the sheet up higher. "Audio only." He accepted the call, and said, "You must be psychic. I was just talking about you."

"That's the reason for the sudden pain in my ass. Do you have a voo-doo doll and a stick pin?" Rocky asked.

"Try washing your ass once in a while, and you won't get pimples, you big nasty," Felix said.

Jonah snickered. "Hey, guys. What's up?"

"We have a break in the case," Felix said.

"*We?*" Rocky asked him.

"Fine. *Major* has a break in the case," Felix amended.

"You're such an asshole. Why do I like you?" Rocky asked Felix.

"I'm irresistible," Felix replied.

"Guys, I have big news too," Jonah said. Avery cleared his throat. "*Avery* has big news."

"*We,*" Avery amended.

Jonah put his phone on speaker. "Okay, *we* have news too."

"See how teamwork goes, Felix?" Rocky asked.

Felix snickered. "Fuck you, Major."

Jonah knew from experience the two men could bicker forever, so he cleared his throat. "Someone is framing Trexler to take the fall."

"Whoa," Felix and Rocky said at the same time.

Jonah caught them up on what Avery had found.

"It aligns with my news," Rocky said. "I can't connect Trexler to anyone at the state prison, but I discovered Bird's real name is Vincent Malcolm."

Jonah felt like someone had punched him in the stomach. "Malcolm? As in related to Charles Malcolm, a deputy director with the GBI?" The man Jonah respected and admired?

"Vinnie is his older cousin," Rocky said. "He's retired now and living in Boca Raton."

Unlike Trexler, Malcolm was the right age to know Earl. How? Were they lovers? Friends? Had Malcolm been a dirty cop, and Earl wit-nessed something he shouldn't have? All Jonah's trouble had started after he talked to the deputy director. As much as he wanted to rationalize away the evidence, he couldn't.

"Breathe, Jonah," Avery whispered, nudging him out of his trance.

"We know what we have to do," Rocky said.

"Tomorrow, we begin setting the first trap," Felix added. "Be at my house at noon to record the podcast. I'll edit and upload it on Sunday."

Even though it felt like his universe had shifted drastically, Jonah was grateful to have his friends and Avery by his side. Jonah smiled at Avery and said, "See, I told you Felix was Fred. He's all about setting the traps."

Avery laughed, while Rocky and Felix talked to each other.

"Fred who?" Felix asked.

"Flintstone?" Rocky guessed.

Felix snorted. "What traps did Fred Flintstone set?"

"It was just a guess," Rocky replied. "What's put you in a bad mood? You think The Straight Shooter is going to solve this investigation before we do?"

"I hate you, Major," Felix groused.

"Fred Jones from *Scooby-Doo*," Jonah said.

Rocky laughed for several moments. "Fuck me. That's hilarious," he said once he calmed down. "Who am I, then?"

"Daphne," Jonah, Avery, and Felix all said at the same time.

Rocky promptly disconnected the call.

"I like your friends," Avery said.

"I do too. Not many people can make me laugh this late at night," Jonah said. Or under these circumstances. *Charlie Malcolm? Could it be?*

"Or this early in the morning," Avery countered. "Depends on how you view it."

"It is morning," Jonah said, tipping his head to the side. "Saturday morning."

"So, you want to watch cartoons now?"

Jonah removed the computer from Avery's lap and set it on the nightstand. "It means my restrictions are lifted. I can drive, among other things."

"Other things?" Avery asked. "Such as?"

Jonah rolled Avery to his back and showed him.

CHAPTER 25

Jonah woke long before the sun started to flirt with the slumbering earth. The possibility of Charlie's betrayal shook him hard, triggering instinctive reactions he'd vowed not to repeat with Avery. During the phone call with Felix and Rocky, their teasing had made it possible for Jonah to table his reaction and hurt. Afterward, sex with Avery distracted him from processing what he'd learned. As usual, delaying the inevitable didn't really make the situation easier.

How the fuck could Charlie Malcolm, a man so dedicated to law, order, and justice, be involved in either Earl's death or the subsequent cover-up? If Jonah had been so wrong about Charlie, was he as equally wrong about Trexler? How much of their antagonism toward each other was genuine? How much was fabricated as part of Malcolm's smoke and mirrors?

Jonah's body tensed with every question that crossed his mind until he thought his spine might snap under the strain. He looked over at the man sleeping soundly beside him in the early dawn light. Avery was lying on his stomach with his head turned in Jonah's direction. He'd shoved the covers low enough so the dimples above his firm ass cheeks played peekaboo with Jonah, distracting him from destructive thoughts. Jonah's fingers itched to trail a path over Avery's backbone, to dip his tongue in those delicious divots, and to count the freckles dotting his nose.

This firecracker had pushed past his barriers, reaching the fragmented pieces of his heart he'd kept guarded for ten years. Avery had used kindness, sass, and unparalleled patience to solder those fragments together. Jonah relearned how to laugh, to trust, and form friendships again. Avery made him want to take chances and live instead of wallowing in what could've been. Most importantly, Avery retaught Jonah how to love.

Acknowledging he was in love with Avery wasn't the lightning bolt to the heart Jonah expected. Instead, the awareness washed over him like a warm summer rain. Rather than fight his feelings, he fucking embraced them.

Avery moaned, jarring Jonah from his thoughts.

"Good God, Jonah," Avery said, his voice raspy and adorable from sleep. "If you're going to freak out and kick me to the curb, can you wait a few more hours? I'm exhausted and need sleep."

"Kick you to the curb?" Jonah asked. "Really?"

Avery's mouth curved into a smile before he cracked open an eye. "Your hard drive is working overtime this morning. If you're not careful, you'll blow a circuit board."

"I have no desire to push you away," Jonah said. To prove his point, Jonah scooted over until they were sharing Avery's pillow. It was one thing for Avery to have knocked down the walls, but it was entirely another not to always trip over the rubble of Jonah's past. He trailed his fingers up and down Avery's back, smiling at the way Avery arched his spine like a cat. "My four friends are dead because I made a big mistake." Jonah slid his hand into Avery's hair, loving the way the silky strands slipped through his fingers.

Avery scooted closer until his hip pressed against Jonah's semi-erection. "You don't have to do this now, Jonah."

Jonah pressed a chaste kiss against his lips. "I really do." He brushed the back of his knuckles over Avery's cheekbones. "War is a terrible thing. You see and hear unspeakable atrocities and do things you never dream yourself capable of. To be brutally honest, I wasn't cut out for it."

Avery made a disbelieving noise.

"It's true. A few weeks before the explosion, my unit engaged in a skirmish with Al-Qaeda in the middle of a village. We had bigger numbers and better equipment, so we quickly gained the upper hand. We gave the surviving insurgents the option to surrender, and they did. As we were rounding up the detainees, I came across a young man wearing traditional Muslim clergy attire in one of the homes. He was reading from the Quran and comforting the women and children in the house. I stared into the man's eyes and only saw fear and a desire to help the family. I backed out of the residence and told Dragon it was clear of enemy combatants. We loaded the detainees into our vehicles and headed back to base. I'd give anything if I could go back to that day and do things differently."

"The man wasn't a clergyman?" Avery asked.

"He was but also a high-ranking Al-Qaeda member our intelligence officers had nicknamed the Radical Mullah. I would learn later his name was Daud Alakozai and that IEDs were his brainchild. When he was eventually captured, he told interrogators about his near capture in Kamdesh. Alakozai laughed about how he made the stupid US soldier pay by killing as many Americans as possible. My team didn't die in the Humvee crash. Those animals took them captive and executed them. They saw my mangled face and blood loss and assumed I was dead instead of unconscious. The rest of our unit found me when they came to recover the fallen."

"Oh, Jonah," Avery whispered.

"When I saw his picture on the news and realized what I'd done..." Jonah took a shaky breath. "Eagle was about to become a father for the first time. Cobra had just gotten engaged. Lion had only been married for eight months."

"And Dragon?" Avery asked.

"He was my boyfriend. We couldn't tell anyone back then because of DADT, but we had big plans for after we got out of the army. Danny wasn't my first boyfriend, but he was my first love. Knowing I failed him..."

Avery held Jonah tighter as tears of regret streamed down his face. "I'm so sorry."

Avery just listened as Jonah talked about the debilitating depression that haunted him for years. He didn't offer platitudes or try to absolve Jonah's guilt. Jonah had heard it all before from the psychiatrists he sought for help and the family members of his fallen friends. Nothing they said seemed to make a difference, and Jonah finally understood why. Ellen was right. Forgiveness wasn't something he needed from other people; he needed to liberate himself. The first step was acknowledging that he was worthy of forgiveness. Then he could work on achieving it.

I am worthy of forgiveness. He'd repeat it as often as he needed.

"Ellie recognized that I needed a purpose and encouraged me to pursue law enforcement," Jonah said. "I laughed and reminded her how much I hated guns and she pointed out there is more than one way to catch bad guys. I combined my love of computers with my desire to understand what makes people tick. I started out taking psychology classes to try to heal the broken pieces of my soul, but it took on a whole new life."

"Listening to your aunt Ellie has worked out really well for you," Avery whispered before kissing Jonah's lips.

"She has the best ideas." Jonah pressed his forehead against Avery's. "Don't give up on me, okay?"

"Never." Avery's resolute conviction was spoiled by a big yawn at the end. God, he was so fucking adorable.

"We don't need to be at Felix's house until noon. Let's try to get more sleep."

"You don't have to tell me twice," Avery said, tucking himself under Jonah's arm and resting his head over Jonah's heart. "First a nap, then we crusade."

Jonah placed his hand on Avery's waist, anchoring him against his body. While cuddling wasn't his dick's favorite pastime, it was quickly becoming Jonah's. He figured his thoughts were too turbulent to permit sleep, but he sank into Avery's heat.

"Are you sure Felix and Rocky won't mind me tagging along to the podcast recording with you?" Avery asked when they pulled up to Felix's house.

"Tagging along? You're not my annoying little brother," Jonah teased. "The guys like you, and I really, really like you."

A light pink blush bloomed across Avery's cheeks. "If you're sure."

"I'm positive," Jonah said, pushing open the door. It seemed like second nature to reach for Avery's hand when he rounded the hood and joined him.

Rocky had arrived before them but was still sitting in his car. Jonah noticed he was talking on the phone when they walked by. Judging by Rocky's stiff posture, his friend wasn't enjoying the conversation. Was the cheating wife case still giving him fits, or was the issue more personal?

Felix met them at the door when they stepped onto the porch. "Where's Major?" he asked.

"Hello to you too," Jonah teased.

"Oh, shut up," Felix said, slapping Jonah on the arm. "I saw him pull into my driveway ten minutes ago. I figured maybe he was avoiding me as long as possible, but here you are and still no Major."

"Major?" Avery asked.

"It's Rocky's first name," Jonah said. He didn't repeat the rest of the story Rocky shared with them because it wasn't his to tell.

"Ah," Avery said. "I don't want to be in the way, so I can duck outside while you guys record."

"Nah," Felix replied, waving off his concerns. "I have excellent editing software. I'm thinking about turning a spare bedroom into a recording studio. It wouldn't take too much to soundproof it."

Jonah nodded. "It's a good idea. Let me know if you want my help."

Rocky knocked on the screen door before Felix could respond. "Sorry," he said sheepishly. "This damn case is going to make me lose my mind." He hooked an arm around Avery's neck and pulled him into a bro hug. "Hiya, cutie."

"Hi," Avery replied shyly.

"You lost your mind a long time ago," Felix countered, leading them into his dining room where his recording equipment was set up. "Are you still working the same cheating spouse investigation?"

"Yeah, but Pete and I are about to shake things up. It dawned on me that the husband is potentially sending me on a wild goose chase for his own nefarious reasons. I've never had a client refuse to accept proof their spouse *wasn't* having an affair."

"Wow. Nefarious. Nice vocabulary, Major," Felix said.

"Aw, shucks," Rocky replied, slipping into an exaggerated southern drawl. "I heard the word last night when I was watching The Straight Shooter's segment on the nightly news. He uses those fancy words and sounds so smart. I looked up the meaning and decided to use it the first chance I got."

Felix tensed and glowered but didn't remark on Rocky saying the name of Felix's nemesis in his home.

"Like one of those word-of-the-day calendars," Avery suggested.

Rocky nodded. "Only Jude Arrow is so much better to look at than any calendar. Don't you think so, Felix?"

"I fucking hate you," Felix growled.

"You're crazy about me," Rocky countered, hooking his arm around Felix as he'd done with Avery. "Not as much as you like Jude Arrow though."

Felix danced out of the embrace and pivoted to face Rocky. He drew his fists up in front of him and bounced on his feet like a boxer. "Those are fighting words, Major."

"The only one fighting anything here is you, pal," Rocky said, grinning wickedly. "Just admit you're jonesing for Jude."

Felix took a swing, but there wasn't much power behind it, so Rocky had plenty of time to duck. He landed a soft jab to Felix's stomach before the reporter brought his hands up and clapped both sides of the private investigator's head, missing Rocky's ears by mere inches. They danced around each other for a few more minutes, taking lousy swings and landing harmless punches.

Avery watched with rapt attention the two men's faux fight for a few minutes before looking up at Jonah. "Is this how your recording sessions always go?"

"It's not usually this bad," Jonah replied. "They're just really showing their asses for you, I guess."

Their voices must've reminded the two scrabbling men that they weren't alone because they immediately froze in place. Rocky had Felix bent over in a headlock and the fist he'd used to give noogies stilled on top of Felix's head. Felix's fist was still pressed against Rocky's stomach from the blow he'd just landed. Both men just stayed locked in their positions for a few seconds before recovering.

Rocky was the first to move. He unhooked his arm and straightened to his full height. "We can't seem to help ourselves."

"We'll try harder to behave," Felix added as he too stood up.

Rocky turned and faced Felix, extending a hand. "Truce?"

Felix reluctantly shook it. "Truce. Just stop saying *his* name. He's my personal Voldemort."

"You started it by calling me Major."

"It's your name."

Rocky released an exaggerated sigh. "You know how much I don't like it."

"You know how much I hate *him*," Felix countered.

Rocky had a wry twinkle in his blue eyes, and Jonah expected more bantering to follow. He gave a jerky nod instead, then gestured to the table. "Shall we get started on setting the trap for Charlie Malcolm?"

"Abso-fucking-lutely," Felix said.

Jonah, Felix, and Rocky took their positions behind the microphones, and Avery sat across from them. They briefly reviewed the agenda to make sure they didn't veer off target, which was a habit they'd fallen into as their friendship grew.

A few months ago, they'd hired a local artist to create an original score and lyrics for their podcast and recorded an introduction they could use with every episode. It consisted of a few lines of the eerie song before the guys introduced themselves as an investigative reporter, criminal analyst, and a private detective. They asked listeners to tune in each week to hear them discuss their beloved city's most sensational crimes and her more sinister citizens. At the end of the episode, the entire Sinister in Savannah theme song would play in the background of the closing recording, where they asked listeners to subscribe, rate, and review the podcast. They also gave previews for future episodes or played funny outtakes Felix had edited out of the episode.

Since the intro and closing sections were already recorded and would be added in edits, they just jumped right into the episode after Felix counted them down.

"Today's episode is called Ride the Lightning," Felix said, starting them off. He had more experience and was much more at ease with the entire process than Jonah and Rocky combined. "The term is slang for execution by electric chair, which wasn't abolished in Georgia until October 2001."

"Wow," Rocky said. "That's hard to imagine."

"It is," Jonah agreed.

"The three of us oppose the death penalty for various reasons, but we're all in agreement on one point," Felix said.

"Probably more than one," Rocky countered. "It's not like I'm going to argue with you that my primary reason for opposing the death penalty is somehow better than the reason you oppose it."

"Maybe you won't today," Felix teased. "I won't hold my breath since you're likely to change your mind."

Rocky laughed. "True. I am a Gemini. What's the one point you feel we agree on?"

"I'll let Jonah explain since it's his main reason for opposing capital punishment," Felix said.

Jonah fought back the momentary panic creeping up on him. *Just breathe and be yourself.* "Well, for capital punishment to work, the convictions have to always be right. That's just not the case. Innocent people are arrested, tried, convicted, and executed for crimes they didn't commit. That is a great travesty."

"I agree wholeheartedly," Rocky said.

"One of the ways people are railroaded by the system is through coerced confessions, which is the subject of our podcast today," Felix said. "Jonah, why don't you tell our listeners about Earl Ison, Bo Cahill, and how you came to know about them."

This was the easy part. Jonah forgot his nerves while he spoke about his dear friend Marla and her friend Earl, whose life was taken much too soon. Jonah was careful not to throw anyone under the bus as he stated the inconsistencies he'd found right off the bat and moved to the investigation the three of them started. Jonah had no idea if Morrissey and Milton were crooked cops. He also made certain he kept Jerry's name private to protect his identity. Jonah's objective was to draw out Malcolm, not wreck other people's lives.

Rocky and Felix interjected with their own observations and experiences. Then they arrived at the part where they set the trap.

"So, you have exciting news about a break in the investigation, right?" Felix asked.

"I do," Jonah agreed. "I located a guard who worked death row when Bo Cahill was incarcerated at Georgia State Prison. He's agreed to meet with me."

"You think he knows how someone was able to coerce a confession from Bo?" Rocky asked.

Jonah smiled and hoped his voice sounded smug when he said, "I know so. He told me he's wrestled with his conscience for over thirty years and wants to make things right."

"When are you meeting with him?" Felix asked.

"Tomorrow," Jonah replied.

"That's really exciting," Rocky said.

They chatted about various aspects of the case a little longer before Felix turned off the recording equipment and called it a wrap.

"Part one is over," Felix said. "Part two will happen Monday after Malcolm has had an opportunity to listen to the episode."

"I've been thinking," Jonah said, making his podcast partners groan. "We can set this trap up, but we're going to need some help if we want to make this legal."

"We do," Rocky agreed. "You know how hard that is for me to say, right?"

Felix and Jonah both chuckled.

"Yeah, what's the point of doing all this if we can't make charges stick? I think we also need a decoy to act as the prison guard. Do you have someone in mind?" Felix asked.

Jonah nodded. "I know the perfect person for each role."

CHAPTER 26

On Monday morning, it was hard to tell which emotion was riding Jonah harder—fear or frustration. Both revolved around one delectable intern who refused to call in sick to work as Jonah had requested.

"I never miss work," Avery had argued the previous night over the phone and again before work this morning. "We need everything to look normal."

"I need you to be safe," Jonah had countered during both conversations.

He reached out to Rocky and Felix for backup on his way to work. He'd argued that calling one of them from his office to confirm the meet time and location would be just as effective as sharing the details with Avery.

"How often does Avery miss work?" Felix asked.

"He doesn't," Jonah admitted reluctantly.

"I think it would look suspicious, especially since it's your first day back after an injury," Rocky said.

"Unless Avery is one hell of an actor, everyone at the office has to know how much he adores you," Felix said.

The remark warmed Jonah, even if he was aggravated his friends were annoyingly hashtag team Avery. "I can't allow Avery to become a casualty of my war."

"*Our* war," Felix and Rocky said at once.

"Awww," Jonah said. "Look at the two of you bonding."

"Bonding?" Felix scoffed. "We agree on one point."

"It's not like you caught us in bed together," Rocky added.

Felix snorted. "As if."

"You'd never be the same," Rocky said smugly.

"Ruined for other men or put off sex altogether?" Felix countered.

"Okay, I'm out," Jonah said.

"Hey, big guy," Felix said, stopping Jonah before he could disconnect.

"Yeah?"

"Keep your head in the game. That's how you and Avery will stay safe."

"Fine," Jonah grumbled as he pulled into the GBI parking lot. "I'll talk to you two nitwits later."

"Nitwits?" Felix and Rocky repeated.

Jonah disconnected the call with a chuckle. Closing his eyes, he counted backward from twenty. Felix was right. He couldn't allow his emotions to cloud his judgment or things would go sideways. Stick to the mission.

A tap on his window startled him. Jonah opened his eyes and found Trexler glaring at him. Jonah knew there would be a showdown but here? Now? Jonah hit the button to roll down his window. "Sir?"

"You either have balls of steel or the hit you took from your mugger last week has addled your brain," Trexler said.

"Good morning to you too, sir," Jonah somehow managed to say with a straight face.

Trexler narrowed his eyes as an angry blush crept up his neck and face. If he were a cartoon character, steam would soon escape through his ears. Ignoring Jonah's cavalier response, his supervisor continued. "Or maybe you just don't value your career. Is that it?" Trexler ambushing him in the parking lot was precisely what Jonah needed to get in the right frame of mind. "You'd piss away the opportunities the deputy director gave you in favor of the podcast with those *losers*?"

"I wasn't aware you subscribed to Sinister in Savannah," Jonah said, finding immense pleasure in goading the man.

"*I don't, but Deputy Director Malcolm does. He's not a happy man this morning, St. John.*"

"I look forward to hearing it directly from *him*," Jonah replied. "Or are you meeting me at my car to inform me I've been fired? If not, I think this approach is very unprofessional."

"*Unprofessional?*" Trexler asked. "You're going to fucking lecture me? I'll have your—"

Jonah rolled up his window while Trexler's tirade continued. He heard the man swear he'd have Jonah's badge, but for once, the threat instilled hope inside Jonah instead of concern. He had the skillset to assist law enforcement in other ways. Computers with artificial intelligence were the tool of the future, and Jonah could carve his own career path. The microchip he designed for GBI? Fuck that. He'd keep the rights and sell it to the highest bidder. Jonah killed the engine, then opened his car door so fast his supervisor had to quickly step back to avoid getting hit with it.

Slamming the door shut, Jonah squared off against Trexler. "Are you firing me?" Jonah asked. Trexler swallowed hard. "If Deputy Director Malcolm wishes to express his disappointment, he knows where to find me."

"He has meetings away from the office all day," Trexler replied. *Of course, he does.*

"Did he advise you to greet me at my car and give me a stern lecture?" Jonah asked.

"No."

"Did he instruct you to fire me?"

Trexler shook his head. Had he rendered the man speechless? A fucking first.

"Then get out of my face," Jonah said.

Trexler's mouth snapped open, and he emitted a stunned gasp. His supervisor continued to gape at him as if his jaw hinges had broken. Jonah pivoted and headed toward the building. That's when he noticed Avery and several other agents and staff members observing his altercation with Trexler. Most wore shocked expressions, while others looked smug. Did they consider Jonah standing up to Trexler as his "Hulk out" moment? Were they calculating their office pool winnings? Jonah's gaze finally landed on Avery, who was leaning against his car, smiling his approval. Avery's opinion was the only one he cared about. Jonah winked playfully at his feisty intern without breaking stride. Once inside the building, he greeted the people who hadn't witnessed the altercation with a serene smile and head nod. He wondered how long it would take for word to spread throughout the building. Like wildfire, not long.

Jonah found a bag of Caramel Bugles waiting for him in the middle of his desk. He dropped into his chair and immediately tore into the bag. "Breakfast of champions," he said before digging in.

Predictably, Avery didn't follow immediately behind him. It was Monday morning, after all, and there would be a ton of gossip for him to enjoy. Jonah was halfway through typing his resignation before his intern entered his office. He imagined every Tom, Dick, and Harriet stopped Avery to talk about what transpired in the parking lot.

"Good morning, Jonah." Avery's professional voice was so different from the one that called out Jonah's name in pleasure over the weekend. Jonah wanted so badly to add to the climax count but wouldn't risk it. For all they knew, Malcolm had planted cameras in Jonah's office.

Even so, Jonah couldn't resist crooking his finger at Avery. "Good morning, Avery." There was no disguising the warmth in his voice or the significance of Jonah pushing back his chair and patting his thighs. Just a few kisses wouldn't hurt.

Avery locked the door and crossed the room, skirting around the desk until he reached Jonah's chair. Jonah wondered about the logistics of where arms and legs would go for Avery's comfort, but his intern demonstrated how often he'd fantasized about sexy times with Jonah in the office. Avery pushed the buttons on the outside of the armrests, which lowered them enough to enable Avery to straddle Jonah's waist.

"You were magnificent," Avery said once he settled comfortably on Jonah's lap.

"You think so? I wish I hadn't let Trexler get a rise out of me," he said, not bothering to keep the desire out of his voice. Let Malcolm think he was too preoccupied with Avery to mount forces against him. Jonah ran his nose alongside Avery's neck, breathing in his fresh scent and detecting faint hints of his favorite spicy tea. Avery wiggled his ass against Jonah's rising erection. Jonah nipped his neck to discourage Avery, but it had an adverse effect. Avery gasped and bucked, making Jonah's eyes roll back in his head.

"The jerk had it coming."

"He did," Jonah agreed.

"Oh, I owe you twenty bucks," Avery said.

Jonah knitted his brows. "Why?"

"Bill and Ashley are back together again," Avery replied.

"Jesus."

"I don't have any cash on me, so do you think we could work out some kind of exchange?" Avery waggled his brows.

Jonah cupped Avery's head and pulled that luscious mouth closer. If this was going to be his last day working for the GBI, Jonah planned to make it a real humdinger. "I think we can work something out."

Just a few kisses. Just a few kisses. Just a few...

Avery pressed his mouth against Jonah's, and the rest of the world disappeared along with his conviction. Jonah would've liked to think he'd have stopped before the clothes came off if his desk phone hadn't rung, startling them apart.

They stared at each other for a few heartbeats before Jonah recovered enough of his faculties to answer the phone.

"Agent St. John," he said.

"Welcome back, Jonah." Charlie Malcolm's voice was warm, friendly, and familiar. The reaction it stirred within Jonah was the exact opposite. He wouldn't let this man fuck with his head anymore.

"Good morning, sir," Jonah replied. To beat a duplicitous son of a bitch, you had to become one. No one would know from his pleasant tone that he was planning to take this man down in ten hours.

"How are you feeling?" the deputy director asked in his best Uncle Charlie voice.

"I'm fine, sir. I don't even have a slight headache."

"Great news, Jonah. I'm glad to hear it. Have the police found a suspect yet?"

"No, sir. I didn't get a look at the guy, so it would be impossible for me to identify him," Jonah said.

"That's too bad," Malcolm said. "Listen, I won't be in the office today, but maybe the two of us could have lunch tomorrow. There are some things I'd like to discuss with you."

"Such as?" Jonah prompted.

Malcolm laughed good-naturedly. "I don't have time to get into it with you right now. We'll chat over lunch. You pick the place, and I'll treat."

"Sounds great, sir."

Malcolm wished him a good day, which Jonah returned before replacing the phone receiver in its cradle.

"The deputy director just wanted to make sure I was doing okay and invite me to lunch tomorrow," Jonah said.

Avery scrunched up his nose adorably. "Trexler has a different story to tell. He's such an asshat."

"Maybe Trexler was telling the truth, and Malcolm is planning to talk to me about my podcast participation tomorrow."

"Maybe," Avery conceded. "Speaking of the podcast, tonight sounds like a big deal."

"It is," Jonah replied. They hadn't rehearsed when they'd have the conversation about the meeting, but this seemed like a natural opening. Felix and Rocky were right about Avery's intuition, but Jonah didn't plan to tell them any time soon. Their egos were big enough as it was. "I'm eager to interview this prison guard."

"What's his name?"

"I can't share the information yet," Jonah said.

"Not even with me?" Avery's pout was adorable.

"Not even you," Jonah said. "I can meet you afterward for dinner though. I might have looser lips by then." Avery's wicked smile said he knew exactly how to make Jonah talk. "I'm meeting the guard at six and should probably be done in thirty minutes to an hour tops." There was no need to give Avery the location since Malcolm was tracking his car. He'd just get in position early enough to allow the traitor to arrive and make his move at the destined time.

"Sounds good. I'm picking the movie and the dinner this time," Avery said. He picked up the notepad and scrawled another message. *What are you eating for lunch?*

Jonah met Avery's gaze with a sensual smile before writing his reply. *You.*

Avery shivered as he responded. *My apartment is closer.*

Adrenaline and courage seemed like strange bedfellows, but one didn't work so well without the other. Courage was the decision to do something in the face of grave danger or great sacrifice. Adrenaline triggers the fight instincts and fuels the brain to execute the plan. The two could feed off each other to increase a man's chance of survival, but too much of either could send him to his death. Jonah strove for the right balance as he pulled into the parking lot of WBM Logistics warehouse on Knowlton Way.

With access to the Port of Savannah nearby, WBM supported some of the largest retailers in the world. The location was isolated enough they wouldn't have to worry about pedestrian traffic and civilians getting caught up in the crossfire if things went south. There were enough warehouses and freight containers onsite to provide excellent cover for their team.

It had been many years since Jonah had felt this amped up on adrenaline, and he took several deep breaths to slow his racing heart.

"Doing okay?" Felix asked through his earpiece. "Sounds like you're breathing awfully hard."

"Exercise to combat the adrenaline," Jonah replied as he turned into the warehouse parking lot.

"I thought he was practicing heavy breathing to get a job at one of those nine hundred numbers since he tendered his resignation," Rocky said.

"Do those still exist?" Royce asked.

"I think everything is web-based these days," Sawyer countered. "Jonah could still rock that though."

"Thanks," Jonah said.

"Can we focus, people?" Ellie asked.

"Oh, fuck. I forgot the commish was listening," Royce said.

"Who happens to be Jonah's aunt," she reminded them.

"Sorry," several male voices said at once, making Ellie and Jonah chuckle.

"I got eyes on Jonah," Felix said. "So far, everything is working perfectly. No sign of Malcolm or any civilians."

Rocky and Felix were staked out on opposite corners of the building. Felix saw the front of the building as well as the right side. Rocky's position allowed him to see the rear and left side, while Ellen, Royce, and Sawyer were hidden inside the warehouse. Each of them was wired for sound. Rocky or Felix would let them know as soon as Malcolm arrived.

"Stay alert," Jonah said as he parked the car. "I've learned from experience that the more perfect a mission seems, the likelier it is to blow up in your face. Literally. Expect the unexpected."

"We got you covered out here, big guy," Felix said.

"My team has you covered inside," Ellen said.

"Let's do this," Jonah said, pushing open his door and climbing from the car. He had an urge to text Avery once more, but that wasn't the deal. Avery made Jonah promise he'd go to his parents' house and stay there until he sent the all clear text. Besides, what would be an appropriate thing to text him before a mission? *Going in. See you on the other side.*

How lame.

I love you.

Jonah's steps faltered as his heart tripped over itself before plummeting to his stomach. He had the insane urge to laugh because holy fuck. He'd been out of the relationship game for a seriously long time, but even he knew that confessing your feelings via text was all wrong.

"It's showtime," Jonah said as he entered the warehouse.

He looked around the space. He couldn't detect any of Ellie's team hiding among the massive shelves holding air conditioners, household appliances, coiled black pipe, lumber, and just about everything else you'd expect to find in a home improvement store.

"There's an ancient Cadillac pulling in. The driver is an older man who looks to be in his mid-sixties."

"Is that your decoy?" Rocky asked.

"Yeah, that's him," Jonah said. "I'd think a person who drives a Woody Wagon would appreciate a classic car like the Cadillac, Felix."

"To each their own, I guess," the reporter replied. "Here comes your guy. He's wearing a light blue polo shirt, khaki pants, and an Atlanta Braves ball cap. Who is this guy? Something about him is familiar."

"I'll introduce you when this is over," Jonah replied, glancing up when their decoy walked in. It had been so long since Jonah had seen Ricky, he probably wouldn't have recognized him if he passed the man on the street until he looked into those dark eyes sparkling with mischief. "What's up, Ricky?"

"What's up?" Ricky, not Richard, Rick, and especially never Dick, repeated drolly as he looked around. "This isn't what I expected."

"That's because you've watched too many police dramas. The team is in place and ready for when Malcolm shows up. Did you study the photo I sent you?"

Ricky nodded. "There were so many boys who came through the clubs back then, so I can't be sure I've met him. If Earl brought him around, it didn't leave a lasting impression."

Jonah stepped closer to Ricky, hoping his proximity would settle any nerves his friend was experiencing. "Scared?"

"Of many things, but not this. Is he going to kill me? He'll have to get in line behind cancer." Jonah must've slipped and let his sorrow show because Ricky reached for him. "I'm sorry, baby," Ricky said, slipping into Marla's persona right before Jonah's eyes. "I don't mean to hurt you."

"I'm not ready," Jonah said, not caring his friends could hear him.

"I know, baby. I know."

"Heads up," Rocky said. "There's a vehicle slowly approaching from the—"

Jonah checked to make sure his earpiece was firmly in place when Rocky's voice suddenly cut out. Tapping on it, he said, "Rocky?" Silence. "Felix?" Nothing. "Can you hear me, Sawyer, Royce, or Ellen?" No response. Jonah met Ricky's concerned gaze. "Malcolm must've deployed a jammer to block our signal. We still have the upper hand because he's not aware some of SPD's finest are covering us right now."

Jonah believed his words until Charlie Malcolm entered the warehouse with one arm wrapped around Avery's neck and the other holding a gun to Avery's head.

CHAPTER 27

Avery stumbled when he met Jonah's gaze. Malcolm's arm tightened against Avery's windpipe, making him choke and gag. Avery's eyes widened as he strained against the hold. He lifted his hands to Malcolm's forearm, but his tightly bound wrists rendered his fingers useless. The deputy director, a man Jonah had admired so much, laughed at Avery's struggle. Rage stirred the tempest within, straining to be unleashed, but acting on his fury would only get someone killed.

Malcolm squeezed tighter until Avery stopped struggling and dropped his hands. "Move," he angrily hissed, pushing the gun barrel harder against Avery's temple.

Avery coughed, sputtered, and gasped for air but did as he was told. With Malcolm using Avery as a human shield, Jonah knew no one on the task force was going to take a shot at Malcolm. This plan had blown up epically and resembled a scene straight out of Jonah's worst nightmare. He couldn't afford to give in to the rising panic, so he focused on regulating his breathing and maintaining his wits.

Buy them time.

Jonah looked away from Avery to check on Ricky, who'd kept his back to Malcolm as they'd discussed. Ricky swallowed hard, but his dark eyes shimmered with determination. He gave Jonah a subtle nod of encouragement.

"Malcolm, what the hell is going on?" Jonah didn't have to fake the surprise in his voice. While he'd factored many contingencies, Malcolm abducting Avery wasn't one of them. He'd been wrong, and now Avery could pay the ultimate price for his mistake. *Please not again.*

Jonah took a deep breath to calm his nerves. He wasn't without surprises of his own and hoped the final point would go in his favor. Keeping everyone alive until the big reveal was his top priority.

"Expecting Trexler?" Malcolm scoffed. "That pathetic ass kisser doesn't have the balls to color outside the lines. He's as much of a Boy Scout as you are, and I was shocked when the two of you didn't click right away. It worked out great for me because I was able to play the two of you off one another. I manipulated Trexler into badgering and bullying you, knowing it would tear you down like your granddaddy used to do."

Jonah cringed and Malcolm laughed, sounding completely unhinged.

"I came along and built you up to gain your trust. You soaked that shit up like a sponge."

Jonah gritted his teeth to keep from interrupting him. He couldn't risk Malcolm getting pissed and taking it out on Avery.

"You should see your face right now. Don't worry. It wasn't all a lie. I am quite fond of you."

"I can tell," Jonah said dryly. *So much for keeping your mouth shut.* "I had a killer headache for nearly a week the last time you showed how much you cared."

Malcolm scoffed. "I wasn't the one who hit you. The dumbass was only supposed to shake you up, not inflict brain trauma. You should've left well enough alone. Once you started digging into Earl's murder, I had to act fast. I realized Trexler made one hell of a patsy since the dumb fuck doesn't understand a thing about the division he supervises, and everyone knows how much he hates you. I thought you cyber geniuses would've caught on, but maybe you're not as smart as you thought."

The deputy director stopped about twelve feet from Jonah. Far enough to maintain separation and prevent Jonah from performing a heroic act to free Avery, but close enough that he wasn't likely to miss

Jonah if he decided to pull the trigger. Jonah wasn't worried about his own life; he wanted to protect Avery and Ricky. If he could get Malcolm to lower the gun or point it at him, Avery might stand a chance.

Jonah held his hands up to demonstrate he wasn't a threat and took a few steps toward Malcolm. Instead of aiming the gun at Jonah, Malcolm tightened his grip around Avery's neck again.

"Don't move," Malcolm said. "Your little boy toy can die quickly, or he can suffer slowly. Which will it be?"

Jonah jerked to a stop as Avery's eyes widened with panic again. "Okay. Okay. Just ease up."

Malcolm narrowed his eyes. "I'm calling the shots, Jonah."

"Yes, you are," Jonah calmly said, taking a few steps backward.

Avery sucked in a lungful of air when Malcolm eased up again.

"You're a fucking pussy," Malcolm hissed. "Or maybe you're a glutton for punishment. Is that it? Do you like it when people demean and humiliate you? Maybe you get off on it." Jonah wasn't sure how he was supposed to answer Malcolm, so he decided to stay quiet. "Are you armed?"

"No, sir," Jonah said, playing along. "You know about my aversions to guns."

"I do," Malcolm said, nodding. "I also know it's going to get your boyfriend killed just like it did your buddies in Afghanistan. How a coward like you survived the war is beyond me. Just proves the good ones die young while the wimps come home in one piece and protest. It should've been you in one of those flag-draped coffins."

Malcolm's words were like daggers to Jonah's soul. Hiding his pain would've made Malcolm suspicious, so he let the man see his wounds.

"Slowly lift your shirt and turn around. I want to make sure you don't have a gun tucked into the waistband of your jeans," Malcolm instructed. "Make any sudden moves, and I will blow Avery's brains out right in front of you."

Jonah did as he asked, dropping the hem of his shirt and raising his hands back in the air once he finished the rotation. "You're just going to kill all three of us?"

"Yes, I am. I'll make it look like a murder-suicide. I'm not sure which one of you is the killer yet, but you make the most likely choice, Jonah. Everyone knows you are a ticking time bomb."

"What reason would I have to kill Avery and Mr. Albert?"

Zachary Albert was the name of one of the prison guards working death row when Bo was at GSP. Jonah borrowed his name, knowing it wasn't likely Malcolm kept tabs on all of them for three and a half decades.

Narrowing his eyes, Malcolm pursed his lips together. "You make an excellent point, as usual." Malcolm shrugged. "The possibilities are endless with the ocean and numerous lakes nearby."

Ricky stiffened and turned to face Malcolm. "Why not a subdivision of homes under construction? It certainly worked out well for you the last time."

Malcolm's face flushed red with rage as he shifted his focus to Ricky. "How do you know that?"

"I didn't recognize photos of you. All you closeted butch boys looked alike. I recognize your whiny-ass voice though. You went by Chuck back then. They called you Chuck the lousy fuck behind your back. Did you know?" Ricky taunted. Jonah wasn't sure whether to applaud his boldness or clap a hand over his mouth before Malcolm killed them all. "You were in the police academy and would lurk around in the shadows of the clubs and bars. You developed a crush on Lola, but she didn't return your interest, is that it? Or was it something more? Perhaps you didn't recognize Earl in drag, but he recognized you."

It looked like it took considerable effort for Malcolm to unclench his jaw. "Who the fuck are you? There's no goddamned way a prison guard at the state penitentiary would know that. What the fuck is going on here?" His gun hand started shaking, and Jonah worried Ricky had pushed Malcolm too far. Jamming the gun against Avery's temple, Malcolm shifted his hostile gaze to Jonah.

"Did you think you could fool me? Trick me into confessing?" Malcolm asked in an enraged voice. Spittle formed at the corners of his mouth, a shocking contrast to the ordinarily urbane man. "The joke is on you, Jonah. Then again, everything you've believed for the past eight months has been a big lie. Hasn't it, Avery?"

Jonah risked a glance at Avery and saw a new kind of terror in his eyes. What could be worse than having a gun shoved against your head?

"No," Avery said in a shaky voice. "None of it was a lie."

"I know Jonah better than he realizes, and there's no way the Boy Scout would've fallen for a common criminal like you," Malcolm said.

"Avery?" Jonah asked.

"I should've t-t-told you before we, um…"

"Fucked," Malcolm supplied. "You should see your face right now, Jonah. Such a prude. I had big plans for you, Avery. I would've helped you reach your full potential instead of pulling off the petty shit you did for The Purists. You chose Jonah. What a waste."

"I-I can explain," Avery said shakily.

"I already know," Jonah said, unwilling to cause Avery any more anxiety.

"You do?" Avery and Malcolm asked at the same time.

"Ellen said she wasn't going to tell you about Mr. Bradford's run-in with the SPD," Malcolm said.

"It wasn't hard to figure out, Malcolm. After all, I did work on the investigation with the SPD. I knew The Purists utilized the skills of a talented hacker. Ellen approached me about an internship for a computer genius right after the investigation ended. The timing was too coincidental."

Avery swallowed hard. "And you still…"

"Fucked him," Malcolm said, raising a brow.

"Want him," Jonah countered. If this was it for either or both of them, Jonah needed Avery to know. "I know the truth, and I still want you."

Avery made the sweet little gasping sound, and Jonah was grateful to hear it, even if it was the last time. If someone was going to die this night, Jonah decided it would be him. "You do?"

Jonah nodded. "More than anything."

"Aww," Malcolm cooed. "So sweet. It's too bad you're going to die."

"Let Avery go. Take me instead," Jonah said.

"No," Avery yelled.

"You should pick me," Ricky offered.

The three of them vying to take the first bullet would've been funny if the situation wasn't so fucking terrifying.

"At least tell me why you killed my friend," Ricky said.

"I fell in love with Lola the second I saw her, but she didn't even know I existed. Getting to know everything about her became my obsession, so I followed her home one evening. I watched through the window as she removed her makeup and wig before taking off her gown and lingerie. I was shocked when I realized Lola was actually Earl Ison." Malcolm's lips morphed into an angry snarl. "Earl wasn't alone either. His lover was my boss."

"I thought you were in the police academy at the time," Ricky said.

"I was, but I still worked part-time for Locke-Tight concrete. Jerry Locke was a proud son of a bitch, and I couldn't stand him. I knew Jerry's dad would've killed him if he found out his favorite son was queer. Earl knew it too, which was why it was easy for me to convince him to end things with Jerry. Earl broke the man's heart to save his life. I should've known a love that deep and pure wouldn't be swayed my way so easily. Earl went on a couple of dates with me, but he did so out of fear, not interest. I would watch Lola flirt on stage and kiss the pretty boys who bought her drinks at the bar afterward, but me? Earl would get stiff anytime I tried to touch him because he couldn't hide his repulsion. Lola would make fun of me in front of the others. She was the one who came up with Chuck the lousy fuck. The whore offered up his tight ass to anyone who offered but recoiled from my touch?"

Malcolm kept switching back and forth between Earl and Lola as well as the feminine and masculine pronouns. Jonah wasn't sure if it was deliberate, or he was confused.

"I gave her an ultimatum. Fuck me or I destroy Jerry Locke. Of course, she agreed to save her precious Jerry. Midway through the act in the back seat of my car, Lola started to cry. A red haze of rage washed over me. I just snapped and punched her in the temple, knocking her out. I just wanted her to love me like she loved Jerry. Why was that too much to ask? All she had to do was love me."

"Then you drove her out to the construction site and strangled her with her silk stocking," Jonah said. "Why did you masturbate with Lola's panties and shove them in her mouth? To teach her a lesson?"

"That wasn't about me. I wanted people to think a deranged lunatic killed her," Malcolm said defensively.

"A deranged lunatic *did* kill her," Jonah said.

Malcolm shook his head. "No. I spent the rest of my life making up for that one bad thing. I'm a good man."

"A good man doesn't hold a gun to another's head," Jonah said, switching tactics from chastising to imploring with the man. If Malcolm thought he had a good side, then Jonah needed to appeal to it. "Let Avery and Ricky go. The two of us can talk this out. Just put the gun down."

Malcolm's gaze hardened. "How fucking stupid do you think I am? Don't use your psycho-babble bullshit on me, Jonah."

A giant rat darted out from beneath a wooden shelving unit stacked with bags of mulch. It headed straight for Malcolm like it was part of the task force. Startled, Malcolm loosened his grip around Avery's neck and swung his other arm to aim the gun at the rat.

"Down," Jonah shouted to Avery.

Avery dropped at the same time Jonah shoved Ricky to the ground and lunged toward Malcolm. He only made it a few steps before Malcolm swung the gun back around toward Jonah and pulled the trigger. The slug hit him in the chest, making him stumble a few steps. Jonah reflexively brought his hand up to cover the area where it struck him, even though he'd worn a bulletproof vest beneath his shirt.

A second gun fired from somewhere in the warehouse, and a bullet struck Malcolm in the shoulder of his left arm instead of the one holding the gun. He yelled out in pain and staggered but somehow found the strength to aim his weapon at Avery, who was running to Jonah's aid.

"Down," Jonah yelled at Avery again.

Avery dove for cover as Jonah quickly dropped to a crouch and retrieved his gun from his ankle holster. Snapping his arm up, Jonah fired off a shot, nailing Malcolm just above the knee. Someone else in the task force shot him in the right shoulder, rendering his shooting arm useless.

Malcolm crumpled to the ground, writhing in pain. Jonah stood up and ran toward him just as Ellen, Royce, and Sawyer advanced from their positions. Jonah reached him first, kicking the deputy director's Beretta away from the man.

Ellen radioed for an ambulance while Sawyer and Royce secured the prisoner and started providing first aid until the EMTs could arrive and take over.

Jonah stood over them, staring into Charlie Malcolm's cold gaze. How could he have ever looked into this man's eyes and seen warmth and compassion?

"I-I didn't think you h-had it in you," Charlie said through chattering teeth.

Sawyer had used a belt as a tourniquet on Malcolm's leg and was helping Royce staunch the blood flow from the shoulder wounds. The quickly expanding pool of blood beneath Malcolm's upper body indicated both bullets had exited through his back. The blood loss and cold concrete were robbing Malcolm of his body heat.

"Just because I don't like guns doesn't mean I can't shoot one," Jonah said. An echo of footfalls slapping against the hard floor caught Jonah's attention. He turned and looked at the approaching man. "Did you catch his confession on tape?"

Malcolm's eyes widened when Jonah stepped aside so the deputy director could see who he was talking to.

"Sure did. I especially like the part where Malcolm called me a pathetic ass kisser," Butch Trexler said, staring down at the prone man. "Guess my skills will come in handy now that your position has come open. Who's the dumb fuck now?"

"The t-t-two of you s-set me up?" Malcolm asked. "Together?"

"We did," Jonah said.

"How?" Malcolm asked.

"I'm going to be the one asking questions, Charlie," Ellen said firmly. "Where the hell is that ambulance? I don't want him to bleed out and die right here."

Malcolm's expression softened when he looked at her. "Thank you, my friend."

"I want you to die in a prison cell where you belong," Ellen clarified.

Rocky and Felix rushed into the warehouse to check on the situation. Jonah met them, and they embraced in a group hug. "You guys can't be here when the cops arrive. Ellen would lose her job if the mayor found out she involved civilians in the takedown."

"Yeah, okay," Felix said, scrubbing a hand over his face.

"Did it hurt?" Rocky asked, poking his finger through the hole the bullet made in his shirt.

"After I finish hours of interviews and paperwork, you can try the vest on, and I'll shoot you. You can see for yourself," Jonah said.

Felix threw his head back and laughed.

"Okay, but not the same vest," Rocky replied. "It's compromised now."

Jonah pulled them into another hug. "Get the fuck out of here. I'll call you later."

"You better," Felix shouted over his shoulder as he tugged Rocky toward the rear of the warehouse.

Jonah walked over to where Ricky and Avery stood huddled together. Avery launched himself into Jonah's arms when he came near.

"Don't you ever do that again," Avery said, hitting Jonah's chest with his bound hands.

"Which part? Get shot or wear a bulletproof vest?"

Avery tipped his head back and looked into Jonah's eyes. "Either one. And the next time a gunman is holding me hostage..." His eyes widened when he realized what he said.

"Let's make this a one-time experience, okay?" Jonah asked, brushing his fingertips over Avery's cheeks.

Avery nodded. "Jonah?"

"Yeah?"

"How can you want someone like me?"

Jonah heard the sirens of approaching police cars and an ambulance. "Can we maybe discuss this after I wrap things up here tonight?"

Avery nodded. "And you can tell me when you and Trexler became conspiring chums."

"I will." Jonah briefly kissed his lips before releasing him to speak to Ricky, who was rubbing his elbow.

"Did I hurt you?" Jonah asked.

"It's no big deal. I just smacked my elbow against the concrete when I fell."

Jonah gently gripped Ricky's bicep and studied the joint. It looked red and slightly swollen. "I want you to have the EMTs check you out when they get here."

"Don't be silly," Ricky said.

Four police officers and two paramedics rushed into the building.

"Oh, honey, that one EMT looks like a stunt double for The Rock," Ricky said, sounding more like Marla by the second. He wasn't wrong. The dude's shirt looked tight enough to split down the middle at any given second. "Maybe I should have him check me out."

"Don't you mean check out your injury?" Jonah asked.

"Same difference, doll. My elbow is part of me."

"Shouldn't Ricky leave," Avery asked. "You wanted Rocky and Felix to leave to protect your aunt's job."

"Hush, child. Can't you see I'm injured? Besides," Ricky said, pulling out a small silver badge. "The commissioner swore me in today as a Savannah police officer."

"Isn't that the same plastic badge they give to little kids when they visit schools?"

"You better take this one over your knee tonight, Jonah," Ricky said before sauntering away. "Yoo-hoo, honey. I got injured in the takedown."

"I'm telling Amos," Jonah said. Ricky stuck his arm behind his back and flipped Jonah off.

Jonah tugged Avery into his arms and kissed him. "Let's get this rope off your wrists. I want the paramedics to check you over too."

"Wait," Avery said suddenly. "Say it again, Jonah."

"I want you."

Adrenaline continued to pump through Jonah's veins, but it wasn't the only thing fueling his frenetic energy. Relief, elation, rage, love, and sorrow were powerful emotions warring for dominance inside him. Individually, they created impressive storm fronts. Together, they formed a superstorm that gave a person two options: seek shelter or ride the lightning.

Jonah was fucking tired of hiding.

CHAPTER 28

"S t. John," Trexler called out before Jonah and Avery could slip out the door.

They had just wrapped up four hours of interviews, waiting, more interviews, and more waiting before Trexler finally cleared them to leave. Now he was stopping them again. Jonah bit back the groan and faced his supervisor.

"Sir?" he asked.

"About your resignation," Trexler said. "I'm shredding it. I know I don't deserve a second chance, but I'm asking for one anyway. I'm truly sorry for the way I treated you, and I'd like the opportunity to earn your trust and respect." Jonah was struck speechless. Trexler extended his hand. "What do you say?"

Jonah shook his hand. "I accept, sir."

"We'll begin our fresh start next week. Both of you have earned the rest of the week off with pay."

Trexler shook Avery's hand also before returning to conduct more interviews.

"What just happened?" Avery asked as soon as they were inside Jonah's car.

"You want to do this now?" Jonah asked, starting the engine.

"Yes, now. I've watched the two of you bicker and fight for eight months, and now you're working secret missions together," Avery said. "I have to know how it all unfolded."

Jonah shifted the car in drive and headed for the exit. "I took a chance and called him last night. I told him about everything we'd uncovered and how it framed him as the fall guy for whatever was supposed to happen to me."

Avery snorted. "I figured that part out for myself. What made you pick up the phone and trust him after the way he's treated you?"

"When I realized how wrong I was about Charlie Malcolm, I started evaluating my other relationships. I started wondering how much of my antagonistic association with Trexler was real and how much of it Malcolm had engineered. I thought back to the day I asked Malcolm for permission to investigate Earl's homicide. It was the only time Malcolm refused to intervene, and I knew there had to be a reason for it."

"He killed Earl," Avery said.

"Yes, but my gut told me there was more to the story. I set aside my differences with Trexler and evaluated the man on how he interacted with everyone else. He is a man known for his intellect and fairness, but his behavior toward me was the exact opposite. I never understood what provoked his hostility toward me. A pattern of behavior emerged. Every time Trexler would tear me down, Malcolm would go out of his way to build me back up. It got to the point where I started disobeying protocol and went directly to Malcolm with my problems or ideas. Then it hit me. Malcolm had purposefully engineered the volatile relationship between us."

"Why?" Avery asked. "There was no way he could've predicted three years ago that you would've asked to reopen the Ison case."

"True," Jonah conceded. "Back in the warehouse, Malcolm insisted he is a good man who spent his life making up for the one terrible thing he did. Malcolm didn't commit a singular crime. What about the stalking, blackmailing, and sexually assaulting Earl before killing him? Someone so devious and deranged doesn't just change overnight. Plus, there were the crimes he committed against Bo Cahill thirteen years later. After getting away with the murder and cover-up, his urges to do other sinister things would've intensified, not lessened. He just got smarter about choosing his victims and inflicted emotional harm instead of physical, or at least in my case. I realized he'd turned Trexler into a weapon against me."

"How'd the conversation with Trexler go?" Avery asked.

Jonah smiled. "Trexler hung up on me as soon as I told him why I was calling. I emailed him the proof you had found, and Trexler called me back immediately. He said, 'I'm listening,' and it was the opening I needed to lay it all out there for him. He told me that Malcolm was the one who encouraged him to come down hard on me, including the warning for insubordination and the subsequent suspension."

"Malcolm is the one who ratted you out to Trexler, huh?"

"Yes," Jonah replied. "We have a long way to go to repair the damage Malcolm caused, but last night and tonight was a big step in the right direction."

Avery hummed. "The two of you decided to stage the parking lot incident, didn't you?"

"We did," Jonah agreed.

"And you didn't tell me ahead of time because you didn't trust me?" Avery asked.

"No, I do trust you. I wasn't certain the confrontation was going to occur. The arrangement was for Trexler to accost me if Malcolm contacted him about the podcast. I needed to be sure Malcolm took the bait."

"You're quite brilliant," Avery said. There was a pensiveness in his voice that troubled Jonah.

"I also wanted to diminish your culpability as much as possible, Avery."

"Because you want me?"

"I do," Jonah emphatically said as he pulled into the driveway. He put the car in park and killed the engine before threading his fingers in Avery's hair and guiding his head to meet Jonah's halfway. "I could've lost you tonight, and you wouldn't have known that you're all I want," he whispered against Avery's lips.

Instead of kissing him, Avery placed his hand on Jonah's chest to stop him. "How?"

Before Jonah could answer, his screen door opened suddenly, slapping against the front of the house. A partially dressed man burst out of Jonah's house like the devil was chasing him. Kendall, apparently playing the role of said devil, stepped onto the porch a second later and flung something at the man, nailing him square in the back before he reached his car parked in front of Jonah's house. When the object hit the ground, Jonah saw it was a shoe.

"What the fuck?" Jonah asked, shoving his car door open.

"I don't ever want to see you or talk to you again, Travis. Don't come back," Kendall yelled across the lawn.

"How many times have I heard the same thing before, and yet, you still call me?" Travis replied.

"Now, I'm telling you," Jonah said. "I don't want to see you on my property, and I better not find out you're harassing him at work."

Travis halted and faced Jonah. "Work? Is that what you call wearing a tiny scrap of fabric while serving drinks and chicken wings to horny men? Lose my number, Kendall," Travis said with a sneer before getting in his car. He gunned the engine so hard his tires squealed before he shot down the road.

"Christ," Jonah muttered. "I'm ready for this night to be over."

"That makes two of us," Avery said, joining him. "I had a gun pointed to my head."

Jonah looped his arm around Avery's waist and pulled him against his side. Having his man so close to him was making it hard to remember precisely why they'd wanted to have a conversation. "I got shot, so I win."

"It's not a contest," Avery hissed. He slid his hand over Jonah's heart, where a bullet would've struck him.

"Good thing because I'd win the prize." Jonah cupped Avery's face and captured his lips for a kiss. "I take it back. I've already won."

Avery elbowed him. "I'm not some stuffed teddy bear from a carnival."

Jonah pressed his mouth against Avery's ear. "Do you want to be stuffed?" Jonah whispered, nuzzling his nose against Avery's soft flesh.

Avery whimpered. "God, yes."

"What the hell is going on here?" Kendall asked from the porch. It sounded like he'd temporarily forgotten his troubles. "Someone held a gun to Avery's head, and someone else shot you, Jonah?"

"It was the same person," Jonah replied.

"It's a very long story," Avery added.

"Sure makes my guy problems seem small," Kendall said. "Are you both okay?"

"We're fine," Jonah told his friend. "I'll tell you all about it in the morning." Kendall nodded and started to head inside. "Kendall."

Kendall turned around and looked at Jonah. "You don't have guy problems. You have *a* guy problem. You can do better than Travis."

"Thanks, J," Kendall replied with a small smile. "See you guys in the morning."

"Maybe I should go home tonight," Avery said. "Kendall looks upset. He could use a friend."

"I will always be Kendall's friend, but there are some battles you have to fight yourself." He hoisted Avery over his shoulder caveman-style and headed inside.

Avery slapped his ass. "Put me down, you Neanderthal."

Jonah just ignored him and secured the house before carrying him upstairs like he weighed nothing.

Inside his room, Jonah laid Avery on the bed, covering Avery's body with his own. "I want you," he said before kissing a path down Avery's neck. Jonah felt Avery's happy purr vibrating beneath his lips.

"How?" Avery asked once more, stopping Jonah in his tracks. "I am a terrible person for getting involved with The Purists."

"You did a bad thing, but it doesn't make you bad," Jonah argued. "How'd you get tangled up with the psychopath?"

"He had proof I hacked into my college's computers and changed my grades so I wouldn't fail a class. I'd come down with mono and missed several lectures. The professor wouldn't work with me, so I made myself even sicker trying to make up for my grades. I fell two points shy. Failing the class would've impacted my scholarship and grant eligibility. It was wrong of me to do, and I regret it as much as getting caught up in The

Purists' schemes. He gave me the option of helping him, or he'd report me to the college. They would've expelled me, and no college would've accepted my application with the transgression on my academic record."

"How'd you end up meeting my aunt Ellie?"

Avery smiled. "One day, I was web surfing on a computer at Bytes and Brew to avoid detection on my own laptop. Royce came in to get lunch, and there was another off-duty cop there too. Royce started asking the owner if he knew any hackers or anyone familiar with the dark web. I knew it was my cue to leave. Like an amateur, I left the café too quickly, which attracted Royce's attention. I ran for it when Royce and the other cop pursued me. I made a wrong turn and ended up in a dead-end alley. Um," Avery said, rubbing a spot behind his ear. "This part is bad."

Jonah kissed him. "I've seen you around Royce enough to know he doesn't harbor a grudge toward you. Just tell me the rest. You'll feel better."

"I picked up a board off the ground and swung it as Royce rounded the corner and ran into the alley. Luckily, his reflexes are amazingly fast because I missed hitting him. He tackled me to the ground and hauled me into the station for questioning. I kept my mouth shut even though they held me there until late that night. I didn't know it then, but Royce and Sawyer set up a stakeout and followed me to the church where I planned to confront the sadistic bastard whose thumb I'd been living under for too long. I don't even know for sure what I was going to tell him, but I intended to confess to the police the next day. When I went inside the church…" Avery closed his eyes and took a deep breath. "The Purists' arsonist had the sick fucker tied up and was dousing him with gasoline. I turned around and ran out of there as fast as I could and nearly collided with Royce."

"I know the rest," Jonah said. "You're the Samaritan who aided the firefighters in saving Royce and Sawyer when they got trapped in the burning building."

"Samaritan," Avery scoffed. "I was so fucking scared. I wanted to run and get away from there as fast as I could."

"But you didn't. You stayed because you're a good person. Royce and Sawyer know it. Ellie knows it. I know it," Jonah said.

"The situation was a horrible wake-up call. I went and spoke to my professor the following week and confessed what I'd done. I was a snotty, sobbing mess by the time I finished and fully expected him to report me to the dean."

"He didn't?" Jonah asked.

Avery shook his head. "He apologized to me. Professor Lafferty explained he had been going through a bitter divorce when I'd approached him for an extension to submit my makeup work. He said that he'd taken his bitterness out on me, and it wasn't fair. We worked out a deal. I tutor students who are struggling with various computer concepts. That's where I was on the night I couldn't talk to you. I wasn't sure how to tell you about that part without confessing to the whole story."

"I don't need perfection, Avery. I just need my boyfriend to be honest with me. Trust is a two-way street."

Avery slid his hand inside Jonah's hair and massaged his scalp. "Make room for me because your boyfriend is no longer willing to stay in his own lane."

"Because you want me," Jonah prodded.

Avery nipped Jonah's bottom lip. "I want you."

CHAPTER 29

It was two days before Malcolm was recovered enough from surgery to be interviewed. Jonah wasn't sure if the deputy director would lawyer up or confess. In the end, he did the right thing and gave a detailed account of what happened with Earl and explained how he was able to coerce a confession from Bo Cahill.

Bo's daughter, Millie, who was a college freshman at the time, got pulled over for speeding in Fulton County. For reasons unknown to anyone, the officer decided to search Millie's car and allegedly found a dime bag of pot. She claimed the deputy planted the drugs in her car, but it was her word against his. Malcolm was a deputy in Fulton at the time. The young lady was enraged and furious instead of afraid, and they sent Malcolm in there to calm her down.

The other deputies thought the girl would chew up the soft-spoken deputy and spit him out, but he was able to calm Millie down. She confided in Malcolm and pleaded with him to help her. Millie talked about her father's pending execution and said her mama needed her. It made Jonah sick to hear the bastard talking about his interaction with the distressed teenager. He knew full well how the man could turn on the charm and inspire a person to trust him. Malcolm showed none of his usual warmth in the hospital room, where he was cuffed to the bed and had an officer guarding his door.

Malcolm was cold as ice, completely lacking empathy and compassion as he talked about staying in touch with people in Savannah after he moved away. He knew Earl's friends still harassed the police department weekly. He worried a rookie officer looking to make a name for themselves would start poking around in the investigation. Milton and Morrissey had zero gumption to solve the case. Malcolm quoted the two men as saying Earl Ison got what he deserved for his perverse lifestyle.

Malcolm had dirt on his cousin Vinnie Malcolm, who was the guard on death row at GPS they called Bird. Through that connection, they coerced Bo into confessing to killing Earl to save his daughter. Millie was an honor student with a full-ride scholarship on the line, so there really was no choice for Bo.

The day after Malcolm's confession, Felix, Rocky, and Jonah drove back to Darnell's house to meet with Bo's family. Jonah wished he could spare Millie the truth, but they'd promised to get answers for the family. Sometimes those answers were painful as hell.

Agnes held her daughter in her arms, and they wept together.

Darnell heaved a long sigh. "I thought proving my dad didn't kill Earl Ison would make me feel better, but it doesn't. Knowing the truth doesn't bring my dad back."

"It doesn't," Felix agreed, "but you can give him a voice now through our podcast. People can learn about the kind of man Bo Cahill really was."

"A man who would go to any lengths to protect his family," Agnes said.

The Cahills asked for time to think about it. Darnell called Felix the following day and said his family had agreed to sit down for interviews for the podcast. The three of them would travel back to Darnell's house in the coming weeks to go over their plans for the episodes and conduct interviews. Felix stressed they didn't just want to make the episode *about* the Cahill family; he wanted to make it *with* them.

By the time Saturday rolled around, Jonah was exhausted and exhilarated at the same time. He briefly thought about rescheduling the barbecue so he could stay in bed with Avery all day and night, but a cookout with friends was exactly what he needed.

"The guest of honor is here, so the party can really start," Royce said as he opened the gate and stepped into Jonah's back yard. He carried a cooler in one hand and a platter of something in another. "Sawyer made fancy-schmancy snacks for everyone."

"Jalapeno poppers aren't fancy. Anything requiring more effort than squirting processed cheese from a can onto a cracker is fancy to Royce," Sawyer said. He snatched the platter out of Royce's hand and kissed his boyfriend on the cheek as he walked by. "Where do you want my fancy-schmancy snacks?"

Jonah helped himself to a few jalapeno poppers, then said, "Marla and Amos are inside setting up a buffet. She can find a place for them."

"Guest of honor?" Felix asked. "Is it your birthday?"

"Nah. That's in October," Royce replied.

"Why would you be the guest of honor, then?" Rocky asked.

"I saved the day," Royce replied. "Didn't Jonah tell you?"

"Royce helped me replace the hot water heater last week after it died," Jonah explained as he brushed another layer of barbecue on the ribs.

"Oh, I thought he was taking credit for the rat again," Avery said.

They all laughed.

"Hey, Robby was part of the plan all along," Royce said. "I deployed him as a diversion tactic, and it worked."

"Robby," Jonah snorted.

"Bullshit," Sawyer said, returning to the back patio. "I saw you do a full-body shiver when my nephew brought out his hamster from his bedroom. You are not friends with any type of rodent, and you sure as hell wouldn't train or name one."

"Must you tell all my secrets?" Royce asked, hooking an arm around Sawyer's neck and kissing him soundly on the mouth. "I did deploy the damn rat."

"How?" Felix asked.

"I startled the fat fucker out of his hiding place when I ninja moved into a better position to get a bead on Malcolm. How I didn't scream like a girl is beyond me."

"Did you have to change your underwear afterward?" Rocky asked.

"Maybe," Royce said with a shrug.

Yep. Having friends over for great food and tons of laughs was the perfect ending to an insane few weeks.

Sawyer hooked his arm around Royce's waist and fed him a jalapeno popper. "So, what's next?"

"For the podcast?" Jonah clarified.

"I meant your career with the GBI, but I'm curious about the podcast too."

"Trexler fed my resignation letter through the paper shredder and asked for a second chance. His apology was sincere, and I still think my skills add value to the bureau. I'm going to give it a shot."

"That's great news," Royce said.

"As for the podcast, we're going to extend the Ride the Lightning episodes to include interviews with Bo's family, so people can get their side of the story," Jonah said. "We haven't nailed down our next project yet. I still think Tess Hamilton is our best bet."

"Oh, the lady who they suspect killed her three husbands," Sawyer said. "That would be a good one."

"I have an idea," Felix said. "I was going to pitch this to you later, but why not now?"

"Go for it," Rocky said.

"You guys all know who Cameron Spencer is, right?" Felix asked.

"The guy who owns like a dozen car dealerships in Georgia, South Carolina, and Florida?" Royce asked.

"That's the one," Felix said. "I have battled with his dealership for months over the extended warranty I purchased with my new car a few years ago. When my transmission blew, I didn't fret about it because I bought the added coverage. I keep getting the runaround about why the bumper-to-bumper warranty won't pay for the new transmission I need."

"That's why you're driving your shaggin' wagon around so much," Rocky said.

Felix rolled his eyes. "Woody Wagon."

Rocky snorted. "Same difference, even though I don't know how you pick up so many dudes in that old thing."

"The guys are more concerned about the driver's skills than what he's driving," Felix told him.

"Touché."

"Anyway," Felix said, "the dealership told me I didn't properly maintain the car, which nullified the warranty. After I provided receipts and service records from their dealership, they still balked. I've talked to everyone in their organization from my original salesman to the service department manager and even the general manager. All I get is bullshit excuses. I tried speaking to Cameron Spencer, but, apparently, he only shows up when it's time for publicity stunts or to shoot commercials."

"Ugh. I can't stand Spencer's commercials," Royce grumbled. "They're like nails on a chalkboard."

"Worse," Avery said.

Royce raised a beer to salute him.

"I started searching the internet for others who had similar problems," Felix said. "I found several instances where customers had issues with both their extended warranties and gap insurance policies. I think something fishy is going on. The kicker is a lady called me yesterday and said she'd taken proof to Jude Arrow—"

"The Straight Shooter," Royce said, mimicking the news reporter's voice. Everyone laughed except Felix. He winced. "Sorry, man."

"This woman said she has proof that the gap insurance policies and extended warranties were issued by Spencer's shell companies," Felix said.

"Isn't that money laundering?" Rocky asked. "That's a serious accusation."

Felix nodded. "It is, which is why Jude Arrow refused to get involved."

"Maybe this woman's evidence isn't as strong as she claimed," Jonah said.

"Possibly," Felix agreed. "Or, Jude Arrow doesn't want to get involved for another reason. Maybe if he starts exposing powerful people, they'll do the same to him."

"Here we go again," Rocky said. "If you really think Arrow has a big bad skeleton in his closet, let me look into the reasons why he left Atlanta for Savannah."

"It will be more fun to torment the truth out of him after I show him up. I owe him nothing less," Felix said. "Listen, there is absolutely no dirt on Cameron Spencer anywhere, and we all know that's a red flag."

Sawyer nodded. "The man has always annoyed me. He's too fucking perfect."

"Mr. Perfect," Felix said. "That would make an excellent title for his podcast episodes."

"Let me get this straight," Rocky said slowly. "You want to use our podcast to settle a personal vendetta with Jude Arrow *and* get your transmission replaced."

"If the evidence shows Mr. Perfect is up to no good, then yes," Felix said.

"I'm in," Rocky and Jonah said at the same time.

"To Sinister in Savannah," Felix said.

The three men clinked their beer bottles together.

Marla opened the door and poked her head out. "Is everyone ready to eat?" Jonah's guests rushed toward the house at once, and Marla barely avoided the stampede. "Lord, those are some hungry boys," she said, walking toward him, toying with the silver pendant she wore around her neck.

When SPD had executed a search warrant at Malcolm's residence, they found the missing evidence and Trexler's stolen laptop tucked under the seat of his car and Earl's necklace hidden in one of his dresser drawers. Jonah had taken it to Jerry, who'd confirmed it was the necklace he'd purchased for Earl. Jonah told Jerry the details of Malcolm's confession because the man deserved to know that Earl had truly loved him.

As far as Jonah was concerned, Marla was Earl's next of kin. Without her, they never would've gotten justice for her friend. She touched the necklace often, and Jonah hoped it would bring her comfort in the coming… Days? Weeks? Months?

Jonah shoved the heartbreaking thought aside. He would not mourn her while she was still alive. "I don't think it's a trait we ever outgrow."

"Listen," Marla said seriously. "I need to extract another promise or two out of you."

"More promises?" Jonah teased. "I agreed to keep your dog, I solved Earl's case, and Marla the Magnificent supercomputer will help me fight crimes for decades to come."

"She's much more attractive than Stella."

"Absolutely," Jonah agreed.

"About the dog," Marla said. Jonah knew what was coming next. "She's Amos's girl now, and I think they'll need each other after I'm gone."

Jonah swallowed hard and nodded. "I think you're right."

"I almost always am," Marla said, looping her arm through Jonah's.

"What are the new promises?"

"I want you to put a ring on Avery's finger and love him until there's no breath left in your body," Marla said huskily. "He's so good for you."

"He is," Jonah said. "When the time is right, I promise to put a ring on Avery's finger and love him forever. Is that all?"

Marla laughed and patted his arm. "I saved the biggest request for last."

"Bigger than solving a crime, offering to take your dog, and promising to marry Avery?" Jonah asked.

"Yes," Marla said. "When HBO comes knocking at your door looking to make a documentary out of Ride the Lightning, I want you to promise me that you'll get Ru Paul to play my part."

Jonah threw his head back and laughed harder than he had all week. "I can't promise you that."

Marla sighed dramatically. "Lie to me if you must."

"I promise."

Marla leaned into him. "That's my boy."

Jonah pressed a kiss to her temple. "I love you, Marla."

"Remember that when HBO wants to cast some basic bitch as Marla."

"Yes, ma'am."

"I love you too, baby. Ready to eat?"

Jonah smiled. "In a minute. You go on and make yourself a plate. I'll be right in."

When Marla went inside, Jonah tipped his head back and studied the fluffy white clouds in the brilliant blue sky.

"Is a storm coming?" Avery asked as he joined him on the patio.

"Not today," he replied, though there was always a storm on the horizon. What was it Granny said about storms and rainbows?

When dark skies bring rain, look for the rainbow that follows.

Jonah didn't have to look anymore. His rainbow was standing right beside him. He cupped Avery's face and fused their mouths together for a sweet kiss.

"Are you okay?" Avery asked when Jonah pulled back.

"I am now." And he was. Not because there would be nothing but blue skies from here on out. He would love, and he would lose. That was life, that was living. He would hurt so fucking bad when it was time to say goodbye to Marla. Jonah had amazing friends and family to help him through the sorrow. He had years of memories to hold on to and more to make before they parted.

Avery smiled up at him. "Because you want me." It was a statement this time, not a question.

"I more than want you, but I'm not sure you're ready to hear just how much."

Avery laughed. "I was born ready."

"I love you, Avery."

Avery's lips trembled before stretching into a brilliant smile. "I love you too. So much."

So long for now...

The Sinister in Savannah series will continue with Mr. Perfect, where Felix Franklin will square off against his nemesis, Jude "The Straight Shooter" Arrow.

Want to be the first to know about my book releases and have access to extra content? You can sign up for my newsletter here: eepurl.com/dlhPYj

My favorite place to hang out and chat with my readers is my Facebook group. Would you like to be a member of Aimee's Dye Hards? We'd love to have you! Click here: www.facebook.com/groups/AimeesDyeHards

OTHER BOOKS BY
AIMEE NICOLE WALKER

Only You

The Fated Hearts Series

Chasing Mr. Wright, Book 1
Rhythm of Us, Book 2
Surrender Your Heart, Book 3
Perfect Fit, Book 4
Return to Me, Book 5
Always You, Book 6
Any Means Necessary, Book 7

Curl Up and Dye Mysteries

Dyeing to be Loved
Something to Dye For
Dyed and Gone to Heaven
I Do, or Dye Trying
A Dye Hard Holiday
Ride or Dye

Road to Blissville Series

Unscripted Love
Someone to Call My Own
Nobody's Prince Charming
This Time Around
Smoke in the Mirror
Inside Out
Prescription for Love

The Lady is Mine Series

The Lady is a Thief
The Lady Stole My Heart

Queen City Rogue Series

Broken Halos
Wicked Games
Beautiful Trauma

Zero Hour Series

Ground Zero
Devil's Hour
Zero Divergence

Standalone Novels
Second Wind

Coauthored with Nicholas Bella

Undisputed
Circle of Darkness (Genesis Circle, Book 1)
Circle of Trust (Genesis Circle, Book 2)

ACKNOWLEDGMENTS

First, I need to thank my husband and children for their constant support and encouragement. It's not easy living with a writer who often disappears into a fictional world for long periods of time. They do so many things to help me out so that I can realize my dream. I love you guys more than words can ever express.

To my creative dream team, thanks seem hardly enough for all that you do. Miranda Turner of V8 Editing and Proofreading, thank you for your tireless work, feedback, and many laughs while editing. Jay Aheer of Simply Defined art is an incredible artist, and I love how she brings my words to life. Stacey Blake of Champagne Formats is also an amazing artist who does incredible interior formatting, illustrating, and designing for e-books and paperbacks. It truly takes a village to whip me into shape. Judy Zweifel of Judy's' Proofreading, Jill Wexler, and Michael Beckett did a great job of proofreading and polishing to make my manuscript shine.

To my lovely PA, Michelle Slagan. I'm not sure how I ever did this without you. I love you to the moon and back!

I want to thank the Brittany for being a wonderful critique partner and Racheal and Melinda for being amazing alpha readers. And to my betas, Kim, Dana, Michael, and Laurel, I appreciate your honest feedback. I love working with you all.

ABOUT
AIMEE NICOLE WALKER

Ever since she was a little girl, Aimee Nicole Walker entertained herself with stories that popped into her head. Now she gets paid to tell those stories to other people. She wears many titles—wife, mom, and animal lover are just a few of them. Her absolute favorite title is champion of the happily ever after. Love inspires everything she does, music keeps her sane, and coffee is the magic elixir that fuels her day.

I'd love to hear from you.

Want to connect with me? All my links are in one nifty location. Click here:
linktr.ee/AimeeNicoleWalker